Laura Kalpakian was born in Long Beach, California and grew up in southern California. She started a career as a social worker, and earned a Ph.D. in literature from the University of California, San Diego in 1977. Since then, she has had residencies at the Virginia Center for the Creative Arts, Montalvo Center for the Arts, and Hawthornden Castle in Scotland. Laura is the award-winning author of thirteen novels and over a hundred stories published in collections, anthologies, literary journals and magazines in the USA and the UK. Her sons are composer Bear McCreary and singer/musician Brendan McCreary.

You can discover more about the author at laurakalpakian.com

THE MUSIC ROOM

1969: Young Marcella and Rose-Renee's parents are divorcing — their mother going to Sweden to sing opera, and their father travelling across the US as a jobbing actor. An inconvenient hindrance to their careers, the two girls are left to live with their enigmatic grandmother Gloria, a renowned violinist, in her decaying New England mansion. Instructed never to disturb the formidable woman as she endlessly rehearses in the music room, the children are left to their own devices. Their cheerful neighbour, Dorothea, convinces Gloria to allow them to be home-schooled with her sickly son, Rodney; and as the girls' gifts are nurtured in ways they have never before experienced, they also receive warmth and care that are otherwise lacking in their lives. But when disaster strikes, and Dorothea is gone, where will they find help?

LAURA KALPAKIAN

THE
MUSIC ROOM

Complete and Unabridged

CHARNWOOD
Leicester

First published in Great Britain in 2015 by
Buried River Press
an imprint of
Robert Hale
London

First Charnwood Edition
published 2016
by arrangement with
Robert Hale
an imprint of
The Crowood Press
Wiltshire

A catalogue record for this book is available
from the British Library.

ISBN 978–1–4448–3102–3

Published by
F. A. Thorpe (Publishing)
Anstey, Leicestershire

Set by Words & Graphics Ltd.
Anstey, Leicestershire
Printed and bound in Great Britain by
T. J. International Ltd., Padstow, Cornwall

This book is printed on acid-free paper

For Sonatine Yarbrough McCreary

'What passion cannot music raise or quell?'

John Dryden
'A Song for St Cecilia's Day'
1687

1

Duets

The train sped northward through a blur of June blue-and-green, whistle shrieking as it paralleled the grey highways. The children sat side by side, Rose-Renee dozing, her head against Marcella's shoulder, Marcella gazing out the window, her body gently rocking with the train's motion. Across the aisle, their mother sat, deep in conversation with a young soldier in uniform. With her softly curling long hair, sassy short skirt, and patterned stockings, Valerie McNeill looked younger than her thirty-one years, and the young soldier was clearly smitten, sympathetic to her story of having left her husband in Richmond just that very morning, starting out all over again, bravely, with her two daughters.

The young soldier regarded the girls critically. At eleven and nearly nine, Marcella and Rose-Renee McNeill had the usual unpleasant assortment of childish woes, scabby knees, snotty noses, and adult teeth too big for their mouths. They had thick, dark, curling hair and dark eyes like their father, Mitch. 'You're too young to be the mother of such big girls,' he said.

'Oh, I was just a kid when I had them,' said Valerie. 'Really, I was just a girl who fell in love with a handsome actor. We eloped like young romantic fools.'

'Wilmington! Wilmington, Delaware!' squawked from the loudspeaker as the train passed through dull and grungy suburbs and slowed on its way into the city.

'We're here,' said Valerie. 'Collect your things, girls.' She stood, reached overhead, and took down two small suitcases scarred with use; she gave one to each girl. Marcella handed Rose-Renee Cubbie, a scantily clad baby doll with floppy arms and plastic hair. She tucked a battered Barbie in a frayed turquoise gown under her arm as Valerie shooed them into the aisle. Valerie reached for her own luggage.

The young soldier stayed her arm. 'Let me get yours, Valerie. I'll carry it out for you.'

'But this isn't even your stop, Danny. You're going on to Philly.'

'I'm in no hurry.'

'But the train will leave without you.' She stood so close to him, her breath might have brushed his chin, and he smiled down at her.

'No one's waiting for me.'

'But what about your family?'

'Why do you think I joined the army and went to Nam in the first place?' He gave a toothy grin. 'I didn't even tell my people I got leave. I'll take the next train north.'

'That's very kind of you, Danny, and I appreciate it. Girls, you girls run along and find your grandmother. I'll be right there.'

Marcella clutched Rose-Renee's hand, pulled her towards the door, jumped down to the platform where they were engulfed by hurrying crowds. Wilmington was not a great international

2

crossroads, like Grand Central or Penn, but kind of a sleepy, urban backwater, a commuter's station where nearly everyone who got on or off wore a suit and tie and carried a briefcase. The platform roof was upheld by lacy, wrought-iron pillars; the iron railings everywhere were fanciful and curling, painted in a strange copper-gone-green tone. Built in 1908, the Wilmington, Delaware station still exuded pre-World War I certainties, though worlds had come and gone in the sixty years since, certainties that now, in 1969, seemed cloying, a little rusty and threadbare like the station itself. Marcella paused, waiting, looking for someone who would notice them, but no one did. Pigeons cooed and strutted, and Rose-Renee chased after them, returning to Marcella, who was watching the big board of destinations where numbers and letters clattered and fell into place.

'Well, where is she?' demanded Rose-Renee.

'Guess we'll have to find her.'

Rose-Renee shrugged and dutifully followed her sister through a door that said *Waiting Room*. Under the vaulted ceiling surrounded by long windows, and festooned with cigarette smoke, thick as bunting, benches lined up, facing one another like pews, as if all the passengers would want to compare notes. Loudspeakers overhead spilled down departures and arrivals.

'Where is she?' Rose-Renee again demanded.

'Dunno. I can't hardly remember her. Can you?'

'I never met her.'

'You did so.' Marcella jabbed her with an

3

elbow. 'You met her, you were just too little to remember.'

In that milling throng of smoke and humanity, debris and candy wrappers, at the back, a tall thin woman rose, a woman upright as a ship's figurehead, though not opulent. Gloria Denham stood straight, and unmoving, clad in pressed pants and a cotton sweater. She had a mass of curly grey hair, reminiscent of steel wool, a narrow nose and keen blue eyes; she was breastless, buttless, thin-lipped as a trout, and nearly as expressive.

'Marcella. Rose-Renee,' she said with royal composure. 'Where is Valerie?'

'She's coming.' Marcella waggled a finger towards the tracks. 'A soldier's helping her bring her stuff.'

'Very well.' Gloria took her keys from her purse. 'I'll get the car. When she gets here, you all come down to the street. I'll pick you up at the corner of Second and French.' She left them.

'What'll we do now?' asked Rose-Renee.

'What do you think? Wait.' They took seats with a view of the doors. 'You and me are like Heidi,' said Marcella after a bit. 'Heidi went to live with the grandfather who she didn't know at all, and she changed his life. 'Member how I read you that book?'

'Sort of.'

'Everyone loved Heidi. We're going to live with our grandmother, and I bet we change her life.'

In reply Rose-Renee wagged Cubbie in front of her sister and made a series of silly noises. Marcella laughed and used Barbie to bonk

4

Cubbie on the head.

At last Valerie came into the waiting room carrying her overnight case, and her handbag, but the handsome soldier, Danny, toted her three other suitcases. Told they were to meet Gloria down on the street, he insisted on carrying them all the way down the stairs. The girls tore down the broad, steep staircase well ahead of their mother and the soldier. A light summer rain fell, so softly it made no noise on the roof that protected the stairs and the sidewalk. Marcella and Rose-Renee left their dolls and suitcases with their mother and the soldier, who talked in low tones.

The girls went swinging on the iron posts, and splashing each other in oily puddles, chasing fat pigeons and collecting the ire of passers-by. Nearby buskers did not even notice them. The violin case lay open at their feet, sprinkled with a few paltry coins. The violinist had thick sideburns, a moustache, a bandana over his long hair, a tie-dyed T-shirt. His whole being seemed channelled into the bow and the instrument. The long-haired girl, who wore dangly earrings, and a skirt that swished around her ankles, lifted her voice and her arms. They were a gorgeous duet, beautiful operatic arias, the boy's playing lilting and lovely, the girl's voice clean and rich and ringing. Marcella stopped the game to listen, to watch, enchanted by the singer who brought such theatrical emotion to the sidewalk. Marcella held Rose-Renee back from a particularly noisy splash, took her hand and drew her over to stand in front of the buskers. Rose-Renee started twirling to the music, as did Marcella, dancing.

The young GI and Valerie regarded the dancing children and the musicians.

'That girl sings very well,' said Valerie. 'In a few years, I'll be singing opera, but I won't be on the street, I promise you that.' She smiled radiantly.

'Too bad I'm a Johnny Cash kind of guy. Don't know squat about opera. Will I see you again?' asked the soldier.

'I don't think so. But I will never forget your kindness.'

Gloria pulled up in the big Lincoln sedan and tooted her horn. Marcella executed a quick little finale, along with a bow that sent coins showering into the boy's open violin case as commuters moved towards the stairs. Then she grabbed Rose-Renee's hand and ran for the Lincoln.

The handsome soldier loaded their bags into the trunk. With the lid still up, he flung his arm around Valerie's back and pulled her into a tight embrace, kissed her long and hard on the lips. She laced her arms around his back. 'You've given me something to remember,' he said with a big grin, 'even if I don't like opera.'

Smiling, though she hoped her mother hadn't seen the impromptu kiss, Valerie hustled her daughters into the back seat with their dolls, as she got in the front. 'Mother,' she said, a bright, expectant look on her face, 'I'm so happy to see you.'

'It's been a long time. Welcome home.'

'Oh, thank you. Thank you. You don't know

what it means to me.'

'Did you pay the musicians?' Gloria had a thin, querulous voice.

'What?'

'Them.' Gloria nodded towards the boy and the girl.

'They're hardly musicians, Mother,' said Valerie. 'Street-corner Mozart? Kerbside Puccini?'

'It's a principle, not an artistic judgement.'

'They're just practising on the street.'

'They seem to me to be rehearsing. They're serious. You can tell. A real musician cares about the music, not the venue. The venue is not always a matter of one's choice.' Gloria did not put the car in gear. The engine hummed.

Valerie opened her purse, took out a dollar bill.

Marcella snatched it from her hand and ran back to the buskers. She dropped the money in the boy's violin case, as he played away, and the girl, in the midst of a lovely high note, opened her arms to Marcella in a gesture of gratitude. 'You're welcome,' Marcella shouted as she hopped into the back seat of the Lincoln, and pulled the door shut.

Gloria was not a good driver, over-cautious, rethinking every stop and start, her foot erratic on the gas pedal, sometimes using the brake and the gas at the same time, as though uncertain which was correct. Other cars honked at her continually until they got out of Wilmington proper, and to the roads leading to affluent suburbs on their way to Chadds Ford. On either side the land gently undulated, and the fields were stubbled with early summer. Marcella rolled down the window and a light rain blew in, and a scent altogether new.

'Roll it up,' said Valerie. 'Too much wind.'

'Rose-Renee'll vomit if I do.'

'I will,' said Rose-Renee. 'I'll vomit. I promise.' She sent a secret grin to her sister.

Gloria regarded the girls in the rear-view mirror. 'I suppose I can look after them for the summer, but I can't amuse them. I have my work, and my work comes first.'

'I know that.'

'But do they?'

'They look after each other, don't you?' Valerie turned in her seat, eyeing them expectantly. Gloria gazed into the rear-view mirror.

'I look after Rose-Renee,' Marcella declared. Rose-Renee grunted.

'Are there any other children in the neighbourhood?' asked Valerie.

'How should I know?' said Gloria. 'I have nothing to do with children. Oh, there is a boy, Dorothea Jones's boy, but he is afflicted, always sick. I hope you don't think I will be taking the girls around to introduce them to — '

'We're just fine on our own,' offered Marcella. 'We don't need anyone else.'

Marcella and Rose-Renee were indeed self-sufficient, their own small cabal. As the daughters of a touring actor, they lacked practice making friends. At each new school (and there were many) they followed the same drill: show up, shut up and go home. Marcella, however, could not quite master the shut up part. Marcella collected applause for her reading, her running, her singing, finger-painting, and anything else she tried to excel at; she was inherently high-spirited, robust, and revelled in approbation. Rose-Renee, her mirror opposite, refused to participate in any activities, including the basics of learning. She would slump, cross her arms, stick her hands in her armpits and close her eyes rather than try to read, or learn to add or subtract. Moreover she refused to take tests that would help to place her. At more than one school, the teacher called Valerie in to discuss her younger daughter. (Mitch was always rehearsing.) Valerie confessed to the teacher that she had nothing to confess, or offer, really; she simply didn't believe Rose-Renee was retarded. Rose-Renee didn't look retarded, did she? Look at her. She had none of that fat face or sloping forehead or tiny eyes. She wasn't the beauty that Marcella was, fine, and she didn't have Marcella's brains, or talent, all right, but Rose-Renee came from a very artistic family, and she was probably just a late bloomer. Teachers did not request a second parental conference. Rose-Renee was always placed into the euphemistic Green Group, or its equivalent, along with children who chewed on their own hair till they gagged, pulled out their eyebrows, who suffered tics and fits.

'When are you flying out, Valerie?' asked Gloria.

'Day after tomorrow. Stockholm.' Valerie savoured the word audibly, as though it were

9

surrounded by cotton candy.

'Stockholm,' Marcella repeated. She did not like the word; it felt hollow on her tongue.

Valerie continued, 'You girls are going to have such a lovely time! The whole wonderful summer lies in front of you!'

She had been saying this for weeks, as they were preparing to leave Mitch, but the girls' experience suggested that when Mitch or Valerie, or any adult for that matter, told them they were going to have a fine time, a good time, a lovely time, a wonderful time, something not-so-fine lay in the offing. Marcella glanced at Rose-Renee; across her face there wordlessly traipsed concurring emotions. The sisters were, in some ways, their own separate country with customs and language known only to the two of them. They communicated with snorts and snuffles, monosyllabic expressions, odd words, hand signals and encrypted looks of the sort that savages no doubt exchanged before humans invented speech.

The children's mutual distrust of the wonderfulness that lay before them was reinforced when Valerie burst into 'Oh, What A Beautiful Mornin''. Valerie had once sung the lead, Laurey, in a Bard College production of *Oklahoma!* Mitch had played Curly. Singing was not Mitch's great forte, and he seldom referred to this experience, but it remained embedded on Valerie's psyche for ever. She could sing every song in *Oklahoma!* (except for 'Pore Jud Is Daid', a dismal anomaly to the otherwise rip-roaring score). The songs from *Oklahoma!*

were a gauge to Valerie's life, the rousing ones when things were going well. Other times — say, when Mitch woke up in an ugly mood, or came home in an ugly mood, or perhaps did not come home at all — the lesser-known plaintive songs sufficed. The girls knew to scatter at the sound of 'Out Of My Dreams'. But now, with a great, a lovely adventure in front of her, Valerie broke into 'Oklahoma!' and 'Surrey With The Fringe On Top'. Marcella and Rose-Renee knew every word to these anthems, and from the back seat they lent their voices.

Rose-Renee tugged on Marcella's sleeve and made a face. Marcella called out. 'Rose-Renee has to pee.'

'Can't she wait?' asked Valerie.

'No. Now.'

'You'd better pull over, Mother. If Marcella says Rose-Renee can't wait, then she can't.'

'You mean by the road?!' Gloria said, aghast, and not even slowing down. 'You let them pee by the side of the road like peasants?'

'Oh, it's nothing. She's just a little girl.'

'It's disgusting. Just because she's retarded you let her get away with anything.'

'She isn't retarded.'

'She has to pee!' Marcella called out. 'Me too!'

The Lincoln pulled to the side of the road, and the two got out and found their way to some bushes where Marcella stood guard for Rose-Renee, and she returned the favour. When they returned to the Lincoln, Valerie was saying to Gloria, 'Well, you don't expect me to leave them with Mitchell, do you?'

11

'He is their father.'

'But he's going on tour with *Major Barbara*. He is a classical actor.'

'Yes, with a second-rate company in a tired revival.'

'At least he's working. He has a play.'

'Will he be sending support?' asked Gloria.

'You mean, like money?'

'I don't need moral support.'

'I don't know about money. I . . . I don't think so. We didn't talk about money.'

Marcella and Rose-Renee exchanged a look of coded disdain. Mitch and Valerie had talked about money, argued and fought about money all the time. Mitch called Valerie a spoiled brat because she had grown up in a wealthy household, with no practice making ends meet. Valerie indicted his egotism and failure to provide. They were both right. Valerie's ends never met and Mitch often failed to provide.

They got back on the winding road, and Valerie rolled down the window and stuck her head out. The June air was moist and fragrant with promise. 'Same old Brandywine smell.'

'Brandywine.' Marcella tasted the word for sweetness or savour or specialness. She liked it. She added it to her cache of secret words and fine phrases, like *Mozambique* and *hover* and *serendipity* and *chandelier* and a hundred other words she had read, but would never have occasion to say. 'Brandywine, what is it?'

'It's a river near here,' said Valerie brightly, 'a whole area synonymous for a century with great American artists, and our house is the centre of

12

its musical reputation. Mother's music room is renowned all over the world for its acoustics. Daddy built it for her wedding present, didn't he?'

'Barry loved me,' said Gloria. 'He really loved me.'

Marcella and Rose-Renee regarded one another quizzically. Maybe Gloria didn't know about Jean, the woman their grandfather Barry lived with. Barry and Jean had a house on a canal in Fort Lauderdale, Florida, where they could park their boat in their backyard. When Mitch had played dinner theatre in Fort Lauderdale, Barry and Jean had taken Marcella, Rose-Renee and their parents out on their shiny big boat, and Rose-Renee managed to get seasick and fall overboard while she was vomiting over the rail. Marcella went in after her. Mitch had to rescue them both.

'You should teach the girls the violin this summer, Mother,' said Valerie.

'Don't be ridiculous. I am not a teacher. I need all my time to rehearse.'

'See you remember that, girls,' said Valerie with a laugh. 'Gloria doesn't practise, she rehearses.'

'Practice is time spent in achieving perfection, which is fine, well and good, but rehearsal is time spent in achieving perfection towards performance, which is the goal of every artist.' Gloria turned and gave Valerie an unforgiving stare. 'If you don't know that, you've no business studying opera.'

'Yes, Mother,' Valerie said obediently, falling silent.

'In any event, opera will be difficult at your age, Valerie. You're over thirty. Too late to become a first-rate singer. You will have to make up for a lot of lost rehearsal time these many years.'

'It's my chance. My dream. Can't you just be happy for me?'

'Why should I be? You're the mother of two children. You have responsibilities. I had to part with my dreams to raise you and Linda. I did my duty.'

There was a short pause in which Valerie debated reminding Gloria that both she and her much younger sister Linda had been sent to a Philadelphia boarding school at the age of nine. She thought better of it. 'Just let me leave here with a good heart, won't you, Mother? I need this summer. That's all. This opportunity. I'm going to work very hard, harder than I've ever worked. Please, Mother. Just say you believe in me.'

Gloria's timorous driving slowed to a crawl as the Lincoln turned on to a hilly, narrow road that passed for a state highway; that is, it had a number and a double yellow line. 'You and Linda both have a musical gift. When you have a gift, it is your duty to cultivate it, but both of you have squandered time, which is more precious than money for an artist. Linda is off in the Berkshires living on a commune with a bunch of filthy hippies, and you! You ran off and married the first good-looking man who gave you a smile and a tumble.'

'He did not give me a tumble. Well, he did, of

14

course he did, but I loved him. I was a girl,' she said again, a catch in her throat, 'who fell in love with a handsome actor.' Valerie Denham, a freshman at Bard College, had indeed met Mitch McNeill in the chorus of Bard's production of *Anything Goes* in 1957. Their attraction was immediate, elemental, all-consuming. Impulsively, they borrowed a car, and eloped to Elkton, Maryland. From Elkton, they drove to Chadds Ford, Pennsylvania, to announce to Valerie's parents that they were married. They expected to be feted, even lauded for their romantic daring. Instead they were chastised for their stupidity and roundly accused of gross ingratitude, but the deed was done. Both families were outraged, each for different reasons. However, the young couple needed an apartment, and their expenses met, and neither the bride nor groom had any intention of quitting school, or getting a job to pay for the other's education. Mitch's family, the McNeills — shopkeepers in upstate New York who had scrounged their last penny to send their only son to Bard — continued to pay Mitch's tuition. The Denhams, a far wealthier family, absorbed the rest of the couple's expenses, at least until they graduated, Mitch in theatre, Valerie in vocal studies. After that, the young couple set off along the rocky path of wedded life. The birth of two daughters early on, a string of furnished rentals, lousy cars, and uncertain pay cheques as the family followed Mitch, touring in various repertory companies, leeched away their youthful elan. Their youth was only part of the

15

problem. For Valerie and Mitch, their whims passed as needs. They were each accustomed to being the brightest star in any firmament, and each expected the other to shoulder the adult burdens. When they finally split up, their paths parted like an elopement in reverse. That they now had two daughters was an inconvenience, but not insurmountable.

'You were a girl then,' Gloria agreed, 'but now you are a mother. You can't just pretend that the marriage, and the two children, didn't even happen.'

'I'm not pretending anything. I just need this summer. Please.'

The Lincoln turned on to an even narrower road, no lines and unpaved shoulders draped with sumac and blackberry bushes. It was unnumbered, potholed, and rose and fell over undulating countryside dotted with stone farm-houses and white barns. Coming over the top of a hill, a car in the middle of the road hurtled towards them. Gloria swerved, corrected, and only just avoided the ditch. Valerie screamed. In the back seat, the girls bounced, and Marcella's arm flew across Rose-Renee's chest, and hit her with a thump.

'They drive like that around here,' Gloria commented grimly.

Gloria followed a peeling white fence, the thin country lane flanked on either side by woods or meadows with low fences tortured by blackberry bushes, and in the distance stands of trees dotted the surrounding hillsides. She came to two flowering cherry trees on either side of stone

16

pillars that marked the Denham place, and turned into a long uphill drive. At the first curve, a huge house came into view. Compared to the farm-houses they had passed, the Denham place was palatial, two long, two-storey wings extended from the centre core of the house. Terraced gardens sloped down to the long drive.

'I remember a pool here!' cried Marcella. 'When I came here last time. Can we go swimming?'

'How could you remember any such thing?' asked Valerie. 'You were only . . . what, four?'

'The pool has been filled in,' said Gloria.

'The gardens look a little . . . ' Valerie's voice trailed off.

'I am not made of money,' said Gloria. 'Nor, unfortunately, is Barry. He sends me almost nothing. I can only pay for the most basic care. I have a couple of boys who come to mow and whatnot twice a month in summer. I live a quiet life. A regular sort of life. I do not expect that to change.'

'They're very good girls, aren't you?' Valerie turned to her daughters, cueing them to agree.

'Oh yes,' said Marcella, ever ready to be agreeable, to charm.

Rose-Renee tucked her hands in her armpits, her chin resting on her chest. She grunted. When there was talking to be done to any adult, Marcella did it.

'See, Mother?' said Valerie. 'They are a duet. Aren't you?'

The McNeill sisters were a duet on the order of brimstone and treacle. Rose-Renee was secretive, suspicious, and in her child's mind and

17

heart there lived a peasant who sneered at her betters, though she might be obliged to bow to their will. Marcella was much too hungry for applause to be either secretive or suspicious. On the contrary, she was reflexively eager to please; she would grin, sing, turn cartwheels, tap dance or tell stories, anything for approval. She thought of herself as wonderfully winsome, rather like Heidi or Anne of Green Gables, or Shirley Temple. She could sing 'Animal Crackers in My Soup' and 'On the Good Ship Lollipop' by the time she was three; however, since she'd turned eleven, she'd noticed her performances did not elicit as many indulgent smiles as they once had. It never occurred to her that at eleven she was no longer the plump, cute little girl she had once been. She thought for sure there was something wrong with the songs.

2

Detritus of the Disembodied

Unlike Heidi's grandfather, who was dour, Marcella found Gloria Denham to be serene and uncurious, so the prospects for effecting life-changing happiness were dim. The morning after Valerie left for Stockholm, Gloria poured herself a cup of coffee from the chrome percolator while Marcella read the back of cereal boxes to Rose-Renee.

Gloria cleared her throat meaningfully, and Marcella quit reading. 'I need to remind you girls of the house rules. There are rules in any house, of course, but mine are very simple. You are not to disturb me while I rehearse, unless it's absolutely necessary, of course. Some emergency. For that, yes, of course, but I can't have my concentration broken by a lot of childish whining or interruption. It takes me a long time to work up to perfection and if I'm interrupted, I must start all over again. You understand?'

'Oh yes, Grandmother,' said Marcella.

'Susan Digges comes three days a week. She tends to things. Laundry and the like. If you put your laundry in the little bathroom there — ' she motioned to her left ' — I'm sure she'll wash yours too. She irons as well. She does a bit of cooking, casseroles, that sort of thing, that I can heat up. Do you like casseroles?'

19

Rose-Renee emitted a series of short, expressive snorts suggesting they detested casseroles while Marcella grinned, and said, 'Yes, Grandmother.' She did not say she had been cooking for the two of them since she was six. Her speciality was hot dogs and beans.

'Susan will come tomorrow. At nine. She has her own key. She lets herself in. You can meet her then.'

'Yes, Grandmother.'

'You must stay around the house. The gardens. Don't go roaming off where you can't be found. I can't be troubled to go looking for you. Especially in the dark. In fact, I won't. So see you're here every evening. Certainly by five.'

'Yes, Grandmother.'

Gloria frowned. 'You should call me Gloria, or Mrs Denham. Grandmother seems too . . . too . . .'

'Gloria,' said Marcella.

'My schedule is very much set and I need it to stay that way.'

'Yes, Gloria.'

'And quit saying yes. You sound like a recording.' She sipped her coffee. 'If you should need me, for some emergency, I'll be in the music room. Would you like to see the music room? Go wash your hands. You can't come into the music room without clean hands.'

They washed their hands, and dutifully followed her through the foyer with its high chandelier — Marcella was glad to have a chance to whisper one of her special words — and down a long hall, lit on one side by wall sconces alternating with framed black and white photographs of intense men in tuxedos. The windows lining the other wall offered a view of terraces with scraggly boxwood borders.

'Pablo Casals played duets with me in this music room,' Gloria said as they followed her. 'Andrés Segovia as well, the Paganini duets. Igor Stravinsky himself wrote deathless music on my piano. I had to tell him he could not smoke here. And Darius Milhaud, he too wrote here, though he had passed his prime by then, and he was always altogether too fanciful for my taste. Too happy.'

Rose-Renee tugged at Marcella's arm.

'Who are these guys, Gloria?'

'Why, they are the premier musicians of the twentieth century! You didn't know that?'

'Sure,' said Marcella. 'We know.'

'Really, before I played with Segovia, I never even considered the guitar a serious concert instrument, though I have since changed my mind, naturally.' Gloria paused at a pair of heavy, mahogany double doors, each with an oval set in the centre and in the oval was a woman in flowing draperies with a lyre in her hand. 'These St Cecilia doors are the originals, made in Italy, in Rome. There's nothing else like them in the whole world. They cost thousands.' Gloria lingered on the last word as she ran her hands over the carving.

'Who is she?' asked Marcella.

'St Cecilia. She is the patron saint of musicians. I, personally, do not believe in such superstitious rot, but the architect insisted.'

'Does she sing?'

'She might have. I don't know. She has a special day, though I don't know what it is. I suppose it's good that musicians have someone who cares about them. God knows they need it.'

For want of any better response, Marcella said 'Uh-huh' and followed Gloria into the darkened space. She snapped on the electric light that shone from a hundred wall sconces and another chandelier lighting the centre of the room, all of them lit with tiny bulbs like flames. Windowless, the ceiling was ribbed with beams of teak, and the shining floors were also teak.

'Barry had this room built specially for me,' Gloria said, warmth suffusing her frail voice. 'It was his wedding gift to me. He really loved me.'

'I can tell,' said Marcella, thinking of Jean.

'It was designed by the premier acoustic architect of our time, well, of that time, certainly. Fabriziano Massimo. He came all the way from Rome. When Barry wrote to hire him to build this room for me, he said yes instantly. I still have the telegram somewhere. Signor Massimo was very flamboyant. Very difficult to live with, though it was worth it.'

'He lived here?'

'He stayed here to supervise the whole time it was being built. A year. Signor Massimo had to have his suits pressed just so, and his silk scarves and his silk vests. He drank nothing but Italian wine, or Campari and soda. He hated everything the cook made for him. He insisted on his own gramophone in his room, and brought his own records. He travelled with five steamer trunks. He was truly difficult. Didn't speak a word of

English and refused to learn. He brought his own interpreter. A Miss Manetti. Very young. Very pretty. Hmmph. We will never forget her!' she said, without quite specifying who we were, or why Miss Manetti was so memorable.

Marcella added *Miss Manetti* and *Signor Massimo* to her secret stash of words and phrases.

'Signor Massimo went back to Rome and disappeared. They say he made an enemy of Mussolini.'

Rose-Renee scratched her nose. *Who cares?* in the sisters' private parlance.

'The acoustics are extraordinary. They insulate me completely against every outside noise, and at the same time, every note played in this room is heightened and brightened and crystalline. It is a marvel, the most perfect small performance space in the whole country. This room was written up in *Architectural Digest* and *Town and Country*, and dozens of music magazines, the *New York Times*.'

At the centre a shrouded harp stood, and nearby a grand piano, a Steinway, covered with an ecru silken scarf with fringe. Between these two instruments there was a long bevelled mirror, a thin music stand, and a drop-leaf table with a violin case on it. Beside the music stand there was a floor lamp with a maroon satin shade fringed in black. Other than these few items, the vast space was empty, except for a tufted divan off in the corner, and a few wing chairs upholstered in creamy blues and greens. The chairs' bodies were set on fat, contoured wooden

23

legs, like overfed patrons of the arts.

Gloria delicately opened the violin case with arched fingers; she removed the instrument as though it were a sleeping baby, and the bow as though it were a magic wand. 'This is 1727 Stradivarius. Do you know what that means?'

'That it's wonderful?' ventured Marcella. Rose-Renee's wrinkled nose meant she did not care.

'I played Stravinsky's violin concerto on this very instrument to a select audience, including Stravinsky himself. People were speechless. Speechless.' She smiled and her sharp features softened. 'I play them all, you know, Mozart, Mendelssohn, Brahms, Beethoven, Paganini, Schumann, Vivaldi, Ravel. Everyone. All the greats. Would you like to hear me?'

Marcella smiled a brightly anticipatory *Yes!*. Rose-Renee grunted in the negative, but Gloria could not understand her.

At Gloria's instruction, they pushed the wing chairs closer to the centre of the room; the chairs slid, unimpeded, on the burnished floor. They curled up in them; the room was cool and the girls were only wearing shorts. Gloria turned the pages of the score on a music stand that was as thin and gaunt as she was. She closed her eyes, straightened her back, took a deep breath and drew the bow across the instrument, and music undulated through the room. Marcella had no idea what she was playing, but she recognized — without the words to say as much — that some sort of enchantment transpired here, that each note seemed to hang suspended in that rarified air, and that the whole cloth of the music

24

itself sailed out from that small instrument like an ornate scarf billowing overhead and leaving indelible shadows on whomever might be present to hear.

Though she had music on the stand, Gloria kept her eyes closed. One piece followed another with no time for applause. She had forgotten the children completely. Rose-Renee, communicating with her right foot, indicated she was bored mindless. Marcella shook her head. Rose-Renee slid from her chair, and started towards the door on all fours. Marcella was half-afraid to follow. What if Gloria opened her eyes and they were gone? Would she be angry? And she was half-afraid not to follow. What if Rose-Renee got lost? How would they find each other in this enormous house? They'd never lived in anything bigger than a two-bedroom apartment. Rose-Renee made it to the door and stood there. She wiggled her left thumb at her sister. Marcella stirred, coughed, coughed again, louder. Much louder. And then again.

Gloria roused from her trance, the music stopped, and she peered at them, surprised to find them there. She spoke the only apology she ever offered, at least to Marcella and Rose-Renee. 'Sorry, girls. Now, run along, and remember I'm not to be disturbed.'

★ ★ ★

Gloria was cordial to the McNeill sisters, as though they were paying guests whose needs must be recognized and met, but with whom no real relationship exists. She took all her meals alone in the breakfast room just off the kitchen, or in the den, her special room. She ate while reading a book and with the phonograph playing. She retired to her room every night by nine, rose every day by eight, ate a light breakfast and vanished into the music room. She might break quickly for lunch, a sandwich and a piece of fruit at midday, and she stopped practising between three and four. Weather permitting, she would take an hour's walk, return, make herself a cocktail, light a cigarette, and either sit on the verandah overlooking the boxwood maze, if the weather were good, or if it were not, she went into the den, and put a record on the turntable. There were record players, and many old gramophones, all over the house. She listened to the same sort of music she had been playing all day. At this time of day, if they wished, Marcella and Rose-Renee could talk to her, but there was no obligation.

This was just fine. The girls could play till night fell, and no one cared, or called them in, or told them to be careful, or be quiet, or be nice. The empty spaces of their grandmother's house delighted children who had spent their young lives living in furnished rentals with one bath and a kitchenette. Here, in these high, empty rooms, the girls jumped on the beds and ransacked the closets, pulling out, dressing up in frocks and evening gowns, fur coats, smoking jackets, scarves, smart hats, high-heeled shoes, rummaging through the bureau drawers, pawing through the contents, gloves and stockings and costume jewellery, hankies that smelled of lavender water, and Chanel N°5, floaty peignoirs, men's pyjamas. There were gramophones and tennis racquets and walking sticks that sufficed the girls for swords. Inspired, they ran riot with this finery; they play-acted, lived out stories of princesses and crones and dashing captains, took their games outside to the vast, overgrown gardens and thick woods, open meadows whose only occupants were stalwart cows.

At twilight they delighted in the fireflies that rose up, brilliant with ephemeral light. The girls chased them through the dusky gardens, and then stood, arms extended, palms out, absolutely still and waited for the fireflies to alight on their thin, bare arms. At first they competed, counting fireflies, but soon left off; they stood that way until their arms grew tired, and they had to go inside.

They rummaged through the tall kitchen cupboards, and the butler's pantry, searching for cans and the can-opener. Gloria had a standing order with a grocer in town. No A&P for Gloria Denham. Stoddard's Provisioners delivered to the house every Tuesday, a day when grumpy Susan Digges was there to put things away. The bill was always left on the kitchen table so Gloria could go over it minutely, be certain that Stoddard's had not cheated her. She had never caught them cheating, but she had certainly brought to their attention the occasional error. When Marcella and Rose-Renee came to live there, Gloria asked the girls what they liked, and duly added to her list hot dogs, buns, pork and beans, ketchup, peanut butter, jam, bananas, Cheerios and Frosted Flakes, Chef Boy-Ar-Dee, potato chips, Fritos, though no candy or Twinkies. Gloria drew the line at that. As an afterthought she added more milk and bread.

Marcella told Grumpy Susan she needn't bother to make casseroles for them. For supper Marcella opened a can of beans, and slit hot dogs lengthwise, and using a fork toasted them over the gas flame. She slit the buns the same way and toasted them quickly. She put a bottle of ketchup on the table, and they doused the hot dogs and the beans. They sat their dolls on the kitchen table while they demolished the hot dogs. The kitchen faced west and the long fingers of twilight reached into every cranny, lighting up the cobwebs.

'Is this a dolls' tea party, girls?' Gloria asked one evening, coming into the kitchen in search of ice cubes for her cocktail.

'Yes, Gloria. This is Barbie. And this is Cubbie,' offered the ever-winsome Marcella.

Rose-Renee took a huge chomp of her hot dog and it stuck out of her cheek while she chewed and scowled.

'Linda used to have tea parties with her dolls,' mused Gloria. 'She was such an adorable child. Very sweet. Much sweeter than Valerie. And what a talent. Oh, Linda could play Liszt when she was twelve. She could have gone to Juillard, but no, she must go to Radcliffe. Just to spite me, and even at that, she wouldn't stay. She lives with filthy hippies on a filthy commune in the Berkshires. She was a sweet, sweet child, and I

28

was sorry to see her become such a wilful adult.'

'Did she have toys?' Marcella gave her Good Ship Lollipop grin.

'Toys?' asked Gloria, suddenly brought back to the moment. She struggled with the ice-cube tray.

'I know how to do that,' said Marcella, jumping up and taking the ice tray, giving it a good upside-down smack on the counter. 'Mitch showed me the trick of it, so I could get ice cubes for him.' She snapped it open with a resounding crack. 'Rose-Renee and I didn't bring too many toys, just Cubbie and Barbie, and we were wondering if we could play with Linda's toys. Or Valerie's, or any old toys, really.' She did not say that they had already pillaged the place looking for toys, for blocks or board games, trains or stuffed animals. But no luck. They found only a shelf with boxes of thousand-piece jigsaw puzzles and playing cards in the sunroom.

'Oh, I gave them all away. They outgrew them. Do you girls have everything you need?'

'Yes, Gloria.'

''Cept for toys,' muttered Rose-Renee.

'You know to stay out of Susan's way when she's cleaning?'

'Oh yes,' said Marcella, stifling a laugh because Grumpy Susan's (so they had named her) cleaning involved a desultory broom and duster; she always brought a book of crossword puzzles and worked on them in the kitchen, and smoked cigarettes while the wringer-washer chugged, or the iron heated up.

29

'And the boys, the gardeners, you know to stay out of their way when they're mowing?'

'Oh yes,' said Marcella, knowing by now they were not boys at all, nor gardeners either, but two men who came twice a month to whack and thwack and mow.

Despite the whacking and thwacking, weeds still sprouted from the bricks and flagstones on the terrace. The pool, filled in, was overgrown, rampant with dandelions, and set about with massive ceramic urns at the corners, the geraniums in them long dead, the weeds triumphant. The Denham house had been created, clearly, for lavish entertaining, though the ballroom was long closed, the chandelier shrouded. Once it was also a centre of equestrian festivities, but the stables had been torn down, the horse runs, fences for dressage were mere meadows now and rented out to dairy farmers whose bovine herds made plaintive calls across the rolling hills, the verdant landscape. Other sounds sometimes reached Marcella and Rose-Renee. When they came to woods that ringed Gloria's property they might hear cheering from some distant baseball game involving children who lived in developments, tracts with long straight streets that had been carved out of what was once Denham property. But the girls never ventured any further to see to whom these voices belonged. They returned to the house.

'You're too stupid even to play Old Maid,' snapped Marcella, using her arm to sweep all the cards onto the floor in Gloria's sunroom. They played at a bamboo card table and sat on bamboo chairs, the cushions upholstered with ghastly maroon and white magnolias. 'You're always changing the rules to make yourself win.' The stakes in these games were arm-farts to be inflicted on the loser's inner elbow.

'Don't wanna play Old Maid. I wanna play Go Fish.'

'You can't play that either. You're lazy and you cheat.'

'You're ugly.'

'I'm rubber, you're glue.'

'Let's play Doll Wars,' suggested Rose-Renee. This was their favourite indoor game, flinging Barbie and Cubbie at one another from behind forts they built in the drawing room, overturned chairs and musty cushions. They shouted *Bonk* when they hit their target.

'Nah.'

'Then Gingerbread Girls,' offered Rose-Renee. 'Let's play that.'

'You always win at that, too,' said Marcella sulkily.

'But I don't cheat.'

At outdoor games, Rose-Renee was invincible; her wariness, her alertness to sound and scent and movement served her well in games of pioneers, or pirates, or princesses, Robin Hood and Indians, ape-girls, but especially in their original creation, Gingerbread Girls. Based on the ill-fated Gingerbread Man — so stupid he got eaten by the fox — Gingerbread Girl was considerably smarter. The game consisted of the chant, *Run run, fast as you will, you can't catch me, I'm the Gingerbread Girl!* You couldn't simply be tagged to be 'It'. You had to be wrestled to the ground, and this presented new dangers: nettles and ticks and poison ivy.

For the nettles and poison ivy, Grumpy Susan pointed them to the bathroom off the kitchen and the bottle of calamine lotion. They painted each other till they looked like peppermint sticks rather than Gingerbread Girls. The itch was gone, but their skin crinkled and flaked. Ticks were another matter altogether. Rose-Renee got a tick in her socks that stuck fast to her flesh and burrowed. Grumpy Susan had to get it out with a hot needle while Rose-Renee screamed her guts out.

'Hush,' Marcella consoled her. 'Hush, Gloria will hear you.'

Grumpy Susan scoffed. 'Go ahead, scream all you want, in that room she'll never hear you.'

There were drawbacks to living at Gloria's. Mitch and Valerie had let the television serve as babysitter. The television at Gloria's did not work. However, there was the library, a sunny, spacious room lined with bookshelves on either side, a fireplace and great comfy, overstuffed couches that felt springy as mushrooms and somehow ingested Marcella, rather like a story ingests you if you remain too long in its pages. The library provided Marcella with a perfect orgy. She had always relied on the public library. Marcella's favourites were all the Wyeth-illustrated children's classics, and many books that harked back to childhoods even before Valerie's and Linda's, books like *Peter Pan* and *Rebecca of Sunnybrook Farm, The Little*

Princess, the *Yellow, Blue* and *Red Book of Fairy Tales,* and an abridged *Uncle Tom's Cabin,* each lovingly inscribed to people whose names remained a mystery to Marcella. Additionally there were bestsellers from Edna Ferber, Taylor Caldwell, J.P. Marquand, books with no pictures and so of scant interest.

Marcella took the books to bed with her too. Gloria had assigned them rooms adjacent to one another, with high, four-postered beds, but Rose-Renee and Marcella had never slept apart, not in all those years while Mitch played Chicago, Minneapolis, Milwaukee, St Louis, Kansas City, Fort Lauderdale, and points in between. On their very first night Rose-Renee barrelled into Marcella's room, jumped up on the stool and into bed with her. 'Morton is after me,' she whispered.

'Morton?'

'Go look. On the back of the door in that room where Gloria tried to put me. He's hanging there. Go on. I dare you.'

'Nuh-uh. I'm not getting out of this bed. I'll look in the morning.'

'He might not be there. He mighta come down off that hook and be stomping around looking for a cat to eat.'

'I didn't see any cats.'

'That's because he ate 'em.'

Morton turned out to be a pair of hip waders, rubber pants complete with boots — fishing gear so a man could wade out into Brandywine River. The rubber was cold and clammy. Morton dangled by his long suspenders from the back of

33

the bedroom door, as though his legs remained, but the rest of his body had vanished. He became their pet spook; they would call to him, each claiming to hear his eerie, anguished reply: *Where is my skin? Where are my eyes? Where are my arms?* Morton's night-time laments counterpointed the creaks and rattles of the old house.

With the music from the phonograph in Gloria's bedroom wafting down the long hall and serving to cue the mood, Marcella told stories, entertained Rose-Renee with tales of Morton, and other bodiless creatures who might have returned: Miss Manetti, Signor Massimo, Pablo, and Andrés, Darius who was altogether too happy, and Igor who smoked and scribbled at the piano. They might have come back, all of them, come back to retrieve all the finery they had left behind — the gramophones, the hats and gloves and walking sticks, and smoking jackets, the long scarves, and high heels — ghosts seeking their skin, their arms, their eyes, the laughter and good times they had left in these abandoned rooms.

Andantino

Lulled by the roar, still sleepless, anxious about what lay ahead, Marcella rested her head against the cold, small window. The night had ebbed from the eastern sky, and cabin lights came on suddenly and speakers squawked that they should put their tray tables up and their seats in the upright position for landing. Marcella gazed

34

out as the plane circled the dawn-dappled land-scape above greater Philadelphia. A thin haze obscured the city, the river, the trees, the arterial ribbon-roads, the slender, thread-like routes lead-ing to woods and meadows, and beyond. 'To Brandywine', she whispered. The word and her breath fogged the glass and vanished together.

Along with other weary passengers, Marcella trudged out of the plane and into the arrival lounge where her Aunt Linda met her, hugged her, and remarked cheerfully, 'They don't call it the Red Eye from LA for nothing. You look terrible.'

Marcella laughed. At forty-two she was sturdy, her dark hair salted lightly with grey; fleshly parentheses framed her mouth, and the Califor-nia sun had crinkled the skin around her dark eyes, but her mouth remained mobile. 'What's the old saying?' she offered. 'At a certain age a woman has to choose between her face and her butt. We can go straight to the car.' She hoisted a backpack. 'I don't have any baggage.'

'Figuratively speaking,' Linda corrected her.

Linda's familial instincts — to incite, rattle, upset — had not changed, though in her line of work she had cultivated considerably more tact. As Director of Development for the Tanglewood Music Festival since 1987, Linda had honed formidable powers of persuasion. Using these she had eroded Marcella's thirty years of resolve never to return to Gloria's house. Linda negoti-ated shrewdly, offering that she, Linda, would take care of all the arrangements, including all lawyer-meetings, and Marcella would not even have to attend the memorial service. Just come for these last two days at the house. Come because Linda could not deal with Valerie alone.

They walked towards the parking garage, exchanging the usual enquiries and news of their children, the trappings of their respective, far-distant lives, Linda's grown sons both living in New York, Marcella's school-age children, Linda's pending divorce, Marcella's twelfth anniversary. The summer morning had already relinquished much of its freshness to smoggy humidity. Marcella threw her backpack into Linda's SUV, got in the passenger seat, and as soon as Linda turned on the soothing air conditioning, she promptly fell asleep.

Thirst woke her, and by this time Linda was well out of the city and its sprawling suburbs, even beyond Kennett Square.

Marcella fumbled in her bag for a bottle of water and her sunglasses, protection against the August light, so different from the dusty bronze sunshine in Los Angeles. 'So tell me all about the memorial service.'

'Which I spared you.' At fifty, Linda looked like Gloria; she was thin with blue eyes, except that Linda had laugh lines, and her often acerbic wit was usually tempered with high spirits if not warmth.

'And I'm grateful,' said Marcella truthfully.

'It was all in extremely good taste and the music was beautiful. What else do you need to know?'

'How did you endure it?'

'Never underestimate the power of alcohol.'

'How did Valerie handle it?'

'Badly. She's still flapping around about the millions she thinks she ought to inherit.'

'She's known for twenty-five years the house would go to Curtis Institute.'

'And Curtis did right by us. They paid for the funeral, burial, and they'll pay for headstone. The entire board of trustees, and faculty, right down to the lowliest professor, was there for the memorial, all of them just as sad as if Gloria had been their own dear mother. They rattled on about her generosity, her artistry, and her commitment to music and her alma mater. On and on and on! Oh, and Mrs Campbell sat in the front pew with me and Valerie. The family, the fucking family.' Linda added, 'And she beamed like a lighthouse every time someone noted her role in getting Gloria to give Curtis this glorious bequest, the Gloria Denham Performance Space and Conference Centre, blah blah blah. Why are you laughing?'

'I was just remembering when I was in grad school at UCLA, I was on the city bus and a woman sat down next to me reeking of Tabu. Suddenly, really, I was twelve all over again, sitting at the piano at Dorothea's, and cowering in front of Mrs Campbell. I had to get off the bus and walk. It was all involuntary, you know?'

'No.' Linda was not renowned for her imaginative empathy.

'Well, then I can't explain it. I never did understand how Mrs Campbell could have wormed her way into Gloria's good graces. She was so cloying and Gloria was so astringent.'

37

'Tut tut, Marcella. Eunice Campbell had nothing but nice things to say about you, about your pioneering work in music therapy, even about your book, A Song for St Cecilia, though she said Gloria was upset to find herself portrayed so harshly in it.'

'I wasn't harsh. I wrote about her playing, about the way music dominated our lives while we lived with her.' Marcella took a swig from the water bottle. 'I never even alluded to the truth.'

'You alluded to it.'

'Listen, it was a memoir about music, not a medical treatise. I asked other people to share their experiences with me, and they were forthcoming. How could I not put my own life in the book?'

'Well, personally, I think Mrs Campbell was upset that you didn't include her.'

'It wasn't about learning 'Turkey In The Straw'. It was about the power of music to flood the brain with memory.'

'And it netted you a nice professorship.'

'Please, Linda, don't make me defend my work to you. I have enough — '

'Never mind. Sorry. Listen, about Valerie, word to the wise: she's mixing up her meds with alcohol. New boyfriend too. Someone named Robert, or Roger, or something like that.'

'What happened to Greg?'

'Who cares? Just treat her carefully.'

'I always do. Well . . . ' Marcella paused. 'I always try to.'

The two sisters, Valerie and Linda, could not have been more unalike. Linda was brisk and

38

earthy. Valerie careened between pathos and folly, shrouding her weaknesses under a mantle of fragility, which made her irresistible to men, and bloody annoying to women like Marcella and Linda.

'Just so you know, Valerie is better in the morning.'

'She always was,' said Marcella. 'Mitch was better at night, but they were both unpredictable, except for their noisy bouts of boodling.'

Linda laughed out loud. 'Oh yes, boodling! How well I remember Valerie's euphemism.'

'In a two-bedroom apartment, there was no question what Valerie and Mitch were up to, no matter what you called it.'

'Speaking of Mitch, Valerie wanted you to call him.' Linda began to dig about in her bag, looking for her phone. 'She'll ask, and she'll get upset if — '

'I called from home. I hate talking to Mitch and having to listen to his sonorous voice. I always feel like he's talking to me while he's watching himself in the bathroom mirror, gestures and all.'

'He's an actor, what do you expect?'

'Yes, the Grand Old Man of the Ashland Shakespeare Festival for twenty-five years. As much a fixture there as Lithia Park.'

'Valerie likes to think that she was his One True Love, that he loves her still. She's always pointing out that he never remarried.'

'His one true love is himself,' Marcella scoffed. 'Why should he remarry? He's lived with about a dozen Cordelias. Some new woman answered the phone. And when I told him Gloria had died, all he said was, 'Gloria was an awful old bitch', and that 'Only meanness had kept her alive into the new millennium'.'

'Didn't he ask after money?'

'He knows it's all going to Curtis.'

'Let me guess. Then he went on to tell you all his successes for the summer season 2000.'

'Yes. I listened and then I said goodbye.'

'Mitch is a simple man.'

'He leaves complexity to the characters he plays.'

'You'll have to tell Valerie that he sent his love.'

Vexed at the thought of all the confectionery phrases she'd need to deal with Valerie, Marcella asked, 'Why are we doing this again? What are we taking from the house?'

'What we'd like, within reason, the sentimental stuff.'

'What a crock.'

'Don't be so cynical. Eunice Campbell is a primary executor of the estate and it was her provision on our behalf.'

'What on earth for?'

'She thought you'd like it.'

'You're kidding.'

'I'm not. She thinks the world of you. Really! She was very disappointed you weren't at the memorial service. Anyway, only the sentimental stuff is left. Even Morton is gone. Stolen. It's been going on for years. There's no point in complaining.'

'I'm not complaining. I don't care.'

40

Linda shrugged. 'There's been a series of nurses over the last ten years, and a lot of Curtis people in and out, so it's all been gradual. There's quite a bit missing, including the Wyeth watercolours that hung over the library fireplace, and the signed photographs, a couple of the silver tea services. Anyway, it's all probably on eBay nowadays.'

'It doesn't matter to me. There's nothing I want from that house.'

'Me neither, but your mother is a different story.'

'What Valerie wanted from Gloria,' said Marcella, 'she was never, ever going to get.'

'Maybe that's why Valerie kept telling the lawyers how we, I mean she, deserved something, money, a lot of money to compensate her for her annual trips to see Gloria. All these years. She was the only one who visited Gloria regularly, no matter what.'

'Until I was twenty she used to try and make me go with her,' said Marcella, 'but I wouldn't do it. I'd go spend the time with Mitch if I had to, but I was never coming back here. She called me pigheaded.'

'You are pigheaded.'

'Yes, and in that I'm more like you than her. At least we're not like Gloria. She nurtured her gift and wasted her life.'

'She didn't think so.'

Certainly, Marcella thought as she gazed out the window at the drying hues of late summer, Gloria Denham had not given — or received — any of those soppy ties of empathy and sympathy, affection and regard, those cross-hatched family loyalties that tug and fray, strengthen and spindle over the years. She was burdened with none of that messy effluvia that makes our lives so complicated, funny or tragic. Or all three. Her cool precision was the more chilling for its lack of overt malice. None of which absolved her.

3

The Pig Sisters

In all their experience of adults — Mitch, Valerie, grumpy stage managers, uninspired teachers, cranky landladies, short-tempered neighbours, drunken prompters, leering actors, crabby waitresses, underpaid clerks — nothing prepared Marcella and Rose-Renee for Dorothea Jones.

She arrived one evening in July, 1969, and rang the front doorbell, a sound Marcella and Rose-Renee had never heard. They forsook Doll Wars to run to the foyer, where they found the door wide open, and Gloria herself standing there, speaking to whomever had been so audacious as to appear and ring the bell.

Gloria was polite, but crisp in her introductions. 'Marcella, Rose-Renee, Mrs Lee Jones. Mrs Lee Jones, my granddaughters.'

'Yes,' said Mrs Lee Jones with a sort of breathless smile, 'that's why I've come. I heard at Stoddard's that your granddaughters were living with you now.'

'Visiting,' said Gloria, 'just for the summer.'

'To be sure,' said Mrs Lee Jones. 'I hate to interrupt. I know you practise every day.'

'I rehearse,' Gloria corrected her.

'To be sure,' Mrs Lee Jones said again. She was a robust, sturdy woman with a round, open face and hair the colour of brown sugar cut short; damp tendrils framed her face. She smelled faintly of chlorine and sweat and banana suntan lotion. She wore khaki shorts and a knit shirt with a collar, athletic socks and athletic shoes. Her tanned calves were moulded with muscles. 'They're lovely girls, your granddaughters. Quite the image of your own self, Gloria.'

Although this was patently untrue, Gloria regarded them as if seeing the girls afresh.

Mrs Lee Jones chatted on a bit, but when Gloria offered no invitation to enter, she got to the point. 'I'm wondering if your little girls would like to come play with my son, Rodney, tomorrow. Often, really. As often as they like. They're just about the same age as Rodney — he's twelve — and he would so love the company.'

Gloria turned to the girls. 'Rodney is afflicted.'

'That's not true!' Then Mrs Lee Jones modulated her tone. 'No more than any childhood illness. He will grow out of his asthma. Would you like to come play, girls? Rodney would love to show you his train set, and we have a pool.'

Rose-Renee and Marcella exchanged looks of raw elation, and replied with an emphatic and collective yes.

'Wonderful! Rodney will be so happy. I will too! You will like him, and I know he will like you. I'll see you tomorrow, then. Come around eleven and stay for lunch. Well, Gloria, I'll see you . . . ' Mrs Lee Jones's voice trailed off. She almost never saw Gloria. Few people did.

'Wait!' cried Marcella. 'Where do you live?

44

How will we know your house?'

'I'm sort of half a mile in that direction, through the fields.' She waved in a vaguely northerly direction, the opposite of the housing developments. 'It's grown over now, though. I came along the road. I could have driven, of course, but I believe in fitness and exercise. Would you like to walk home with me? So you'd be sure not to get lost?'

They accompanied her. The road, narrowly bordered by brambly hedges, was thick now with summer and dust. Mrs Lee Jones's stride never lost its pace, though she slowed in deference to their shorter legs. She talked about her son. Rodney Lee Jones. He was named Rodney after Caesar Rodney, the signer of the Declaration who was related to her husband's family. Did Marcella and Rose-Renee know the story of his famous ride to Philadelphia, eighty miles on horseback, probably over these very roads, to put his signature on the Declaration?

'What declaration?' asked Marcella. Both girls were a little breathless keeping up with her.

'Why the Declaration of Independence, of course. Caesar Rodney didn't have any children of his own, but he had scads of relatives and they all lay claim to him.' She added with a rippling laugh, 'But why should it matter who you are related to? People should be proud of their own accomplishments, not what the long-dead once did. I'm a Californian, and I prefer a rosy future to some sort of hallowed past. I find all this glorifying the past tedious, don't you?'

'Dunno,' said Marcella for both of them.

She chattered on, how she had grown up in Claremont, California, daughter of a geology professor at Scripps College for Women, and a physical fitness enthusiast. She had been swimming all her life. She had been Athlete of the Year at Scripps, and competed in the 1952 Helsinki Olympics, though she hadn't placed. 'I practised every day. That's the only way to be good at anything at all. Practice.'

'You mean rehearse,' said Marcella.

'Yes. I was a champion swimmer.'

'We don't know how to swim.'

'Don't know how to swim! What's wrong with your parents! I assure you, you girls won't be getting in this pool until you've had some lessons!'

'We don't need lessons. We're never going to have a pool.'

'Everyone needs to know how to swim! Swimming is not just an art, it's a skill. And it could save your life.'

'Couldn't we just stay in the shallow end and splash?'

'Would you say that of life, Marcella?'

'What?'

'Would you say of life, oh, I won't learn how to cope with danger and challenge and excitement, I'll just stay in the shallow end and splash?'

'I don't know,' she said truthfully.

'Well, of course you wouldn't. That would be, well, unbrave, unadventurous. And besides, life is full of depths you must explore. Just like the pool.'

Rose-Renee shot Marcella a look in which

they concurred that Mrs Lee Jones was weird.

Mrs Lee Jones turned from the narrow road onto the somewhat wider state highway. On either side meadows sloped down to long, white, well-kept fences, some with barbed wire. Huge dogs raced downhill, seemingly coming out of nowhere, barking ferociously as if they would eat people alive. The girls both screamed, but Mrs Lee Jones just took their hands and marched past.

Cars zoomed by, paying scant attention to the solid yellow line, and honking at them if they walked three abreast. Rose-Renee ran along the side of the road, chasing a bird, hooting, following it as it fluttered to the other side.

'Come back here, Rose-Renee!' called Mrs Lee Jones. 'That's dangerous! People drive way too fast on this road. Please, be careful. You could get hit by a car!'

Rose-Renee ignored the warning, so Marcella marched to her, grabbed her arm and was about to bring her back to the shoulder when another car crested the hill, and barrelled towards them, the echo of its horn left hanging in the air, like exhaust, though the speeding car had long since vanished over the next rise.

'My knees are cold,' said Rose-Renee when they faced the prospect of another hill.

'Well, you can go back,' said Dorothea. 'Our house is practically right on the road, just up ahead. You can't miss it, an old white fieldstone farmhouse, nothing like Gloria's place. There's a mailbox at the road that says Jones. We'll see you tomorrow, then. Eleven. Rodney will be so happy.'

They turned and ran back the way they'd come. A car zoomed by.

'Nah! Nah! Nah!' cried Rose-Renee, jumping out into the road, waving her fist. 'Run run, fast as you will, you can't catch me, I'm the Gingerbread Girl!'

'Get back here!' Marcella shouted. 'Jeez, what if there'd been another car coming?'

Rose-Renee ran headlong into her sister, laughing as Marcella stumbled off the shoulder and splayed into the road. A bark sounded and a snarl. Marcella scrambled up off the pavement, grabbed her sister's hand, and they ran as fast as they could. *Run run, fast as you will, you can't catch us, we're the Gingerbread Girls.*

★ ★ ★

Leaving Gloria's the next day, carrying Cubbie and Barbie, they started down the hill towards the stone pillars. Rose-Renee stopped. 'I don't like the dogs,' she said.

'I don't either. I bet there's a short cut. Their place can't be that far, can it? I bet it's not too far from the pond. Come on, let's go that way.'

They turned and went back beyond the gardens out towards the woods and the pond. They had explored much of Gloria's property, but they got lost just the same, or took a wrong turn and kept walking, surrounded only with endless vistas of untroubled cows. At last they came to a farmhouse. A pickup truck was parked in front with a big sign on it that said *Bowker's Septic Service*, and the cackle of hens and the snorts of pigs could be heard from a side yard they could not see. They were tired and dirty, sweaty, thirsty and quarrelling when they knocked on the door.

A huge German Shepherd bounded at them when a middle-aged woman in rumpled clothes answered. 'Sit!' she barked, and he sat.

'We're looking for Mrs Jones.'

'You're lost. She don't live near here. She's over there.'

'Could I have a drink of water, please?' asked Rose-Renee.

'Sure. Come on in.'

Though the day was sunny and hot, the kitchen was dim and cool. A man stood up in the shadows; he was paunchy and grizzled and his shirt was stained and sweaty. He lifted the front of bib overalls and snapped them at the shoulder. 'You gone a-ways off course if you're looking for the Jones place, little ladies. I'll drive you there,' he said, putting a cap on his head. 'Go on and get in the truck. I'm just leaving.'

The truck smelled something fierce. They were breathing through their mouths, and Rose-Renee held her nose, but Mr Bowker just laughed. 'I guess I don't even smell it a'tall no more,' he said, as he drove along the narrow road. 'Where're you coming from?'

'Over there,' Marcella said. 'The Denham place.'

'Oh, we heard Gloria's granddaughters come to live with her.'

'Just for the summer. Our mother is in Sweden studying opera. It's her destiny.'

49

'Fine destiny. Opera.' He seemed to chew on the word 'opera'.

'And our father is touring in *Major Barbara*.'

'What about you two?'

'What do you mean?'

'Well, you girls probably got lotsa talent,' he said. 'Just like your granny.'

'Yes,' said Marcella, pleased with the praise, 'we do.'

'I never heard your granny play, not myself, but oh, lotsa people did, come from all over to hear her and lotsa others play their fine instruments. There used to be some fine doings there at the Denham place. Septic troubles all the time, they had so many people a-coming and a-going. Mostly going.' He laughed at his own joke. In his nasal twangy accent, he chattered about the septic systems in the area, how artists and farmers alike needed their systems tended. Then he downshifted and the septic truck pulled off the road and immediately on to a short, rounded driveway. 'Here's Mrs Jones's place,' he said. 'That house was built two years afore my house. There's a cornerstone you can still see, 1789.' It looked less like a farmhouse and more like a white fort with five deep windows on two floors across the top and dormers on the third floor. Ivy crept up and clung to the stone, and red climbing roses framed either side of the covered porch. 'People built stuff to last in them days. My people been round here for a long time. You see the porch around this here house? My great-grandfather added that porch in 1855. He was a fine builder.' He leaned across and

50

opened the door for them.

'Thank you, Mr Bowker,' said Marcella.

'Any time, little ladies.'

'I druther take on the dogs than ride in that stink wagon,' said Rose-Renee as they ran to the front door. 'You shoulda found it in the first place. You are a sissy and a no-good explorer.'

For that Marcella bonked her with Barbie and she defended herself with Cubbie. Mrs Jones opened the door in mid-scuffle.

'I was so worried!'

'We got lost, Mrs Lee Jones. We tried for the short cut and got lost.'

'I've been calling your grandmother to see what could possibly have happened to you. But there was no answer.'

'She can't hear anything in the music room,' said Marcella. 'And it's not Grumpy Susan's day.'

'Well, never mind. You're here safely! Rodney is so looking forward to this. Oh, and you must call me Dorothea. Mrs Lee Jones sounds so . . . so like your grandmother, doesn't it? Come along!' She led them through a hall with a shining floor, and into the kitchen. There was a huge fireplace on one wall, and the four gleaming windows had deep sills which were thick with African violets. Sunlight spilled in, though the place remained cool. 'Ethel,' she said to an older woman with a furrowed face and a stained apron, 'meet Marcella and Rose-Renee. They are staying with their grandmother, Gloria Denham.'

'I know the Denhams,' said Ethel.

'Only that's not your name, is it, girls?' said

Dorothea. 'What's your last name?'

'McNeill.'

'We're going to have lunch out by the pool,' said Dorothea, 'but first I'll take you to Rodney's room.'

The whole second floor of the house belonged to Rodney Lee Jones. On one side of the stairwell was his bedroom with his own private jungle painted along the walls. And suspended all around, on slender, invisible threads, were model airplanes, mostly vintage bi-planes and delicate mobiles of paper cut into fantastic shapes. These swayed in the air currents from the open windows. The walls were lined with shelves and the shelves were lined with every toy imaginable, trucks and stuffed animals, most of them pristine and loveless. He had games and a box of Lincoln Logs and an Erector Set. He had every Little Golden Book known to man, and a beanbag chair to read them in. From the high, uncurtained windows the view looked out over rolling hillsides, dotted with cows and distant trees. Right below his window the sight took Marcella's breath away: a swimming pool, a flagstone patio, a wide lawn with a trampoline, all of this fenced to keep the animals out.

The pasha of all this splendour was a spindly kid with his mother's light-brown hair, though his was thin, and lank and dry. He had her blue eyes, but he was so gaunt that they looked bigger. His nose looked bigger too. Where Mrs Lee Jones was tanned and fit and rounded, Rodney was pale and wan and thin. He sat at a desk, which was vast, and covered with papers and model airplane parts. The room smelled sharply of glue. He barely looked up; nodded as his mother introduced the girls.

'Now, Rodney! You must say hello and show them around!'

He said hello with a semi-smile. His wrists were knobby, and his back curved slightly, his shoulders rounded over his innards. When his mother left them, the smile drained not simply from his mouth, but his blue eyes seemed to go empty and grey.

'What a great place you have here, Rodney,' said Little Miss Treacle. 'And you have a pool!'

'We have a pool.'

'And a train set?' said Rose-Renee.

'Yes.'

'Where is it?'

He motioned for them to follow him across the landing and into a sunny schoolroom with a teacher's desk and a single desk facing it, with maps on the wall, and easel, and a drinking fountain; just like a regular school, thought Marcella, only cleaner. At the back, on a child's-height table there was a train set complete with miniature painted brooks, trees and bridges, a town with a railroad station that had lacy iron pillars holding up the roof, just like the Wilmington train station. Altogether perfect.

'Turn it on,' said Rose-Renee. 'Please.'

'It doesn't work very well,' said Rodney. 'There's something wrong.'

'Why don't you fix it?'

He shrugged, unwilling to expend the energy to explain himself.

'Want me to fix it?' Rose-Renee offered.

'No, you'd just break it. You're just a baby.'

'Am not.'

Just then Mrs Lee Jones came in, all smiles and talking about lunch outside and fine summer weather. 'Wash your hands and come along.'

She led the girls through the kitchen to the flagstone patio that surrounded the pool, all the way out to the fence. The pool, patio, and broad fenced lawn were clearly all recent additions, and very much incongruous with the farmhouse itself, with its assorted outbuildings, woodshed, cider house, smokehouse, all testifying to what must once have been demanding physical labour extracted from the generations who had once farmed here. In contrast, the patio was set about with pots of lavender and geraniums, and the pool itself gleamed and twinkled, a sapphire blue, oblong, like a perfect gem, completely sunny at one end and shadow-shady at the other. Two small changing rooms stood beneath an elm, neatly painted white with green trim, like stables for toy horses.

'Now, here, Marcella, Rose-Renee.' Dorothea showed them their places at a table covered by a jaunty green-and-white-striped umbrella.

Marcella set Barbie on the table, her legs splayed for balance, and Rose-Renee leaned Cubbie against her. Cubbie fell over. Marcella and Rose-Renee nearly fell over as Ethel walked around the table and loaded up plates with mountains of mashed potatoes with rivers of butter running down their sides, great big hamburgers on fluffy buns, great slabs of tomatoes alternating with leafy lettuce, and an array of pickles and peppers and mounds of coleslaw. Rose-Renee's nose twitched, and she offered not merely a grunt, but a groan of pleasure as the sisters picked up their spoons and dug in.

Mrs Lee Jones reached across, and touched each of their hands, pressed them down slightly towards the table. 'It's customary,' she said, 'to give thanks.'

'Thanks,' said Marcella.

'To God.'

God was someone not very well known to the McNeills, never having been to church in all their lives, but they thanked him just the same, silently, as Rodney and Mrs Lee Jones offered up their prayers. And then they went at it, shovelling that food in like their lives depended on it.

'Look at those girls eat, Rodney!' Mrs Lee Jones cried, her face alight with pleasure. 'I like to see girls eat. Enough of this Twiggy business! Where I come from, people know how to eat. Rodney, you should follow those girls' examples.'

Few could have followed their example. Dorothea realized these girls had been hungry for weeks. Clearly Gloria Denham had no notion whatever how to care for two children. Rose-Renee and Marcella were too engaged with the mashed potatoes and hamburgers to offer response to Dorothea's cheerful banter, which centred mostly on the pleasures of the pool, of swimming in general, and how she intended to coach them.

'Is that coach like in Cinderella?' asked

Marcella between gulps.

'Not quite,' said Dorothea gently. She beamed at her son. 'I hope you've saved room for dessert. You've done very well, dear. You've eaten a very good lunch. I'm proud of you.'

Rodney smiled at her, pleased to have made his mother happy. She cleared the dishes, put them back on the cart and wheeled it through the door into the mudroom, and then into the kitchen.

The three sat there, listening to the blue water lap noisily against the sides of the pool.

'How often do you beat your dolls?' asked Rodney.

'We don't beat them.'

'They're all beat up.'

'Are not!'

'Look at that one.' He pointed at Barbie. 'Look at her hair and her torn-up dress.'

'We have Doll Wars,' said Marcella. 'And that's all we're going to tell you.'

'Why would I want to know anything about either of you? You think I care? My mom wanted you here, I didn't. You think I wanna play with two stupid girls?'

'We're not stupid.'

'Rotney,' Rose-Renee blurted out. 'That's your real name. Rotney.' She gave her squinty smile, said it over and over, lingering. 'Rot . . . ney.'

He accepted the ignominy of the name. He said nothing.

Dorothea brought out a half-gallon of ice cream, a can of whipped cream and a jar of chocolate syrup. Rose-Renee gave a barely audible squeal, and Marcella had to hold her arm, to keep her from falling over, face-first into the dish as Dorothea scooped the ice cream and told them to eat up.

★ ★ ★

For the first time in their lives, Marcella and Rose-Renee were not treated as mere impediments to adults' needs and wishes. Dorothea Jones was ongoingly delighted with the McNeill sisters. She found them charming, lauded their small triumphs and listened, chin resting in her hand, to Marcella's stories, the true and the false, never asking which was which. She watched them jump and twirl and fall and jump and twirl and fall on the trampoline, bumping into one another and shouting out, 'Bonk!' She said Marcella was a natural athlete, that she should take up gymnastics. She seemed completely content to have them underfoot. Dorothea personally fixed the train, and did not care if they wrecked it again and again. She thought it was funny when Rose-Renee cut her waffle in half, folded it again, and stuck it in her mouth. She actually applauded when Marcella took an orange slice between her teeth and then bared her lips in a grotesque smile. She got into the spirit, and one day tossed a little Brussels sprout at Rodney, who was at first alarmed but then he tossed one back at her, and she broke into peals of laughter. She was happy when he followed the girls' piggish example, and he ate well to see her smile.

Rodney Jones, on the other hand, just

57

tolerated the McNeill sisters. As a playmate, he was neither engaged nor engaging. He watched the train wrecks without contributing to the various stories Marcella concocted. They used his paints and toys while he watched them, as if they were actors whose task was to amuse. Occasionally they got into proprietary fights with him in which he reminded them he was sole owner over all this domain. Emboldened by her victory that first day, Rose-Renee called him Rotney all the time (though not around Dorothea). He did not repudiate the name, nor retaliate for that matter.

When Marcella told Dorothea they were afraid of the dogs on the walk to her house, she instantly wrote a note to Gloria (on cream-coloured paper embossed with *Dorothea Jones* in gold script) asking to have the thwackers mow the short cut between the two houses. She made the case for the additional expense by saying how the cars went by so fast on the road. The road was known to be dangerous. Marcella delivered the note, slid it under the St Cecilia doors and ran away.

When Gloria came in for the ice for her cocktail, she said, 'I will pay for this first time, but if it needs to be done again, Mrs Jones can pay for it.'

The short cut, once hewn down, provided a wonderful path that took them past a large, scummy pond, and through woods and meadows where they learned to steer clear of the cow pies and the cows. Monday through Friday, they arrived around eleven and had swimming lessons

58

with Dorothea before lunch. She jumped into the pool with them, demonstrated, and they followed, learning proper breathing and kicking and strokes. Dorothea called them little champions with great form, and called on Rodney to applaud. She said both girls had untapped talents, and Marcella tucked the phrase into her cache of secret words. *Untapped talents.*

Once they learned to swim, the two girls took to the water like tadpoles, exploring and imagining among the pale shadows, magical places, whole watery kingdoms. Underwater, free of every constraint, propelled by their own strong bodies, moving smoothly through the ripples, air bubbles escaping their lips, they dipped and twirled, enjoying a finite freedom that would only last until they must come to the surface and take a breath, not knowing, not then, that all happiness is finite, and sooner or later you must come up to the surface and take a breath.

Rodney never went into the water; he sat in the shade, and dangled his feet in the pool. Rodney always wore a baggy swimsuit and never took off his long-sleeved T-shirt. His knees were bony knobs and his feet in the water looked green. He was always slathered up with sun cream and he wore a baseball hat. Rose-Renee and Marcella splashed him, but he didn't seem to mind, and that took the fun out of it. He was like a little old man.

But as the weeks passed, Marcella began to reassess Rodney. He was a weakling, but he was a thinker. You could tell. He made elaborate model airplanes, but he did not play with them. Dorothea hung them up for him, and he seemed content to watch them blow about in the breeze. He folded paper into unique shapes, animals mostly, and linked them with slender threads into mobiles and Dorothea hung these as well.

'What do you call those?' Marcella demanded of him one afternoon.

'Origami.'

'What's that?'

'I can't explain it. I have to do it.' He folded creased paper, his hands blocking the actual process from view, and eventually he handed her a paper peacock. He did it again and handed Rose-Renee a paper elephant.

'Can you teach me to do that?' asked Marcella.

'No, you're too dumb, and your sister's even dumber.' He settled back into his chair.

'What's wrong with you anyway?' Marcella asked, flopping on the beanbag chair. 'How come you're always so sick?'

'I'm not sick.'

'Ha ha! Look at you. You're sick as a . . . ' She glanced over to her sister who silently offered up a wonderful epithet. 'A dirty donkey.'

Rodney did not have the strength for the fight. 'I have gastroenteritis and asthma. Childhood diseases. Anybody could have them.'

'We don't.'

'Yes, but you're putrid. You are Putrid and Stinko, the Pig Sisters.' He made a snorting noise.

Marcella did not know what putrid meant,

though clearly it was something disgusting. She called him Rotney for lack of anything else to say.

'Rotney,' Rose-Renee echoed.

'You're going to grow up to be fat and ugly and no one will marry you,' he went on. 'Both of you.'

'Oh yeah?' Rose-Renee stood up, suddenly emboldened. She pointed an accusing finger at him. 'Well, at least we're going to grow up. Look at you! Look at you! You're sick, and you're going to die! We're going to live, and you're going to die!'

Marcella pulled Rose-Renee away from him, fearing suddenly and inexplicably that the death she wished on him was catching. Rose-Renee broke free and continued to taunt him, ignoring Marcella's attempts to intervene, darting, evading Marcella's grasp, moving in closer, yammering all the while that they were going to live and Rotney was going to die.

When she got close enough (and he waited till that moment; he was still calculating his energy), he smacked her. A good one. 'Now, go cry, you putrid baby.'

'Cry? You think you can make me cry? I been bit by ticks, buster. I had a tick taken out of my leg with a hot needle and I didn't cry. Try, try, hard as you will,' she sang out, 'you can't make me cry, I'm the Gingerbread Girl!' But Rose-Renee's lip trembled, and she clutched her cheek where the imprint of his hand was beginning to rise. She glared at her sister, and nodded, *Go get him*.

Marcella did not move. She sensed that Rodney

61

had squandered every bit of energy he possessed. One retaliatory blow would have flattened him. 'Let's go.' Marcella took her sister's elbow.

'Go? And let him win?' Rose-Renee struggled to free herself. 'Lemme alone! I wanna make Rotney cry!'

'You can't.' Marcella dragged her away.

'Can too.'

'Shut up.'

'Go away,' Rodney said, rising from his chair, and moving in his rickety fashion, back to his bed. 'I'll tell my mother to send you away for ever. I hate having you come here. I just want to be left alone. I wish you'd both go away and never come back. I hate you.'

Marcella pulled the protesting Rose-Renee down the stairs, through the kitchen and the mudroom, and without a word to Ethel, who frowned at them grimly, she shoved her out the back door.

Rose-Renee stayed stomping mad all the way home, angry that Marcella hadn't fought him, that she'd just let him smack her, that Marcella was a stupid fraidy-cat, and rattling on about all the ways she was going to make Rot cry.

'Will you just shut up about Rot,' Marcella said at last. 'He got you good, that's all. Accept it.'

'No.'

'Then shut up just the same. Jeez, I mean it, shut up.'

They walked the rest of the way in stony silence, Marcella struggling with a complex welter of shame, anxiety and pity. She could not shake off the yucky feeling that something irreparable had happened, that Rodney would tell Dorothea what Rose-Renee had said, that he was going to die. Marcella knew — not just in her heart and mind, but in her very guts that now roiled with fear — that Dorothea would never tolerate the presence of anyone who believed Rodney was really sick and dying. She would never forgive anyone who was unkind to him; she would ban the Pig Sisters from ever returning. Marcella could not bear that thought, though whether her anxiety had to do with the pool or the train set or the food, or the basking in Dorothea's admiration, she could not say.

The next morning, though Rose-Renee seemed to have forgotten their quarrel, Marcella had not forgotten its cause. When they arrived at the Jones house she went cautiously up the stairs to find Rodney as usual at his desk, twisting paper.

He looked up. 'Putrid and Stinko,' he said in a good-natured way. He smiled. 'The Pig Sisters.' He gave them each an origami pig, complete with little tail.

4

The Audition

Rodney Lee Jones was the first person ever to tread inside that metaphorical fort over whose walls Rose-Renee and Marcella had watched the world. The three moved towards tolerance, then trust, then an odd, sometimes wobbly friendship, for each of them their first experience with three-way loyalties. Rodney taught Marcella to play chess, a game in which Rose-Renee had no interest whatever. He made special origamis for Rose-Renee, any animal she wanted, and before long, a paper menagerie collected atop the dresser in their bedroom. Slowly, Rodney lost much of that old-man wariness that had made him so comic. He got more adventurous in the pool, and splashed back. The game quickly turned to Rodney and Rose-Renee against Marcella. Marcella was the strongest. Rodney was the smartest, but Rose-Renee was the most adventurous.

One intolerably hot, sticky afternoon, too hot even to go outside and swim, Rose-Renee suggested they make a fort and play Doll Wars.

'It's too hot for a fort,' Marcella said, turning back to her book.

Rodney looked up from his airplanes. 'I've never made a fort.'

'What? Never?'

'What's the good of making a fort alone? You

64

have to make it with someone.'

'You want to play Doll Wars? It's a fun game,' said Marcella.

'How do you play?'

Rose-Renee walked over to the shelves of furry friends, their expressions unchanging, some with toy tags still in their ears. 'Rot's got plenty of ammo.'

'Easy. You make a fort and then you throw things, and whoever gets the most bonks wins.'

'How do you know if you've been bonked?' he asked.

The sisters smiled knowingly.

They pulled the mattress and pillows off his bed, and upended the beanbag chairs and tiptoed downstairs into the living room to steal the cushions off the sofas to make three forts. They cleared the furry friends off the shelves, dividing them up equally, and went at it, a fierce competition that set the airplanes overhead in motion. A few of them got hit and little bits broke off. Rodney stood up to protest, and Marcella bonked him good.

'Not fair! My plane! I — '

'You can't stand up in the middle of the Doll Wars unless you give up.'

'But my planes!'

'Get down and fight.'

'Bonk! Bonk!' shouted Rose-Renee, hitting him again before he dove behind his fort.

They were trouncing him royally, and their victory cries rang out until Dorothea came in and gave a little gasp. 'Where's Rodney?'

'In here,' came the voice behind the sofa cushions.

Dorothea hurried over to her son's fort and, kneeling, pulled the cushions away gently. Her every feature knotted, as though a ribbon tied her face into a big package of pain. She took a pillow from the floor, and put it under his head. 'What on earth were you doing, girls?'

'Doll Wars,' said Rose-Renee.

'I won,' said Marcella. 'You both lost.'

Dorothea stroked his hair, and then tore the sheet off the mattress and covered him. He was sweating and pale. 'Water?' she asked him.

'It's just a game,' Marcella said.

'For you,' she snapped. She went into the bathroom and brought him out a glass of water, stroked his hair tenderly while he drank. 'Come, girls, I'm going to drive you home. I need to speak with your grandmother.'

'We're sorry, Dorothea. Honest.'

'No, not about that, though you ought to be more . . . well, you ought not to be so rough. You'll be fine, won't you, Rodney? Ethel's here. Call Ethel, dear, if you need anything. I'm just going to run the girls home.'

'I'll be fine.'

'Gloria's probably still rehearsing,' said Marcella. 'We can't bother her.'

'This is important.'

They got in her car, an old boxy Mercedes that smelled of leather and a smoky engine and Dorothea's banana sun-tan oil. Rose-Renee had the back seat to herself. Marcella took the front, feeling very grown up.

'I think you girls had better stay home for a couple of days.'

66

Marcella figured quickly. Wednesday. That meant four days with no pool, no toys, no train wrecks, and no ice-cream sundaes. 'But can't we —'

'Rodney needs to rest after a game like that.'

'He wanted to play. It was his idea.'

'Come back in a few days. You girls are good for him. But soon, of course, things will change. They will have to.'

'Why?' Was he dying? Marcella feared for him.

'Soon it will be the end of summer. Haven't you noticed? There are leaves in the pool and look along the roadside how everything is drying up. See? The sumac is turning scarlet.'

Marcella wouldn't have known sumac from shortening, but she dutifully looked out the open window where a thickly humid breeze blew in.

'Soon, in a week or so, after Labor Day, the pool will have to be drained and covered. The patio furniture will be put away in the old cider house. School will start in a week. Have you given any thought to school, Marcella?' She added, 'Have you girls been registered at the school?'

'My mother's coming back. It was just for the summer,' Marcella said, wishing she could see Rose-Renee and consolidate their stories. 'She's in Sweden, rehearsing to be an opera singer.'

Dorothea smiled. 'Practice, that's the only way to excel at something. Both of you girls might be first-rate swimmers if you practise.'

'You mean rehearse,' Marcella said.

'Yes. I rehearsed every day. I was a champion swimmer once.'

'You probably wish Rodney would swim every

67

day and be a champion.'

She turned her guileless blue eyes to the girl. 'Rodney is a champion. Rodney is the bravest person I know. I want him to be whatever he wants to become.'

She wants him to live, Marcella thought, struck, yet again, with the foreknowledge that he would not. For that moment, it seemed to be a secret that she and Dorothea shared as equals, as peers, not as a grown woman and a little girl. In that spirit, Marcella asked, suddenly curious, 'Where is Mr Lee Jones?'

'He is with the angels in Heaven.'

'My father's on tour with *Major Barbara*,' said Rose-Renee from the back.

'I'm sorry to hear that,' she replied. 'He should be with you.'

'He's a classical actor,' Marcella explained, using Valerie's line.

'Parents should be with their children. If they can. Rodney and I miss his father very much.'

'Was Mr Lee Jones sick like Rodney is sick?'

'Rodney is not sick.'

Marcella thought for a few minutes how best to phrase the question, and maintain the grown-up exchange. 'When did his father join the angels in Heaven?'

'Eighteen months ago. There was an accident. On this road, in fact, a little further down. The road was narrow and icy and he lost control of the car. It was very sad.'

'It sounds sad. I'm sorry.'

'Thank you, Marcella. He was a good father and a good lawyer. Everyone loved him. We loved

68

him.' Her voice brightened. 'Lee and I were such an unlikely couple. Lee's college roommate, Tom, was also on the Olympic team in Helsinki, and though Lee was not at all athletic, he came to cheer Tom on. That's how we met. I was used to being around men who were athletic and competitive and, well, brash, and here was this lawyer, very studious, and rather quiet, unlike anyone I'd ever known. And for Lee, meeting me was like . . . well, he always expected to marry a girl from his own social set, you know, a girl from around here, from a family like his, related to the Signers and all that.' She turned to Marcella with a wink. 'But once we fell in love, well, we were in love for ever. He had to wait for me to graduate from Scripps, two years, but then we got married, and I moved to Chadds Ford with him, and we bought this beautiful old farm-house, which I didn't like at first. It was so old! But Lee promised to build me a pool and a patio. And two years later Rodney was born, so everything was wonderful, except for the cold.'

'The cold?'

'Well, I froze! I had no notion of winter! I'd never seen snowfall. Never in all my life. In Claremont the camellias bloom even in January.' She seemed dreamy for a few minutes. 'But I've learned to appreciate winter. Lee had a new heating system put in the house, and I learned to skate! Do you girls ice skate?'

'No.'

'Well, then, you will have to learn, won't you? Just like you learned to swim. No more dallying about in the shallow end, right, Rose-Renee?' she called into the back seat.

'Right,' Rose-Renee chirped.

'You girls have worked hard, and I'm proud of you. I love to watch you, to watch anyone work hard and play hard and be rewarded for what you do well. That's what we all want, isn't it?'

'Yes,' said Marcella. 'We all want that.'

She pulled to a stop in front of Gloria's, turned off the engine, and smiled.

Marcella suggested, 'We should go round to the back. You know, the kitchen door. You can drive under the arch in the hedges over there.'

'I think it's best to deal formally with your grandmother,' Dorothea said, getting out of the car and crossing the wide porch. Marcella and Rose-Renee followed. 'I think she's that sort of person.'

'Well, I guess,' said Marcella. ''Cept if it wasn't Grumpy Susan's day, you could stand here and turn into a skeleton before Gloria would hear you and come to the door.'

But it was Grumpy Susan's day, and she answered Dorothea's persistent ringing of the bell, grumbling, 'Why can't you just go round to the kitchen door? Everyone goes to the back.'

'This is a formal call,' said Dorothea. 'Marcella, would you go find your grandmother so I can have a word with her.'

'She's rehearsing,' said Grumpy Susan.

'We'll wait,' said Dorothea, taking Rose-Renee's hand.

Grumpy Susan pulled a postcard from her pocket and handed it to Marcella. 'I went and picked up the mail at the post office box. It's

70

from Sweden. Remember to save me the stamps, willya? My grandson, y'know. He collects 'em, though why I can't imagine.'

Marcella read aloud. ' "This is a picture of the Opera House!!! Isn't it beautiful? I am working very hard, singing, studying, rehearsing every day. I hope you are having fun and being good! I love you!!' '

'She always says that,' Rose-Renee explained.

'I thought she was just gone for the summer,' said Dorothea.

Marcella shrugged, and turned to her little sister, and in their secret code they conveyed to each other, *We don't know when she's coming back, and we don't care; we don't care about the opera house, or that she loves us; we don't want her back.*

Putting the postcard in her pocket, Marcella set off towards the music room. As she walked down the long hall, wisps of music beckoned, small miscreant notes that somehow wiggled beyond the room's acoustics just long enough to ricochet down the hall. At the ornate doors, Marcella put her hand on the brass handle, then took it away. Gloria was playing a piece that was fierce and jubilant and unrelenting. Marcella dared not interrupt. Instructions aside, the very passion of the music itself was forbidding. She put her forehead against St Cecilia and listened. When at last Gloria finished, Marcella knocked. Again and again. Louder.

Gloria came to the door. 'Marcella?'

'Dorothea would like to talk to you.'

'Whatever for?'

'I don't know, but she's here. She's in the front hall with Rose-Renee.'

'Is everything all right?'

'I don't know,' she said again, and it was true.

Gloria greeted Dorothea formally, coolly. Dorothea, in her usual bouncy manner, waxed on about what lively girls they were, what good swimmers. She was a bright warm wind rattling Gloria Denham's frosty boughs. Finally she said, 'Have you thought about school, Gloria?'

'School?'

'For the girls. After Labor Day, in about a week, school starts.'

This observation seemed to perplex Gloria, but she replied that Valerie would be home soon. 'She said she would only be gone the summer.'

'That's lovely, and I'm sure she will, but if she's not, these girls must go to school. Surely you don't want the girls to go to the public school, do you? Surely Valerie and Linda did not go to the public school.'

'They went to Miss Butler's School in Philadelphia. They came home on weekends.'

'Well, what about these girls? They can't go into Philly, can they?'

'Certainly not. Miss Butler's costs a lot of money.'

'Well, you surely can't want Marcella and Rose-Renee to go to the public school. The public school is so . . . so . . . what's the word I'm looking for? You know what I mean, don't you?' Had Dorothea known her better, she would never have asked a question requiring Gloria to make a leap of empathy. When Gloria failed to respond, Dorothea declared, 'I've heard that some of those kids at Lafayette School have nits.'

'Knits?' Gloria made motions with her hands.

'Head lice. The thought of head lice! My skin crawls!'

'Why, that's disgusting.'

'The public school has no music programme at all. And physical education! Kickball, dodge-ball. That's it! Don't you find that shocking, Gloria? Especially for your granddaughters. Why, they might be great musicians if only they were taught.'

'I hope you are not suggesting I teach them.'

'Of course not,' Dorothea was quick to assure her, 'but we, that is, I, have an old piano. An old upright. Quite nice. It belonged to my husband when he was a boy. He used to play. I will find a teacher, and the girls can have lessons. They can practise there too, so you won't have to hear them. They should go to school with Rodney.'

'And where does he go to school?'

'Why, at home. We have a schoolroom that will be perfect. He gets a first-rate education: reading, math, social studies, and naturally art and music and sports. It will be perfect for Marcella and Rose-Renee. The kids are so good for each other. It would warm your heart to see them.'

But Gloria Denham was not easily warmed. 'Who is the teacher?'

'I am!'

'And how much will it cost?'

'Nothing. Lunch is included, and afternoon snack.'

Lunch and snack were the magic words for the Pig Sisters. Rose-Renee peered around Dorothea and gave her sister the waggled thumb. Marcella replied in kind.

Dorothea used other persuasions for Gloria, stressing that as well as being free, their going to school with Rodney would be no trouble at all for Gloria. 'They're already used to getting up and coming over in the morning five days a week. Now they must come at 9 a.m. sharp. Can you do that, girls? You see, Gloria, your days will stay the same, nothing needs to change for you.'

'Valerie will be home.'

'Yes, but until she is, they can go to school with Rodney.'

Gloria agreed without further protest and Marcella walked Dorothea out to the car. 'What do we need to go to school, Dorothea?'

'You need to be on time. You must ask your grandmother for an alarm clock, and set it each night for eight in the morning, Monday through Friday for school.'

'Why not Saturday and Sunday too? We get real bored here on Saturday and Sunday.'

'Saturdays Rodney needs to rest,' said Dorothea, 'and Sundays are reserved for church.'

'Our Sundays were always matinees,' said Marcella.

'Have you never been to church?'

'No. I seen them, but I never been inside one.'

'Church is a place where God is, or would be if He could be. Of course, God being God can be anywhere He wants, and that's why we pray to Him, but in church, you can be certain He is there.' Struck by the quizzical expression on Marcella's face, she added, 'Have you no spiritual life at all? Do you know the meaning of Christmas and Easter?'

'Presents and candy?'

Dorothea shook her head. 'I would be happy to take you girls to church with us, but every family wants their children to follow their own religion. Do you know what religion Gloria is?'

'No.'

'What church were your parents married in?'

'No church. They ran off, and got married by a judge in Elkton, Maryland. It was all very daring and romantic,' she added, again taking her cue from Valerie.

Dorothea laughed, kissed her forehead, and passed her chlorine-scented hand on Marcella's cheek. 'Well, certainly your parents have very daring and romantic daughters. You brighten up everything you touch. You make Rodney happy.'

'And you, Dorothea?' Marcella asked expectantly, hopeful. 'Do we make you happy?'

'Very. I'm so happy you're going to go to school with Rodney. We are going to have such a fine time!'

And for the first time when an adult told her that good times lay ahead, she believed; she did not doubt or recoil or wonder what might happen next.

★　★　★

On the first day, the day after Labor Day, 1969, Dorothea announced that they would be called

75

the Flag School. Rodney was in the White Grade, Marcella in the Red, and Rose-Renee in the Blue. Then they recited the Pledge of Allegiance, a generalized sort of prayer, and sang 'My Country 'Tis of Thee'. The schoolroom had been newly outfitted. Two new easels had been delivered, two new desks, complete with new pencils, notebooks, and coloured pens. Dorothea had already sought out a music teacher and she would be coming to visit soon. 'And now that we're in school, just to make it official, you must all call me Mrs Jones.'

'Even me?' asked Rodney.

'Yes, dear.'

Mrs Jones taught school like Dorothea taught swimming: *I'll show you how to do it, you do it, I correct, you do it again, I applaud and you keep at it till you get better.* When Rodney was her only student, all went well. He was careful and neat, and smart; he was not temperamental. But Dorothea had no teacherly tools to deal with the depths of the McNeill sisters' ignorance. For Marcella, despite her many gifts as a reader, writer and painter on the easels, math eluded her. Beyond the limits of her ten fingers lay a thicket, a forest of numbers whose relationships to signs and symbols she could not fathom. When presented with a story problem, Marcella cared nothing for the math of how Jimmy and Susy might pool their funds and buy three oranges and three apples; she wondered instead how they came by the money and why they would buy apples or oranges when they could buy Fritos or Twinkies. Time and again she defeated Dorothea's attempts to make her memorize the multiplication tables. She simply didn't care.

Rose-Renee presented her teacher with even greater challenges, and even more frequent defeats. Dorothea would chide Rose-Renee for being lazy, but never for being stupid. The word 'retarded' was never mentioned. Rose-Renee had mastered the concept of reading left-to-right and the notion that certain letters together created words, but beyond those rudiments, she remained illiterate. She sometimes seemed to take actual delight in her inability to learn. She would cross her arms, shove her hands into her armpits, slump and rest her chin on her chest, refusing to even try. Sometimes, however, to win the M&Ms Dorothea used to reward her students (and a chance to stand on the Winner's Box beside the teacher's desk), Rose-Renee might exert herself. But when she repeatedly failed to get M&Ms she would have small brimstone fits, intense tantrums. Before these Dorothea was helpless. Only Marcella could assuage.

Marcella would move her flailing sister to a quiet place, the beanbag chair in Rot's room, pull Rose-Renee's head against her shoulder and hold her tight, even if Rose-Renee resisted. Sometimes Marcella would sing, anything soft, sweet, slow. Sometimes she'd just talk, stories about the circus, or pirates, or princesses, the places the Gingerbread Girls would go together. On those occasions the school day was effectively over, but the next day, all would begin again, afresh.

Students in any school will make mischief, and when Mrs Jones turned to write on the chalkboard, Rodney scrawled quickly on a piece of paper PIG SISTERS OINK and held it up, sliding it swiftly back into his desk before she turned around. Marcella wrote out signs for herself and Rose-Renee, ROT SPOT GOES TO POT. Rodney created pictures of pigs' behinds, curly tails and all. Rodney's spirits rose. He threw the occasional spitball. With her back to the schoolroom, and writing on the chalkboard, Mrs Jones smiled and pretended to see none of this.

They ate lunch now in the dining room and there was no more flinging of peas or Brussels sprouts. The girls learned the prayer that Dorothea always offered up, and recited it before lunch. Her religion was of the vanilla variety, pale and sweetly comforting. They learned their manners as well, Dorothea often tediously insisting that Marcella and Rose-Renee hold their utensils correctly; they were not to talk when they were chewing, nor shovel food into their mouths. They didn't eat like pigs any more, but then they weren't as hungry as they had been. Still, their plates were always clean at the end of lunch, and Dorothea held them up as a shining example to Rodney. His appetite improved and he grew stronger.

At the end of September Dorothea announced that after lunch there would be a very special visitor. 'Your new piano teacher! She wants to come up and meet all three of you. She wants to be certain that it will be worth the drive for her.

She comes from Greenville.'

'It isn't that far,' Rodney said.

'Nonetheless, she wants to meet with us. So everyone will be on their best behaviour.'

'Is this an audition?' asked Marcella.

'Yes, I guess you could call it that. I guess your father has had all sorts of auditions. I guess you're used to this.'

Yes, thought Marcella, and when Mitch got the part, everyone went out to dinner and there were Shirley Temples for the little girls, vodka Martinis for Mitch and Valerie. And when he didn't get the part there were slammed doors and noisy accusations. 'What if we don't get the part? What happens then?'

'How can any music teacher turn down the granddaughters of Gloria Denham? There'll be no painting or rough games. You will all read and sit quietly till she gets here at two. Everyone needs to look their best. Rodney, I've laid out a white shirt for you on your bed. You go change. Girls, we'll go into the bathroom and I'll help you fix your hair. I've bought you some barrettes.'

But the McNeill girls' rough, thick curls could not be entirely tamed by little plastic barrettes, and their tangles resisted Dorothea's hairbrush.

'You ought to wash your hair more often, Marcella. Rose-Renee too. How often do you take a bath?'

'Whenever we feel like it.'

'Do you wash your hair?'

'If we feel like it.'

'Do you have shampoo?'

'I don't know.'

'Well, you should take more baths and wash your hair. Champions are always clean, and you girls are champions, aren't you?'

'Yes.'

'And what about some new clothes? All your clothes are summer clothes. Soon you'll need warm ones.'

Marcella shrugged. 'There's plenty of clothes at Gloria's.'

'Children's clothes?' Dorothea looked perplexed.

'No, but we can wear 'em. There must have been tons of people come and stay and leave without their clothes. Isn't that funny? Maybe they left in their underwear.'

'They must have belonged to old Mrs Denham, and her husband, and Ellie, her daughter, and I have heard there were legions of visitors, and parties. But you girls should not be wearing grown-ups' castoffs. You should have your own clothes, children's clothes. There, that's the best I can do. Go watch TV with Rodney, will you? I want everyone calm and clean when she gets here. No rough games.'

It was after three when the doorbell rang, and Ethel answered the door and led Mrs Campbell into the living room where Dorothea greeted her enthusiastically. She called for the children to turn off the television and come meet the piano teacher.

Mrs Campbell exuded the odour of cloves, Tabu and irritation. She had the longest fingers Marcella had ever seen. A stout woman of perhaps thirty-five with pink cheeks, Mrs Campbell wore a treble-clef brooch on a beige

80

wool suit. Her hair was lacquered, high and impossible, like a great sandy cliff overhanging her face, and she wore wing-like glasses that continually slid down her nose. She was cranky, having got very lost on these back roads and wasted an hour, a half-tank of gas, she was certain, and now she was running late the rest of the day. She could not stay long. Dorothea nodded to Ethel, who went to the kitchen and returned with a plate of sandwiches and a pot of tea. She set them in front of the brightly snapping fire, and Mrs Campbell allowed herself to pick at one. As the tea and sandwiches had their slowly soothing effect, Mrs Campbell talked fondly of her own musical education and the pianists she had studied with at Curtis Institute, all of which Dorothea found endlessly fascinating. When the time was right — that is, when Mrs Campbell had relaxed, unwound from her journey and bathed in her own little glow — Dorothea mentioned that the girls' grand-mother, Gloria Denham, had been a student as well as a teacher at Curtis. 'Gloria Denham.' Dorothea's voice clothed the name in signifi-cance. 'These are the granddaughters of Gloria Denham, the famous violinist, so their musical education is important.'

Unimpressed, Mrs Campbell continued, 'I have expectations of my students. They must practise at least one hour a day. They must practise the pieces in the order that I lay it out, that is, your scales first before the songs. They must learn theory as well. Theory and practice are united.' She continued on while Rodney

81

squirmed, but Rose-Renee and Marcella were used to people who took their music seriously.

Mrs Campbell asked to see the piano. Her face fell to behold the battered old upright; she played a few notes and declared it too out of tune to be useful.

'Oh, I'm sure it's not what you are used to. I promise, I know it's not a wonderful piano, but I'll get it fixed before next week!'

'It's called tuning the piano, Mrs Jones.' Mrs Campbell shifted her attention from the upright to the three children — a scrawny, pale boy, two dark-eyed girls with dirty hair and crooked teeth and scabby knees — and regarded them all with unvarnished condescension. 'The distance is too far. I can't take on three new students.'

Dorothea looked crestfallen. 'Oh, but they have such promise! Truly, Mrs Campbell, they have untapped talents. If you can't take all three, at least take on the girls.'

'Impossible.' Mrs Campbell thanked her for the tea and picked up her bag.

'We are a family of musical geniuses.' Marcella stepped forward, unwilling to let this bespectacled fat lady defeat Dorothea Jones. 'My aunt Linda played Liszt at twelve, and my mother's an opera singer. My grandmother's music room is the best music room in the whole world. Anything played there sounds like it came from the angels. Igor and Pablo played there, and Andrés and Darius. They're all geniuses and so are we, my whole family!'

'Genius is not a word to be tossed around lightly, little girl,' Mrs Campbell chided.

Dorothea clarified, 'That's what I've been trying to tell you, Mrs Campbell. Surely, as a musician, you've heard of the music room at the Denhams.'

'Do you mean that concert room at the . . . ?' Mrs Campbell's damp mouth fell open. 'But every musician on the east coast knows about . . . The acoustics are unparalleled! Famous musicians used to come from all over the world, oh, a long time ago now. They say, that is, I've heard when Andrés Segovia played in that room, that people sat sobbing in their chairs, but afraid to move, to make a sound because each sound was so . . . so . . . so . . . Is that your house?' She regarded Marcella with new admiration.

'No,' said Marcella, 'I mean, yes. We live there with our grandmother, Gloria.'

'I have always longed to see that music room.'

'Maybe when Rodney and Marcella and Rose-Renee have their first recital, you can have it at Gloria's!' Dorothea offered joyfully.

'We could have our recital there?' Mrs Campbell's pink face suffused with pleasure.

'What do you think, Marcella?' asked Dorothea.

'What do you mean?' This had all taken a turn Marcella could not quite fathom.

'Do you think Gloria would agree? You know, to have the recital there.'

Marcella glanced at Rose-Renee, whose expression was eloquent: *Are you out of your mind?* Marcella's bravado withered, but for Dorothea's benefit, she said, sure, she would certainly ask.

'Will you?' asked Rose-Renee by the time they

bolted from the Jones house, and were on their way home. 'Will you really ask Gloria about letting a bunch of strangers in her house? You think that would ever happen?'

'Jeez, don't be stupid. I just said that to make Dorothea happy.'

Music lessons began the following Tuesday and every Tuesday thereafter. Rodney wasn't equal to the extra exertion, and dropped out, but Marcella and Rose-Renee were excused from school one hour each day to practise. Rose-Renee sometimes thumped a few scales, sometimes played 'Chopsticks' till her fingers hurt and occasionally battered out her lesson, 'Three Blind Mice'. Marcella dutifully did her scales, but moved so swiftly beyond 'Three Blind Mice' into easy pieces of the beginner's repertoire, and mastered them. Dorothea gave her an extra handful of M&Ms after each lesson.

Monday and Thursday mornings were reserved for physical education. The pool had been drained and covered, and the huge trampoline put away, but what once had been a spacious smokehouse had been refurbished into a mini-gym, heated, insulated, floored, with newly installed big windows to let in the light. There was a shelf with barbells and jump-ropes, and exercise mats; there were balance beams and chin-up bars. On one wall there were framed blue ribbons and photos of a very youthful Dorothea wearing one-piece swimsuits and slick, tight-fitting swimcaps, with the strap hanging down while she held up trophies. Dorothea Lassiter, champion swimmer, including Athlete of the Year for Scripps College

84

in Claremont, California. With the US Swim Team in the 1952 Helsinki Olympics. With her referee's whistle, Dorothea blew like a real coach, talked to Marcella and Rose-Renee, about technique and form and Untapped Talents. Rodney's efforts elicited her happy enthusiasm.

As the days shortened and chilled, and the afternoons closed in, the summer clothes the girls had brought were inadequate to the weather. The many closets they had originally pillaged for fun now yielded jackets, and heavy satin blouses that they wore over their summer clothes. They found sweaters too moth-eaten to wear, and smart day-dresses from the Thirties that they simply cut so the hem came to their knees. For warmth Marcella at first favoured an evening cape, but by mid-October it wasn't enough, and so she traded it for a man's motoring jacket that came to her knees, and a smart fedora. Rose-Renee, with considerably more panache, chose a woman's fur jacket that had the heads of little animals hanging down. She said that these were animals Morton had killed and eaten, all but the fur and the heads.

Their new raiment smelled powerfully of mothballs and the girls trailed naphtha wherever they went. Rodney remarked they really were Putrid and Stinko. Dorothea's nose wrinkled when she came near them, but she did not comment, not on the way they smelled, and not on their weird attire, not even when, Rodney's stamina permitting, Flag School took the occasional field trip, and the three children ventured into a world beyond their schoolroom.

Other visitors to Winterthur Museum, Hagley Museum, Brandywine Battlefield and Longwood Gardens looked askance at these oddly clad children, but neither girl seemed to notice, and with Olympian aplomb, Dorothea ignored everyone else.

On these outings, they took turns sitting in the front seat of the Mercedes while Dorothea drove. Rose-Renee and Marcella taught them the entire score from *Oklahoma!*, at least all the songs that Valerie sang, finishing up with a heartfelt 'Oklahoma, OK!' just as the Mercedes pulled up the long drive, and through the hedges to the kitchen door. They came in singing, knowing that Gloria, deep in the embrace of the music room, would never hear them.

In Marcella's memory, these ordinary days ran together, like chalk drawings in the rain, one undifferentiated afternoon following, flowing into another, tinted in warm lights, dipped in satisfactions and melded into a general sense of well-being. Though each day is its own individual entity as it is lived, once past, few can be reconstructed or remembered, or peeled from the rest. The past is not a sheeted plane, all tucked down with hospital corners, but ordinary days get ironed into flatness. The extraordinary ones loom up, obscuring all others.

Andantino

Speeding through the green and rolling countryside, Linda's SUV passed through a landscape dotted with beautiful homes, some of them

86

McMansion new, some very old, all set far back from the roads. 'You won't believe what Curtis has done for Gloria's house,' she said, 'for the outside anyway. Everything looks like it used to, like that house in The Philadelphia Story, built to impress, to exhibit wealth and dazzle. The Denhams were the first family in the Brandywine to scream: 'We're nouveau riche and we don't care!''

'Yes,' Marcella said, 'just imagine what people like the Bowkers thought. Here they'd been, living in the same eighteenth-century stone farm-houses their great-great-grandfathers had built, and suddenly all these people are talking about art.'

'Oh, I laugh to think of the Bowkers, and their septic tank service,' said Linda breezily, 'the old man cleaning out people's shitholes, all the while sitting on a gold mine. Their kids sold the place for millions. I'm not exaggerating. Millions!' She frowned. 'Though I can't remember who bought it. Someone rich with artistic pretensions.'

'Wasn't that always the assumption? Living here, breathing the Brandywine air would make you an artist. You could live around artists! You could rub shoulders with the Wyeths! Howard Pyle! And all their schools of students and hangers-on and wannabes and would-bes. A hundred years of that?'

'Don't knock it. How do you think I got hired at Tanglewood in the first place? I am the daughter of Gloria Denham, the renowned violinist. I could say that my mother and Andrés Segovia had played Paganini duets in my home, that Pablo Casals had touched my hand. Who else could say they'd seen the great Stravinsky write works of genius in my music room? That Darius Milhaud had hammered out Le Boeuf sur la Toit on my Steinway, with my mother playing violin! Such cachet!' Linda snorted in derision. 'Of course, I only barely met Segovia and Casals, and I was too young to give a shit, but what the hell. I got the job. Tanglewood hired me to work in the ticket booth, and now I'm the Director of Development. I've earned my keep with them, don't get me wrong. I'm good at what I do, but it isn't artistic.'

'It could have been.'

'Not for me. Mother wanted me to live her life, and I wanted my own. I can't complain. I've got two great kids, and my husband was all right before he started boffing that twit. I have a beautiful home — which I'm keeping out of the divorce, by the way. I have a great job. People respect me. I'm not unhappy, Marcella. I fought Gloria and in my own opinion, I won.'

'Gloria was an enigma,' said Marcella. 'That's the kindest thing I can say.'

'That'll do,' said Linda.

'Drive me past Dorothea's, will you?'

'Now?'

'If not now . . . '

Dorothea's house had not substantially changed. The farmhouse still stood, a three-storey white fieldstone fortress, lonely as a Wyeth watercolour. Long ribbons of sky, awash in morning light, were woven with narrow bands of clouds. The farmhouse windows shone, though whether

88

from within, or reflecting the sunshine, Marcella could not tell. The red climbing roses were gone, but the porch was hung with two colourful geranium baskets. The SUV turned, and rumbled down the short driveway, and the tyres crunched on fresh-laid gravel. A child came out of the front door and stood there, watching them, a boy. Marcella gave him a slow wave, and he waved back. 'We can go now,' she said. 'There's really nothing to see.'

As Linda backed out and barrelled down the narrow road, Marcella rolled down her window; the flat, air-conditioned air flew out, and the thick moist air of the Brandywine blew in and over her face, the scent redolent of earth and grass and blowsy, high, refulgent summer, the Brandywine smell. Wyeth country, Marcella thought, the landscape of longing, of loneliness, of prim desire, and splintered exhalation in winter, the landscape of the mute and alone, that's what Tim had called it in winter. He had never seen it in summer.

Linda chatted on about the changes to the gardens. 'Ever since she willed the house to them after Barry died, Curtis has been paying the property taxes and the utility bills, and Gloria let them reconstruct the gardens, but not repair the inside. Not until the memorial service did most of them even see the place. At the reception in the drawing room, and the foyer, there were all these important people from Curtis, sipping white wine, and nibbling canapés, and watching the mice running over their shoes, and the cats bounding right behind the mice! You should have seen their faces!'

'Cats? Gloria wouldn't tolerate cats.'

'She had to finally. She wouldn't let anyone fix anything inside. But she had to let people in, finally. She pretty much wasted away and lost a lot of mobility. Ten years ago, maybe 1990, 1989, something like that, Eunice Campbell hired some guys to basically bring her bedroom downstairs, and set her up in the den. She never went upstairs again. After the walker, she used the motorized wheelchair, and hired full-time nurses who came in shifts. Curtis even paid for the nurses.'

'They probably didn't expect her to live so long.'

'I'm sure they didn't. She was frail, but she just wouldn't die. Then, one day last week, Gloria didn't come out of the music room, and the nurse found her there, asleep in the wheelchair, the violin lying in her lap, the bow on the floor, as if everything had been peaceful. They called Mrs Campbell immediately.'

'Gloria was lucky to have Eunice Campbell. Someone she couldn't intimidate, I suppose.'

'She didn't intimidate me,' Linda protested.

Marcella let this pass without comment.

They came to the stone pillars and the drive lined with flowering cherry trees, but the effect of the house's splendour was blunted by the camouflage offered by the trees. Not till they turned at the top of the drive was the house in full prospect. Two long two-storey wings extended from the centre core; the wings were not evenly balanced because Gloria's windowless music room, built at the end of one, had thrown off the symmetry. The other wing had a ballroom with crystal chandeliers and French doors that opened on to formal gardens and a boxwood maze. The house Marcella beheld before her had been restored to its original grandeur, painted, repaired, gutters fixed. Even from this distance, Marcella could see that roses and day lilies speckled in the distance, small blurry smears of peach and scarlet-hued flowers laid out in formal gardens and roses looped along the terrace fences.

Linda drove on past the grand front entrance to the house, and on through the hedge archway that led to the garages and the kitchen entrance where lesser mortals came and went. She turned off the car at the kitchen door. 'Welcome home.'

'It's not home to me,' Marcella retorted, knowing that once, to return to this place had filled her with the joy of homecoming; this was once the scene of such happiness that her unwilling heart still filled with remembered pleasure.

5

The Arkansas Traveller

Marcella and Rose-Renee shared a big black umbrella, for the rainy-day walks back and forth to Flag School, but it wasn't enough to protect their passé finery, which was stinky and sodden by the time they arrived home in the afternoon. Chilled to the bone, they stepped into the kitchen, and quickly stripped down to their underwear. Marcella stood on a chair to fling their coats and clothes over the laundry lines Susan had strung at the back, while Rose-Renee dashed into the bathroom to get their matching maroon robes with wide satin lapels, pillaged from the closets. They'd only just put the robes on when they heard a car stop at the back door, idling; the door squealed open, and many voices tumbled out, all of them unknown. Strangers. Marcella gave a quick nod to her sister, and they both dashed into the butler's pantry, leaving the door just ajar so they could peer out.

The back door opened, and closed, and there were footsteps, and a couple of suitcases thudded to the floor.

'Holy shit!' A girl's voice. 'I thought they'd never shut up.'

'Just goes to prove,' said a male voice with a deep drawl, 'shouldn't ever take a ride with speed freaks.'

'I'd have got in the car with Richard Nixon to get out of the rain.'

'Well, they brought us all the way out here, didn't they? That was something. We'd have never got a ride on that little road. So, this is home, babycakes? Far out.'

Babycakes? Rose-Renee's face twisted. Marcella put a finger to her lips.

'Spiritually speaking, it's a dump. Take my word for it. You were better off on your family's sharecropper's farm.'

'Well, it's warm anyway.'

'Some of it is warm. Mother only barely heats part of the house in winter. Just enough to keep the pipes from freezing, no more than that.'

'Is she here? You oughta tell her you're home.'

'Oh Tim, Tim, Tim . . . ' She laid a big smacking kiss on him. 'No one, and I mean no one, interrupts my mother's rehearsing. She'll come out of that music room when she's damned good and ready to, and not before.'

'Far out,' said Tim.

'Hey, Linda,' Marcella said, emerging from the butler's pantry, Rose-Renee behind her.

'Jesus!' Linda clutched her heart. 'You scared the shit out of me! Hey yourself, squirts! What are you doing here?' Linda looked a lot like Valerie only more careless of her appearance. Where Valerie curled and teased and sprayed her fair hair, Linda's was long, straight and framed her face without a single curl. She wore low-slung purple bell-bottoms, a long vest of loud colours, and a fringed jacket with green suede boots. 'Valerie's still in Stockholm, huh?'

'Opera.'

'Tim, these are my nieces, Marcella and Rose-Renee. Girls, this is my old man, Tim.'

'That isn't your father,' Marcella frowned. 'He's in Florida.'

Linda gave a rippling laugh. 'What do you want me to say? He's my beau? Tim and I are together,' she added.

'That we are, babycakes.' He smiled. 'I'm happy to meet you girls.' He was tall and hairy, his hair and beard so wiry and coppery red, and there was so much of it that his face was obscured, though his eyes were a bright, welcoming blue. Tim, too, wore wide bell-bottoms, a fringed leather jacket and heavy boots. He had a scarf of many colours, and a slouch hat.

Rose-Renee gave him an intense squint. 'You talk weird.'

'Tim's an Arkie,' chirped Linda. 'Won't that just fry Mother's onions!'

'What does that mean?' asked Rose-Renee.

Linda laughed. 'Hey, is there anything to eat? We're starving.'

'Go on, sit down,' Marcella said, feeling quite grown up. 'I'll fix you up something good.'

Rose-Renee got the hot dogs and buns out of the fridge and Marcella filled the big kettle, put it on the burner, and opened an extra can of beans. She took down the Limoges teapot and found three teabags.

'Yes, well, you've certainly grown,' said Linda. 'You especially, Marcella; why, look at how tall you are. And how you've filled out. And you,

94

Rose-Renee, how old are you now?'

'Going on ten.'

'Aw, she just turned nine in July,' said Marcella.

'Imagine that,' said Linda to no one in particular. 'When did I last see you? Where was that? Your dad had a gig in . . . '

'*Death of a Salesman.*'

'Their dad is an actor,' Linda said to Tim. 'A mediocre actor who thinks he's Laurence Olivier. Where is Mitch these days?'

'*Major Barbara*, but that was a while back. We don't hear from him.'

'And Valerie, how's she doing in Stockholm?'

Rose-Renee and Marcella seemed to consider this jointly. Marcella said, 'Dunno. She just writes postcards and tells us that she loves us and we ought to be good.'

'I thought she was just going for the summer,' said Linda. 'I didn't know you'd still be here.'

'Well, we're here.'

'Well, Tim and I are here too, just for the winter. We've been living on a commune in the Berkshires.'

'What's a commune?' asked Rose-Renee.

'Don't you know anything? A commune is a place where free spirits all come together to live in peace and harmony.'

'Why'd you leave?'

'Because we were freezing our asses off,' drawled Tim.

While they ate the hot dogs and beans and drank the hot tea, Tim and Linda offered up their story. Linda was studying music at Radcliffe, and Tim

95

was on an engineering scholarship at MIT, and a year behind her in school. They might never have met but for a big anti-war and anti-ROTC protest. Linda tried to explain to the girls what the ROTC was, how the military was wholly corrupt and the war in Vietnam was evil and the President was a lying pig, then gave up, and moved on to the rest of their story, which ran along the lines of them getting it on, and then, tune in, turn on and drop out. Linda and Tim had dropped out of college, and with a group of other like-minded souls and free spirits, moved to a commune in the Berkshires where they had lived until last week when the butt-biting cold convinced them to leave. They planned to go back to being free spirits in the spring.

Tim took a pack of ZigZag papers out of the pocket of his flannel shirt. 'What do you think, babycakes?'

'Please, Tim, don't call me that in front of people.'

Tim turned to the girls. 'Are you people, or are you Munchkins?'

'Munchkins,' said Rose-Renee.

'See, the Munchkins don't care if I call you babycakes. What about the joint?'

'Let's wait. Mother will be here any minute, if I'm not mistaken.'

'Yep. Quarter of six,' said Marcella.

And, as if on cue, Gloria swung open the door and came into the kitchen, her face registering only mild surprise, as if she'd found a missing button. She held a glass with two fingers' worth of Scotch.

'Look who's here, Gloria!' cried Marcella as Tim stood up.

'Tim Farleigh, Mrs Denham. I'm pleased to meet you. I've heard a lot about you.'

Gloria put her glass on the counter, ignoring him altogether. 'Barry phoned two days ago and told me you had called him, Linda. He said you'd asked to stay in Fort Lauderdale with him all winter, but he didn't want you.'

'It was Jean who didn't want us,' said Linda. 'Not Daddy.'

'Barry said you'd probably call me next. But you didn't. I suppose you didn't call because you knew I'd say no.'

Linda quickly went on the offensive, declaring that any ordinary mother would be happy to have her daughter home for a bit, that most families were happy to have a little time together, but she stopped just short of saying if Gloria didn't want them, they'd leave.

Gloria let Linda run out of steam while she looked Tim up and down. 'Where are you from?'

'Arkansas, Mrs Denham.'

Gloria returned her attention to Linda. 'I suppose you and the Jolly Red Giant want to shack up here for the whole winter.' Gloria took a fortifying sip of Scotch while Marcella did her little trick with the ice-cube tray. 'Really, Linda, how can you and Valerie think that I should run a hotel for you, and your Arkie boyfriends, and your deserted children? Will you next be sending me your mutts? Will you bring along your hippie friends who also think that everything in life is free, that work and discipline are nothing, mere trifles to be scoffed at, while you all sit around and smoke pot? How can you and Valerie make such huge mistakes and then just walk away from them?'

'Going to the commune was not a mistake.' Linda tugged Tim's hand and he sat down.

'Ah, is that why you're here? Because it was such a wonderful idea to drop out of Radcliffe and go live with a bunch of free-thinking weirdoes? You're twenty-one, aren't you? You're supposed to be grown up.'

'We're prepared to earn our keep here, aren't we, Tim? Tim can fix things, Mother. And I can look after Marcella and Rose-Renee.'

'We don't need looking after. We're not babies.'

'Not babies,' echoed Rose-Renee.

'Maybe we should leave,' Tim offered in his drawl. 'Tomorrow, if it's all right, Mrs Denham. It's too late to get a ride now.'

'To get a ride? To call a cab?'

'We hitch-hiked.'

'We're not leaving,' said Linda . . .

'Very well,' said Gloria. 'Will you practise the piano while you're here? Will you at least acknowledge that you have a gift, and it ought to be fostered, cherished?' Gloria gave Linda the same unforgiving stare she'd given Valerie the day she had collected them at Wilmington train station. Valerie had withered under it, but Linda radiated defiance. Under the table Marcella pressed Rose-Renee's foot and they both braced. Life with Valerie and Mitch had attuned them to the moment that a squall was about to become a storm.

Tim reached over and placed his hand on

Linda's. 'You know, Linda, I've only ever heard you play on those old upright pianos in the practice rooms. It'd be a great pleasure to hear you play on your mother's piano. I've heard so much about your music room, Mrs Denham. It'd be a real honour to hear Linda play there, and to hear you play the violin.'

'I'm sure where you come from it's called a fiddle.'

'Yes, ma'am, matter of fact, it is. But I'm sure you play the violin.'

'Absolutely. I rehearse. Rehearsal is not for an audience. Performance is for an audience.' She turned again to Linda. 'You can have the two rooms across the hall from Rose-Renee and Marcella.'

'We won't be needing two rooms,' said Linda.

'Well, I hope you're on the Pill. I don't want any Arkie grandchildren.' And with that Gloria left them, took her cigarette and cocktail into the den and put a record on the stereo.

'Ravel's *La Valse*,' said Linda, just as if nothing — and no one — had happened.

Gloria's routines were like the tides and unlikely to be altered, but her struggles with Linda were vivid, ongoing and, unlike the tides, unpredictable. Gloria jabbed and chastised Linda for throwing away gifts that required devotion. Linda heaped abuse on the dead composers Gloria revered, calling their music irrelevant, condemning anyone who valued them to the dustbin of history, the rubbish heap of European assumptions of superiority, the tired, old, clawed hand of the imperial past. She and

Gloria collided like two ocean liners of arrogance, and afterwards the wreckage lay strewn for days till it could sink to the bottom and some semblance of placidity be restored.

Rose-Renee and Marcella secretly referred to these battles as Doll Wars with Music. They knew enough to evade them, to slink away when a quarrel threatened to erupt. Tim had to learn self-preservation, but he had endless patience, aided no doubt by the endless joints he rolled and smoked slowly. He did everything slowly. He and Linda were an odd couple, Tim like a 33 1/3 record compared to Linda's 78.

He liked to puzzle things out, and he was delighted with the thousand-piece jigsaw puzzle in the sunroom, a Monet seascape in a million nuances of green and grey and blue. He brought to this endeavour a weedy stoicism, and within a few days it had a frame. Marcella too pored over it. Rose-Renee had no interest in the puzzle and resented the time Marcella spent on it, insisted they quit and play cards with her. Even the card games changed with Tim there. He was less forgiving than Marcella, and he wouldn't allow Rose-Renee to change the rules whenever she wanted, even on a game as basic as Old Maid or Go Fish. Besides he wanted to bet real money. The cards snapped under his fingers. He tapped the deck. 'A nickel, a dime?'

'We don't have any money,' said Marcella.

They sat at the green baize card table with the little drawers and Tim shuffled expertly. 'Well, bet something else, then.' His blue eyes twinkled between his mass of red hair and his mass of red beard. 'Bet something you would miss if you lost it.'

'Cubbie?' asked Rose-Renee.

'Nah. I don't want a doll.'

'Does it have to be a thing you could lose?' asked Marcella. 'Can it be something you do or get done to you?'

'Like what?' Tim dealt the cards.

Rose-Renee started to crack up laughing. She rolled up her sleeve and held out her arm, looking away, as though someone were about to puncture her with a vicious needle while Marcella planted a fat arm-fart on her, blowing against skin with delightful blubbering fart sounds that held out as long as she had breath. A long time.

'I will meet your arm-fart, and raise you a nickel,' said Tim.

'Go Fish,' said Rose-Renee.

He liked to wander the basement, and Marcella and Rose-Renee often followed him as his flashlight lit circuits and fuses and thick black pipes that criss-crossed the roof; there were puddles on the floor, sodden rags wrapped round the pipes, the sound of dripping, and the place smelled bad. 'Look at that,' he would say. 'Will you look at that?' He liked to explain how things ought to work. He gave the girls the occasional toke of his joint, not more than that since he said pot would stunt their growth. He made them promise not to tell anyone.

'Even Rodney?' asked Rose-Renee.

'Especially Rodney. Why, what would his mother think?'

101

'Yes,' said Marcella. 'Dorothea wouldn't like it. Champions don't smoke pot.'

One evening Tim enlisted Marcella to go with him to broach Gloria literally in her den. 'Someone's gotta back me up, and I don't dare bring Linda. You know what she's like.'

Marcella nodded, proud to be his ally. 'What do you need from Gloria?'

'Well, I'm just not the kind of guy to be sitting around and watching the place go to hell in a handbasket. I think I can do some good around here, but I need some materials, and I'll need to borrow her car to get them We'll wait till after she's had her first Scotch. It'll be better then. I built up a nice fire in the den. There's lots of great wood, dry but no one's split it, I guess, for years.'

When they entered the den Gloria was just changing the record on the record player, a smooth piece Marcella recognized but could not name. It made her think of water. Gloria actually thanked Tim for building the fire. Marcella thought that a great start. She sat down. Tim remained standing. He read from a list, a number of things he thought he could fix, a long list which he handed to Gloria. He said he'd need some parts and some tools and he assumed there was a hardware store, or a Feed and Seed or some such place in Chadds Ford. He'd go tomorrow if he could use her car. And her account there.

'I do not have an account there.'

'Well, I'm sure you could if you telephoned, Mrs Denham. I'd like to fix things up here. I'd like to earn my keep, or at least do something for the place. It's kind of crumbling around you.'

'Very well. But I assure you, I will be going over the receipts. Do not think you can put anything past me.'

'Never, ma'am.'

'I want itemized receipts for everything.'

'Yes, Mrs Denham. Itemized.'

In the next few weeks, faucets that had dripped for decades were silent, and the toilets quit singing. Tim reamed out the drains, and the water went down swiftly. Light fixtures that hadn't worked because the chains had broken off suddenly had new chains, new bulbs; and outlets that didn't work, suddenly did. He split wood that had been sitting in a shed, untouched, for years and hauled logs into the breakfast room and the sunroom, which, even if it wasn't sunny, at least was warm. He cleaned the grates, and used a long broom to unplug the chimneys. He came away from this work covered in soot. He took long hot baths (usually with Linda) in the second-floor bathroom near their bedroom. They sang Bob Dylan tunes and smoked joints in the tub. On sunny days he found a ladder and cleaned out the gutters that rimmed the house, at least those on the first floor. He'd need a taller ladder for the second. He set traps for the mice and took care of them once they'd been snapped. He advised getting a cat, but Linda told him not to say so to Gloria. Gloria hated animals and would not admit that there were mice.

At first Tim helped Marcella with the cooking,

then he took over the task. He even drove into Chadds Ford to pick up Gloria's grocery order, and saved her the delivery fee. Grumpy Susan still made casseroles twice a week for Gloria, but for the rest of them Tim did wonderful things with cornmeal, flour and eggs, some ham or bacon; he made great biscuits, pancakes and stews. He told them stories of his Arkie family while they ate, of the chickens and pigs they kept, of his father's shooting rabbits and ducks and wild turkeys, and handing them to the children to pluck and pick the pellets out. 'But we'd still spit out shotgun pellets when we ate, and we used to shit shotgun pellets too,' he added to his admiring audience while he hand-rolled a cigarette. 'Day after we had duck, you'd hear the pellets, ping, ping, ping in the toilet bowl, that is, when we had indoor plumbing. When we had the outhouse, you didn't hear nothing.'

'How come?' asked Rose-Renee.

'Because it was just a hole, Munchkin, a hole in the earth with a board over it, and a hole in the board for your butt.' He told them about the ham radio his father kept in the front room tuned to the police frequency. 'Whenever it would come on the police band radio that someone hit a deer on the highway, no matter the time of day or night, my father would say, 'All right, Timmy, Jimmy, boots and butts! Get out to the truck, boys!' He'd grab the keys and we'd be outta there, driving like hell to get to the accident before the state patrol or the sheriff or the game people could get there. My dad would

104

tell the woman — it was usually a woman or a drunk who'd hit a deer — '

'Don't be such a male chauvinist pig,' Linda objected.

'I'm not, babycakes. It was always a woman or a drunk.'

'Go on,' said Rose-Renee.

'My dad would tell her we were from the State Game Commission, sometimes he'd say he was the County Game Commissioner himself, and these two fine young men here were his deputies, and it wasn't our policy to write up tickets or nothing, but we had to remove the dead animal. And she'd be so happy to have it gone and no ticket.' Tim did her voice in a tremulous falsetto: 'Yes, *yes, officers! Please take the animal. Oh, thank you, sir, thank you so much* . . . And me and Jimmy would work and sweat and cuss and finally heave that deer into the back of the truck, and we'd go on home, hang the deer, skin it, gut it, and eat like kings for a month.'

'That is a disgusting story,' said Linda.

'Not if you were hungry,' said Tim.

'Were you hungry?' asked Marcella, mopping up gravy with one of his biscuits.

'Sometimes. My old man hated farming, but it was all he knew. He didn't even own the land he farmed, so profits went first to the owners. Bad years — and there was a number of them — my mother'd go be a waitress in town just to have food on the table. He'd be dangerous then, tetchy, on edge, as soon smack one of us as look at us. My sisters got married young, just mainly to get out of the house. My twin brother Jimmy

105

joined the marines. He was always a scrapper.'

'Why was he scrapping?' asked Marcella.

'We weren't named James and Timothy, like you'd think. No, my mother named us Timmy Dee and Jimmy Lee, really, like we'd never grow up. We took shit for our names from the time we went to school, the other kids sing-songing *Oh Timmy Dee . . .* But after a while, there came a time when Jimmy had whupped so many of them that no one teased him any more. That's why he became a marine.'

'And you?' asked Linda. 'Did they go on beating up on you?'

'Me, I say make love not war.' He gave a slow grin. 'Anyone who wanted to give me shit about being named Timmy Dee, they knew they'd have to tangle with my twin brother, Jimmy, and not too many people wanted to do that. We graduated high school and the very next day Jimmy signed up for the marines. That fall Jimmy went to Nam, and I went to MIT. Massachusetts Institute of Technology. Yes, ma'am, a scholarship to the Massachusetts Institute of Technology.' He said the word as though biting into it, as though he could tear off a chunk with his teeth. 'And honest, when I got there, I wished I'd joined the marines. I was so alone and so outta my . . . I don't even know what to call it. It was like a foreign country. I only met one other guy from Arkansas, and he was from Little Rock, and his daddy was a banker. So, that was that.' He smoked gently.

'Why'd you choose that place?' asked Rose-Renee.

'I had this dream of going or doing or being something like none of Farleighs ever, not just some little Baptist college, but someplace great. I had big dreams, Munchkins.'

'Were you a good student?' asked Marcella.

'Well, I was, and not because anyone was beating me to study. I just liked it. Of course, I liked fixing up old cars, and racing them on country roads too, drinking beer, chasing girls.' He grinned at the memory. 'My math teacher told me about MIT. *Massachusetts Institute of Technology*, it just sounds some big important science-fictiony place. And it was far away. Not just Memphis or Fayetteville, or Little Rock, but really, really far away. No one in my family had been that far away, except for when my dad was in the marines in the Pacific, and he wouldn't ever talk about that. When I first got that far north, I wished I had never left Arkansas, but the longer I stayed in Massachusetts, I quit missing everyone, and pretty soon I started to think of them in a different light. I can never go back now.'

'Why not?' asked Marcella.

'It's like I know too much.'

'Why would you want to go back to Arkansas anyway?' Linda demanded.

'Well, I don't wanna go back, and I won't. But at least now I can see the good with the bad. I have some respect for them. My father, he was just as tough as an old boot heel, but he took shit from no man. He was afraid of nothing.'

'Are you afraid?' asked Rose-Renee.

'Sure. Any responsible man knows to be afraid.'

'Of what? What are you afraid of?'

107

'The draft,' he answered without a second thought. He was rolling a fine, pencil-thin joint. The more he smoked pot, the more pronounced became his Arkansas drawl.

'Everyone's afraid of the draft,' said Linda.

'Yes, but now I'm prime draft bait, babycakes. I'm not in school any more. I'm not doing anything socially responsible. Soon as they find me, I'll be 1A and they'll have my ass in Nam.'

Linda scoffed at this. 'If they call you up, we'll just go to Canada.'

'Well, I don't think I can do that, Linda. No, if they call me up, I'll have to go.'

'I hate it when you say that! There's nothing wrong with going to Canada. Canada or prison, anything's better than fighting in an unjust war.'

'Maybe.' He lit the joint and inhaled thoughtfully, not sucking the smoke in, just leisurely. 'But Jimmy is a marine and he's in Nam, and I just don't think I could ever go home again and see him or my folks if I ran away.'

'Why would you care?'

'Well, Jimmy, that should go without saying why I'd care. He's my twin brother. And my folks, well, if I ran away, they'd be so ashamed of me, they'd . . . well, hard to say what they'd do. It wouldn't be pretty. Of course, my folks aren't like yours, Linda. They're not great at anything, nothing to admire. Now, your mother, there's a woman to admire.'

'Oh, Tim, you are just impossible. Isn't he girls?' Linda said with enormous affection, and they agreed he was impossible. She took the joint from him and puffed. 'But you don't know shit

108

about classical music.'

'You're right.'

'Sometimes, when you're at Dorothea's, girls, he just goes and sits on the floor by the St Cecilia doors, and listens to Gloria play.'

'She takes my breath away. I never 'spected to hear anything like that except on a record, and of course we can hear it on a record, but here, right in the same house where I'm living? Me, Tim Farleigh, living in the same house with someone who can play like that? Genius. Like you, Linda. You know you can do things to any piano that will shudder the rafters.'

'But I don't want to.'

'You sure?' He passed her the joint.

Linda picked up her dish and took it to the sink. 'Just because you are so fucking deferential to my mother doesn't mean I have to be.'

'No one would ever accuse you of that,' said Tim with a straight face, though he winked at the girls.

'Mrs Campbell says I have a musical gift,' Marcella announced. 'She says I am so good that I ac-cede expectations.'

'That's exceed,' said Linda. 'To excel.'

'Yes, well, that's what I do. She says she can't wait to hear me play in the recital.'

'Save it for a surprise,' Rose-Renee butted in.

'Yes,' said Marcella quickly. They had agreed they would tell no one of Marcella's foolish offer that Mrs Campbell's students could have their recital in Gloria's music room. If Linda knew, she might even tell Gloria just to make her angry.

109

'I'd like to hear you play, squirt,' said Linda. 'When?'

'Now. It's after eight. Gloria's upstairs. Let's all go to the music room. She'll never hear us. Let's do it.'

The four went down the chilly hall to the music room, turned on the light and closed the St Cecilia doors behind them. The room was warm, heated by giant silver radiators at strategic places and warmly lit from the wall sconces. The bulbs were all small, like fake flames. Marcella had not actually been in this room, except to deliver a message, since that first day months ago, when Gloria had sat them both down, and then lost them, in a manner of speaking. The two wing chairs were exactly where the girls had left them in June.

Linda took the ecru silken scarf off the piano and flung it around her shoulders. She opened the keyboard and lifted the long arm to open up the piano. It looked as if it might take flight. Linda sat in one wing chair, and Tim in the other. Rose-Renee sat on the floor. 'Do it right,' Linda advised Marcella. 'I mean, really play it. Announce it, then play it.'

'I am going to play — '

'Don't you need the music?' asked Tim.

'I have it in my head,' said Marcella. Then she bowed to the audience. '*The Waltz* by Messer Armand.' She took her seat and played the piece, not well but caring less as she went on about the mistakes and more about the way the familiar music sounded. So different from Dorothea's upright! The deeply resonant Steinway seemed

110

to offer up each chord singly, amplifying every mistake Marcella made, but mistake or not, each note seemed to hang briefly in the rarified air, almost until it had achieved brilliance, and only then did it give way to the next. Everything she played was clarion and enhanced, music, mistakes, the whole. When she stopped, they all applauded.

'You should sit on the floor,' said Rose-Renee. 'I could feel it in my butt.'

Everyone laughed, and Tim moved to the floor. 'All right, people,' said Linda, walking to the piano. 'Feel this in your butt. This is Monsieur — not Messer, squirt — Ludwig van Beethoven's *Sonata Pathétique*.'

Marcella sat on the floor too, feeling the music move through her whole body, right up her spinal column and all along her arms as Linda attacked the piano and the piano seemingly fought back; strength and struggle roiled round the room, the arpeggios shimmering, each note ringing on the air and then eliding into the upper reaches of the music room until it vanished, and the other notes chased it into oblivion. Marcella began to understand why Gloria would want to live here, indeed, why she might not emerge from these teak walls where all was forgiven.

Linda finished, waved away their applause. Though they were all three clapping enthusiastically, she brought down the cover on the keyboard and put the arm down. She looked completely wrung out, but there was a kind of peace about her, odd and unsettling in a woman who was usually so sharp-tongued and wound

111

up. 'Sometimes I miss it,' she confessed. 'I'd never give Gloria the satisfaction of saying so.' She lay the ecru silken scarf atop the piano, the pale colour glowing in the warm light.

'Do you think this is what people feel in church?' Marcella asked.

'Church?'

'Dorothea says that church is a place where you knew God was, or would be if He could. Do you think God would be in this music room if He could?'

'Dorothea gives you girls a lot of strange ideas,' said Linda.

'This is what people feel like in church,' said Tim. 'I was raised Baptist, and though I left it behind a long time ago, I can tell you for sure that you can feel things in church you can't feel anywhere else. Things that sometimes might scare you, or make you want to lift up your hands and your voice, or maybe just sit there and not move, not so much as your little finger, and let some kind of spirit fill you up.' He stood, extended his hand to Marcella and pulled her to her feet. Rose-Renee too. 'You got a real gift, Marcella. Just like Linda has.'

'I'm going to sneak down here and practise at night when Gloria can't hear me,' said Marcella.

'You mean rehearse, don't you?' Linda linked her arm through Tim's and put her hand on Rose-Renee's shoulder. 'Let's go before we get swallowed up here, or seduced, or drugged or whatever happens to you in this room.'

They turned off the lights and closed the doors behind them; they made their way upstairs

112

and everyone said goodnight.

After brushing their teeth, Marcella and Rose-Renee walked down the hall towards their room, turning off the lights as they went. When they passed Tim and Linda's room they heard laughter and squealing.

'Boodling,' said Rose-Renee. 'They don't boodle as much as Valerie and Mitch.'

'We don't know that. Their room is far from ours. Valerie and Mitch were always nearby.'

'Do you miss them, Stinko? Valerie and Mitch, I mean?'

'Nah. Do you?' The two climbed up and into the big bed.

'Nah.'

'I like it here,' said Marcella, nestling down, 'I like living with Tim and Linda and Dorothea and Rot.'

'Yes,' agreed Rose-Renee, rolling over, turning her back to her sister. 'If we had a television and a puppy, it'd be just about perfect.'

6

A Question of Vision

Even at a school as unconventional as Flag School, autumnal rituals recurred, predictable as the little miniature train on its endlessly looping tracts. Autumnal colours — umber, orange, maroon, and gold — appeared on cue; ghosts and ghouls and witches, pumpkins and black cats adorned the bulletin boards. For the Flag School Halloween party, Rose-Renee wanted to be a Munchkin, so Tim rigged her a costume from an old yellow dressing gown with big buttons. He stuffed out the shoulders with padding made from what he'd cut off the hem. He found an old rain hat and painted it yellow. Marcella insisted on wearing a beautiful satin evening dress in shades of peach and plum that might once have had feathers on the shoulders, but they had moulted or been eaten by moths. The dress had thin, beaded straps and a beaded bodice and they caught the light and many tiny noises, and the beads felt cold and smooth. She found a paper parasol to carry as well.

'You'll freeze your ass off in that,' counselled Linda.

'I don't care.' Marcella preened in the long bevelled mirror in Linda's room while Tim and Rose-Renee looked on. 'I think I look pretty.'

'Actually, you do,' Linda conceded. 'You might

actually grow up to be a pretty woman, squirt.'

'I think I'm as pretty as Miss Manetti. I bet she wore this dress.'

'Miss Manetti! How did you hear about her!'

'Gloria told us how she came with Signor Massimo, who built the music room. How he didn't speak English and she had to speak it for him.'

'Oh yeah, and that's not all she did for him.'

'Did you meet them?'

'Hell, no. They were way before my time. But I was introduced to Pablo Casals once. Yes — ' Linda held out her hand and minced about the room ' — this is the hand that touched the hand of greatness.'

Tim gave her a swift pat on the ass. 'And this is the hand that touched the ass of greatness.'

'Oh, girls,' Linda laughed. 'Isn't he impossible?'

They agreed that he was. Linda rouged their cheeks, and told them not to freeze on their way to Dorothea's, and to be certain Dorothea took their pictures.

Dorothea greeted them at the back door dressed as a witch with a pointy hat and a blacked-out tooth. 'Heh-heh, my pretties!' she screeched.

Rodney wore an old tuxedo of his father's with the pants cut short for him, and long trails of red paint down the front. He had drawn stitches across his forehead and great green circles around his eyes, and blacked up his lips with crayons. 'I'm Frankenjones,' he declared. 'Mom hates my costume, but I think I'm scary.'

'You are. You're scary, Putrid's yellow, but I

am beautiful,' Marcella said with some pride, twirling so the pale beads caught the light and twinkled. 'I am like a firefly.'

'And now, my pretties, you must all follow me!' cried Dorothea after she had taken half a dozen Polaroid pictures. She led them out to the small gym.

Once inside, Ethel suddenly jumped out, jabbing at them with her broom, and wearing a pointy hat like Dorothea's and a black cape, and one front tooth blacked out. 'Heh-heh-heh,' Ethel cackled, 'welcome to the haunted house . . . You will never escape.'

Dorothea drew them in where ghosts — sheets tied around balls — hung from the old smokehouse meat hooks; a fan stirred enough wind to move them. Dorothea and Ethel had curtained off tiny spaces with black cloth. Each child got led behind the cloth, their hand grabbed and plunged into a tub of guts (cold spaghetti). Ethel and Dorothea rasped out horrible laughter at their shrieking responses. Beyond the tub-of-guts partition, the room was decorated with paper skeletons and cardboard black cats and in the centre there was a big copper washtub filled with water and bobbing with small red apples.

'I don't know why this should be fun,' Dorothea admitted, 'but it's what everyone does at Halloween. So, youngest first!' She took off Rose-Renee's Munchkin hat, and tied her hair back with a rubber band. 'Have at it, you Munchkin!'

'What do I do?'

'Have you never bobbed for apples?'

116

'Uh-uh. Neither of us.'

'Just get an apple with your teeth. No hands.'

Rose-Renee splashed into the washtub, came up, splashed again, her mouth open wide, gnashing fruitlessly at the water. Rodney and Marcella and Dorothea cheered her on, but then Dorothea quit cheering. She just watched. Finally, she drew the little girl back. 'That's enough.' She smoothed her cape over Rose-Renee's upturned face. 'That's enough.'

'Guess I lost that game, huh?'

'You can't really see the apples, can you?'

'Sure I can. Just not where they are.'

'What's that, over there in the corner?' Dorothea pointed to one of the cardboard black cats.

'The corner.'

'But what's in the corner?'

Rose-Renee glanced to Marcella, but Dorothea told Marcella to say nothing. 'Dunno,' said Rose-Renee. 'Dunno, and don't want to. Don't care.'

'Oh, Rose-Renee, I understand everything now. Everything.'

'What? I want to understand everything too,' said Marcella.

'She can't see,' said Dorothea. 'That's why Rose-Renee is so . . . so . . . why school is so hard for her.'

'Putrid's blind?' asked Rodney.

'Not blind. She just can't see well, and she thinks that's the way everyone sees, don't you, Rose-Renee? You think the whole world is vague and indistinct.'

'Ask Marcella. She knows what I think.'

117

After lunch Dorothea drove them all, including Rodney, back to Gloria's. She parked the Mercedes at the front.

'We ought to go round to the back,' said Marcella. 'But I guess this is another formal call, huh?'

'Yes.'

'The front door's always locked,' Marcella offered. 'The back door isn't.'

'You knock. Someone will answer.'

Marcella knocked. More than once. She pulled her oversized coat close around her; she was freezing in the beaded evening dress, and beside her Rose-Renee shivered in her Munchkin costume. Dorothea in her witch's outfit did not so much as tremble in the cold. Finally Linda answered, Tim right behind her.

Marcella knew the drill. She left them all there and walked through the dusky, unlit corridors to the music room. She came to the St Cecilia doors, and as she always did, even when she sometimes crept down alone at night to practise her lessons on the Steinway, she ran her fingers over St Cecilia's beautiful face and lyre. She might have knocked, but Gloria's music was so intense and tender, she did not dare. She paced for a bit, but finally she just slid down the wall, her head on her knees while the music circled round and over her, like an embrace, or the promise of an embrace, and then it stopped. She jumped up and knocked on the door.

Gloria answered, carrying her violin. 'Why are you dressed in that ridiculous gown?'

'It's Halloween. Dorothea's at the front.

Dorothea would like to see you.'

'What for?'

'I don't know.'

When they returned to the foyer, Linda and Tim sat on the bottom step talking to Dorothea, who held tight to Rose-Renee's hand, as though she were a small, yellow balloon who, once untethered, might float for ever out of reach.

'Really, Dorothea,' said Gloria, 'you look silly in that outfit. And your tooth!'

'Well, yes, it is just for Halloween.'

'And your boy! He looks awful! He looks like the dead!'

Dorothea quickly used her witch's cape to wipe his make-up. 'Linda was just telling me all about her musical studies at Radcliffe,' Dorothea went on a little breathlessly. 'How proud you must be. Both she and Valerie have inherited your talent. And Marcella too. Rose-Renee too,' she added.

'Linda let all of that go,' said Gloria. 'She could have had a brilliant future. Even genius must be nurtured with work. Linda has a genuine gift. Linda was playing Liszt when she was twelve. The same age as you, Marcella. Just imagine being that gifted to — '

'Oh God.' Linda stood up. 'Not that again. Come on, Tim. I'm sick of this bullshit.' Linda pulled Tim to his feet and up the stairs.

'I've come about Rose-Renee's vision,' said Dorothea.

'Vision?' Gloria looked perplexed, as though Rose-Renee might be seeing angels dance on the head of a pin.

Dorothea cleared her throat, and began again. 'I mean her eyesight. She can't see properly.' And then Dorothea launched into a rapid-fire declaration of her observations, her conclusions, her prescriptions for righting these wrongs which included contacting Rodney's Philadelphia doctor for a referral, making an appointment with an eye doctor, and taking her to Philly for the appointment and the glasses. 'It's a question of vision,' she concluded passionately. 'A pair of glasses will change the whole world for her.'

'Glasses?' said Gloria. It had taken her a while to absorb all this, so breakneck was Dorothea's recital. 'Who will pay for glasses?'

'Valerie and Mitch are her parents. I'm sure they'll be happy to see her sight corrected. It should have been attended to long ago. Don't you understand? That's why she's slow in school.'

'She isn't retarded?'

Dorothea's round, open countenance clouded, suddenly grim, the look she wore at the Helsinki Olympics when she didn't even place. 'Rose-Renee's difficulties in school probably result from her not being able to see clearly what other children see. Her vision can be so easily corrected and the whole world will open up to her.'

'I doubt Valerie can afford glasses,' said Gloria. 'I most certainly cannot.'

'Well, her father, then?'

'He's an actor,' Gloria scoffed. 'He can't pay. Valerie is a student. She can't pay; besides, she's far away. It will take a week to get a letter to her, and another week to get a reply.'

'This cannot wait. I'll make the appointment,

120

and I'll carry the cost for the moment. Valerie and Mitch can pay me back.'

'You understand, Mrs Jones, I cannot answer for them. I can't pay. I can't promise — '

'The child needs glasses. I shall see to it that she has them, and when Valerie comes back, she and their father can repay me then. That's fine. When will Valerie be back?'

'I don't know. She hasn't said, well, she did say not this year. Her last letter said not this year. Next year, I suppose.'

Rose-Renee and Marcella exchanged encoded, wary glances; they had not known Valerie wrote to Gloria separately from the bi-weekly postcards she wrote to the girls.

Dorothea in her witch's outfit looked truly dangerous. 'I think your daughter is making a terrible error in leaving her children alone.'

'I don't like it any better than you do. Valerie is shirking her responsibilities.'

'But she thinks like you do, Gloria. She's acting on the values you taught her and Linda, and now you're teaching Marcella and Rose-Renee these same values.'

'I do not teach,' Gloria maintained. 'I am teaching them nothing.'

'Teaching by example! Don't you see? Can you truly justify sacrificing everything, just so you can serve only some notion of genius?'

'Yes,' said Gloria simply and without apology.

'What if you're wrong?'

'How could you possibly understand?'

Dorothea seemed poised to retort, but didn't. 'I'll see you tomorrow at Flag School, girls.'

121

She nodded to Rodney, Marcella opened the door for them, and they left. By the time Marcella had closed the door, Gloria was gone. Rose-Renee plopped on the floor, a great yellow puddle in her Munchkin costume. Marcella, in her beaded finery, sank down beside her. They sat in silence, their old innate communication radiating anxiety.

'We got to make a promise, Putrid,' said Marcella. 'Right now, and for ever. Promise that we'll never grow up to be like Linda or Valerie, or Gloria.'

They completed their pact, licking both thumbs, tapping them three times together, each hand left and right. Nothing could break such a solemn oath as that.

★   ★   ★

Rose-Renee's new glasses — round granny glasses, very fashionable, though very thick — altered her relationship with the world, or as much of the world as would care about Rose-Renee McNeill. At first they made her a little dizzy, off balance, and she was easily startled when things loomed up in front of her. She sometimes held out her hand to steady herself. Marcella reflexively took her hand. But with the glasses Rose-Renee did not need Marcella to make all her choices, did not need to rely on her so completely, or follow her cues or wishes, to echo Marcella as though the two shared the same nervous system. This altered dynamic left Marcella sometimes confused, as the easy assumptions of their long partnership shifted. Sometimes Marcella thought she could actually hear the separation taking place, like long sheets of paper ripping.

Dorothea had hoped for a dramatic, perhaps an Olympic leap, in Rose-Renee's learning abilities. This did not happen. Rose-Renee was easily challenged, and unlike Marcella, easily defeated. She learned to read, haltingly, not swiftly, but she learned, and Dorothea made certain she stood on the Winner's Box and collected her M&Ms. Now that she could see the maps and pictures and numbers better, Rose-Renee was a more responsive student, but sometimes the onrush of sensation, visual stimuli, was too much, and she would take her glasses off, put them on her desk and put her head down. Dorothea never demanded that she sit up and participate. More often than not Dorothea ended the school day early, and let the girls run into the woods to play Gingerbread Girls. Their voices sometimes reached Rodney, who had to rest in the afternoons; his energies were swiftly spent, and once spent, not easily restored. Dorothea stood at his bedroom window and watched Marcella and Rose-Renee dart through the thinning woods, the leafless trees, calling out their chant: *Run run, fast as you will, you can't catch me, I'm the Gingerbread Girl* . . .

Mrs Campbell, however, had no such lenient scruples. Though she had early on lowered her expectations for Rose-Renee, once she got her glasses, and better learned to read music, Mrs Campbell demanded more. Mrs Campbell was often sharp with her, and made her endlessly redo passages till there were no mistakes.

Rose-Renee was at the piano one Tuesday with Mrs Campbell. She was banging out 'Turkey In The Straw', or trying to, when Rodney called to Marcella from his room. At first she didn't see him because he wasn't at the desk with the model airplanes, but in bed, under the covers. 'Get me another blanket, will you, Stinko? Don't let my mother see you. Just ask Ethel.'

So she went to Ethel and asked for another blanket. Ethel handed her the blanket with a sharp warning. 'See that you don't upset him or tax him, young lady. Not everyone's like you, you know.'

Marcella recognized the rebuke, though not quite what she had done to deserve it. She brought the blanket and lay it over him and sat down on the bed. 'How can you be cold? This room is toasty warm. The whole house is warm.'

'I'm cold inside.'

'Childhood diseases. You'll grow out of them.'

'Maybe not this time. At least it's not cancer. That's what they've told my mom, but Crohn's disease might be worse than cancer.'

'Will you turn into a crone?'

'Boys can't be crones, stupid.'

'Well, why is it worse than cancer?'

'Everyone knows what cancer is, but Crohn's is different. No one knows why you get it or how to cure it, but it's like your body hates itself. Your guts. My guts. Mom doesn't like me to talk about it.'

'That's OK, I won't tell her.'

'We're going to Boston. To a children's

hospital there because I have to have some tests and a surgery where they open me up and see what's wrong, and if it's Crohn's, I might have to have an operation where they take out my guts, and give me a bag.'

'What kind of a bag?'

'It's called an ostomy.' He teared up. 'My body hates me and I hate it.'

Marcella ran her fingers through his thin, pale hair. 'Don't cry, Rot. Dorothea wouldn't like to see you cry. It would make her sad.'

'Don't tell her I told you.'

'I promise. I want you to be well, Rot.'

'Yes, so we can have aerial combat in Doll Wars.' He smiled weakly.

Marcella heard Rose-Renee call her from the foot of the stairs. 'Want Putrid to come sit with you while I have my lesson?'

'No, but ask her not to wreck the train, will you? I have a headache.'

When Marcella went down to the piano, she found Mrs Campbell shuffling the music. Marcella didn't really need the music; she'd memorized the piece. She was about to put her hands on the piano when Mrs Campbell said she had been thinking about Gloria's music room and the spring recital. She beamed.

Marcella felt a little knot tie itself in her throat but she coughed and said, 'I asked Gloria, and she said no. Absolutely no. Never. I'm very sorry, Mrs Campbell, but she isn't going to change her mind. She got very angry. She said never ever mention it again.' And then Marcella looked soulfully down at her hands, lying still in her lap.

Mitch McNeill could have done it no better.

'She should be delighted to share her performance space with young musicians,' Mrs Campbell retorted, unimpressed with Marcella's dramatic delivery. 'After all, she once taught at Curtis.'

'She doesn't like to teach. She needs all her time to rehearse.'

'Perhaps you didn't put the proposition to her correctly. Perhaps you are too young to do it. Perhaps I ought call her myself.'

If that upright piano had opened its maw, bent over and inhaled her on the spot, Marcella would have been grateful, but she slurred and furred her words, and promised to talk to Gloria again, that Mrs Campbell should not call, that Gloria was sick and needed to get well before she could bring the subject up again. After that, her lesson was terrible and Mrs Campbell chided her for her poor performance.

Dorothea, who had been waiting in the den for the lesson to be over, met Marcella and Mrs Campbell at the door. 'I wanted to tell you that there won't be any lessons next week,' she said, 'nor the week after. Rodney and I are going to Boston next week.'

'But Thanksgiving's two weeks away.'

'Yes, we are taking an early holiday, all of us. We are an independent school, after all,' she said brightly, stroking Marcella's curly mop of hair.

'Yes,' said Marcella, standing tall, basking in Dorothea's Olympian aplomb. 'We can do what we want.'

★ ★ ★

On Thanksgiving Day for the first time Gloria would join the four of them for a meal. Tim lit a fire in the breakfast room. Linda showed Marcella and Rose-Renee how to set a table properly, going so far as to unearth the Denham Spode china and tall crystal flutes from the butler's pantry. Rose-Renee put an origami turkey Rodney made in the centre of the table. In all, they agreed the place looked festive.

Tim had talked Gloria into letting him choose a turkey at Stoddard's Provisioners and he made a corn-bread and pecan stuffing that he remembered (sort of) from what his mother made. Linda made a pumpkin pie. He made sweet potatoes and biscuits too, and some kind of greens that Marcella found both bitter and bracing. They all effusively complimented his cooking, which was one way to steer clear of topics that would set Gloria and Linda at one another's throats. Linda and Gloria seemed to have agreed to the truce. Marcella watched her grandmother, fascinated, never having seen her eat anything. Gloria carefully hedged off each thing on her plate, as if creating hostile borders. She balanced her biscuit on the edge, and sliced her turkey into tiny little slivers, as she spoke in her thin voice.

Rose-Renee kicked her under the table, and Marcella jumped. 'What?'

'Christmas,' said Rose-Renee, scowling. 'Gloria's talking about Christmas.'

'What were you saying, Gloria?'

127

Gloria, who disliked any waste of effort or motion or time, repeated, somewhat testily, that she could not and would not be doing Christmas for two children. 'That is your parents' responsibility. Mitch's, I guess, since Valerie is in Sweden. The two of you should be with your father for Christmas. It's not for me to have a tree and all that. This house is long past that.'

'I'll do it, Mrs Denham,' offered Tim. 'I mean, I'll get the tree and do the work if you want.'

'We both will,' said Linda. 'It'll be fun.'

'Yes!' cried the effervescent Marcella.

'I can't be bothered with all that folderol. Shopping. All that effort. It's all so false and stupid, all that ho ho ho. No, I've made up my mind. Valerie writes that she won't be back from Sweden till next year. But Mitch is in Dallas. I'll write to him tomorrow. He's in some play there. Valerie says you girls always liked the theatre.'

'We want to stay here. We don't want to go to Dallas.'

'See that he buys you some winter coats,' said Gloria, ignoring Marcella, 'and some decent winter clothes. I can't stand to see you in that mink stole with the little heads.'

'But we're coming back here, right?' said Marcella.

'Mitch will have to pay for your tickets.'

Ten days later the girls returned from Flag School in the chill December dusk, happy to come into the warm kitchen where Tim was peeling onions for his famous Arkansas chili and Linda was reading a book. She had a joint in her hand.

'Hello, squirts,' said Linda. 'Mitch called. Yes, I actually spoke to Sir Laurence himself. Lear on the heath. Hamlet on rye. Gloria put it to him good. He's buying your tickets and sending them here. You'll stay with him in Dallas, December fifteenth to the thirty-first. He's playing in *A Streetcar Named Desire*. He's sweaty Mitch, not sexy Stanley.'

'He is Mitch,' Marcella said.

'That's the character's name too. You know, Karl Malden played him in the film.'

'How would two little girls know that?' asked Tim.

'Hey, they're an actor's daughters. I bet they know more characters than you do.'

'That's a weird name,' said Rose-Renee, peeling off her fur coat with the little heads. 'A Streetcar Named Dorothea.'

Linda howled at this, and a rousing game ensued, fuelled by a rising tide of stoned humour. A Streetcar Named Agnes, a Streetcar Named Gertrude, a Streetcar Named Gloria, but a Streetcar Named Dorothea remained the funniest of all.

'It's true though,' Marcella said, 'Dorothea is like a streetcar. She's always going someplace happy. She takes everyone with her.'

Andantino

Carrying her backpack, Marcella entered the kitchen, which, except for the cigarette burns at the edges of the wooden table, and a big white cat that sat there licking its paw, remained

129

unchanged. Dry, brown and tattered dishcloths hung suspended on the string over the sink, and Grumpy Susan's clotheslines still sagged from the pantry all the way across to the other wall. Marcella went to the bathroom off the kitchen, scene of many a childhood crisis. Ticks, for instance. The plumbing was still sluggish when she pulled the chain on the toilet. The ceiling was patched with dampness and mould grew in the corners of the huge claw-foot tub. Thick cobwebs, grey with dust, linked the toilet plunger to the wall. The wringer washing machine she remembered had been replaced with a model from the 1970s, and there was a dryer. She turned on the tap to wash her hands; the water was discoloured with what looked like rust or copper. When she came into the kitchen, Linda was getting eggs out of the ancient fridge. 'How soon till Valerie comes down?'

'Depends on what she took last night to help her sleep, and how much she drank to wash it down. Remember what I said about treating her gently. If you don't, she'll just fall apart again.'

'Yes. Of course. I'll be back in a bit.'

Marcella meandered through the rooms, unpeopled now, just as they had been thirty years before, unchanged save for the air, which was heavy, stagnant and musty. Perhaps it was always that way, and she simply had not noticed. She crossed the main hall, the foyer where the staircases for each wing converged in a flaring circular room, with a crystal chandelier hung high up, catching the morning light, reflecting it in prisms. For all the high-ceilinged splendour, a

130

damp, slightly fetid odour wafted. Cat pee, perhaps. Mould? Mildew?

The library, once her favourite room, was darkened by deep green shades blocking the natural light from the windows. She did not remember the shades ever being down, or indeed, if they had been there at all. Raising them, she could see there was little to protect here. The two pale Wyeth watercolours that had hung over the fireplace, those were gone, as were some lesser framed Wyeth and Howard Pyle sketches. The shelf that once held the entire collection of Nathaniel Wyeth-illustrated children's classics — first editions — that was empty. Long rows of Edna Ferber, Taylor Caldwell and J. P. Marquand novels still stood, and there was a dog-eared copy of her own book, the hardcover. A Song for Saint Cecilia: Music and Memory. She lifted the cover: For Gloria, with all good wishes, Eunice Campbell, Christmas 1994.

Marcella left, and closed the door behind her, walking down the long hall as morning light flooded through the windows, mercilessly exposing the stained carpets, dusty walls and empty squares where framed pictures of the greats — Segovia, Casals, Stravinsky, Milhaud — had once hung. She paused at the music-room doors, as though she ought to knock. Then she reminded herself that Gloria was no longer here. Marcella Brailled her fingers over St Cecilia's face, her full figure, flowing classical robes, her every feature so perfectly wrought, so well-remembered. She took a deep

131

breath before she pushed the handles, brass that had been shaped, one into a treble clef, one into a bass. The door unresistingly opened, giving on to a vast sea of darkness until she snapped on the electric light and the wall sconces lit all at once.

The room was windowless, but it did not feel airless, quite the contrary. In this magnificent space, the high ceiling ribbed with beams of teak, Marcella felt as if she were on the deck of a vast ship with golden beams for sails. The floors, too, were teak, and they gleamed in the warm lighting. Towards the edges of the room, assorted, orphaned bits of furniture stood, a divan, a few wing chairs, a long bevelled mirror. Perhaps twenty Spartan, metal, folding chairs formed an informal circle around the piano. That they were already, even haphazardly set up, suggested that in the few days since the memorial service musicians had already gathered here to try out the fabled acoustics. Marcella moved slowly through the rarified space, remembering the thrill of surreptitious practice in this room when, as a child, she had sneaked downstairs late at night, and played her basic piano pieces, alone.

The folding chairs faced the shrouded harp, proud and isolate, and the grand piano, a Steinway, covered with a vast, fringed, ecru silken scarf, a scarf so fine and filmy, it fluttered in the last remnants of the draught Marcella had created. Nearby stood a drop-leaf table, a thin music stand, and a tall floor lamp with a fringed shade, and that too swayed with the slightest current, creating small shadowy patterns on the floor. The 1727 *Stradivarius* in its ornate case, that of course was already gone; no doubt the board of trustees took possession of that before Gloria was cold.

Marcella walked to the piano, opened the keyboard, and plunked out a few notes; even these seemed to shimmer. Emboldened, she sat down and played a few well-known chords that registered through the floor and into her very feet. She played portions of Debussy's Underwater Cathedral, The Girl With The Flaxen Hair, of Ravel's Sonatine, pieces she had always loved, and then halted quickly, mid-measure, and looked up, aware, uncomfortably aware, that she might not be alone. She surveyed the chairs.

In life, the process of rehearse-and-perform reverses. Childhood, that small, intense shard of time, is the short rehearsal for the long years of performance ahead. When that short rehearsal ends — ready or not — you are thrust into the adult world to perform. You must gratify and vindicate all those people from your childhood who will continue to wield power over you with their unequal measures of guilt and praise as long as they live. Longer. As long as you live. They remain an unseen audience, for ever assessing your performance, your abilities, your successes and failures, your crashing stupidities, your transcendent moments, your ongoing defects, and occasional gaffes, your courage in adversity, your grace in the face of indignity, your conduct measured against impossible and always unmet standards. You, the performer of your adult life, cannot see across the footlights

133

into the darkness, but you can hear their phantom coughs and whispers, the restless creak of empty seats, the scrape of empty shoes, the untethered sighs.

7

The Last Taco on Earth

Mitch McNeill needed no velvet curtains, no prompter, no Laban method to create theatre. He could easily cast his deep, sonorous voice well beyond his impressive body: six feet tall, broad-shouldered, solid, handsome with slightly drooping eyelids and a mobile mouth. He had a shock of dark hair that just brushed his collar, and he was clean-shaven except for heavy sideburns. In contrast to the cowboy-hat-clad crowds in the Dallas/Fort Worth airport, he wore a smart blue suit with wide lapels and a loud-print shirt, like a character out of *Yellow Submarine*. He did not gather in the airport lounge with other families awaiting the Philadelphia flight, but stood a way off, smoking thoughtfully until the passengers began to come through the door. He threw away the cigarette and waited till he saw the statuesque stewardess shepherding two girls through the door and into the crowd. The stewardess, beaming, looked around. Mitch's only move was to kneel and open his arms and call out their names. The children bolted from the stewardess, cried out 'Daddy!' and ran to him, and he enfolded them both in his embrace. The entire airport lounge — if they did not burst into spontaneous applause — knew they had witnessed something

135

wonderful and heartwarming, a Christmas family tableau.

Mitch held the girls in his arms, and then stepped forward, revealing behind him two enormous teddy bears, one green and one pink, seated in the airport chairs, with wonderfully happy grins on their faces.

Marcella was annoyed. Didn't Mitch know she was too old for a teddy bear? She felt silly carrying a big stupid pink teddy bear through the airport to baggage claim. Worse, Rose-Renee thrust Cubbie into her arms so she could properly hug and carry her green teddy bear.

'Rose-Renee,' said Mitch, holding her hand, 'you look so different with glasses.'

'I can see now. Everything.'

'And you, Marcella, how you've grown in such a short time!'

'It wasn't such a short time,' said Marcella, still stung that she should be stuck with both the teddy bear and the battered baby doll. She was hoping he would say something about the smart new skirt and sweater sets Linda had bought for them. Linda insisted they couldn't go to Dallas looking like refugees from a Noël Coward play, and Gloria begrudgingly gave her money.

But Mitch did not mention their clothes, or anything else, as he collected their two bags and walked them out to the parking lot. His car was not the old Chevy, the one they'd left him with. This car was a Pontiac Firebird and the engine growled when he turned it on. 'It belongs to my girlfriend, Cherie. You're going to love her.'

In the back seat, Rose-Renee and Marcella

exchanged an encrypted, *We'll just see about that*.

Mitch's home was just like the ones the girls remembered. Metal stairs clanged underfoot as they walked up to a second-floor apartment where doors fronted a long walk. A furnished one-bedroom rental with a window in front, a window in the bedroom and a kitchenette. However, here there was a sewing machine tucked in one corner and an ironing board beside it. Mitch said Cherie was the wardrobe girl for *A Streetcar Named Desire* and a talented fashion designer.

Cherie burst into the apartment just then, carrying grocery bags, full of apologies; she had meant to be there to greet them but she'd got in line behind someone who couldn't speak English. She was blonde and bubbly with a strong jaw and short nose. Her blonde hair was straight, her bangs came to her eyes, and she was constantly brushing them away. Her clothes were colourful and daring: a fringed shawl, a mini-skirt, hoop earrings.

'There's only one bedroom,' Cherie explained, 'so, look, we've set you up with two sleeping bags and two pillows, everything's new, right here on the floor in front of the TV.'

'Does it work?'

'What?'

'The TV. The TV at Gloria's doesn't work.'

'Nothing works at Gloria's,' said Mitch. 'Not even Gloria, that bitch.'

'Really, honey,' Cherie said gently, 'she's their grandmother.'

137

'Sure,' he laughed and mussed up Rose-Renee's hair. 'See, it works.' He turned the TV on to prove it. Then he turned it off. 'We can't stay long. We have to go out and eat so we can get to the theatre. We're going to a Mexican restaurant,' he said as they all trooped back down the concrete stairs. 'You'll love it.'

Mitch said he loved Mexican restaurants because they were all like small theatres. Inevitably, coming in from the bright Texas sunshine, your eyes would take a moment to adjust to the dimness and then, following a costumed señorita in a low-cut blouse and a flouncy short skirt, you passed through a stage set that was always some artful combination of Aztec sun gods, piñatas, sombreros, serapes, and huge paper flowers in brass vases, and mariachi music playing in end-less loops on the muzak.

Mitch ordered beers for himself and Cherie, and Shirley Temples for his daughters. They all clinked glasses. 'I'm so happy to see you girls, to have all my girls together.'

Marcella beamed, the indignity of the teddy bear forgiven, delighted to be eating out. This was the first time she'd been to a restaurant since they had left Mitch in Richmond, and she'd never been to a Mexican restaurant.

'You girls will have to come to the theatre with us,' said Mitch after they had ordered. 'We couldn't find a babysitter for you.'

'We don't need babysitters,' said Marcella. 'We're not babies.'

'Not babies,' Rose-Renee echoed.

'Well, all right then,' said Mitch, 'you can wait

138

in the green room. They were brought up in the green room,' he explained to Cherie. 'Born in a trunk.'

'What's that mean?' asked Rose-Renee.

'It means you are an actor's daughters,' he replied, slicing Valerie from the equation. 'You want to see the play tonight? *A Streetcar Named Desire*. You'll love it.'

'*A Streetcar Named Dorothea*,' they laughed.

Mitch looked perplexed. He knew nothing of Dorothea or Rodney, and he sipped his beer while the two rattled on about Flag School.

'A private school?' asked Cherie, interrupting. 'Doesn't that cost a lot of money?'

'Don't worry,' said Mitch, 'it's free. Some friend of theirs runs it.' Then he returned to the original thought. 'You'll have to be very quiet and grown up there in the audience, but I think some good seats are still available.'

Many good seats were still available, as it turned out. The house was perhaps half full. Rose-Renee and Marcella sat stage left in the front row. They each had programmes.

A Streetcar Named Desire
by *Tennessee Williams*
4 December 1969 through 18 January 1970

Mitch McNeill's headshot showed a virile, intense actor, though he did not play the sexy Stanley Kowalski, but rather the rumpled, spurious-genteel Mitch. Rose-Renee was bored and restless. Marcella put her hand on her sister's arm to still her. Marcella herself had only

139

one reaction to *Streetcar*. She felt sorry for Blanche DuBois, knowing what it was to live with people who didn't want you, and that the kindness of strangers is overrated.

After that first night, the girls sat out the performances in the green room, four nights a week and Sunday matinee. This green room had bordello-red flocked fleurs-de-lys on the wallpaper and Spartan plastic furniture. Someone had looped an abject silver tinsel swag along one wall, and a sprig of plastic mistletoe hung from a light fixture. There was a speaker in one corner that blared out unvarying messages: *Fifteen minutes. Fifteen minutes till curtain. Places, please. Places.*

Mitch was not the sort to hang out in the green room. He said it interrupted his character interpretation, but less dedicated actors came in there to smoke, or knit, or read the trades. They ignored the girls, who made faces behind their backs, and played games of Go Fish or Old Maid. They were unable to bet arm-farts because even on that first night, the stage manager came down on them for noise. The actress who played Stella, in her very pregnant costume, came into the green room to use the pay-phone one night, a not-so-subtle conversation with her agent, whom she scolded for tying her to this lousy production. When she was done, she turned to Marcella and Rose-Renee, who were reading *Variety*. 'You are a pain in the ass,' she announced, and then left.

Within days the girls were bored mindless; the card games paled, the teddy bears had long since

140

lost their lustre, and they took to writing letters to Rodney. They signed them Stinko and Putrid. They told him all about Dallas: Dallas was flat, except for buildings. The weather was nice, warm. They didn't go out very much because Mitch and Cherie slept late. There were a lot of Mexican restaurants in Dallas and they had eaten at every one of them. They did not like the food or the mariachi music. They got to watch TV till they were cross-eyed. They loved 'Sock it to me' on *Rowan & Martin's Laugh-In*. They laughed and laughed. Sometimes when they woke up in the morning, the TV was still on. In the mornings they ate cereal in front of the TV. During the day Mitch would sometimes go out, and sometimes he took them to the movies. They went to see *Butch Cassidy and the Sundance Kid*. They loved it, but Mitch didn't. Cherie taught them her favourite song, 'The Ballad of John And Yoko', and they promised to teach it to Rot. They tried to teach Cherie some songs from *Oklahoma!* but Mitch forbade it. No *Oklahoma!*. Mitch brought home a teentsy-tiny fake Christmas tree they set on the dinette table. Cherie was nice to them. She worked at her sewing machine all the time and made decorations for the tree with scraps of cloth. She let them sew on sequins, but they got bored. They hated the green room and the play. They sent Rot a playbill of *A Streetcar Named Desire*, though Marcella crossed out *Desire* and wrote *Dorothea*. They drew moustaches and blacked out the teeth of the actors' headshots, except for Mitch. Beside Mitch's picture Marcella wrote Daddy. The word was fine to

141

write, but it did not fit their lips and so, like Cherie, they called him Mitch.

He called Cherie 'Girl' as an endearment. They were all three 'The Girls'; more to the point, 'His Girls'. Marcella took some contrary pride in knowing that Valerie would never have permitted herself to become one of The Girls. Valerie always contested Mitch's right to centre-stage, but Cherie accepted his assumption that he was the sun god of any universe he chose to inhabit. She had lived with him since June, and by now recognized that people who questioned Mitch's right to be the centre of the universe (or even people who annoyed or thwarted him) fell into simple categories. All such men were bastards. All such women were bitches. Any such children were brats.

One afternoon Mitch gave Cherie some money and she took the girls to a department store and bought them each new shoes and tights. She bought them each a winter jacket and a new dress. She told Marcella she would soon outgrow the children's department. She took them to see Santa, who sat enthroned in a big chair on a dais enclosed in a red and green bower and attended by elves in little green caps. The elves were silent, but Santa boomed 'Ho ho ho!'

'I'm too old for Santa,' said Marcella. 'I don't want to talk to him.'

But Cherie said everyone liked Santa; she liked Santa, and to please her, Marcella took Rose-Renee's arm and stood in line.

'Ho ho ho! What's your name, little girl?'

'Putrid.'

142

'And what do you want for Christmas?'

'A pony.'

'A pony! Well, well! I hope you've been a really good girl to get a pony.'

'I haven't been good, and I won't be either.' Rose-Renee crossed her arms, and stuck her hands in her armpits. 'You stink.'

'What?'

'Like menthol cigarettes, you stupid, stinking fake.'

Marcella yanked her off Santa's lap, and they followed the angry, unspeaking Cherie back to the car, secretly laughing in their silent fashion.

Accustomed to the freedoms of Gloria's big house, games in the woods, to Flag School, and the lively company of Dorothea and Rodney, Tim and Linda, the girls grew restless and cranky as the days passed. The thrill of the television wore off. Even the big teddy bears were only good for boxing matches, which were forbidden after they knocked a lamp off an end table and it broke into a hundred pieces. Cherie's warm welcome cooled. Mitch, unused to considering any but his own needs, was sometimes short with them, snapped at them, called them brats. Later he would make up, not apologizing, exactly, but handing out dollar bills for nothing in particular.

Marcella's instincts, as well as her experience, taught her to be grateful for his genial attentions, and to avoid him when he was grim. Rose-Renee's instincts were of a different sort, and she had not learned from experience.

She sometimes broke into bits of *Oklahoma!* just to taunt him.

On Christmas Eve there was no performance, and they were all at the apartment. Rose-Renee started sing-songing 'A *Streetcar Named Dorothea*' over and over. From the bedroom Mitch called out to her to shut up. She did not. She did not refuse, or say 'Make me', or any such thing, she just kept it up till he came barrelling out of the bedroom, filling up the door, Cherie right behind him, as he boomed out, 'That play is a great work of art, and you will show some respect!'

Rose-Renee darted underneath the dinette table and crouched there. 'A Streetcar Named Agnes! A Streetcar Named Gloria! A Streetcar Named Valerie! A Streetcar Named Dorothea!'

Marcella, on the couch, tensed, readied herself for action if needed; he had been known to smack them now and then when they all lived with Valerie.

Mitch moved to the dinette table, stood, legs apart, poised, like Stanley in the play. 'Say it right. It's a great goddamned play, and you will say it right.' His words fell down upon the tiny Christmas tree.

'Oh, Mitch,' said Cherie, 'now who's being childish?'

'Stay out of this. I'm not going to stand here and allow my own daughter to belittle a great work of art. Now, say it right, goddamnit.'

But Rose-Renee fearlessly darted out from under the table, laughing and shouting, 'A Streetcar Named Dorothea!'

He caught her by the arm, smacked her a good one across the bottom, then another across the face, when Marcella barrelled into him, full force, butted him in the side so he lost his grip and staggered backwards. She grabbed Rose-Renee's hand, and they both scrambled into the bathroom, slammed the door, locked and leaned against it, sliding down to the floor, their feet pressed against the tub. The guy in the next apartment thumped the wall and shouted for all of them to shut the hell up.

For twenty minutes Mitch stood at the bathroom door and banged on it with his fist. Cherie yelled at him. The guy in the next apartment said he was calling the goddamned cops. The apartment manager pounded on the door, and Cherie placated her before turning to Mitch, and calling him a stupid sonofabitch. The door slammed, and Mitch's feet pounded down the metal stairs. Cherie leaned over the banister and called out, 'Where do you think you're going in my car, Mitch? You can't leave me here to look after your kids! You get back here, you sonofabitch! Bastard!'

They heard the Firebird growl and then peal out. They heard Cherie dial the phone and talk briefly. She went into the bedroom and ten minutes later she called out, 'I hope you brats are happy.' The door closed behind her on the way out.

'You bonked him good, Stinko.' Rose-Renee grinned happily. 'You socked it to him.'

'Don't you ever learn, Putrid?' Marcella grinned, and nudged her in the ribs. She would not admit to being scared.

Mitch stumbled home about 2 a.m. He walked

145

past the girls sleeping on the living-room floor, and went to bed. Cherie didn't come home till the next morning. Her make-up was streaked and her stockings hung out of her bag. Marcella and Rose-Renee, eating cereal in front of the television, wisely said nothing, though they listened to the noisy boodling bout in the bedroom as Mitch and Cherie made up, full of regrets for last night and promising eternal love.

They came out of the bedroom, and Mitch said he was sorry. Marcella agreed she was sorry too, and with a few encoded glances convinced Rose-Renee to say the same. So everyone was sorry and they could open their Christmas presents. Cherie had sewed outfits for the oversized teddy bears. Mitch gave them each twenty dollars, and hand puppets, and roller skates for which they were both effusively grateful, though they knew that at Gloria's, there was no place to skate, except down on the narrow road with the snarling dogs, and fast-moving cars, which they would never do.

That afternoon they all went to the home of the actress who played Blanche. Her husband made Christmas dinner. The adults drank too much and smoked too much and Blanche went on a crying jag. Everyone was very glum because they'd been given notice on the twenty-third that the play would not have its full run; it would be closing the first week in January. Marcella and Rose-Renee, monumentally bored, used the hand puppets. 'Stella! Stella! Where is my liver? Where are my eyes? Where are my clothes?

146

Where is my skin?' They laughed till they had tears in their eyes. The actor who played Stanley told them to shut the hell up.

Mitch said, 'Ditto.'

The following day, they were eating in a Mexican restaurant before the performance and Rose-Renee announced to the waitress in the frilly costume that she wouldn't eat any more Mexican food. She hated it. She called it slop.

'She'll have a taco,' said Mitch.

'Will not.'

'Eat your taco and shut up.'

'I want a hot dog.'

'She'll have a taco,' he repeated.

Rose-Renee spoke to her father very clearly. 'I wouldn't eat your old taco if it was the last taco on earth, and I was starving.' She reached across the table and flipped the whole basket of chips on the floor.

'Say you're sorry.'

'Sock it to me.'

'I'm going to take you out to the car,' Mitch growled, 'and leave you there unless you say you're sorry.'

Marcella and Rose-Renee exchanged a glance. 'If Rose-Renee goes, I go too.'

He slid out of the booth, ignoring everyone else (or possibly enjoying this bit of family theatre in the Mexican restaurant; certainly all eyes were upon them) and grabbed their hands and marched them outside.

They went without tears, but not without a fight and there were a lot of harsh childish cries of *I hate you*'. Once at the car, Mitch said, 'I

147

hate you too.' He put them in the back seat, and slammed the door.

Rose-Renee thrashed all around the back seat while Marcella tried to hold her, soothe her while she wept and blubbered about how much she hated it here and wanted to leave.

'Where would we go?' said Marcella. 'There's nowhere to go.'

'Home.'

'It's too far away. We can't. We only have a few more days.'

'How many?'

'I don't know. Five or six.'

'I hate it here, Stinko.'

'I do too.'

'I hate Mitch and Cherie both.'

'Me too.'

'I miss Tim and Linda and Dorothea and Rot.'

'Me too.'

'I'm hungry.'

Marcella tried to imagine the two of them going back into the Mexican restaurant, a lovely father-and-daughters reunion with tacos and everyone being sorry. But she couldn't. 'We're staying here. We'll make them come to us.'

'I think I miss Gloria.'

'Hush, Putrid, hush.' Marcella put her arms around her.

Half an hour later Cherie came out, and drove them to a 7-Eleven where they bought peanut butter and all the Twinkies they could carry. She said not one word. Then she drove back to the Mexican restaurant and picked up Mitch. He was standing outside, smoking.

On that cheerful note, they drove to the theatre. The girls were deposited in the green room without a word from either Cherie or Mitch. The girls were silent, but in their own code they congratulated one another on their victory over the adult world. They ate the Twinkies and scooped peanut butter out of the jar with their fingers. They played a noisy game of tic-tac-toe and whoever lost would have to say 'Sock it to me' and get bonked off the chair.

The stage manager came in. 'Any more noise out of you two and I put you in the alley. I've had it with you two. I've had it with McNeill too. Thinks he's fucking Lear on the heath, does he? He can go to hell and take you two with him.'

'A Streetcar Named Dorothea,' Rose-Renee snotted-off. The man's face suffused with colour and he left. Marcella laughed and laughed.

When the performance ended, Cherie came to get them. 'Mitch is really pissed off.'

'Sock it to me,' Marcella said, and they both rocked with laughter.

Mitch came out and started the car up. 'They've forbidden me to bring you back. What the hell am I going to do with you now?'

'Think of something,' said Cherie, 'because I'm not living with you or your brats any longer than I have to.'

The next day Marcella and Rose-Renee flew back to Philadelphia. It was an ugly farewell with the teddy bears and the roller skates all left thrown down on the apartment floor. Mitch, pressed beyond endurance, asked Cherie to take his daughters to the airport, and she refused.

149

Once at the airport, he argued with the ticket clerk, saying he should be able to change their tickets without paying a fee. Then he paid the fee, and left them in the departure lounge.

Stewardesses on every flight checked their name tags as if they were runaway luggage. These young women spoke in dulcet, high-pitched voices, asking how was the girls' Christmas. Marcella said it was lovely. Rose-Renee said it was putrid. Everyone laughed. Imagine, a little girl using a word like putrid.

In Philadelphia a stewardess led them off the plane into the lounge. No one appeared to meet them. Others all around them had their small reunions and drifted downstairs to baggage claim. The stewardess's lovely smile faded. Rose-Renee shot Marcella a cryptic look. *Have they forgotten us? Are we alone, really alone?* The stewardess's jaw tightened as she went to the telephone at the ticket counter and started dialling.

Just then, careening down the long hall, laughing madly, their fringed coats flying, came Linda and Tim.

The stewardess hung up the phone and gave a stiff nod. She would have handed them over to Lurch and the Addams Family at that point.

'So how was Mitch?' asked Linda.

'Putrid,' Marcella said.

'Stinko,' said Rose-Renee.

'Where's Gloria?' asked Marcella.

'Where do you think, squirt?

'Practising?'

'Don't be a dumbshit. Gloria rehearses. You know that.'

150

Once in Gloria's Lincoln, Linda and Tim sat up front, passing a joint back and forth, Tim at the wheel navigating the curvy country roads and driving slowly while Linda played with the radio. Marcella and Rose-Renee in the back seat were spent, exhausted, beyond tears or whining. As darkness fell over the patchy snow, the narrowing roads, the rolling hillsides and stands of bare-limbed trees, Marcella tingled with a wholly new sensation. A sense of coming home. Of belonging. A feeling so new and powerful, Marcella felt woozy. Rose-Renee threw up.

'We should stop,' said Tim.

'And do what?' said Linda. 'It's dark, it's cold and there's nothing we can do about it now. Open the window back there, will you, or the smell will kill us all.'

Marcella opened the back window halfway and the night and the frigid wind blew in, and they huddled together, Rose-Renee's head on her shoulder.

'I really am putrid, Stinko,' she said with a little whimpering hiccough.

'Go to sleep,' Marcella whispered, stroking her hair. 'Go to sleep.'

'Sock it to me.'

★　★　★

They were both sick for days, a grisly, intense bout of flu, throwing up, shivering, and running high fevers. Tim and Linda moved them into separate bedrooms and looked after them. They put Marcella in Morton's room, and put Morton elsewhere so he wouldn't frighten her.

'Linda called Dorothea,' said Tim when he brought Marcella a tray with some soup and toast, and 7Up. 'She says you two can't come back to school till you've been all well for ten days. She can't risk Rodney getting sick. Come on, sit up.'

'I don't want to.'

'Eat some of this. It'll make you well. Here, drink some 7Up.' He gave her the glass, dipped the spoon in the soup, and held it to her lips. 'I guess Rodney had a bad time of it over Christmas. He needs more rest.'

'Do you think Rodney will die, Tim?'

'No. He just needs to be careful.'

'He has crone something and he might have to have an operation and take his guts out.'

'He'll be all right, squirt.'

'Don't call me that. I can stand it from Linda, but not from you.'

'All right, Marcella. Here, have some more soup.'

By New Year's Eve Marcella and Rose-Renee were well enough to wrap up in blankets and come downstairs to the library where Tim had built a snapping fire, and pulled five chairs up to it. There was a plate of sandwiches, bottles of Nehi orange soda, and champagne as well on the table in front of the fireplace. Marcella looked up at the Wyeth watercolours, and said they made her feel lonely. 'I never noticed before how they could make you feel.'

'Mute and alone,' said Tim.

'That one, the winter scene, was a present

152

from Andrew Wyeth for Linda's birth,' said Gloria.

'Really?' said Linda. 'I didn't know that.'

'He brought the painting over and gave it to Barry in honour of your birth. It makes a nice story, but I also think Barry had done something for him, some bit of investing information, perhaps. I can't remember.'

'It's beautiful,' said Linda.

'Yes, and one day when you actually grow up and have a real home, you can have it, if you like.'

'Let's have a toast,' said Tim quickly, not wishing the truce to be imperilled. There were five crystal flutes on the table, and he poured the girls some Nehi soda and popped the champagne. 'Here's to a new year, and a new decade. 1970.'

They all drank solemnly.

'Here's to Tim,' said Linda, 'who doesn't have to fear the draft any more. Thank God for the lottery and his birthday coming up Number 351.'

'Does that mean you'll stay with us?' asked Rose-Renee, her voice still weak.

'Till spring. Then we'll go back to the Berkshires. The draft can't get me now.'

'To Marcella and Rose-Renee,' said Linda, lifting her glass again. 'To their getting well.'

'We missed you both,' said Tim.

To everyone's surprise Gloria said, 'Yes. We did.'

Ten days later, braving swirling snow, Marcella and Rose-Renee raced over fields and past the creek. The old well-known path had been rendered foreign and magical; the pond, the

153

fences, the woods were all shades of pale under a pewter sky; the wind blew, stinging their faces. Skimming along, low over the whitened field, Marcella saw a brilliant red bird who disappeared, flitting into the bare, black branches of the woods. She wished suddenly, a wish so vivid it felt visceral, that she could have caught that bird and held him always fluttering against her heart. As they came in sight of the farmhouse, icicles draped from eaves as far down as the windows, like bedraggled ball gowns, all raggedy at the hem. A second-storey window flew open, Dorothea waved from afar and their names rang out across the cold air.

'Hello!' Rose-Renee called back.

'Hello!' Marcella waved her mittened hands, and together they ran, doubling their speed.

Dorothea flung open the mudroom door, and enveloped them each in a hug. Even Ethel seemed happy to see them as Dorothea drew them quickly into the living room. 'Girls, don't you think Rodney's looking well?' she asked, though he was thinner, bundled up in sweaters despite the fireplace warming the room. He had dark rings under his blue eyes. 'I know the Christmas tree is gone, but we have been saving our presents for you. School can wait. School tomorrow. Today we'll celebrate. Right, Rodney?'

'Right.' Rodney got off the couch and gave them each a tentative hug, as though he had to measure out the energy for each.

'We didn't bring any presents for you,' said Marcella with a stab of regret.

'Of course you did! You're here, aren't you? We

154

can put ribbons on you. Here.' Dorothea reached into a box and pulled out some bows, and placed one on each girl. She told them to stay right there while she got the Polaroid.

As they all stood huddled over the Polaroid camera, watching the picture magically emerge, Marcella smiled to think how easily Dorothea created happiness all around her. Then she wondered if it was that easy, or if, like Mitch and Gloria, Dorothea had to rehearse. She rehearsed daily.

Dorothea gave them each two boxes of exactly the same size. She told them first to open the small one, where they found silver charm bracelets with a silver dolphin. 'That's for your swimming. Now, open the big boxes. At the same time. Go on.' She grinned.

The big boxes, once unwrapped, revealed shiny ice skates.

'We don't know how to ice skate,' Marcella said.

'You didn't know how to swim last summer, did you? You learned. You'll learn to skate too. We'll all go skating.'

'What about Rodney?' asked Marcella. 'Did you get skates too?'

'Rodney has weak ankles,' said Dorothea.

'I won't skate, but I'll come and watch and laugh while you two fall down.'

And he did. Bundled to the teeth, he sometimes accompanied them to the pond where Dorothea Jones was as graceful and fluid and lovely on ice as she was in the water. Patiently all that month she led the girls across the ice, wobbling, clinging to her hand. Marcella and Rose-Renee skated and fell, and skated and fell, and got up and skated again. They stayed out long enough for Rodney's cheeks to get pink, and for his hands to get cold, and then Dorothea took her skates off, threw her arm around his shoulder, and they walked back to the house while the girls made patterns on the thick grey ice, and Marcella kept wishing there was a word for the sound their skates made so she could put it away, safely, with her other secret words, and keep it for ever.

8

A Song for St Cecilia

One morning in early February, Marcella and Rose-Renee were shocked to find that Gloria awaited them in the kitchen when they dashed down for a bowl of cereal on their way to school. Gloria already had a cup of coffee in one hand and a cigarette in the other. It was unlike her to smoke in the morning. 'I got a rather strange phone call last night. A Mrs Campbell. She wanted to talk to me about a recital. Do you know anything about this?'

'Nuh-uh,' they agreed in unison, shovelling Cheerios into their mouths as they exchanged the cryptic *We're in for it now . . .*

'She asked me to reconsider.' Gloria let that hang in the air along with a billow of smoke. 'She wondered if her students, including the two of you, could have their spring recital here.' Gloria's voice spiralled upwards. 'Here in this house. In the music room.'

'Jeez, I don't know where she got such a stupid idea.'

'She says she got it from you, Marcella. Playing in my music room! I told Mrs Campbell that was a mad idea, that she was mad to think that I would ever permit such a thing, and that you were mad to offer it.'

The phone rang and Marcella dashed to the

157

kitchen wall to pick it up. 'Hmmm,' Marcella said into the phone. 'Yes. Sure. OK. Thank you.' Marcella hung up. 'That was just Dorothea reminding us to bring our homework, and come right now, Rose-Renee!' She flung her bowl in the sink. Rose-Renee left hers on the table as they dashed towards the mudroom door and their coats. Marcella called out, 'Mrs Campbell was lying about me, Gloria. I'd never offer your music room.'

'Dorothea Jones put her up to it. I'm sure she did.'

Marcella thrust her arms in her coat, tempted to let the absent Dorothea take the blame, but some fledgling instinct, whether of honesty or self-preservation, made her reconsider. 'No, Gloria, I gotta admit. It was me. I did it. Not Dorothea. I'm sorry. Really. I never thought — '

'Never thought what?'

'We gotta go!'

'Never thought what?'

'I wasn't thinking. I was stupid. I should've known. Really. Sorry, OK, Gloria? Please. We have to go right now!'

They dashed out the door, running headlong through the snowy landscape until finally Rose-Renee faltered, and said her tummy hurt from all this running. 'What's going on?'

They were well beyond the Denham house. Marcella, panting, slowed to a walk. 'That was Ethel on the phone. She said no school today, Dorothea took Rot to the hospital in Philly.'

Rose-Renee walked a little further in silence, her feet crunching in the snow. 'I wish I hadn't told him he was going to die. I'm really sorry. You think he'll remember I said that, Marcella?'

'Nah. Come on, we'll go get our ice skates.'

They knocked at the kitchen door and Ethel greeted them. 'I told you no school today.'

'We'll be good if you let us in,' Marcella vowed.

'And if you don't let us in, we'll be really bad,' said Rose-Renee.

'Children with no one to look after them can't never be too good,' she retorted, but she let them in anyway.

'What's wrong with Rotney this time?' asked Marcella, sitting at the table. Rose-Renee sat across from her, swinging her legs.

'Poor tyke, I can never keep it all straight what they're doing to him. You, on the other hand, the two of you, with the health of an ox. It isn't fair.' Ethel filled the sink with hot water. 'You have to leave by noon. That's when I'm leaving. I won't be driving you home neither. Not driving any more'n I have to on that icy road. Not in my old car. And there won't be no one here tomorrow, girls,' she added, in her nasal tang. 'You can't be coming here when Mrs Jones is gone. You'll just have to stay at Gloria's. Weather's so rotten, everyone should stay home. Of course, Gloria Denham don't ever leave home, so she don't count.'

'She's rehearsing.'

Ethel made a sound of contempt. 'What's she rehearsing for? Do you know?'

It seemed disloyal to say they hadn't any damned idea. Marcella shrugged.

159

'Once people like my family and people like the Bowkers and the Digges, we farmed here, lived and died here, and did just fine here for two hundred years. Then, all of a sudden, why, all this land here, round here, it's suddenly grand and pitcher-esque, and full of artists tramping round the countryside looking for what to paint next, artists buying up barns — barns, mind you! — and turning them into studios. Living in them, some of 'em did just that. Lived in barns and thought they was artists for doing it. And after the Pyles and the Wyeths and their bunch of paintbrush-waving maniacs, comes the Denhams, chasing foxes, upsetting the dairy herds, damming up the creeks for trout ponds. At first,' Ethel conceded, 'I do have to say, for all the upset, the Denhams brought work. They hired local. That was before Gloria come.'

'What do you mean, before Gloria?' asked Marcella. 'Tell us about before Gloria.'

Ethel set about scrubbing a particularly dirty saucepan, then stopped, and wiped her brow.

'Would you like me to dry dishes?' offered Marcella in her best saccharine tones.

'Sure. Pick up that towel and see you get the water spots off. Just stack 'em up on the counter. I'll put everything away. I like my kitchen just so. Well, Rose-Renee, what's wrong with you? Get a towel and help your sister.'

Marcella silently seconded the command, and Rose-Renee complied.

'My mother was a fine cook,' said Ethel. 'No Frenchy chef, but a fine cook, and she worked for Mrs Denham for thirty years.'

'For Gloria?'

'Gloria? Perish the thought. Mrs Charlotte Denham, Barry's mother. Charlotte Denham's parents went down on the *Titanic* and she made sure everyone knew it too. Barry's father was a Philadelphia banker, and they had a big house in the city, and then they come out here and built this place for a country house. Glory days, really. They'd have twenty, thirty-five people for sit-down dinners! All kinds of dances and sporting stuff, and balls and recitals, and teas. They hired lots of help.' Ethel turned up the flame under the kettle. 'My mother used to say, the gowns those girls wore were fit for princesses or butterflies. The balls and suppers and private recitals, oh, and the horses! They had stables in them days, and Barry and Ellie — that was his sister, Ellie — and their friends all rode just like fiends, but your great-grandmother, Charlotte Denham, she was mad for music. Barry and Ellie, they didn't give two hoots about anything 'cept horses, and fast cars, but Charlotte Denham . . . ' Ethel leaned against the sink and folded her tea towel into a neat foursquare. 'There was music in that house before Gloria Denham, I can tell you that. Old Mrs D used to have private recitals, concerts, really, in the drawing room with candlelight suppers afterwards. Old Mrs D, Charlotte, she sowed the very seeds brung her to grief. She made Barry and Ellie come to all her musical evenings whether they wanted to or not. Barry and Ellie, they was all for riding and tearing around the countryside on horseback, Ellie especially was a daredevil, and Barry, he liked fast cars and rich women.' She smiled, reached in her apron pocket, and took out a cigarette. 'He was all set to marry a Wanamaker girl. A real Philadelphia belle. His mother, she was just as pleased as could be. A Wanamaker.'

'Wanna-make-her!' scoffed Rose-Renee. 'What kind of name is that?'

Marcella hushed her with her glance. 'How come he didn't marry her? How come he married Gloria?' Marcella finished drying her last pan and, like Ethel, folded the tea towel neatly and sat down. Rose-Renee did the same.

'My mother was the cook in them days, and one night Mrs D said she wanted something special for the supper, that she had invited a special musician from Curtis to give a concert in the house. She'd heard this girl was just miraculous, that her playing could make the angels weep and the devils sing.'

'Gloria,' said Marcella.

'Gloria.' Ethel's water boiled and she put the tea in the pot, and filled it. She got them each a cup and saucer, two cookies for each girl, and brought the sugar bowl and creamer within their reach. 'I guess if you can behave like ladies now and then, you can get treated like ladies.' She found an ashtray and sat across from them. 'It musta happened that very night. Young Barry was struck, yes, just as surely as if there'd been a thunderbolt come down from the sky, through the roof and hit him. He fell in love with Gloria, just like that.'

'What happened to the Wanamaker girl?'

162

Ethel shrugged and puffed on her cigarette. 'Who knows? For a year Barry Denham chased after Gloria. Imagine! Rich Barry Denham, slavering after a fiddle player! A girl who just couldn't make up her mind . . . Dear me. Oh, should she marry him or not? Marry him and give up her music? She turned him down. Twice. Can you imagine? Turning down someone rich as a Denham so you can go on playing a fiddle!'

'I can imagine,' Rose-Renee said stoutly.

'Well, that shows you're Gloria's girl, don't it?' Ethel seemed to take offence, and Marcella hastened to smooth things over so she'd go on with her story. Ethel poured their tea. 'Charlotte Denham was broke up. I mean, musicians are fine and all that, but she didn't want her son to marry one, not when he coulda married a Wanamaker girl.'

Marcella added *Wanamaker Girl* to her list of fine phrases, to go with *Miss Manetti*.

'Charlotte Denham, she was pretty undone, though she was too much a lady to say so. She doted on Ellie and Barry, loved the ground they walked on, even though they was both disappointments to her, Ellie for her wild ways, and Barry because he married Gloria. Old Mrs D tried to talk him out of it, but Barry Denham was smitten beyond all words. He got engaged, and they was to get married in June, but old Mr D died in May, and they had to put everything off. They got married in December.'

'Were you there?'

'At the wedding? Of course not.' She smashed out her cigarette. 'But I served at the reception. I

163

was just a girl, maybe fourteen. Ma got me hired on as staff for that day. I wore a uniform and cap, and I had instructions on how to do everything just so, or I'd have paid for it! I can tell you that.'

'What was it like?'

'Well, it was like something out of a Fred Astaire movie. Here was the rest of the world crawling through years of Depression, and this wedding was like a fairy tale. The Denhams had money in them days! Oh, they footed the whole bill, and they did it up right. Gloria didn't have no say, even if it was her wedding. Her people were all Philly music teachers. Who was taking music lessons in 1938, '39? Gloria's people didn't have a pot to pee in, so to speak. After they got engaged, Gloria's people come out here for lunch, the mother and father and sister, Marga or Margaret. My cousin was waiting the table that day and she come back to the kitchen and said Gloria's father told the Denhams he and his wife and Marga wanted to play for the reception, and they wanted to be *paid*. Just like they was waiters or something! Oh, Lord! The bride's own family getting paid. It was probably Gloria's idea. She pinches pennies till you can hear Lincoln scream.' Ethel sipped her tea.

'Did they,' asked Marcella, sugaring her tea, 'play the reception and get paid?'

'Old Mrs D had heart failure in private, but she was a real gracious lady, and she talked them out of it. They settled on that Gloria's people would play at the church. No pay.'

'Where'd they get married?'

164

'Episcopal church, of course. It was Mrs D's church. Gloria didn't have no church. Gloria wanted a judge, but Mrs D wouldn't hear of it.'

'Was Gloria a beautiful bride?'

'Oh, she was! Slender and pale in that beautiful white dress. They got the dress at Wanamaker's.' Ethel chuckled. 'She had a bouquet of purple and white orchids and a tiara of orchids holding her veil in place, and the bridesmaids wore little tiaras of purple and white orchids. Her sister, Marga, was a bridesmaid and Barry's sister, Ellie. It was just about the most gorgeous thing I ever seen, that wedding and the reception. They all danced till dawn, and then the bride and groom went to the Bahamas or some island down there in the Caribbean. Right the next spring, that's when that Italian come out here with his lady friend and they started building Gloria's music room. Took 'em a year, a whole year.'

'Signor Massimo,' said Marcella. 'She told us all about him. She said he was difficult.'

'That ain't the half of it! Oh no, he had his own floozy with him. Miss Manetti. Don't suppose we'll be forgetting her! Still, Signor Massimo was always pinching girls' bottoms and talking nasty to them. You just knew what he was saying, even if it was in Italian. The girls just loved it, but my ma said it was plain nasty.'

'He sounds awful,' Marcella consoled her, 'but he must have been good at building music rooms. I mean, he was good at that, wasn't he?'

'Oh yes. The music played in that room just about made the whole house lift up. Everyone said, well, the Brandywine Valley had its artists, Mr Pyle, Mr Wyeth and their people, they made the place famous, but after Signor Massimo built that music room for Gloria, them painters, they was only part of the show in the Brandywine. Now the world's most famous musicians were lining up to come here. Oh, the doings! Them and their women, and some of 'em not wives, either, and their instruments that had to be babied, to be carried on silken cushions! I was working there too by then. I was seventeen.' Ethel looked pleased with herself. 'There was high, fine times for a while. Concerts with foreigners. There'd be limousines all the way down the driveway and chauffeurs in the kitchen, flirting with the housemaids.'

'Like Signor Massimo?' asked Rose-Renee.

'No. The chauffeurs wasn't foreign, only the musicians. More tea?'

The girls both nodded, and Ethel filled all three cups, and put on some more hot water. 'But finally, it all come crashing down on the Denhams. Barry's father knew how to make money, but alls Barry knew was how to spend it. Barry'd spent all their money on the music room. The doors alone cost thousands! They lost their Philadelphia townhouse and old Mrs D, she didn't have no place else to live 'cept with Barry and Gloria. She and Gloria, they could not abide one another. They was like oil and water, flame and ice. I doubt Barry even noticed. He never was too smart, if you ask me; good-looking and rich, though.'

'I thought old Mrs D loved music. She should

have loved Gloria too,' Marcella said.

'Mrs D could have loved Gloria. She was a good woman, fair, you know. But Gloria thought she was better than everyone. Gloria thought she was a blazing genius and they should all fall at her feet. Barry Denham did, but Charlotte Denham wasn't about to lie down at no one's feet, howsomever beautiful they could play. Charlotte Denham's parents went down on the *Titanic*, don't you forget. And her husband owned a bank! Anyway, couldn't no one warm up Gloria.'

'What about Barry?' said Rose-Renee. 'Didn't he warm her up?'

Ethel gave them an astringent look. 'I s'pose he did, but you know he never . . . well, let's just say this.' Ethel lit up again. 'Those Wanamaker sorts of girls, they was their own breed, their own sort of lovely, debutante girls. That was the only kind of girl Barry Denham knew. And living around girls like that, his own sister Ellie included, though she was a daredevil, they taught Barry Denham nothing — I mean it, absolutely nothing — for living with Gloria. It was like — ' Ethel smoked thoughtfully ' — without the violin, Gloria was only a half-person, a beautiful half-person, but only half, and then, once she picked up the violin, she was like a hundred different people, whoever she was playing, that's who she was. I never seen the like of it. No one has. Probably no one will. You ever know anyone like her?'

'I'm only nine,' said Rose-Renee. 'I might meet someone like her one day.'

'Well, missy, you get to be ninety-nine, and

167

then you come back and tell me. Besides, as I say, your grandfather, Barry, he was handsome and all that, but he wasn't no wizard for brains, and when it comes down to it, he wasn't much for backbone either.'

'Well, what happened?' said Marcella. 'Come down to what?'

'Sometime after the war, 1950, '51, maybe — Linda was just a tyke, and Valerie just a little girl — Ellie died. Barry's sister. She was a ball of fire, that girl, and she ran with a wild crowd and she died in a car crash on Capri. Just like the song. 'The Isle Of Capri'. You know that song?'

The girls shook their heads.

Ethel hummed for a bit. 'Old Mrs D, she never did recover from that. Just kind of shut herself up and withered away. She died, a year or so later. Charlotte Denham was scarce cold in the ground when Gloria fired all the staff. She knew they was all loyal to the old lady, and didn't none of them like her — and it was true, none of us did. She hired the new people, not asking locally, you know? Called up services in Wilmington and Philly. And she didn't hire near enough people to run a house that size but, as I say, she was a tightwad. She niggled every penny. She couldn't keep anyone, always nicking people for a cigarette break, and marking the levels on the brandy bottles, but she was still having lots of company in them days, and you can't just stick some famous guy with a guitar to wash out his own socks, can you?'

'I guess not.'

'So people quit right and left, and there wasn't

168

no . . . what's the word I want? Nothing flowed smooth, though I don't think Gloria much cared. Anyway, after a time, Barry quit coming back from Florida, and soon, there wasn't no more parties, no nothing, just Gloria and her practising.'

'Rehearsing,' said Marcella.

'She only keeps on Susan Digges because Susan don't care if she works for peanuts. She's lucky to have the job.'

'Grumpy Susan.'

'What's she got to be grumpy about? I ask you. Ain't no one there. Ever.'

'We're there.'

'You don't count.' Ethel poured herself some more tea.

'She does crossword puzzles in the kitchen,' Rose-Renee said.

Ethel snorted, finished her cigarette and waved away the smoke. 'You don't see me doing no crossword puzzles.'

'I wish there'd be another big party at Gloria's,' Marcella offered up wistfully. She stood and waltzed around the room, one arm out, as though holding up the hem of a gown. 'I wish there'd be all kinds of people and they'd fill up the bedrooms, and wear all the fine clothes just hanging there in the closets. I wish they'd have a great big performance in the music room and I'd wear that beaded dress, and we'd all come and dance, Signor Massimo, and Miss Manetti, and the Wanamaker girl . . . '

'Don't go holding your breath on that one. Gloria have a party?' Ethel gave a resounding harrumph. 'No one's seen the inside of that house, much less the music room in . . . well, since your parents, Valerie and Mitch, when they got married. They come back from eloping, just bubbly with love, but Gloria and Barry had heart attacks. On the spot. They couldn't believe Valerie could do something that stupid. But her and Mitch McNeill, they were in terrible love, give 'em that. Not that it lasted. Not that it ever does. Valerie just begged her daddy to have a big party for her wedding. She knew better than to ask Gloria.'

'Did Valerie get her party?'

'Not what she wanted, not what she imagined, not any great ball, but Gloria and Barry did invite some of the better-known people here roundabout, the artists and the like, for cake and champagne. Maybe fifty people. I served for it, and I can tell you this, I don't think Mitch McNeill had any idea what Valerie come from till he stood in that house. Nor his parents either. His parents, they keep a shop in upstate New York somewhere, and you just know they never seen anything like where the Denhams lived. Them, and Mitch, they just sort of stood around with their tongues out.' Ethel sighed. 'Gloria and Barry were none too fond of Mitch, not ever. They thought he was too good-looking.'

'Mitch is very good-looking,' said Marcella.

'That and a nickel,' Ethel replied cryptically, dropping a sugar cube into her tea.

'Why did Barry move to Florida?' asked Marcella.

'Well, the Denhams always had a Palm Beach

place, and for a long time Barry and Gloria would spend winters there, even after they had Valerie, even after Linda was born. When the girls was real little, they'd take them too, along with a nanny. Then they sent them to school in Philly, and Gloria and Barry went down by themselves. Then, oh a few years after Valerie married Mitch, Barry went alone. Then he went, and one year, he just didn't come back. They had to sell off big chunks of the Denham property so they could live apart. Why do you think there's all them housing developments so close by? All that land had to get sold.'

Rose-Renee asked, 'Why didn't they just get divorced? Our parents got divorced.'

'People didn't get divorced in them days. Least not people like the Denhams. No, if you ask me, Gloria didn't want no divorce, but she didn't want Barry neither. She wanted that music room. Like she'd married the music room, and she spent all her time there, like it was her husband, her children, everything. She loved it more than she ever loved anything or anyone else. Valerie and Linda had nannies when they was just little tykes. Then she sent them to boarding school in Philly. Gloria used to drive up and get them on Fridays. She'd fired the driver too, by then. She'd drive to Philly, and see her sister who lives up there, and get her daughters and drive home. You call that being a mother?'

She seemed to want an answer and so Marcella said no. She did not.

'I can tell you this,' Ethel stated emphatically.

'Old Mrs Denham is spinning in her grave as I speak, if she could see what Linda dragged in with her, that red-headed hippie boy.'

'Tim,' said Rose-Renee.

'Gloria calls him the Jolly Red Giant,' said Marcella.

'Call him what you like, girls. How can Gloria abide him in her house?'

'He's not so bad,' Marcella said. 'Gloria pretty much ignores him. She pretty much ignores all of us.'

'We like Tim.'

Ethel lowered her voice. 'He does drugs. Yes, that's what I've heard in town. They say when he comes into the hardware store, or Stoddard's to buy groceries, you can smell the marijuana all over him! I'm not one to meddle,' she added confidentially, 'but I gotta tell you, the narcs might come to Gloria's house any day and arrest him.'

'What's narcs?'

'Narcotics police. There's a law against smoking marijuana and people who break the law, well, they get arrested. You want to beware of him, girls. He's dangerous.'

'We will,' they promised, barely able to contain their laughter.

Ethel seemed to know she wasn't being taken seriously. 'The narcs could take you too, just for being a part of it. Gloria too. For allowing it.'

'What would they do with us?' asked Rose-Renee. 'We're just kids.'

'Separate orphanages,' said Ethel.

Marcella was about to laugh, but seeing her

172

sister's face, she instantly became serious. 'She's just telling you a story, Putrid. She's making it up. They'll never separate us, don't you worry.'

'I did make up that part,' Ethel confessed. 'But they might take Gloria.' The thought seemed to give Ethel pleasure.

On their way home that morning, they saw Tim wandering towards them. He said he'd heard in town that Andrew Wyeth walked these hills and valleys carrying an easel and paints and sketching materials, and Tim said he was going out walking, hoping to see Mr Wyeth, even from a distance, just to watch him paint. Rose-Renee asked why.

'Why? He's a great American artist. Are you a ninny that you can live here, in the Brandywine Valley, and not know that?'

That shut her up. She did not want Tim to think she was a ninny.

'I know who he is,' declared Marcella. 'He did all the pictures in those books.'

'No,' said Tim. 'That was his father. Andrew Wyeth did those pictures that hang over the fireplace. Don't you remember?'

'Sure,' Marcella lied. She too did not want to be thought a ninny.

For two weeks after that, Marcella and Rose-Renee walked out on winter mornings with Tim, scouting Mr Andrew Wyeth. They never did see him.

'But if we do,' Marcella said one brisk, snowy morning, 'I'm going to go right up to him, and say, hey, put me in your picture!' She struck a pose, head cocked, hip thrust out.

'He wouldn't do that,' said Tim.

'And why not? Aren't I pretty enough?'

'Andrew Wyeth doesn't care about pretty. His people, when he paints them, they're all mute and alone. You're not mute and alone, Marcella.'

'Ha ha! You're not either,' she whooped as she scooped up a wad of wet snow, flung it at Tim and ran in the other direction, pursued by Tim and Rose-Renee.

A few days later they were all in the kitchen, late afternoon, Tim and Linda peeling potatoes, Marcella and Rose-Renee playing checkers. The phone rang, and Linda moved to answer it, but Marcella, suddenly fearing it might be Mrs Campbell again, dashed in front of her, nearly knocking her over, and took the call. The voice on the other end was strange, thick and furred. They wanted to speak with Tim Farleigh. Gripped by fear — perhaps this was the narcs — Marcella was about to say he's not here, but thought better of it. The phone had a long, coiled cord and she took it over to him. 'It's for you.'

'Me?' He took the phone slowly. He said hello. He rose from his chair, but made no other move. His responses were monosyllabic and he cleared his throat often.

Linda, Marcella and Rose-Renee watched him intently. Linda dusted her hands on her jeans.

'Yes,' he said at last. 'Yes. Tomorrow. Goodbye.' He dropped the phone and sat down heavily in the chair. 'My brother. My twin brother, Jimmy.'

'The marine?'

'Yes.' Tim stared over their heads. 'He's been killed in action.'

'Oh, Tim. Oh, Tim,' Linda cried. They all three wrapped him in an embrace while the sobs racketed through his big body, though no sounds came out.

Finally he mopped his face with his hands. 'I'm going home.'

'I'm coming with you,' said Linda.

'No, Linda. Thanks, but no. I'm leaving tomorrow.'

'But I want to come with you.'

'No, you don't. You don't understand. It's nothing you can help, or be part of. It's me and them. My people.' He ran his hands through his long hair. 'I got to get to Memphis, Little Rock if I can. It'll take me days to hitch-hike.'

'I'll give you all the money we won off you at cards, and you can have my Christmas money from Mitch. I didn't spend it yet,' Marcella said. 'Twenty dollars.'

'Mine too, Tim!' said Rose-Renee. 'It's yours and you don't have to pay it back.'

'What kind of man would take money from a child and not pay it back?' He rose. 'I just need some time by myself.' He put on his hat and jacket and left them, walked into the snowy dusk just as Gloria came in for her ice cubes.

'Tim's leaving,' Linda began.

'Good riddance.'

'Mother! Tim's brother's been killed in Vietnam! How can you say that?'

'I'm sorry about his brother,' said Gloria in her inflectionless way; even if she meant it, or felt

175

emotion, the verbal expression of it was beyond her. 'He was a soldier, I take it.'

'He was a marine. They were twins.'

'I suppose he wants money.'

'Not from you!' cried Rose-Renee, jumping up from the table.

Marcella silenced her sister with a fleeting glance, opened the ice-cube tray and gave Gloria an ingratiating grin along with the ice. 'He needs to take the train to Little Rock, Gloria.'

'I will give him ten dollars,' she said. 'Worth it to be rid of him.'

'Oh, Gloria . . . ' Linda seemed to simmer. 'You really have no . . . '

'I only meant that at least we needn't fear the narcotics squad coming to arrest him. To arrest both of you for that matter.'

'You know about the narcs, Gloria?' Rose-Renee asked, breathless.

'Don't be ridiculous.'

That night as Marcella and Rose-Renee lay close together, Rose-Renee demanded a story, a really good story, not just Morton. Thanks to Ethel, Marcella had added to her collection stories of the Wanamaker girl. Wanna-maker cry? Wanna-maker laugh? Wanna-maker lost and looking for her true love? These were funny stories, but tonight Rose-Renee said she did not want to laugh; she was too sad to laugh, sad for Tim's brother and sad they were losing Tim. So Marcella invented fantasies of the narcs descending, carting Tim and Linda away in shackles while they cried out, *Help us, Gloria!*, as everything was swept away while Gloria madly played in the music room. *Help us, Gloria!* Gloria hearing nothing except the sounds she herself created, the fierce, the crazy music, *fantasia ala narc*, that came spilling from her violin, flowing through and under the St Cecilia doors.

* * *

The following morning Linda came into the kitchen, made the coffee without a word. Marcella stirred oatmeal on the stove, and Rose-Renee buttered toast, the knife scraping audibly on the crisp surface.

'When is Tim coming down?' asked Marcella.

'Shut up,' said Linda. Her face was red, puffy and she had been crying.

Tim came downstairs, scowling. He was clean-shaven, and his hair cut short, cut badly, sawed off in the back, and unevenly above his ears. His jaw was pale, though pocked, red and rough where he had nicked himself, and his neck was white. With the awkward haircut and the bad shave, the fringed jacket on his tall, lanky frame, he looked comic, pathetic, a figure of fun, though no one laughed.

'I don't know how you could do such a thing,' said Linda while the percolator bubbled behind her. 'Cut off all your hair and make yourself look so weird.'

'I look weird to you, but not to them. I couldn't go back home looking like that. Not with Jimmy dying for his country. I couldn't go back home looking like I had nothing but

177

contempt for everything he died for.'

'But you surely don't believe in the war, do you?'

'The war's not Santa Claus, that you can believe in or not. No matter what I think, I'm not going back home and telling my people that Nixon is a pig, and my brother was a misguided grunt, and died for nothing.' His voice caught in his throat. 'I won't do that. I'm going home to honour Jimmy. Call me a hypocrite. I don't care.'

'What's a hippo-crit?' asked Rose-Renee.

'Shut up,' said Linda. 'It's someone who says one thing, and does another. Like Tim.'

'Think what you want, Linda.' He thanked Marcella for the oatmeal, but took only a few bites.

'So, you're really leaving me?' Linda asked. 'Just taking me off like a dirty shirt. Like I was nothing to you but just a chance to get laid.'

Marcella returned to the kitchen counter where she was making sandwiches for his trip. She shot Rose-Renee a glance: *Stay out of this.*

'You know that's not true, and it's not right to say it in front of the girls. You have all been good to me — your mother too.'

'My mother! God! My mother thinks you're an Arkie asshole, Tim!'

'She's been good to me.'

'And I haven't.'

'Linda, I keep telling you, I been trying to explain, telling you all night, babycakes — '

'Stop that! You're leaving me now and you're not coming back to the commune in the spring. That's what you said.'

178

'Yes.' He put the spoon down as though it weighed ten pounds. 'I need to do something with my life. I know that now. The commune, and living here, it's been . . . time serving, water treading. I can't go home and face my people after being thrown out of MIT.'

'You weren't thrown out. You quit. We quit. Tune in, turn on and drop out. Remember?'

'Yes, and now I feel like a fool. A real fool. The first person in my whole family to go to college, a scholarship to MIT! And I just dropped out because it seemed like a good idea? Like fun? All that summer after high school, I kept thinking, my stupid brother, Jimmy, he's going to be cannon fodder, and I'm going to be an engineer. How can I go back home for my brother's funeral, and tell everyone I'm strumming guitars and growing vegetables with a lot of high-minded souls in the Berkshires? Do I tell them I'm living here in a rich girl's house, doing nothing, no work, no — '

'You work! Look at everything you've done around here!'

'I wanted to be an engineer, not a handyman, Linda. I've been wasting my life.'

'You mean the time you've spent with me?'

'It's nothing to do with you. I've got to think things through. I've got to make amends.'

'Amends. Like what?'

'Who knows? Maybe I'll join the army.'

'What!' Linda shrieked. 'Just because of your brother? You'd — '

'It crossed my mind.'

'Oh, Tim . . . '

'But right now I'm going to go home and help them bury my brother, and then I've got to find a life I can be proud of, that has some dignity. My old man, for all his bitching and hating and hardscrabble life, his drinking on Saturday night and praying on Sunday, his quarrels with the weather, and the growers' association, and all the time he and my mom went at it, tooth and nail, he has some dignity. Give him that.'

'Do you think I don't have dignity? Is that what you're telling me?'

'You have talent. That's better than dignity. Talent tells you what you have to do. I mean, you can do it or not, Linda, I'm not judging you, but it's there.'

'I can't believe you! You sound like Gloria!'

'But I'm not Gloria.' He finished the oatmeal quickly, rose and put the bowl in the sink. 'You have a gift, and you make your own decisions about how to use it. I'm speaking only for myself now. I don't want to die without doing something in this world.'

'But you're not going to die, Tim, we're young!'

'So was Jimmy.'

'You're saying I'll never see you again?'

'Yes, Linda. That's what I'm saying.' He thanked Marcella for the sandwiches and apples.

Linda remained defiant. 'I thought we were in love,' she said at last. 'We have a thing.'

'A thing is not enough.'

'I thought you loved me.'

'What you and I are calling love, that'd dry up and die in an Arkansas autumn.'

180

'You're saying I'd never fit in with your life.'

'Yes. Just like I never fit in here with yours.'

'This isn't my life! I'm not like these people!'

'Marcella and Rose-Renee?'

'They don't count.'

'Well, they count by me.'

'I meant people like Mother.'

'So who are you like?'

'What?'

'What good is it if you only know what you aren't, Linda? You gotta know what you are. Who you are.'

Linda made a face, but he had taxed her imagination, or asked a question deeper than she was prepared to answer. She lashed out at him, 'And who are you?'

'An Arkie, my little chickadee, and now I'm going home to Arkansas to mourn my twin brother. He's dead and I have to live for the both of us.'

'Here, Tim,' said Marcella, handing him a heavy envelope, bulging with coins. 'Here's all the money we could scrounge for you, all the money we won off you, and our Christmas money.'

'I'll pay you back.'

'And here's a tenner from my mother,' said Linda, oozing arctic disdain. 'Wages for the handyman.'

He thanked them, put the money in his knapsack and shouldered it. It was all he had brought with him; it was all he took away.

In Gloria's Lincoln they drove him to the Wilmington train station. Linda, at the wheel, was angry. Tim uncharacteristically silent, the girls in the back seat tense. They drove through the increasingly grungy downtown and came at last to the station. Linda stopped the car at 2nd and French, by the steep stairs.

'Goodbye, Tim. I'm leaving you off. I'm not coming up.'

'Jeez, Linda,' Marcella said, 'how can you be so mean to Tim?'

'It's all right,' said Tim. 'She's not being mean. She's just being Linda.'

'I only brought you home to piss off my mother, and look! I succeeded.'

'Well, babycakes, if that's your only ambition — '

'Don't call me that!'

'Goodbye, Linda.' He held out his hand. 'Friends? Come on. You know you can't resist me. Let's be friends.'

'We're not leaving him off,' said Marcella. 'Come on, Rose-Renee, get out. We're waiting with Tim till the train comes.'

'There's no place to park,' said Linda. 'I swear I won't come back for you.'

'So leave us,' said Marcella, scrambling out, Rose-Renee right behind her.

A cold March wind blew grit in their faces. Tim held on to his slouch hat, which did not fit him as well with such short hair. The three started towards the stairs. 'Look!' cried Marcella, pointing to a musician, a violinist, pouring out a sad, sweet melody, his case open before him, glittering with a few coins, his hands clad in fingerless mittens, a cap pulled low over his ears. 'It's him!'

'Who?' asked Tim.

'He was here when we came before. When we first got here. Only he had a girl with him then. She sang opera and he played. Hey, Mozart.' She went up to the busker. 'I 'member you. I remember your music. Only it was opera. What's that you're playing?'

He finished his piece with a mournful flourish. 'Ravel's *Pavanne For A Dead Princess*.' He removed the violin from his chin, and lowered his bow.

'Where's the girl? The girl who sang opera with you? She had such a beautiful voice.'

Behind his glasses, his eyes were whorls of sadness, and his pale face was darkened by a stubbled beard and he looked much older than the boy who had played last June. 'She left me,' he said. 'She left me and she broke my heart, and I'll never be the same.'

For the second time in twenty-four hours Marcella confronted unvarnished sadness. She stammered out, 'I'm sorry. You were beautiful together. Maybe she'll come back.'

'She won't.' He replaced the violin beneath his chin and, bringing his bow into position, took a deep breath. 'But thanks for remembering us like we were.'

He began to play again, a piece Marcella recognized as one that Gloria played, measured, melodic and indelibly sad. She ran after Tim and Rose-Renee, who had already started up the broad stairs. She tugged at Tim's sleeve. 'Gimme a quarter, will you, Tim? We gotta pay the musicians. Gloria says you have to pay them, no

183

matter where you find them.'

He dug in his pocket and gave her a quarter. She ran back and tossed it in his case. 'That's from St Cecilia. You know who she is?'

The violinist lowered his instrument. 'The patron saint of musicians. A thankless job.'

'Don't be sad,' said Marcella, knowing somehow her words were futile. 'Maybe St Cecilia will take care of you.'

He began to play again, and she ran up the stairs to the tracks, which were bustling with coat-clad commuters carrying briefcases and noisy loudspeakers.

Tim sat on a bench, his back to the wall, his knapsack resting on his knees, his big hands folded over it. Rose-Renee ran up and down the platform chasing pigeons, but Marcella sat beside him. He was strange and silent and Marcella wondered if he always would be. His brother was never coming back. All Tim would ever have of Jimmy, he had. As with the heartbroken musician, the look on Tim's face belittled anything she could possibly say, but she was congenitally incapable of silence. 'There was a soldier with us on the train when we first came here. He wore a uniform and his hair was stubbly all over his head, but he was real nice to Valerie and us. He was real helpful and nice. I bet Jimmy was like that too. I wish I'd met your brother.'

'I do too. He was a tough marine, but he had a good heart, Marcella. You would have liked him, and he would have liked you.'

She put her hand over his, and they both

184

stared ahead, afraid they might cry.

The train roared in; the loudspeaker called out, the platform of commuters came to collective life, people standing up, tucking newspapers beneath their arms, the great ebb and rise of everyday lives caught in a thousand transitions. Marcella and Rose-Renee clung to Tim's hug, and then he released them, stepped onto the train and vanished, leaving the two girls to wave frantically at windows framing the faces of people they would never meet or know as the train pulled away, and just as Linda, breathless, got to the top of the stairs.

Andantino

Marcella McNeill was nineteen years old, a sophomore psych major at UCLA, when she suffered one of those cataclysmic moments that altered the course of her life, and the lives of others, an incident that would finally appear in and inspire her to write her first book, A Song for St Cecilia, that brought her work to national attention. What happened to Marcella was not an earthquake, or a traumatic accident, or falling in love with the wrong man. Quite the contrary. She got in an elevator.

She was going to interview for a part-time job, receptionist for a therapy group, in a shiny, high office building not far from the UCLA campus. The elevator had three other people in it, and they all looked away from each other as strangers do. She stepped in, punched the button for the sixth floor. The elevator jolted upwards while the

185

elevator music played. Only, this was not the usual pap of elevator music, old standards badly homogenized, this was classical muzak and the piece that came on — she did not know the name of it — only that Gloria had played it in the music room, that Gloria had played it on the record player in the den, that Gloria had played it on the phonograph in her room, that this music had wrapped around Marcella's life at Gloria's like an audible scarf, that as she stood there in the elevator, that scarf was choking her, tightening its relentless grip. The past came upon her in such force and fury that suddenly Marcella began to weave on her feet, to strangle out tears, not mere little gasps, but great, aching sobs she could not contain; she coughed and choked and her knees buckled under her, and the blood drained from her head, and she passed out.

She was on the floor of the elevator when she came to with two strangers crowding over her, and someone holding open the elevator doors, and keeping others from entering while people helped her up gently, making hushed enquiries, and supporting her between them, escorting her out, and towards a chair in the little waiting area on the fourth floor. Someone else fetched a glass of water from a nearby office, and put it in her trembling hands. They all wanted to know if she needed a doctor. One of the women dug about in her purse and gave her a stale cookie. Another asked if she were pregnant. A man volunteered to drive her home. She drank the water. She nibbled the cookie. She thought to herself: the

186

kindness of strangers.

She was too shaken to go to the interview, and besides, she could never work in this building. And ride that elevator every day? Never. She collected herself, thanked everyone, and slowly, gripping the handrail, took the stairs down to the street.

Marcella had, in effect, been mugged by Mozart, ambushed by a piece of music, unexpectedly engulfing her. She had been flung down and roughed up for the small change of a few memories that were hers alone, and of no use to anyone else. But when she recovered, she recognized that her brain had neurologically short-circuited, that music could function as a weapon. If so, why not as a tool?

In the years that followed, she spent countless hours in the music library seeking out more of the same, the music that had so brutally waylaid her, not because she was eager to be mugged again, or that she wanted to suffer, but to understand the process. To begin with she did not know the names, or the composers, though she started with Igor, Pablo, Andrés and Darius, seeking out the compositions that had wafted over her life for all those months that she and Rose-Renee, cast off by everyone who was supposed to care for them, had lived in the Brandywine Valley. Each time her searches led her to something she recognized, she succumbed again to these crippling bouts of clarity, the past roiling before her as the music played.

To come upon these pieces was to revisit that past in all its pain and splendour, and if it could

187

happen to her, Marcella reasoned, that process could probably happen to anyone, and not necessarily via Gloria's rarefied repertoire. It could happen probably just as easily with 'You Are My Sunshine', or Dave Brubeck, or Marvin Gaye, or The Temptations; it could happen with 'What A Friend We Have In Jesus', 'Folsom Prison Blues', or silly pop songs; it could happen with the score from Oklahoma!. Music could quell or unleash passions, could go to places long shuttered, could touch where words were useless. Music could pinpoint meaning, elicit emotion instantly.

When she embarked on her graduate studies in counselling, she asked to create, in effect, a new field for herself: music as a therapeutic tool. Her advisor was dubious, regretful, but she pressed him, put together not merely an account of what had happened to her in the elevator, but a theoretical premise around that incident, suggesting that music could short cut through the brain.

When she got her doctorate in psychology from UCLA in 1986, she had already pioneered methods in the uses of music to treat, to reach patients — Alzheimer patients, stroke victims, troubled children — who, for whatever reasons, were locked in their singular prisons. Her methods did not always meet with success, but when they did, results were dramatic. As a therapist, she was able to elicit response — emotion, smiles, laughter, talk, tears, voice! — from patients, some of whom had been silent for years.

Whether she succeeded or not, she often met

with administrative resistance. In dealing with any number of colleagues, directors, administrators, Marcella tried to be agreeable, undemanding, pleasant, but the eager-to-please child she had once been, that person was gone for ever. As an adult Marcella McNeill did not suffer fools gladly. Nor had she much tolerance for the staid, the safe, the timid. Her willingness to venture into new paths stemmed from a restless, energetic intellect, but often came across as arrogance. She was not good in committees. In this, she knew herself to be like Gloria Denham: a born soloist.

Marcella did not want to go through life solo. Not personally. Not professionally. She always wanted to belong to someone beloved, and to something larger, to be part of an undertaking with others. Though she became engaged to a hard-working ER doctor, and joined a prestigious practice, that sense of belonging eluded her. But then, she told herself, perhaps she would not even recognize belonging. The pleasures of being, belonging, connectedness, these satisfactions always wavered from afar as the mirage of oasis water shimmers before the thirsting desert wanderer.

9

Savages

When they returned from the train station, Linda went directly into the sunroom and swept the Monet seascape jigsaw puzzle from the table to the floor, a harbinger of things to come.

Without Tim's steadying presence, Linda's temper ignited over any small thing, and between her and Gloria, the very air at the Denham house was charged, thick and heavy with reflexive recrimination. Marcella and Rose-Renee recognized that these ongoing contests, just like those between Mitch and Valerie, would escalate, intensify, but never quite to the point that one or the other could declare victory. Everyone nearby must walk on eggshells that cracked and splintered and the gooey innards of family betrayals spilled everywhere.

One morning, Marcella and Rose-Renee heard an unfamiliar car pull up in the paved yard outside the kitchen. Gloria came in just as Marcella opened the back door to find a VW van disgorging a motley crew, dressed in outrageous clothes. They'd come to collect Linda, and return to the commune in the Berkshires. They were not invited in. Gloria sent Rose-Renee to get Linda.

She came downstairs carrying two suitcases and wearing a moth-eaten mink coat she had found in one of the closets and a cloche hat. She

190

reeked of naphtha as she hugged each of her nieces.

'One day you will regret all this time you've wasted,' said Gloria without preamble. 'Valerie already regrets it. She's past thirty, and now she wants to study seriously. One day you will grow up too, Linda, and you'll see what you've lost and you'll be sorry. You have a gift and you have failed to honour it.'

Linda laughed. 'What's honour got to do with it? You want me to spend my life, night and day, practising in tiny, draughty little practice rooms? Like a monk's cell. Playing the music of dead people! Always rehearsing, towards what? Some great day when I'll dazzle the world? One day when it will all be worth it? When will it ever be worth it for you? When did you last perform in public?'

'When that day comes, I shall be prepared. And it will come.'

'Groovy, Mother. Just groovy. But for me, I don't want to wait for some great day. I want to live every day. I don't accept your values. The whole world's out there, Mother! The whole fucking world! Music isn't everything! Goodbye, Mother.'

Gloria reached out as though she would hug her younger daughter, but the attempt was awkward, like watching a bird with a broken wing learn to fly.

Linda finally made up the distance for her, and though she seemed to want to say something more, she just called out 'See ya, squirts!', opened the door, and climbed in the van with her compatriots.

'It's my birthday next week, Gloria,' Marcella said, as they closed the door. She thought she should take advantage of the moment. She had Gloria's attention, after all. 'March tenth. I'm going to be twelve. I hope there'll be something special for me.'

'Are you really! Twelve years! Imagine!' She poured some coffee and took it into the breakfast room.

Marcella expected to have better luck with Dorothea than with Gloria when she announced that her birthday was imminent.

After lunch, when ordinarily the girls would have been sent home when Rodney needed to rest and conserve his strength, Dorothea asked Marcella to stay. She sent Rose-Renee back upstairs with Rodney, with the proviso of no rough games, and no train-wrecking. When they had gone, she turned to Marcella seriously. 'Did your mother ever have The Talk with you?'

'The Talk?'

'Perhaps Gloria did.' She frowned. 'Probably not. What I mean is The Talk explaining what it is to be a woman.'

'Oh, that's a long way off.'

'You shouldn't be growing up without parents, without your mother. Truly.'

'We have you and Rodney.'

'You need your own mother. Gloria just isn't equal to the job, and I don't think she wants it, though I'm sure she loves you,' she hastened to add. 'But no one can be your mother, except your mother. Your very own. You need someone to love you as much as I love Rodney.'

'Don't you love us too?' Marcella asked with a small, vivid tightening of the heart.

'Of course. Go get your jacket. We'll walk out to the pond.'

On her return from this walk, The Talk, and in possession of many M&Ms and much adult knowledge, Marcella felt very superior to both Rodney and Rose-Renee, and once in the schoolroom when they questioned her, she refused to tell them what had been discussed. 'You're too young,' she said, flopping down on the beanbag chair. 'You're just babies.'

'I'm older than both of you,' said Rodney, working on an origami tree at his desk. Since his return from the hospital, he had put on a little weight, enough that his face filled out slightly, and his nose did not look so large, nor his hands so bony, but he still moved with the studied economy of an old man, not squandering energy, nor wasting effort. 'I'll be thirteen in August. A teenager.'

'So what?' retorted Marcella. 'I know what it means to be a woman.'

Rot brought his pale blue eyes up, and regarded her with a grin exactly like Dorothea's. 'You'll never be a woman. You're a Pig Sister and you'll grow up to be fat and ugly, and no one will marry you.'

'Ha ha ha.' Rose-Renee flung her papers into her desk, jumped up, ran to Marcella and flung herself at her.

'Except for me,' Rodney added. 'I'll marry you, Stinko.'

'Well, I won't marry you, Rot.' Marcella

pushed Rose-Renee off of her. 'Unless we can go on living here, swimming in the summer, skating in the winter and having dessert every day and wrecking the train over and over.'

'Sure,' said Rodney. 'Why not?'

★ ★ ★

Her twelfth was the best birthday Marcella McNeill ever had. Dorothea gave her a small golden locket with an M on it, and paperback copies of *Huck Finn, Tom Sawyer, Treasure Island* and Willa Cather's *My Antonia*. Rodney made her an origami zoo, and Rose-Renee gave her a certificate for five free arm-farts. They had cake and she got to wear a paper crown. Dorothea gave them the rest of the cake to take home to share with Gloria. They did take it home; they did not share it. The Pig Sisters ate it all themselves.

Following the best birthday ever, however, Marcella endured the worst toothache ever. She woke with what she described as a 'yowling' in her teeth, so much so that once she got to Flag School she could only moan with pain.

'How long since you've been to the dentist?' asked Dorothea. 'Either of you.'

They could not remember. Kansas City, maybe. Minneapolis?

Dorothea sighed, and resigned herself to spending the day at the dentist's office. She telephoned and got an emergency appointment with her dentist. She left Ethel with Rodney and Rose-Renee, and took the suffering Marcella into Chadds

194

Ford. When the ordeal was over, and she drove Marcella back to Gloria's, she drove round the back. No confrontations in the foyer today. 'Is Grumpy Susan here today, Marcella?'

Marcella, holding her jaw where the novocaine was wearing off, just shook her head.

She helped Marcella into the house and from the kitchen telephoned her own home, and told Ethel to send Rose-Renee home. She turned back to Marcella, and regarded her assessingly. She said, 'You girls need your own parents. Your own mother. Someone to look after you.'

'No we don't, Dorothea. We look after ourselves.'

'You are children. Someone should be looking after you.'

'We're fine. We like it here. We like going to Flag School and you and Rot.'

'No one can take the place of a parent.'

The pain in Marcella's jaw gave way to a pain in her heart. 'We're fine on our own,' she insisted. 'We're the Gingerbread Girls.'

'That may be,' replied Dorothea, uncharacteristically grave, 'but you heard the dentist. You need braces, Marcella, and eventually you'll need that tooth pulled. You can't go on wearing clothes you scrounge out of old closets, and you need to practise better hygiene and better manners. You need new clothes, new shoes, your shoes and socks are filthy, a disgrace.'

Marcella cringed; disgrace was not a word Dorothea ever used.

'You need . . . well, there are so many things you need, Marcella, I can't begin to — '

195

'We need you!' she cried, jumping up, and flinging her arms around Dorothea. 'Don't you love us?'

Dorothea smiled, and touched Marcella's hair. 'I do. Of course I do. We'll talk about all this later. I'll see you at school tomorrow morning, Marcella. Just have something soft for dinner.'

'Is a hot dog soft?'

'No. Soup or a boiled egg or something. Can you find me some paper and a pen? I want to leave a note for Gloria. You must give it to her when she . . . when she . . . comes down or comes out or whatever she does. She is an enigma to me.'

'What's that, enigma?'

'A puzzle. A question mark. A walking question mark.'

When Rose-Renee came home, Marcella read the note aloud. ''Dear Mrs Denham, I am writing on behalf of your granddaughters, who will soon be young ladies, and who are much in need of their mother's love and guidance. You must write to your daughter, Mrs Denham, and tell her to come home and care for her children. No responsibility is more sacred. No performance will equal these satisfactions. These girls are rehearsing for adulthood. They need their mother more than Valerie needs to sing.''

'Not true,' said Rose-Renee. 'Valerie needs to sing, and we don't need her.'

'But we have to give Gloria the note. I can't lie to Dorothea like I did to Mrs Campbell.'

'Mrs Campbell is a sorry old frog and I hate her. I'd like to bonk her, and maybe I will,' Rose-Renee said.

196

When Marcella gave Gloria the letter, she immediately said she could see that the envelope had been opened. 'Did you read it?'

'Yes,' said Marcella.

'Don't you know that's rude?'

'I do now,' she said, faking contrition.

Gloria read the note. 'So you know what it says.'

'Yes, but I'm sure Dorothea doesn't mean it.'

'I'm sure she does, though she has absolutely no right to. What does she know of seeking perfection, of working towards performance? What has she done with her life except to marry a lawyer who was driving drunk when he ploughed his car into a tree, and to have a child who is sickly and afflicted.'

Dorothea, the Olympian, would never have let these observations pass uncontested, and Marcella wanted to object on her behalf, but she didn't. Instead she asked, 'Driving drunk?'

'Didn't she tell you that?'

'She told me Mr Lee Jones was with the angels.'

'Stupid,' said Gloria, reaching for the phone. 'What is her telephone number?'

Marcella and Rose-Renee stared at each other, their horror accelerating throughout this short conversation. Gloria spoke briefly and then listened for quite a long time. Finally she said, 'What they need is none of your concern. They will not be coming to your house again ever . . . Your house is not a school. It's a farce. They will not be coming back.' She said goodbye, and hung up the phone.

Behind her glasses, Rose-Renee's eyes grew

wide; her mouth opened, she threw her head back, and let out a mournful wail. Marcella began to blubber and protest.

Gloria told them both to shut up, her voice cracking with emotion, like a long-unused instrument played in the cold. Her grey curls were trembling with suppressed rage. She took her glass of Scotch without ice cubes and left them where they stood.

Marcella's instinct was to chase after her grandmother, to fling herself at her feet and implore her mercy and forgiveness. Rose-Renee's instinct was to go into the rehearsal room, and kick over the harp and bust up the piano and tear the scarf and knock over the lamp. They did neither. They both knew that Gloria would not be swayed by orgiastic emotion of any sort, neither pleading nor temper.

'Let's just stay out of her way for a few days.' This was Marcella's only inept suggestion. 'We'll hide in the house. Sneak around. We'll be like bandits, like Robin Hood in Sherwood Forest.'

The next morning, to their jaw-drop surprise, when they came into the kitchen there were two spoons and two bowls and a box of cereal and a bottle of milk on the table. The toilet flushed and Gloria came out of the bathroom. 'Eat up,' she said. 'We're going shopping.'

She drove to Wanamaker's in Philadelphia. Rose-Renee stared at the sign, and crowed with laughter. 'Wanna-maker laugh? Wanna-maker cry? The girl who — '

Hush! Marcella warned her in their secret, silent lingo.

Amid the unfamiliar dazzle of the department store, they followed Gloria up the escalator to the children's department where she bought them a lot of underwear and ordered them to try on dresses in their sizes. The saleslady remarked that Marcella really needed the teen department. And perhaps even a trainer bra. Gloria maintained they would stay with undershirts for both girls. The saleslady said no more on the subject. The girls tried on clothes, but Gloria did the choosing, selecting finally frothy dresses for each. The saleslady obliquely asked if perhaps the girls might need some more casual clothes as well; clearly the frothy dresses were only for very fine occasions. She brought out a few pairs of bell-bottoms, shorts and T-shirts, two light jackets.

'Fine. Yes. Fine. Ring it up,' said Gloria.

When the salesgirl handed her the bill, Gloria was incredulous, astonished; she seemed to tremble like a leafless birch in a strong wind. She insisted the whole be rung up again, that the department manager be called, that there must surely be some error. But in the end, she paid it. She wrote a cheque, though her lips were set in a grim line, and she did not speak all the way back to Chadds Ford. She put the Lincoln in the garage. 'I have a dreadful headache, and I am going to bed,' she announced. 'Take this stuff inside. Take a bath. Both of you. You smell terrible.'

They climbed in the huge claw-foot tub together. Marcella washed Rose-Renee's hair while she whined and complained. Marcella told her to hush. 'There, you're done. Go stick your head under the tap.' Marcella was glad Rose-Renee did not have her glasses on. What it means to be a woman might be coming on her sooner than she'd thought; little hairs were sprouting where they didn't used to be. Marcella lay back in the tub and put a washcloth over her face.

Looking bedraggled and forlorn, Rose-Renee spluttered out from under the faucet. 'What'll happen, Stinko? You think Gloria will call Valerie? Tell her she can't be doing opera? She has to come look after us?'

'No one calls Sweden. It's too far away.'

'We could call Sweden and tell her we don't need her.'

'Didn't you hear me? It's too far away.'

'Will she send us back to Mitch?'

'No. Well, I hope not. That would be awful.'

'What, then?'

'I dunno.'

Rose-Renee let the water from the tap drip its sad solo. 'Maybe the narcs will come, and take us all away.'

'Tim's not here any more smoking pot.'

'I wish he was,' said Rose-Renee. 'If he was, we could go to Arkansas with him.'

'Oh, don't be silly. Tim doesn't want us.'

'What about Florida, where Barry lives with Jean? He's our grandfather, isn't he? We could be like Heidi.'

'Just shut up about Heidi. I hate Heidi. I hate Anne of Green Gables and Rebecca of Sunnybrook Farm and Little Eva, and I hate Shirley Temple, and the drink named after her. I hate everyone.'

'How far is Florida?'

'I don't know. How do I know? Anyway, you think they want us? You think anyone wants us, Putrid? Anyone at all?'

'Dorothea wants us. Dorothea loves us.' When Marcella did not reply, she added, 'Doesn't she?'

'Sure. She loves us. But . . . '

'But what, Stinko? Come on, talk to me.'

'I dunno. Even if she loves us, it's like we belong to someone else.'

'I don't belong to nobody. I'm not a piece of furniture.'

'You belong to me,' said Marcella, splashing her.

'Sock it to me!' she replied, splashing back.

The next morning Gloria again greeted them in the kitchen. As usual, she was dressed in pressed silk pants, and a cotton sweater. She wore a long silk scarf at a rakish angle and a pair of pearl earrings. She smoked. She drank coffee. She seemed especially irritable. Marcella wordlessly conveyed to her sister that they should just eat their Cheerios and shut up, see what happened. Reluctantly Rose-Renee followed her lead. The spoons pinging against their bowls sounded like ominous percussion in the silence.

'Go put on your new dresses, girls,' Gloria said when they had finished. 'And come out to the car.'

She drove in the direction of the developments with names like Fox Run, and Lafayette Estates, the houses differentiated only by those yards with straggling daffodils, and those without. The roads were smooth and wide. Gloria got lost looking for the public school. They drove around for forty minutes before they found Lafayette Elementary, a one-storey building shaped like an L and built with narrow, brown bricks. The flagpole out front had a few shaggy clumps of heather and some plastic flowers at its base. Gloria parked in the space reserved for the vice principal.

They walked into the main building. Gloria quickly put her hands over her ears as a bell shattered the air, more like a buzzer than a bell. All along the hall, both sides, the doors were flung open at once and the hall monitors streamed out, holding aloft paddles with room numbers, followed by hordes of noisy children in straight but shuffling lines who followed them out of the building. Marcella, who had had more experience in schools, recognized the superior look on the hall monitors' faces, their officious voices carrying out the authorities' edicts.

'We are looking for the principal,' said Gloria to a teacher who was locking her classroom door.

The teacher pointed them round the corner. PRINCIPAL in blocked black letters on frosted safety glass. A woman of ample proportions sat at an imposing desk behind a low rail guarding a door that said PRINCIPAL on it. She wore horn-rimmed glasses, bright lipstick and her hair was teased and varnished to a high gloss. 'Can I help you?'

Gloria said, 'I've come to see the principal.'

'Do you have an appointment?'

Gloria pointed the girls to a line of chairs against the wall and they took their seats beside two other kids, one holding an ice pack over his eye, and one picking his nose and scraping the snot under the chair. Marcella stared at him. He picked another dried chunk from his nose and ate it, grinning.

'My name is Gloria Denham. I do not have an appointment, but I need to see the principal about these students.'

'Sorry, he's busy.'

'I want to register two new students in the school. I must speak with the principal.'

'Look — ' she spoke as though Gloria were deaf or senile ' — you don't have an appointment, and the principal can't see you. He doesn't need to see you. If you just want to enrol a new pupil, I can help you.'

'Two,' said Gloria. 'Two new pupils.'

'Ages?'

'Twelve and nine or ten.'

'Twelve? Well, she'll probably go to a different school, the junior high.'

Underneath their frilly skirts, Marcella and Rose-Renee clutched hands, their backs pressed against the hard chairs. They had always gone to the same school. They had never been apart.

'Still, you can use the same forms for both schools.' The lady handed Gloria a mass of forms to fill out, a set for each child, and a ballpoint pen. Then she added that they'd need the girls' immunization records and birth certificates. She had to explain, more than once, what an immunization record was and why it was important, but Gloria got no M&Ms for comprehension.

'I don't have that information!'

'Who does?'

'Their parents, I guess. Someone must.'

'Where are their parents?'

'Stockholm.' Gloria looked around the office, fastening on the kid with the ice pack and the snot eater.

'Really! Stockholm? Like Sweden? Are these girls foreigners?'

'Don't be absurd.'

'Are you their guardian?'

'I am their grandmother.'

'It's not the same thing as a guardian, is it? And anyway, we can't admit them without immunization papers and birth certificates, no matter who you are.'

'But they weren't born here. They were born far away.'

'Sorry, ma'am. That's the rules. Oh, and here's the pages with the bus routes if you live more than two miles from the school. The children have to be at the bus stop — see the little Xs here on the map, that shows you where the bus stops — ten minutes before the time that's listed here. The bus waits for no one. Here's one map route for our school and one for the junior high.'

The bell blazed again like a chainsaw. Gloria's hands again flew up over her ears until it stopped. The school nurse opened the door to her office, and called out for the kid with the ice pack. The principal, a stern man, balding and with a heavy overbite, opened his door and glared. He crooked his finger, and the snot eater followed him back into the office.

'Until we have that information, and all those

forms,' said the officiating lady, 'there's nothing the principal can do.'

'Couldn't they start today? Just to — '

'These forms, their birth certificates and immunization papers. I've told you.' The woman was losing patience. 'It's that or nothing.'

'I shall get this information,' said Gloria, 'and we will be back.'

They drove home and she took to her bed.

In the kitchen, Marcella got out the peanut butter, the bread and a butter knife. She opened the jar, and thrust the knife in, licked it, thrust it in the jar again, and passed it to her sister.

Rose-Renee licked the knife. 'I'll never go to that school, Stinko. And sit next to a snot eater? Never. I'll run away. I'll join the circus. I hate that school.' She passed the knife back, and her face fell. 'What'll we do?'

'I don't know,' Marcella confessed, spent and troubled. She wanted to cry, but she told herself Dorothea would not cry. Dorothea would find a way to be happy.

'And you, they said you couldn't even go to school with me! Not be in the same school? Not be together? I wanted to tell that old lady you'll never split us up, you old hag. I should've told her. I could've called her names like Mitch calls people, old bitch, I could have called her old bitch and got us kicked out of school even before we got in.'

Marcella started to laugh. 'Yes! Hey, we'll do like Linda does and say bullshit and goddamnit, and get in lots of trouble, and I'll tell them we've smoked marijuana and we like it and we're going to do it again and again.'

'Yeah! We'll make that school lady so mad she'd fall on her head and break her hair.'

Marcella waved the peanut-butter knife overhead. 'We'll be savages, and terrorize those stupid kids and their stupid teachers!'

'Yeah! We'll break that snot eater's nose!'

'We'll tell them all, we're outta here! We're getting on the streetcar named Dorothea and we're going someplace where we'll all be happy and you can't come!' She made Rose-Renee a sandwich and passed it triumphantly, but the mirthful moment had passed, and the wonderful joke that had amused them for months was no longer funny. They ate their sandwiches in silence.

Rose-Renee, swinging her legs under the table, rested her head on her hand. 'OK, then, the circus. How can we find the circus?'

'Look! I don't know! What makes you think I have all the answers?'

'You always do.'

Mollified, Marcella said, 'Let's wait.'

'For what?'

'Let's just see what happens.'

'She'll send us to that school and we'll have to march in lines, and fight our way out of the principal's office. They won't even let us be together.' Rose-Renee's voice escalated to a wail.

'Maybe she'll just forget.'

'I'm not going to any damn public school!' Rose-Renee choked up and burst into a volley of tears and saliva flavoured with peanut butter.

'Please don't cry.'

'I love Dorothea and Rot and I want to go back there, and Gloria will never let us.'

'Don't cry, Putrid. Don't cry. Please.' But when Rose-Renee took her glasses off, put her head in her arms and cried, Marcella let her. When Rose-Renee wanted to cry or laugh or rage, no one could dam her emotions, and anyone who tried did so at their peril. When finally her sobs had subsided to hiccups, Marcella said, 'Maybe we ought to pray, you know, like Dorothea and Rot pray.'

'You pray. I don't remember it.'

'It always starts out with food.'

'Well, we have peanut butter.'

So Marcella prayed and Rose-Renee wept and neither made the least bit of difference because finally Gloria Denham did what was best for Gloria Denham. Which was nothing.

The following morning rain poured down, but there was no Gloria to greet them in the kitchen, and they scurried out of sight, careful to keep out of the arc of her known paths, trying to be like Morton, present but not obtrusive, like the mice in the ballroom: the scratching in the wainscoting might make you alert and uneasy, but it was not enough to tear down the walls. They knew Gloria's routines, where she was likely to be and when. They made a game of it once the rain let up. Hiding in the boxwood, watching her from a distance as she smoked on the terrace, pretending to be spies. Gloria was most certainly the enemy.

On the third morning Gloria still had not showed up in the kitchen to march them to the public school. 'Let's try it,' said Marcella. 'Let's see if she fights us, or finds us.'

Rose-Renee grabbed their coats and thrust Marcella's at her.

'We have to leave a note.'

'What for? Let's just go.'

'No, it has to be official, clear-like, so she can't pretend like she didn't know.' She scribbled a note and left it on the kitchen table. *We are going to school. Back this afternoon.*

They tore across the muddy fields smelling of spring, though winter held its grip on twig and tree, the denuded blackberry bramble, the sumac pulsing red and ready to burst, across the brown and yellow grasses. They ran to the white fieldstone farmhouse with its peal of grey smoke rising from the chimney and drifting against the cloud-scudding sky.

The Flag School reunion was joyous and noisy, and Marcella was once again filled with that vivid but elusive sense of homecoming happiness. Even Ethel, when they burst in the kitchen door, cheered to see them. Marcella and Rose-Renee tore to the foot of the stairs and called out for Rot and Dorothea. Rodney's sallow face lit as he beheld them on the stairs and he whooped with joy. Dorothea came rushing down, enfolding them both in her embrace, communicating her sheer physical strength, her capacity for joy, the fragrant lemon scent she wore.

'What made Gloria change her mind? Did she see that the public school was just, well . . . '

'She didn't change her mind,' Marcella said truthfully. 'She didn't do anything. She didn't

208

know how to fill out the forms, or where were our birth certificates or how to catch the school bus, or if she'd have to drive us every day. Can you imagine Gloria doing any of that?'

'So she let you come back?'

'She didn't say no,' replied Marcella. Tonight would be the crucial test, but there was no reason to say so now. No reason to impugn this festive moment that was just like Christmas, only better.

That evening, rather than avoiding Gloria, Marcella insisted they wait in the kitchen. Rose-Renee was against it, but Marcella said she'd wait alone if she had to. 'I have to know. I have to know what to do.'

'What to do when?' asked Rose-Renee, dutifully taking her place at the table.

'What to do if.'

'If what?'

'That's what I don't know, stupid.'

'I'm not stupid.'

Gloria came in for the ice for her evening cocktail. 'I suppose you've returned to that awful woman's house,' she said, opening the freezer.

Marcella popped up, reached into the freezer and took out the ice tray. She carried it to the sink and worked her little magic trick and with a gratifying crack the ice cubes came free. She held the tray out to her grandmother. 'Is that enough ice? You want more?' she added, smiling; she would have done a little pirouette if she thought it would help. She was shameless.

'Yes,' said Gloria, taking three ice cubes. 'That will work just fine.' She thanked them and left the room following the music twirling on the record player as it wafted down the hall.

'What if what?' asked Rose-Renee when she was gone.

'I don't know. I still don't know.'

What if what remained a mystery, but in the following weeks, though Gloria did not forbid their return to Dorothea's, something subtle had altered. Gloria's indifference to them, that was over. Nothing was too minor to elicit her attention, and when she chose to bring her baleful eye upon them, she was pernickety, demanding, and angry. Their sloppily tied shoes, or dirty clothes, their raggedy, uncut hair tied back with rubber bands, fingernails rimmed with dirt, slouching. Noise of any kind. Leaving a mess in the kitchen. Towels on the bathroom floor. Things Gloria had never noticed, much less commented upon. The sisters suffered under the weight of her scrutiny, which had a fierce undercurrent of condemnation, and Marcella began to better understand Linda's defiance and Valerie's cringing. Marcella reined in Rose-Renee's instincts to sass back; better to sulk in silence than to run the risk of . . . what? Marcella wasn't quite certain of the price they might pay, but she knew for a fact she did not wish to pay it.

Valerie's colourful picture postcards ceased, supplanted by frantic letters admonishing the girls to BE GOOD!!! *You must do exactly as Gloria asks!! I will be home soon!!* Marcella and Rose-Renee tossed these letters aside. They didn't want her home. They didn't want her at all. Their life with Mitch and Valerie was like

Rose-Renee's vision before the glasses, a blur, and as long as they knew nothing else beyond that blur, they had neither questioned nor complained. Now they knew better.

All that spring Marcella and Rose-Renee lived like code readers, looking for signs and symbols, like savages pawing through the chicken entrails trying to figure out whether to appease or evade. Living with Gloria was like living with mercury in the house: once upset, once tilted either direction, the result would be unpleasant and far-reaching.

10

Rite of Spring

May burst open in a great lilac blaze. Shiny blue dragonflies lilted over the surface of the pond, and a veil of dust and earthy debris scummed the grey-green waters. The surrounding woods exhaled after winter; tiny tight fists, brown knobs on twigs, opened, expanded in fusillades of green. Birds cleared their throats and learned to chirp, and the frogs came back. In the evenings, the occasional firefly blinked to life. The world seemed to shake off its shaggy winter clothes and want to dance.

Sunshine raised Dorothea's spirits, the first daffodil brought her to rapturous exclamations, and in the riot of lilac that was May, she flourished, forgiving winter everything, making new plans for the school. Her students, despite the lengthy winter hiatuses for Rodney's illness and hospital visits, had made progress. Rose-Renee could read and write, though she still used her finger to follow the words and her math skills were not what they ought to be. Nor were Marcella's, but Dorothea forgave Marcella's lapses since her music was so exceptional. Moreover, Marcella had a novel underway, scribbling something about pirates and Indians. Whatever Marcella's lack of originality, Dorothea confined her critical remarks to spelling and punctuation and gave emphatic encouragement and a handful of M&Ms, and a round of applause as Marcella stood on the Winner's Box. Dorothea herself felt like standing on the Winner's Box; she had justified herself as a teacher. Best of all, with the spring Rodney strengthened, visibly, audibly. Though he could not keep up with the Pig Sisters playing outdoor games, the pain subsided, and he was able to eat and gain weight, as though the girls' high spirits and Dorothea's Olympian bravado were contagious.

Mrs Campbell, on beginning their lessons again, was less than delighted with Marcella and Rose-Renee. With the dream dashed that the recital might take place at Gloria's music room, Mrs Campbell's patience waned. With Rose-Renee in particular, she could be sharp. Rose-Renee plunked down a discordant chord and Mrs Campbell's swift reprimand wafted upstairs where Marcella, Dorothea and Rodney were in the schoolroom.

'See what I mean? She's mean to Rose-Renee,' Marcella said, thinking that Dorothea would exert herself against injustice. She started for the stairs, but Dorothea stayed her with a simple hand on the shoulder.

'You won't always be able to stand between Rose-Renee and the rest of the world. She has to learn to defend herself. She's always relied on you, and you never let her down, but she will be her own woman one day, and she will need to deal with the world in the way that everyone else does. Let her be. Go back to work on the book you are writing. By the way, how are you getting along with Gloria?' she asked offhandedly.

'Everything's fine.' There was no point in bothering Dorothea with Gloria's new hyper-critical attitude towards them. Marcella made Rose-Renee promise not to tell either, to say nothing of the wariness they daily practised, the evasions, and when those weren't possible, the restraint obliged of them.

At last Rose-Renee's lesson was over, and she stomped upstairs and flung herself into the beanbag chair. 'I hate 'Turkey In The Straw'. I wish that turkey would eat some straw and choke on it.' She crossed her arms and tucked her hands in her armpits. 'She's waiting for you, Stinko.'

Marcella went down for her lesson, but before they began Mrs Campbell reached into her huge purse and drew out a cream-coloured envelope with a lyre embossed on it. Marcella recognized the lyre from the St Cecilia doors.

'This is an invitation to our year-end recital. Give it to your grandmother, will you?'

'Sure. Don't we get one?'

'You are the performers. You don't need an invitation.'

'Did Dorothea get one?'

'She doesn't have a child in the recital.'

'She does so. She has us. We're her students. Same thing.'

Mrs Campbell reached down into her music case and pulled out another envelope. 'You may give Mrs Jones this one.'

After Mrs Campbell left, Marcella took the

invitations upstairs. 'Here's yours,' she said to Dorothea, 'and this one's for Gloria. Let's just throw Gloria's away. She'll never know the difference and me and Rose-Renee will sneak out and go with you and Rodney.'

'There will be nothing underhanded. You will not sneak out.' Dorothea opened the envelope and drew out the thick, cream-coloured card. 'How lovely. Mrs Campbell has such good taste. Anyway, you know how your grandmother loves and values music. She will be delighted to come and hear you perform. She will be delighted to know you've rehearsed. You must tell her this very afternoon. Don't wait. You must put it to her in a way that . . . in a way that will let her see you're practising her values. That will change everything. I'm sure,' Dorothea added. 'I feel certain that this recital will be a wonderful success and clear up any little misunderstandings we've had in the past. She'll be so pleased.'

On their return from Flag School that afternoon, Marcella and Rose-Renee both slumped to the floor outside the doors of the music room and waited, knees drawn up while Gloria played. Music, both fierce and sweet, escaped from under the St Cecilia doors.

'Tim always said she played like a frigging angel,' said Rose-Renee. 'And she does.'

'Don't say frigging.'

When she came to a halt, they scurried to their feet and knocked on the door, and pushed it open. Gloria looked shocked to see them. 'Here, Gloria.' Marcella held out the envelope as she crossed the room. 'This is from our music teacher, Mrs Campbell.'

'The woman who called here wanting to use my house?'

'Oh, that was a mistake, my mistake and hers,' Marcella rattled quickly lest the conversation turn to blaming Dorothea, 'and it's all cleared up now, and it's going to be somewhere else. See? Read it. Some church in Greenville, Delaware. Wanna come?' Marcella hoped she would say absolutely not, and the ordeal be finished there on the spot.

'Have you been rehearsing?'

'Oh yes. All the time. Every day.'

'We have Untapped Talents,' said Rose-Renee.

Gloria folded the invitation and put it back in the envelope; in the brilliant acoustics of the music room, even those sounds were crisp and clear. 'Very well.'

'Very well what?'

'I will go, though it will be musically excruciating.'

In the ensuing two weeks Marcella bore messages back and forth between Gloria and Dorothea working out logistics for the night of the recital. Gloria finally consented that Dorothea should drive because Dorothea knew where the Episcopal church was, only as it turned out that was another church, and Dorothea got lost.

In the back seat, uncomfortable in their finery, their frilly Wanamaker dresses, white socks and new shoes, wearing hair ribbons that matched (Dorothea's gift), the girls were silent. Rodney wore a bow tie and a starched white shirt and starched pants. Their clothes chafed and nettled,

216

and they were doubly uncomfortable with the unstable cocktail of Gloria and Dorothea in the same confined space.

Gloria persisted in calling her Mrs Jones, and Dorothea gave little bursts of replies like sprays of carbonation that failed to moisten Gloria's dry tolerance. Driving through the spring twilight, Dorothea asked after Valerie, after Linda, eliciting monosyllabic responses. When she enquired after Gloria's own music, the replies were slightly more forthcoming, though hardly descriptive. As they drove around Greenville — a town of much money and many colonial markers, a bastion of complacency, political conservatism and social contentment — Dorothea rattled on about her late husband's family, the Rodneys, descendants of the famous signer of the Declaration. In the back seat the three children exchanged looks that said, *She must be desperate.*

The more they drove around Greenville, the more lost Dorothea got looking for the church, the more desperate she became. Her voice scaled upwards, and Gloria sat in glowering silence. To be late for a performance was a heinous crime in sports as in music.

Finally they found the correct Episcopal church, and the five of them entered like emissaries from a foreign country, ambassadors of some weird potentate. They drew stares from the other students and their families who congregated in small lively groups, the students laughing and chatting, sharing gossip and games and schools of which Rose-Renee, Marcella and Rodney were ignorant. Rodney, scrawny and round-shouldered, and dressed in his pale white shirt and bow tie (askew), hardly looked like a boy at all, more like an old man in miniature. Rose-Renee kept scratching a nasty-looking spider bite on her knee. Marcella's Wanamaker dress was not at all what anyone else was wearing, and it pinched her armpits. She felt suddenly painfully self-aware: she and Rose-Renee and Rodney were unendurably bizarre and probably stupid. She caught sight of one bright-eyed girl pointing at Rodney, whispering to her friend until the two of them burst into giggles. Marcella did not even bother to stifle her pangs of envy and shame. Was there not some way she could disembody herself from her sister and Rodney, and float over to these confident people, so vivacious and connected, share their secrets and their laughter? Among the snot eaters of Lafayette School she had not questioned her own superiority. But here?

Marcella turned her attention to the grown-ups. They too were looking askance at Gloria, regal in a black sheath, high heels and wearing the voluminous ecru-fringed piano scarf across her shoulders. She wore a long pearl necklace, and cream-coloured gloves that came to her elbow. Dorothea, like an athlete, walked on the balls of her feet, which made her ungainly in high heels. She seemed altogether too physical to be in this over-upholstered gathering, and her crisp white Oxford cloth shirt and slim skirt only somehow seemed to accentuate the muscles in her calves. The other women present, young and old, were variations on the Mrs Campbell theme, varnished hair sprayed into high, impossible formations. Stout or slim, they were expensively clad in Good Taste with gem-crusted brooches and handbags with brass fixtures. The men were suited and tied, bored, anxious, and trying not to look bored or anxious. Everyone knew one another, and had for ages. All these adults participated in a lively sense of anticipation, blunted by well-bred restraint.

On espying Gloria Denham, Mrs Campbell came down upon them like a fresh wind, snatching her elbow, and blowing the frigate *Gloria* away from her small tugboat entourage and sweeping her towards the open seas, introducing her to one and all as *The Gloria Denham*, effusing over her musical abilities, her reputation at Curtis as violinist *extraordinaire*, her music room, and the immortal musicians who had played there in the past, immortal musicians with whom the immortal Gloria had played immortal duets. Gloria did not seem to object overtly to these intimations of intimacy. In any event she was borne along on the tide of Mrs Campbell's enthusiasm. She was shown to the best seat in the house, a front pew, beside Mrs Campbell herself. Mrs Campbell beckoned Rose-Renee and Marcella to come forward with their grandmother. Dorothea gave them a little push. Dorothea and Rodney took a pew at the back. Mrs Campbell clapped her hands and the recital began. Mrs Campbell seemed not to notice that Gloria winced visibly at the tortured performances, and she did not applaud.

Sitting beside her Marcella too cringed as the

other children pounded out the old warhorses, *Für Elise* and 'The Spinning Song'. She wondered momentarily why she cringed; could she be becoming more like Gloria and less like Dorothea? The thought did not please her, but it might well be true. She positively ground her teeth when one girl played and sang 'Somewhere My Love', crooning wistfully. Marcella noticed, too, that the more a student screwed up, the louder and more emphatic the applause. At first she thought she'd mistaken or misheard, but she hadn't. The student who played well, competently, got a nice hand. But the student who forgot in the middle, and returned to the beginning, or who hit the same chord five times in a row and still got it wrong, or stopped, and turned to Mrs Campbell looking like a scared rabbit, then started again? For that student the audience went wild with applause. Why is that? she wondered. Why were their efforts all the more wonderful if they failed to execute? Marcella could not imagine anyone in her own family clapping under such circumstances. If you failed to perform, then what good was your effort? The reason for the failure didn't matter. Either you performed adequately, or you did not. She looked up to Gloria for some possible indication of her response, but Gloria had on her Sphinx face.

When it was their turn, Marcella and Rose-Renee did things dully right. Rose-Renee's 'Turkey In The Straw' and 'Three Blind Mice' went off without a hitch. Marcella performed Monsieur Armand's *Waltz* creditably, though not brilliantly, as well as a simplified Bach. At least she didn't screw up. She glanced at her grandmother, whose gloved fingers tapped each other unenthusiastically. From the back of the church came wild applause that could only have been Rodney and Dorothea.

At last the evening's entertainment was at an end. Marcella jumped up, ready to make a break for the door, but Mrs Campbell personally took Gloria's arm and escorted her into the church hall for coffee and cookies. Rodney, Marcella and Rose-Renee sat on metal folding chairs along the wall, ate their cookies in dispirited silence, and wished for the whole grisly thing to be over. Dorothea, equal to anything, was having a spirited conversation with a silver-haired gent. They were talking about Signers. Rodney sighed.

Gloria, under Mrs Campbell's enthusiastic tutelage, was escorted about the room, plied with coffee and cookies. She listened while Mrs Campbell extolled her genius and blatantly asked to come to see the music room, to hear Gloria play one day very soon. Gloria resisted the latter, or at least evaded a direct answer. Perhaps she was enjoying the attention since she did not free herself from Mrs Campbell's ministrations, not for a full hour.

On the drive home Dorothea bubbled along about what a wonderful recital it was, and how she looked forward to next year. Dorothea said again and again what a fine job both girls had done, and how proud she was of both of them, pausing only long enough that Gloria might offer up some indication of assent, though this was not forthcoming. Dorothea said how both girls

221

had got their talent from their grandmother, and how much Mrs Campbell clearly admired Gloria, and to this Gloria assented. At last the car reached the flowering cherry trees at the foot of the Denham driveway, drove up the long hill. Dorothea dutifully went round to the yard, the service entrance by the kitchen.

At last Gloria turned to Dorothea. 'You may, of course, do as you wish — you have proved that — but I shall never again sit through anything so dreadful.'

'I thought they did very well.'

'What do you know of music?'

'They worked hard, and they performed beautifully,' Dorothea maintained.

'Clearly, we have different standards.'

'Clearly,' Dorothea replied with Olympian poise.

'I may as well tell you, all of you, I have written to both Valerie and Mitch. I've told them I will no longer be responsible for their children. Mitch is impossible, of course, though he ought at least to be paying child support. But Valerie will come home and take her children. Were those not your very words, Mrs Jones? That Valerie was shirking her duties and should give up her opera career and come and take care of her children?'

'Yes, I suppose,' said Dorothea in a small, strangled voice. 'When?'

'June.'

'That's very soon. Two weeks.' Dorothea turned to the back seat, her gaze resting on her crestfallen son. 'What will she do when she returns?'

'I have no idea. She will not be living with me. Nor will the children.' Gloria got out of the car, and wished them all goodnight. The door of the old Mercedes thudded shut.

'Oh, Rot!' cried Marcella. 'What'll we do?'

Rodney, fighting tears, wiped his eyes and nose furiously.

'I hate her.' Rose-Renee's fists clenched in her lap.

'Oh, Rodney, sweets, don't. Don't cry.' Dorothea reached out towards him. 'Rose-Renee, you mustn't say that. She loves you.'

'Gloria?'

'I meant your mother. Your mother loves you.'

'No, she doesn't. We're just in the way.'

'Ugly and stupid,' said Marcella, who had been feeling ugly and stupid all night long.

'I won't hear such talk! You are none of those things. You are beautiful, talented girls, and we will not despair of this. Please, Rodney, don't cry. Don't get upset, dear. Don't. I have great plans for Flag School for next year. French. Science. A microscope. Doesn't that sound wonderful?'

'Not without Putrid and Stinko,' he said.

'Maybe it's a lie,' said Marcella. 'It was a big lie before, wasn't it? I mean, she said just for the summer and look . . . She doesn't want us any more than we want her.'

'Of course she wants you. You are her children. She's your mother.'

'Gloria said she was coming back a long time ago. Maybe she'll never come back, just stay in Sweden and sing.'

'We will wait for Valerie to come home and

then we'll see what her plans are.' Dorothea looked around as though some plan might be lurking in the Mercedes. 'We will not be defeated by despair. I'm sure this will all work out. Everything is going so well. Rodney's getting better and you girls are doing splendidly. It will all be fine.'

Marcella and Rose-Renee shrugged and got out of the car. When Dorothea Jones wanted to believe things would go well and happily, her stubborn optimism was unshakable.

★   ★   ★

For all Dorothea's brave words the night of the recital, the prospect of Valerie's imminent return had a curious effect on her. As an academic undertaking, Flag School faltered. Dorothea was restless and unfocused and her ambitions fizzled; she handed out fewer M&Ms for achievement because the students weren't called upon to achieve. There were no lessons after lunch any more, and very little before, certainly nothing difficult or demanding. The children drifted into their own various pursuits, some outdoors, some indoors. Rodney made model bi-planes to exacting World War I specifications. Rose-Renee and Marcella amused themselves on the trampoline which had been set on the lawn. Marcella played the piano whenever she felt like it. Rose-Renee played with the train. Amid the usual small schoolroom crises, like Rose-Renee losing her glasses for a time, that spring flowed out into the great bay of early summer. June. The days passed, each with a sharpened edge of discontent.

Ethel's son filled the swimming pool, and watching the water twinkle under cloudless skies seemed to give Dorothea new momentum. Like a sunflower she blossomed into the warmth, and once in the pool, she found scope for her enthusiasms. She smiled to watch Rodney play Doll Wars with Cubbie and Barbie in the pool. Both dolls began to smell.

Marcella's swimsuit no longer fit her and Rose-Renee inherited it, but Marcella had nothing else till Dorothea found one of hers and fixed the straps for Marcella. It was a red, white and blue one-piece; Dorothea said all the great swimmers wore one-piece suits, less to worry about and better fluidity, and that she had worn this in her Olympic days. Marcella was proud to wear it, even if it didn't quite fit. She now insisted on her own changing room, instead of sharing with Rose-Renee. Strange things were happening to her body. Hair. Her chest was no longer her own chest, but someone else's. Some woman's.

One afternoon, returning to Gloria's, they found on the kitchen table a letter from Mitch addressed to both of them. Marcella opened the envelope and two five-dollar bills floated out. Rose-Renee scooped them up and danced around while Marcella read the letter aloud.

''Dear Girls, How are my two best girls in the world? I'm in Michigan now, in Ann Arbor, and I'm working every day. Unfortunately won't be able to see you for a while, but your mom will be back soon, and I know she'll be happy to see you. I love you and miss you. Here is a little play money for each of you. I hope you're being good girls and no trouble to your grandmother. You ought to be grateful to her. I'm sure we all are. Be good and give Gloria my love.''

'Give Gloria my love?' asked Marcella.

'My love, Gloria.' Rose-Renee held out her arms. 'Dahlink.'

'Dahlink Gloria, I so love you.' Marcella took up the refrain. 'Will you be mine for ever?'

'Oh Mitch! Mitch!'

They drove themselves into gales of laughter improvising love scenes for Gloria and Mitch with Dahlink dialogue and expressive gestures, all of which came to a swift close when Gloria unexpectedly came in.

'What did Mitch have to say?' she asked.

Marcella, grinning, cracked open the ice tray for her. 'He said you've done a wonderful job looking after us, and we ought to be grateful.' She smiled her treacly best. 'And we are, Gloria. We're grateful to you.'

'I suppose he said there'll be no child support from him.'

'Here, Gloria, you want these five dollars?'

'Yes,' said Rose-Renee, 'here's mine.'

'You should save your money. You should learn to save now.'

'Oh yes,' said Marcella, dropping the ice cubes in her glass.

'You must teach me how to do this one day

226

soon, Marcella, to open the ice tray,' said Gloria in an even tone. 'After all, when Valerie comes back, I won't have your help, will I?'

'You heard from Valerie?'

'Yes. I hear from her often. She's coming back in June.'

'It's June now. She said June a long time ago.'

'I look for her any day now.'

But many days passed and still Valerie did not come. One evening, in the midst of a game of Gingerbread Girls, Marcella (who was 'it') crouched in the bushes, hiding from Rose-Renee. In the distance she saw Gloria on the terrace, sitting on a grey wicker chair, smoking a cigarette. Her thin knees were crossed and her beige silk pants and beige sweater seemed to muddle into the colour of the faded paint and dirty sandstone terrace, as though she were actually part of the house itself. A long plume of smoke hung heavy on the damp air. Gloria dropped her cigarette, the butt one among several, and stomped it out with her foot. She seemed poised, as though listening for some word, some voice she sought, some note she wanted to hear.

Rose-Renee cracked through the bush to tackle her sister, but Marcella put a finger to her lips. She pointed to Gloria.

'So what?' sulked Rose-Renee, squatting on her haunches. 'She does that every day.'

'Yes, but . . . '

'But what?'

'Don't you ever feel sorry for her?'

Rose-Renee scoffed audibly. This game was

clearly over. 'Why would I feel any such thing? You are a stupid old frog, Stinko, and I'm leaving.'

Marcella stayed, watching from her hiding place, experiencing an involuntary spasm of sympathy or pity, or some emotion she did not yet have the word for, and yet which she recognized as an adult insight. The tug of pathos, the sense that though they had lived with Gloria for a year, they knew nothing of her. Nothing. Not who she was, or whom she had loved, or hated, or what might have made her laugh, or made her cry. Marcella could not imagine Gloria's laughter or her tears. She was utterly opaque. As Marcella watched, she saw Gloria not simply as children see the adults in their lives — sources of power to be outwitted, appeased, or evaded — but as a creature composite of experiences. What did Gloria think of there, alone, her face tilted to the setting sun? Her husband, Barry, lived far away with another woman. Her daughter Linda denied, refused the very gifts she had inherited. Her daughter Valerie would try to live up to those gifts and standards, and would never succeed. Her parents were dead. Her sister, Marga, also a musician, lived in a Philadelphia suburb, but never ventured to visit. So who did Gloria commune with when she sat with her cigarette, Marcella wondered. Did she regret or revisit the past? Had her great gifts been a blessing or a curse, taking from her those satisfactions most people hunger for? Marcella tried to imagine her as the great beauty who had stolen the heart of Barry Denham, so much so he defied his family to marry her, and finally bankrupted the Denhams to build a music room for her. Was her life a perfect prison, or a perfect palace of contentment?

Andantino

August, 1987, and nearly thirty years old, Marcella McNeill, PhD — pioneering advocate of music therapy, a woman who ought to have been launching a successful medical or academic career — was working at the same job she'd had the first summer after high school. She sat in the ticket booth at Tanglewood with a paperback novel under the counter. She had got the job, both times, thanks to nepotism: her aunt, Linda Denham. Marcella's cycle of stagnation was even more complete since she was staying in the guest room at Linda's, living with Linda, her oboist husband Mike and two sons. In short, Marcella felt a total failure, paddling stupidly through one of life's troughs where the Old has ended and the New has not yet presented itself, when one was painfully conscious of what has been lost and not at all certain what lies ahead.

In May, 1987, the administrator of the clinic where she practised had told her that her contract would not be renewed. He said she did not suit the 'clinic culture'. At first she thought she'd misheard him; after all, she'd complied with everything asked of her (indeed when many others had not!) and look at her record! She had been successful! The more he talked (and nodded, grinned, grinned and nodded, blathered and burbled), Marcella knew she had been too successful. She had made enemies of the old guard, men and a few women jealous of their positions, people hunkered down over little plots of mediocrity which they cultivated and reciprocally admired. Anyone more bold, more ambitious, less willing to settle for ... She listened as this weasel wished her well in all her new endeavours.

Marcella went back to her apartment, and called Linda, who pronounced them all fuckers, and told Marcella to come east for the summer.

She told her aunt she could not leave Eric, not for the whole summer. When she got off the phone, Marcella went into the bathroom where she found a puddle of water in front of the sink. Looking for the source of the leak, there behind the big bottle of Drano she stumbled on a cache of prescription bottles, uppers, and bags full of multicoloured pills. This ill-timed discovery precipitated the cratering of her love life. Within the week, she had left Eric, the ER doctor she had lived with for nearly five years.

Linda's offer was too perfectly timed to pass up, even if the Tanglewood ticket booth wasn't exactly a new endeavour. All that summer Marcella went out with men Linda introduced her to. Of the men, a few were interesting, but none stirred in her anything more than mild lust; certainly none appealed to the imagination.

Marcella was at the ticket office, deeply ensconced in another Maeve Binchy novel, when her phone rang. 'Tanglewood ticket office, how may I — '

'Oh, shut up!' Linda's voice was breathless. 'You'll never guess who I just talked to. Don't even try. Tim. I know, it's incredible.'

'Who?'

'Tim Farleigh! The Jolly Red Giant? Remember?'

'Tim!'

'I couldn't talk long. I still can't. I'm on my way out the door to a meeting.'

'How long since you've seen him?'

'Never, not since he left Gloria's! I haven't even heard from him since he sent back my twenty dollars in 1970. God! How long ago is that? Have you heard from him?'

'Me? Why would I hear from him? He sent us back our money when we were still at Gloria's. That's it. What's he doing up here? Where has he been all these years?'

'I guess we'll find out, won't we? You and I are meeting him for pizza and a few beers after work. I already called Mike, and it's fine.'

'How did Tim find you?'

'I guess some old friend from the commune saw him in DC and told him I was here. He called Tanglewood and asked for Linda Denham. Good thing I kept my maiden name. He's been at a conference in the Berkshires and he's on his way back to DC.'

'What's he do?'

'I don't know!'

'Is he married?' said Marcella, her heart giving a little thump.

'We'll find out at six. I'll swing by and pick you up at the ticket booth.'

As the three tentatively greeted each other at the pizza place, they laughed at how seventeen years had changed everyone, Marcella, most dramatically, though the girl might yet be seen in the woman. She still had the dark colouring of the McNeills, the mobile mouth, the broad Denham forehead; she was slender but solid with long dark hair, permed now, and fashionably curly-wild. Linda wore colour-contacts and was devoted to L'Oréal, so her forty years showed less than they otherwise might; if anything she was thinner than she used to be. Tim at thirty-eight was still broad-shouldered and lanky; his red hair (well cut) had faded, and retreated from his forehead, but not thinned. He still had big competent hands, and wry, muted laughter. His drawl remained pronounced, and the lines around his blue eyes were those of a man who has worked outside, squinting against the sunlight. However, he lived in DC now, reduced, he said, to being a bureaucrat for the Tennessee Valley Authority. He planned to quit, and take his hydro-engineering talents out west, though nothing was firmly set. He bought the first round of beers, and had no sooner returned to their table with the pitcher when Linda asked, 'Are you married?'

'Well, I was for a while. My high-school sweetheart, Sharon. I saw her at Jimmy's funeral, but she was married by then to another guy from our class. He was an asshole, but Sharon was still real sweet and pretty, and she had a cute little girl, Carrie. By the time I got out of the army, Sharon was divorced, and — '

'You joined the army!' cried Linda, incredulous.

Tim shrugged. 'After my brother died, I did a lot of things I wouldn't have done otherwise.'

'Did you go to Vietnam?' asked Marcella.

'No. I spent my tour freezing my butt off guarding the Korean border where nothing was happening, unless you count being horny and bored to death. I read Tolstoy. That made it even worse. Felt like I was wasting my life. When I came back from Korea, Sharon was divorced, and she and I got together. Sharon was real good to my mother, to both my parents after Jimmy died. She and I both wanted to be settled and secure, and I liked having the ready-made family with little Carrie. We got married and moved to Fayetteville so I could go to University of Arkansas. She got a good job as a dispatcher with a trucking firm.' He sipped, and seemed pensive. 'We were good for a long time.'

'But?' asked Linda.

'Well, it's not like anything big happened, nothing terrible.'

'Kids?' asked Linda.

'I would have liked kids, but Sharon said she didn't want to start all over again. One was enough for her. Carrie was a little sweetheart. We probably would have broken up sooner, but for Carrie. I was real fond of her.'

Linda was merciless. 'Well, why did you break up?'

'We had different ideas what settled and secure meant,' he replied in his slow drawl. 'Sharon never wanted to leave Arkansas, and I

233

never wanted to stay. Nothing tied me to Arkansas, not after my parents passed away, her parents too, but Sharon didn't want to move, so we stayed. It was just easier. Then I got a chance to go work in Brazil for a couple of years, and I was all ready to jump on it, but Sharon didn't want to give up the retirement she'd collected with the trucking firm. Not even for the chance to go to Brazil.' He shook his head. 'I passed it up, but the writing was on the wall. We kind of fell apart after that.'

'How long were you together?'

'About ten, twelve years. Broke up a few years ago. I gave Sharon the house.'

'Really?' said Linda. 'Isn't that kind of unusual in a divorce?'

He shrugged. 'I was leaving. She was staying. It wasn't too bad, as divorces go. I've had worse experiences. Quitting smoking. That was bad.'

'Then I won't tempt you with a cigarette,' said Linda. 'I've been trying to quit too.' The number for their pizza was called out, and Linda insisted on getting it.

'Do you smoke, Marcella?'

'Not since I smoked pot with you.'

'I did way too much weed for a long time, I'm afraid.'

'I didn't do any weed, nor even drink while I was a swimmer.'

'Like Dorothea.'

'Yes.'

'You ever go to the Olympics?'

'No, I was never very good. I just trained really hard.'

234

A smile tugged at his lips, and his gaze rested benignly on Marcella. 'You were always a real interesting kid, and Linda told me on the phone you're a PhD too. She says you're real smart, and that you work using music to help people, doing new and interesting things.'

'At the moment I'm in the Tanglewood ticket booth and living with Linda and Mike, and neither of those counts as interesting.'

'You married?'

'No.'

'Well, I bet you have a whole string of boyfriends all lined up round the block, just begging you to marry.'

'Oh, Tim, please.' Marcella waved his comment away as like second-hand smoke. 'Don't treat me like a kid. I'm almost thirty.'

'Don't tell me you don't have a boyfriend or a fiancé.'

'I broke off an engagement in May. A man I'd been living with for almost five years,' said Marcella as Linda returned with the pizza and plates, and dished it out.

'I'm real sorry to hear that, Marcella,' he said in his laconic fashion.

'Don't be,' she replied.

'Marcella's well out of that,' Linda concurred.

'Eric was an ER doctor, so it's understandable, of course, he lived under lots of stress, and that's what I always thought it was, his moods, his manic highs, and then he'd crash. But I found a bunch of pills under the sink, and suddenly everything became clear. We had a huge fight. He promised he'd go through rehab,

235

and it would all be different. Blah blah blah. In five years I would have hated him.'

'I always hated him,' Linda offered. 'Supercilious prick. Just because he was a doctor he thought he was God.'

'You have to admit,' Marcella offered, 'the pills might have had something to do with his arrogance. Anyway, I didn't want to spend my life with someone who would be bouncing in and out of rehab. I moved my stuff out, and came here.'

Tim seemed to consider all this while he munched on a piece of pizza. Linda peppered him with questions about his life and work in DC; he replied in his slow, thorough manner, but after a while he turned to Marcella. 'Will you stay here, you think?'

'Selling Tanglewood tickets and living with Linda and Mike? Not on your life. I'm going back to LA in September.'

'What's waiting for you in California?'

'Nothing.' She sipped her beer. 'Everything.'

'What'll you do?'

'Well, I haven't really . . . ' Thought on it, she was about to say. An evasion. No, a total lie. She lay awake nights thinking about her career: had it crashed or just stalled? Should she have been more patient with Eric? Given rehab a chance? She did not want to be a soloist like Gloria. She wanted to belong. She looked into Tim's bright-blue eyes. 'I'm going back to LA in September, and I'll find a new apartment, and get my stuff out of storage. I'll look for a job in a clinic or a hospital or even part-time faculty somewhere where

I won't be corseted to a bunch of outmoded theories, and shackled to a bunch of inbred medi-ocrities. I guess you could say I need to restart my life.'

Tim gave his old slow smile. 'Well, Marcella, I never doubted that you can do just about anything you set your mind to. You always were a go-getter.'

'No, Tim, I was always looking for applause. It's not the same thing.'

He grinned, and settled back into the booth. 'Now tell me about Rose-Renee. What's she up to?'

11

The Kindness of Strangers

June passed into July with no sign of Valerie McNeill. No word from her either. After a summer flurry of fireworks and fireflies, Dorothea and Rodney left for a vacation in California to see her parents. Rodney wrote often, addressing his letters to The Pig Sisters c/o Gloria's PO box. He sent postcards from Disneyland with stick figures of Putrid and Stinko standing next to Snow White and Cinderella. He missed his friends. He enclosed an origami animal for each in his next letter, a horse and a giraffe, and the girls fought over who would get the giraffe. He wrote about his boring grandparents and their boring house in boring Claremont. He said their pool was having filter problems and his mother couldn't wait to get it fixed. He wanted to come home. Then five days passed with no word at all. A short letter arrived on stationery from UCLA Medical Center. Rodney wrote that he was hooked up to an IV. No more letters.

The summer turned sour. The two sisters sulked and chafed at one another and their usual pastimes paled. Outside they were hot, filthy, eaten alive by bugs, thirsty and hungry. Inside, there was nothing left to do. The only place they wanted to go was Dorothea's and they had been forbidden to go there, especially forbidden to

238

swim until Dorothea and Rodney returned.

Nonetheless, that's where they went. The house was locked up, drapes drawn, no Ethel. The gate was locked, but easily vaulted by two agile girls. The pool waters twinkled in the sunshine, silent save for the slurping sound of the drain. 'Oh, I don't care that we promised we wouldn't,' said Marcella, slipping off her sandals. 'I'm burning up.' She dove in and Rose-Renee followed. They played a splashing version of Gingerbread Girls till Ethel showed up.

'Get outta that pool! Right this minute. You know Mrs Jones said you wasn't allowed to come here when she was gone, and you're specially not allowed to swim. Why do you think that gate is locked? Mrs Jones don't want no one, not you, not any animals getting in the pool and drown!' She laid especially vehement emphasis on the last word, conjuring up death floating in the pool. She nodded in agreement with herself. 'Oh, you two are Denhams, all right. Thinking the rules don't apply to you! Now dry off, and go home. And don't come back.'

'No towels.'

'There's some in the changing room. Anyway, my son's coming over next week to drain the pool.'

'Why? It's still summer.'

'They're not coming back right away. Rodney's real sick. He's in the hospital still. He's having some kind of operation.'

'But he'll get better,' said Rose-Renee. 'He always does.'

'His disease will turn him into a crone,' said Marcella.

'I don't know nothing about diseases, but what he's got's bad, poor tyke. I come to collect my recipe book, and I'm gonna stand right here and watch while you girls go home. You wanna do something for the Joneses, you write Rodney a letter and tell him to get well, that you miss him.'

'We do,' said Marcella, 'but what's there to say after that?'

'Don't ask me. You're the clever one. Now go on home and don't come back.'

If they only had a few more days until the pool was drained — and despite Ethel's ominous warnings — they decided to use them to good advantage, and they went over to the pool and swam every day, even the day that Rose-Renee said she didn't feel like going. Marcella said she'd go alone; she'd leave Rose-Renee with Gloria and Morton. Rose-Renee roused herself, but once they got to Dorothea's, she sat in the shade, elbows on her knees and refused to get in the water. Marcella dove in, splashed her from the depths and shallows, called her names, but nothing would move her.

'You're just like Rot!' Marcella called out. 'He just sits in the shade and won't move.'

'Maybe I got it from him.'

'What?'

'My tummy hurts too. Just like his. Hurts bad.'

Marcella scrambled out of the water and stood beside her, dripping. 'Are you going to throw up? Like in the car that day?'

'No. Hurts bad.' She lifted her face, and started to cry.

Marcella sat beside her, arm around her

shoulders. 'Fart? Do you need to fart? That can hurt.'

'Not like this. Never had nothing hurt like this.' She rolled on her side against Marcella's body and began to whimper. Marcella held her till the spasm passed, but another one followed, and another after that one. Marcella led her to the chaise longue by the pool and made her lie down. She grabbed some dusty beach towels and put them over and around Rose-Renee and held her till she quit shivering, but another bout of pain seized her and she doubled up and cried out in pain. Marcella felt its force shuddering through her sister's body as she wept and tensed and her breath came in short, harsh gasps.

As the pain eased, Rose-Renee went pale and a little green; her mouth was pursed against another bout. 'This is bad.'

'Yes. Maybe you ate something bad.'

'We ate the same stuff. You're not sick. Maybe this is what Rot has.'

'No. He has crones disease. Could it be that?'

'Could be, You think I got it from him?'

'I don't know,' Marcella replied, remembering with a guilty thump their early taunting of Rodney and her fear that the death he had might be contagious. 'Maybe.'

Rose-Renee spat from the side of her mouth. 'Don't leave me.'

'I'll never leave you.'

Time measured itself out in waves of pain, escalating pain, each leaving Rose-Renee spent, and Marcella increasingly helpless, anxious and fearful. 'Stay here,' she said, as though

241

Rose-Renee could have done anything else. Marcella ran to the house, pounding on the windows, knowing there was no one within, but the phone was there. She tried to break the window, hammering on it until Rose-Renee cried out again, and then she ran back to her sister and held her, thinking who would she call anyway? Gloria? Grumpy Susan wasn't there today. Gloria would never hear the phone. Who would she call? A doctor? What doctor? Who? Ethel? She didn't know Ethel's number. She wasn't even sure of Ethel's last name. She held Rose-Renee while she wept and moaned and shivered. *Oh please please please take this pain from her and give it to me, to me me me me,* Marcella pleaded silently, but no one listened. She wished like mad Dorothea was there. Dorothea would know what to do. 'Maybe I should go for help.'

'Don't leave me, Stinko. Don't. I'm afraid.'

'I'm afraid too, but I can't . . . what can I do by myself? We need help.'

'Who'd help? Who would you get?'

'I don't know.'

'Stay with me.'

'I have to get help.'

'Where? Who? Don't go. Don't leave me.'

Where? Who? If she ran all the way back to Gloria's, how long would that take? Would Gloria come? It was a long way back to Gloria's, not just the distance between the stone farmhouse and the Denham mansion, but down the long, long hall to the music room which in Marcella's mind suddenly expanded, lengthened,

242

stretched out before her in a straight but ever-elongating path to a tiny, distant door. How long would all that take? Would Gloria jump in the Lincoln and blast over here to Dorothea's? Lift Rose-Renee over the fence and call the doctor? What doctor? Could Gloria be made to rush to get here? Be made to rush at all? *Who else?* Where could she *run run, fast as you will...?* The road? The road was just here. In front of Dorothea's house. Nearby. 'Wait for me.'

'Don't!' Rose-Renee doubled up, screaming, and Marcella stayed, but the pain was unremitting. Helpless in the face of such pain, Marcella's own muscles seemed to grip round her bones, and her heart pounded percussively. She put her lips to her sister's ear when at last the bout subsided, and whispered, 'I'm going for help.' Marcella freed herself, not heeding Rose-Renee's pleas and cries. She slid her feet into sandals, and vaulted the fence.

Run run, fast as you will, you can't catch me, I'm the Gingerbread Girl! She dashed to the front of the farmhouse, and sprinted to the mailbox at the main road, where she jumped up and down, flailing her arms, though no cars passed. She glanced back at the farmhouse, and then started to run. She turned in the direction of Gloria's house and tore along the narrow road. She stayed in the centre so someone would have to stop or hit her. She tripped and stumbled and fell, scraping abrasions on both knees, got back up again and *run run fast as you will, you can't catch me I'm the Gingerbread Girl!* She heard snarls and the vicious barking of the dogs as they hurtled themselves against the fences howling at her as she *run run fast as you can, you can't catch me you can't catch me you can't catch me* . . . She fell again, and got back up, breathless, and ran on, willing herself not to hear the dogs, to hear nothing but the pounding of her feet on the asphalt and willing there to be a car that would come over the hill, that would stop and not mow her down, but she heard only the steady slap of her own sandals, the rasp of her breath as she tore along the road until she heard an engine coming from behind, over the hill. She started jumping up and down, arms waving in the middle of the road. 'Help! Help!' A truck.

The driver slowed, to a crawl, stopped beside her, a man in a soiled T-shirt, with an unshaven, florid face, a greying buzz cut under his duck-billed cap; a cigarette hung from his lips, the fumes obscuring the wretched smell all around him. The radio was blaring till he turned it off.

'Please!' Marcella flung herself against the driver's side. 'Please help me! It's my sister, my sister, my sister Rose-Renee. Come on. Come with me!'

'What's a matter with your sister, little lady? Slow down. Say, aren't you wonna them Denham girls?'

Marcella ran round to the passenger side, opened the door and jumped in. 'Go!' She pointed wildly behind them. 'The Jones place! Please. Please. She's awful sick. The Jones place!'

He worked the floor shift a couple of times,

putting the truck in reverse, making a U-turn in the narrow road and started back towards Dorothea's while Marcella bounced up and down and yelled at him not to ask her stupid questions like where were her parents. 'Just drive. Fast. Go!' The truck smelled awful, and then she remembered, recognized Mr Bowker who had brought them there that first day. July. A year ago.

'Ain't no one here,' he said as he rumbled up the driveway to the house. 'They gone to California.'

'Never mind! Just come with me!'

A scream rent the air, and he hustled after Marcella as much as an overweight, out-of-breath, 60-year-old man could. She vaulted the short fence at the side, but he was too big and portly, and the gate was locked. Marcella ran to Rose-Renee, who was blubbering and couldn't get her breath for screaming. Abel Bowker considered the gate. He ran back to his truck and pulled some tools from his box, went back to the fence and lifted his hammer to the lock once, twice, then he swung the hinges, and with one more blow, and a powerful kick, the low gate gave way. He flung the hammer down, opened the gate and ran towards the pool.

'Here! Here!' cried Marcella.

Abel Bowker stood sweating, breathless and speech-less before the girls, one writhing in pain and the other writhing with fear. 'Where's your mother, little girl?'

'Gone! Don't you see? Please, please help me! Please, please help me. Please.' Marcella pressed

Rose-Renee's head in her arms and her eyes beseeched Mr Bowker.

In one swift movement, Abel Bowker swooped Rose-Renee up, towel and all, into his arms, while she cried out for Marcella, who ran beside him, all the way back to broken gate. Abel Bowker stepped over the wreckage and made his way to the front of the house, one child in his arms, one at his heels.

Once back at the truck, Marcella flung open the passenger side and got in, held out her arms for her sister. Abel put Rose-Renee in her arms and hustled back to the driver's side, jumped in, and put the gear in reverse. The tires squealed and exhaust billowed dust as the truck bounced on to the main road while Rose-Renee screamed, and Marcella wept. He drove, honking his horn like a madman, and waving his arm out the window for cars to pull over and get out of his way so he could get past them.

Marcella had no idea where they were going, or how long it would take, or did take. It was the longest ride of her life until at last she saw a big sign: EMERGENCY.

Mr Bowker parked the septic truck in a no-park zone. His door squealed on dry hinges as he jumped out. He pulled the protesting Rose-Renee from Marcella's embrace, and carried the scream-ing child in his arms — Marcella right behind, alternately shouting and soothing — as he pushed through the revolving door. And then the three of them just stood there, no one knowing what to do or whom to call.

'What's the problem?' asked a woman, an

intake worker perhaps.

'How the hell should I know?' Bowker shouted. 'Look at her!'

'Is she your daughter?'

'No, no, I don't know her name.'

'Rose-Renee!' Marcella cried. 'She's Rose-Renee McNeill. I'm Marcella McNeill.'

'Where are your parents?'

'Sweden. Please, please make her well.'

This woman disappeared behind some swinging doors and a white-clad nurse followed her out, pushing a wheelchair. Gently Mr Bowker put Rose-Renee in the chair.

'You wait here,' said the nurse to Marcella.

'No!' Rose-Renee cried as if all her ten years of surly sullen stubbornness were but a rehearsal for this single moment. She fiercely gripped her sister's hand.

'You must let go,' said the nurse. 'Make her let go.'

'No.'

Rose-Renee flung her head back and her eyes rolled into her sockets, and the nurse made no further protest. Marcella went with her through swinging double doors into a cavernous room with curtains closing off spaces here and there, everything spare and lit so brightly her eyes hurt. The nurse pushed the wheelchair into an enclosure, and pulled the long white curtain and it sang along the metal rails. She left them briefly, and Marcella knelt in front of the wheelchair and took both her sister's hands in her own.

'Don't go,' said Rose-Renee, shivering, her teeth clenched.

The nurse returned with a wheeled gurney; she locked the wheels and lowered the bed. She asked Rose-Renee to get on.

Rose-Renee shook her head. Another bout of pain assailed her.

'Help her on the gurney,' said the nurse when the worst of it had passed.

'Here,' said Marcella gently. 'I'll help you. Get on the bed.'

'Don't let go,' she whispered fiercely. 'Don't.'

'I won't.'

Together Marcella and the nurse moved her to the gurney; the nurse wheeled the chair out and brought some blankets, tucking them around Rose-Renee. She gave one to Marcella as well, who till that moment had not realized how cold she was in the air-conditioned confines of the hospital.

'We need your mother and father,' said the nurse, speaking very slowly.

Marcella replied or tried to, but it all came out as gibberish, Sweden and Michigan and none of that mattering, and Gloria not being able to hear the phone, and who cares? *Make my sister well.*

That nurse left and another came. She slapped a cuff on Rose-Renee's arm, and stuck a thermometer in her mouth. Rose-Renee's eyes behind her thick glasses were whorls of pain and fear. The nurse gently removed Rose-Renee's glasses. 'I'll put these at the front desk. All right?'

'She can't see without them,' said Marcella.

'She won't need to see right now, and you don't want them to get lost, do you?'

The first nurse returned and blathered about

248

the two girls being found at the Jones place, like they had dropped from another planet, saying that Mr Bowker said they were Gloria Denham's granddaughters. Was that true?

'Yes, yes, it's true.'

'Where is your grandmother?'

'There! Home. Her house!'

'We've called. There's no answer.'

'She can't hear! There's no phone in the music room!' Marcella screamed, suddenly seized with *fantasia ala narc* stories she had told Rose-Renee: *Help us, Gloria!* Gloria hearing nothing except the sounds she herself created, the fierce, the crazy music that came spilling from her violin, flowing through and under the St Cecilia doors. *Help us, Gloria!* Marcella wanted to grab the nurse's shoulders, shake her, but she dared not let go of Rose-Renee. 'Don't you understand? Gloria can't hear! Nothing can touch her in there. Nothing can get to her!'

The nurse must have thought that Gloria was deaf, because she quit asking. She left and pulled the white curtains and they sang their silvery song along the metal rail.

'Stinko,' said Rose-Renee, gulping when at last the pain abated, 'I'm scared.' Her face was grey, and her dark eyes were big.

'I'm here.'

'Stinko, don't let go of me. No matter what happens.'

'I won't. I promise. I promise a thousand times. I will never let you go, Putrid.'

Marcella climbed onto the narrow gurney, and the two pressed together. 'I promise. I'm here.

We are the Gingerbread Girls.' Marcella started to cry, and stopped herself. Licked one of her thumbs, and tapped it to the back of Rose-Renee's hand, or maybe her cheek or her neck, their old, I Swear code. Marcella embraced her as another thrust of pain accosted her. 'I swear,' Marcella whispered throughout the spasm, 'I'll never let go. Never let go.' Rose-Renee fell back and took a few short, shallow breaths, as if testing her ability to breathe at all. She never took her eyes from Marcella, and in that moment Marcella feared, believed that maybe she should extract a solemn promise from Rose-Renee that she would not leave either. But surely *it was impossible that we should ever be separated, not the Pig Sisters, not Putrid from Stinko. We are the Gingerbread Girls who cannot be caught run run.* Fear, rising, coiled in her throat.

Marcella started singing, like she always did when she needed to comfort Rose-Renee, or quell one of her tantrums. She broke into 'Surrey With The Fringe On Top', quietly, gulping back tears, forgetting the words, with her lips at Rose-Renee's ear, sang bits and pieces of 'Beautiful Mornin'' and 'People Will Say We're In Love', all of them scrambled up with screaming when the pain came on again. Rose-Renee squeezed Marcella so tightly Marcella thought surely all that pain must pass into her body. But it did not.

'Get this girl out of here,' said a white-coat-clad man when he burst in. 'Get her off this gurney!'

'Do as the doctor says,' said the nurse.

'I won't let go.'

'Please,' said the doctor, 'you want to do what's best for your little sister, don't you? Don't you?' he asked again as someone pried at her fingers. 'You want to do what's best for her. We need to treat her. You need to let go.'

'Go away, you bastard! I'm not leaving!'

'Marcella, stay! Stinko!'

'You need to leave us to make her well.'

'I'm not leaving and you can't make me!'

The doctor stepped back and nodded to the nurse.

Minutes later, another man pulled back the curtains, and put his big hands over Marcella's shoulders and another pair of male hands pried her fingers from Rose-Renee's as they lifted her up and off the gurney. *No. No.* Marcella grasped quickly, held to the rim of the gurney while they pulled at her, both girls shrieking, Marcella tightening her grip on the gurney, as harsh voices instructed her to let go, to get her off, to get her out, and once again a man's hands covered hers, and unpeeled her fingers from the rail. Two men pulled her by her arms while she called them bastards and bitches, and Rose-Renee screamed again, though in pain or anger Marcella could not tell. She tried to scramble back to her sister till one of the men simply picked her up off the floor, held her in his arms, though she fought back, beating on his chest and shoulders. Rose-Renee and Marcella's wails filled the air, ricocheted everywhere, brought more white-clad people running, some to subdue Rose-Renee, some to quiet other patients, some to open the double doors and get Marcella out.

Once into the waiting room, the orderlies put her down, though they did not release their grip on her arms as she swore and screamed, cursed them, even when, suddenly surrounded by a phalanx of intake workers and more nurses whose disapproving faces and harsh words blurred and melded in her vision, they tried to put her in a chair. She fought back.

'Let her go,' said Abel Bowker, pushing through the small throng. They refused, but he knelt at her feet, patting her knee, his rough voice gentle. 'Marcella, you gotta quiet down, honey. You gotta listen to me. Listen to me. I'm gonna stay here with you. See? You 'member me? Abel Bowker. I brought you here.' He brushed her dark hair from her face gently. Mr Bowker's dirty hand removed the orderly's fingers from Marcella's small wrists.

Marcella bolted to her feet. The orderly pushed her back down, saying, 'They'll throw you out of here if you try to go back to your sister.'

'They won't take care of her if you try to go back there,' the other said as they left.

Someone thrust a blanket at Mr Bowker and he wrapped it round her shoulders, and pulled her close to him. She shivered, and her teeth chattered. 'Hush, now,' he said as she wept and hiccupped. He spoke softly. 'I need your help. Marcella, they've been calling your grandmother, Gloria Denham. Right?'

'I let go of her hand. They made me. Those bastards.'

'Where'd a little girl like you learn a word like that?'

'Mitch.'

'Your grandmother, Mrs Denham, but she's not home. Gloria Denham, but she's not there. Who else can they call, Marcella?'

'She is there! She can't hear! There's no telephone in the music room!' She was wailing at him. 'Don't you see? I told them already! *She can't hear anything in there!* Nothing can touch her in there. Nothing can touch her in the music room! Nothing can touch her and she can't hear anything but music! Nothing can touch her ever!'

Mr Bowker glanced over to the desk where a nurse watched with interest. 'Are you saying your grandmother's there, in that music room, but she can't hear the phone?'

'It's not Grumpy Susan's day!'

'You mean Susan Digges?'

'I let go of her hand! I promised her I wouldn't! Why'd they make me do that? I promised. I promised I'd never let go, that I'd stay. I need to go back to her, Mr Bowker. Make them let me.' Marcella hoped whatever Rose-Renee had was catching and she would get it too and have so much pain they'd have to take her back. She waited for a great thunderclap of pain in her stomach or guts, but only her head hurt and she was intolerably thirsty. She wiped her nose with the back of her hand.

'I'm gonna help you, Marcella. You wait here.' Mr Bowker went to the desk and conferred with the woman who had greeted them on their arrival. When he returned he said, 'Marcella, you know Ethel Wilcox, don't you? She works for Mrs Jones.'

'Everyone knows Ethel.'

He gave a small laugh. 'Yes. Ethel is my wife's cousin. I've called her and she's coming here to be with you and your sister.'

'Ethel is?'

'She's gonna go to your grandmother's first. That's good as I could do, honey. I can't do no more. I don't know what's wrong with your sister, but you are a quick thinker and you did right by her. You run into the road and stopped me, and now your sister's here in this hospital, and she's gonna be all right, you see, look all round you here.' He turned to the waiting room as though it were a theatre and they were about to be massively entertained. 'All these good doctors and nurses are looking after your little sister. And Ethel's gonna go by your grandmother's place and get her. Ethel'll be here. She's coming.'

'I don't want Ethel.'

'I know, you want your mother.'

'I don't want her either. Don't you see? I want Rose-Renee. I promised I'd hold her hand! I promised!' She cried into her hands.

Mr Bowker left her and came back with another blanket and put it around her. He pulled it up to her chin. Still whimpering, Marcella stared into his blue and bloodshot eyes. She wanted to remember his coarse, unshaven face, his stained cap, even his smell.

He sat beside her. He put an arm around her and pulled her close, her head on his foul-smelling shoulder. 'Ethel'll be here. And you'll have your sister back. Don't you fret.'

254

The next few hours were a welter of sensation and emotion, none of it clear, none of it orderly, or sequential. Marcella stayed in the chair beside Mr Bowker, clutching the blanket while people came and went in front of her eyes and Mr Bowker was called to the telephone while hospital intercoms blared out names and directions, like the green-room squawk box blaring *Fifteen minutes! Places, please. Fifteen minutes till curtain.* She remembered the curtains in the room where they had taken Rose-Renee singing along the rail. *Fifteen minutes! Places, please . . .* But Marcella had left her place. Let go. Marcella's own guts hurt, knotted in a painful tangle, and her teeth chattered, and she felt woozy and wretched as if she were experiencing whatever they were doing to her sister, though she had *let go let go let go, left* and not kept her promise. Her hands were freezing. She wobbled out of the chair, still holding the thin blanket, and asked the nurse where was the bathroom.

She pointed with a pen, and then said, 'Oh, you poor kid.'

Another nurse, a young black woman with a halo of curly hair, came up behind Marcella, put her arm on her shoulder and led her to the bathroom. She held the blanket while Marcella went into the stall and pulled down her shorts and saw blood. Not just on her knees where she had fallen, but in pink streaks along her thighs. Marcella started to cry.

The young nurse came to the stall door. 'There's nothing to cry about. The blood is perfectly natural. You've got your period, honey.

Has your mom explained this to you, about getting your period once a month?'

'What if I don't want to be a woman?'

'You'll get used to it.' She damped down some paper towels and handed them to Marcella under the door. She put a coin in a machine and underneath the door she passed Marcella a big bulky cotton pad. 'Put it in your undies, honey. I'll be right back.'

Marcella sat on the toilet, mopping up the blood and mopping up tears, as if she were bleeding and crying from orifices she didn't even know she had, till the nurse knocked again at the door.

'Open up, Marcella. That's your name, yes? Marcella. I got a robe here for you. You put the pad in your undies and put this nice warm robe on, and we'll go find out how your sister is doing. Would you like that?'

'Yes.'

'Are you hungry?'

'No.'

'Wanna go to the cafeteria and get you something to eat?'

'No. I told Rose-Renee I wouldn't leave and I did.' Marcella started to hiccough. 'I let go of her hand.'

The nurse wrapped the robe around Marcella. 'My name's Odette. I'm a nurse's aide. I'm going to get you a sandwich and bring it to you in the waiting room. Would you like that?'

'I guess. I don't know. No. I want to see my sister.'

'They said to tell you that your sister is

comfortable and they're waiting for your grandmother.'

'Comfortable? What does that mean? I need to go to her. Hold her hand. I want her glasses back. They took her glasses and I want them back. She can't see without them. What if we forget them? I need them. She needs them.'

Odette led her back to the waiting room and sat her in a plastic chair. She said she would get Rose-Renee's glasses. She left and returned with a sandwich wrapped in cellophane and a Coke. She left again and returned with Rose-Renee's glasses in a plastic bag.

'Thank you,' said Marcella. 'We can't forget these. Where's Mr Bowker?'

'I told him he could leave. I told him I'd sit with you.'

Spent, Marcella turned away, pressing the glasses gently against her chest.

'Go ahead. Eat your sandwich.'

Marcella tried, but couldn't. She had forgotten how to chew. She put the sandwich on the chair beside her, swilled the Coke, put her head back, and closed her eyes. She was still cold.

The double doors whooshed open and Ethel and Gloria walked into the waiting room. Ethel had a hand on Gloria's elbow like a tugboat steering an ocean liner. She led Gloria right up to the desk, and said this was the little girl's grandmother. 'Mrs Denham,' said Ethel firmly, 'tell them who you are.'

'Where is Marcella?' Gloria's blue eyes squinted against the fluorescent glare.

'Here! Here I am!' Marcella bolted among the

chairs and ran to her side.

'Gloria!' Ethel shouted at her like she was deaf. *'Tell them who you are, Gloria, so they'll tell you what happened!'*

'What happened, Marcella? What happened? What did you do to her, Marcella?'

'Gloria! Tell them!'

'I am Gloria Denham.'

'Ma'am,' said the lady at the desk. 'Are you the grandmother?'

'Yes.'

'Where are the child's parents? Ma'am? Where are the child's parents?'

'Stockholm.'

'Like Sweden, ma'am?'

Gloria seemed to ponder this.

Marcella pushed herself in front of Gloria, and grabbed her arms, shook her. 'Wake up, Gloria! This is not a rehearsal! Perform! Where is Valerie?'

'Yes, like Sweden. Their mother is in Sweden.'

'Their father?'

'Michigan, or one of those places. These girls live with me.'

'Are you the guardian?'

'Yes. I think so.'

'Yes, Gloria!' Marcella yelled.

'Yes.'

'Sign this,' said the lady, showing a form in front of her. She took the signed form and went behind the double doors.

The three went back and sat in a row of chairs along the wall. Ethel pulled a chair in front of them and sat down, her elbows resting on her knees. Her furrowed face was bleak and her eyes were dark, her voice thick with anger. 'You done it, now, Marcella. I told you girls not to swim. I told you not to go there while Mrs Jones wasn't home, and she told you, and now you gone and done it.'

'Done what?'

'I told you not to use that pool.'

'It wasn't the pool! She never went in the pool.'

'Then what happened?'

'I don't know.'

'Abel don't know either, Marcella. It's up to you. What happened?'

'Her tummy hurt. And then she was screaming. What else could I do?' Marcella started to weep. 'I let go of her hand. I promised I wouldn't.'

'Why didn't you run to Gloria's for help?' demanded Ethel.

'It isn't Grumpy Susan's day.' She was blubbering, snot and tears mixing as she smeared them across her face.

'I'm not talking about Susan. I'm talking about your own grandmother. Her.' Ethel pointed to Gloria, who was watching all this with interest, her blue eyes wide and blank. 'Marcella, talk to me.'

'I couldn't get in.'

'Couldn't get in your own house? I got in. The kitchen door was open.'

But Marcella did not speak to Ethel. She spoke to Gloria. She said fiercely, 'Nothing can get in the music room. Nothing can touch you in there, nothing, and what if I did run home?

259

Huh? What if I ran down the hall to the music room? Huh? What then? Think you'd have come running? Jumped in the car and come running for her? Think so? Would you? Would you? Fat chance.' Her voice cracked. 'I'm all she's got and I let go of her hand.' She bent double and wept.

Ethel patted Marcella's back, but she spoke to Gloria. 'You understand now, Gloria, what's happened? They wouldn't do nothing for Rose-Renee till you come because Marcella's just a kid. See? Do you, for God's sake, see? Speak. Say something.'

'Do you have a cigarette?' asked Gloria.

Ethel shook her head. 'You think the rules aren't for you. I tried to tell you what this little girl mighta tried to tell you, but you wouldn't hear. Just like Marcella said, you don't hear nothing but that damned violin, and what the hell good is it? I ask you. Now you mighta cost — ' Ethel shut up. Then she said, 'Marcella, you done the right thing to get Abel. He's a good man.'

'I didn't get him. He got me. I let go of her hand. I said I wouldn't, but I did. They made me.'

'You want a cup of water or something?'

'No.' Her hair was dry by now and she had warmed up, but the pad in her underwear was sticky and uncomfortable. She wiped her nose with the sleeve of the robe.

Ethel reached over and took Marcella's hand. Marcella's gaze scored over Ethel's well-known face as she tried to explain, and again and again, that she had let go of Rose-Renee's hand, that

260

she had broken her promise. 'Hush,' said Ethel, gently, all anger drained from her voice. 'Hush.'

Gloria seemed to want to speak, but she just kept licking her lips. Finally she eked out, 'Marcella, you should have . . . '

'Just shut up, Gloria,' said Marcella. 'Just shut up because there's nothing you can say.'

A different nurse came out, looked down at the clipboard she carried, and asked to speak to Mrs Gloria Denham.

Gloria rose, as if the nurse were the conductor and Gloria the first-chair violinist. She might have bowed. She followed the nurse through the big double doors, leaving Marcella and Ethel there. Time swam and leaked around them, bodies moved, and overhead squawk boxes rained down words — *Fifteen minutes; places, please* — but Marcella had lost her place with Rose-Renee.

When, finally, they brought Gloria back out, she was in a wheelchair, her head was down, her fist pressed against her lips. Odette was pushing the wheelchair, which she parked there in front of Marcella and Ethel, and said she'd be right back.

'Gloria,' said Ethel, 'what happened? How's Rose-Renee?'

'Gloria,' Marcella begged, 'Rose-Renee, please, did you see Rose-Renee?' Marcella jumped up, and took Gloria's narrow shoulders in her hands and shook her again and again, astonished at how frail she was, how like all those empty clothes left by Miss Manetti, Signor Massimo, the Wanamaker girl and all the rest of them, as though her flesh was as uninhabited as their clothes. 'Answer me! Did you see her? Where is she? How is she? What did they tell you?'

Odette returned, walking behind a doctor, a different doctor from the one who had ordered Marcella to be dragged away. This one was older, with fluffy grey sideburns on either side of his face, thick-rimmed glasses and a white jacket. He asked Marcella to sit down. He sat down, pulling his chair into a little semicircle with theirs.

'Her name's Marcella, Doctor,' said Odette.

'Marcella,' he repeated. 'You're the one who brought your little sister in. Marcella and . . . ' He glanced over and Odette supplied Ethel's name. 'Marcella and Ethel, we have some difficult news. It was difficult for Mrs Denham, and it will be difficult for you as well. The little girl, your little sister, had peritonitis. A burst appendix, and before we could get her on the operating table, she passed away. I'm very sorry to tell you this, but — '

'No,' Marcella said, 'she's been sick before. In the car. She threw up in the car and she got sick. She's been sick before. We both got sick. We both had it. I'm sick too.'

'No, Marcella,' his voice a soothing monotone, 'this is not just being sick. This was a burst appendix. It burst and sent poisons flooding through her little body, and she . . . she went.'

'No, she didn't. Where could she go? She's here. She didn't go anywhere.'

'I'm sorry. That's all I can say. She had peritonitis and she went.'

'Where? Where'd she go?'

'She's gone. She died.'

'No, that's Rodney. He's the one who's going to die. He's sick. We're not. We're the Gingerbread Girls, the Pig Sisters. He's the one who's sick . . . '

'Your sister has passed away, Marcella.' The doctor seemed to want to reach out for her hand, but she snatched her hands back, grabbed the bag with the glasses and waved it in front of him. 'I have her glasses. She can't see without them.'

'Marcella, honey,' said Ethel, 'they're trying to tell you she can't come home with you. She's died.'

'That's Rodney, Ethel! You know how sick he is!'

'No, honey, it's Rose-Renee. She's passed away. I'm sorry, Marcella, but — '

Marcella started up, bounding towards the doors they had dragged her through just hours before. She called out her sister's name and promised she would never let go before someone wrapped her in a firm embrace, held her as she plunged, as if underwater, kicking and creating a vortex of bubbles that followed her all the way to the bottom of the pool and the suppression of all sound, where she was enveloped in shadows and shifting currents of light that held her until she had to come up for air, and when she did, the arms that held her were Odette's, and Marcella depended upon the kindness of strangers.

12

The Pathetique Sonata

For two children who had been of little note and no concern, death made the McNeill sisters suddenly precious. Their very names were endowed with unthinkable pathos, *poor little Rose-Renee, poor little Marcella*, their every funny or exasperating expression now poignant, and much loved as the family scrambled to assemble from afar.

The immediate burdens fell on Ethel. From the hospital Ethel summoned her son to meet her at the Denham place. She got two orderlies to help as Gloria had to be wheeled out to Ethel's car. When they tried to move Marcella, she flailed and fought, and Odette could not contain her; an orderly came and carried the weeping girl to the car, and from there Ethel drove to the Denham mansion, and came round to the back where her son awaited her. With Marcella, asleep, unconscious, speechless and tearless anyway, in his arms, he and Ethel followed Gloria up the dimly lit staircase to the second floor. He put Marcella in her own bed, and covered her up. Ethel helped Gloria into bed, but first she demanded to know where her address book was, and Gloria yielded it without protest.

Her son left, and Ethel sat in the kitchen

remembering her own mother once lording over this domain, and wondering why she should still be serving the Denhams, who could not care for themselves, who were careless and arrogant. She lit a cigarette, and made two calls, Susan Digges locally, and Dorothea in California. Then she pillaged through the address book and telephoned first Barry in Florida and then Gloria's sister Marga in Philadelphia. She could not find a phone number for Valerie in Stockholm. The number for Mitch in Dallas was no longer in service. Fine. Let one of the Denhams do those honours. She called Barry again and asked if he had a number for Linda. She called Linda. Ethel did not leave till noon the next day when Susan Digges at last appeared. Susan had reason to be grumpy, suddenly beset with the prospect of people flooding a house that had been empty for years, save for one mad musician and two little girls.

Barry Denham immediately flew up from Florida, alone, without Jean. He was fleshy and tanned, and his blond hair had thinned and gone grey, though a lock still fell boyishly across his forehead. He had Valerie's blue eyes, sloping nose and soft features. He was undone to find out that he was expected to call his daughter in Stockholm. He had assumed that someone else would have done it. But no. The burden fell on him. Barry made the international phone call to Valerie with the terrible news, and once he put down the receiver, he poured himself a drink. After the drink he knocked on Gloria's door. He sat on her bed and patted her shoulder as she

265

told him what had happened. It would have been different, Gloria said, if only Marcella had come for her, if only Dorothea Jones hadn't turned the girls against her. After assuring Gloria that she had done her best, Barry went back downstairs, and poured another drink. This was the extent of his effectiveness. Without a boat nearby, or a game of bridge, or a Republican fundraiser, Barry mostly drank and smoked and paced.

The truly onerous responsibilities fell on Linda. She left Tanglewood, where she had a job in the ticket office, as soon as Ethel's call came. Linda's boyfriend Mike drove her down, drove all night, but once they arrived and Linda saw the extent of the chaos, the emotional rubble, the wreckage present — and that still to come — she could not imagine translating for poor old Mike the family dynamic. Hell on the fucking half-shell, she assured him; you don't want to be here; go back to Tanglewood. She drove him to the Wilmington train station, but she kept his car. The getaway car, she told herself. Insurance in case the whole horrible scenario overwhelmed her.

But Linda did not run away. She rose to this sad occasion. She dealt with crises large and small, dealt with the immediate family, and made the necessary arrangements with no help and little input from anyone else. She thanked those who came and called, who left flowers and notes and food, people Gloria had not seen or dealt with in years. All along the social strata of the Brandywine — from the wealthy and artistic Wyeths to the Bowkers and their ilk — people

266

offered tokens of sympathy to Gloria Denham, the unknown, enigmatic Gloria Denham who had sequestered herself in her legendary music room.

Linda was good to Gloria, tender, persuasive, physically supporting her down the staircase when after two days she finally go out of bed, and rejoined the family. Barry took Gloria in his arms and she rested her head on his shoulder. Linda treated Mitch and his girlfriend Jackie gently when they arrived. She gave them Morton's room. She took the one where she had stayed with Tim. She made sure there were meals for everyone who came and stayed, including Marga and Marga's married daughter, Sylvia, both of whom were unused to emergencies, and unprepared for such palatial surroundings, as were Mitch's overwhelmed parents, Sam and Elsie McNeill. After driving down from Elmira, New York, they were tearful, and kind, but they hardly knew their granddaughters; they came to support their son who, they were certain, would need his own family among these supercilious Denhams. But Mitch had so outgrown his parents, he could scarcely stand the sight of them, the narrowness of their awful lives. He shunned their embrace.

On the day Valerie was to fly in from Stockholm, Mitch wanted to go with Linda to collect her at the Philadelphia airport. Linda refused. She knew she would have all she could possibly handle with Valerie, and in this she was correct. Valerie, stunned, jet-lagged, asked the same questions over and over, sometimes in Swedish. Once back at the house, Valerie sought out her remaining daughter, Marcella, to love, to hold, to cry against her shoulder and be comforted, but Marcella struggled, and ran away like the Gingerbread Girl that she was.

Marcella ran away from everyone, rebuffing every sympathetic appeal, repelling every adult, from Valerie and Mitch to Marga and Sylvia, and Barry, Elsie and Sam, from people who came to the house, from anyone who tried to mollify and soothe. To hell with pleasing adults; adults had pried her hand from Rose-Renee's. Marcella put on Rose-Renee's glasses and refused to take them off. She wanted to be blind. She raged and kicked and cried her way all over the house. She hid in the cedar-scented closets, the butler's pantry, locked herself in the unused bathrooms, and in the garage and the potting shed that had long since gone to pot. When compelled from these or other hideouts, she hurtled through the halls, fighting off people who tried to stroke her cheek and pat her back; she pushed past their subdued voices, their sentiments like peppermint, bracing and palliative at the same moment, like the breath mints that veiled the alcohol and cigarettes, the hairspray on the women, the after-shave of the men. Their sympathy was genuine, and their words flattered and absolved Marcella McNeill of guilt for having let go of her sister's hand, for having broken her solemn promise. Any other time Marcella would have delighted in the attention showered upon her; she would have danced the 'Good Ship Lollipop' for these adults, basked in their affection and applause, but now she wanted to slap them. All of them. To hell with brave Eliza and Heidi and Anne of Green Gables and Rebecca of Sunnybrook Farm and Shirley Temple and 'Animal Crackers In My Soup'. Marcella was a Gingerbread Girl and she could not be caught. She was putrid and stinking and rotten to the core. She snarled and wept and had savage tantrums from which she emerged a wreck, hiccoughing with squandered emotion. She collapsed into exhausted sleep.

Linda could not ease Marcella's suffering, but she tolerated her tantrums. Linda did not call her squirt. Linda did not tell her everything would be fine. But Linda would not for one moment agree that Marcella could have saved Rose-Renee if only she had kept her promise. No one blamed Marcella.

But blame lay like a spectral scarf around the Denham mansion. Like a banner of cigarette smoke, or a low-lying fog, it roiled underfoot and coiled overhead, arose in the whispers of family and twittering visitors alike, people who assembled and departed, brought food or flowers and left with *No! Really?* and *So shocking, she was just a little girl* . . . . In Chadds Ford blame wafted along the aisles of Stoddard's Provisioners, and in the smart art galleries. *She was at a neighbour's house* . . . *Yes, the one with the sickly son. Jones. Dorothea Jones* . . . *Yes, the one whose husband was killed when he drove into a tree that winter, yes, he was drunk* . . . *Suicide? Well, maybe* . . . *The McNeill girls were at the Jones house all the time. And I do mean all the time* . . . *They went to school there,* not a real school. Mrs Jones doesn't let her son go to regular school, and so the girls went to her house . . . Gloria couldn't stop them. They were there every day, I've heard . . . in the pool . . . Dorothea let them use the pool without adult supervision . . . No one told poor Gloria for hours . . . Yes, Marcella didn't call Gloria . . . Abel Bowker found her in the middle of the road screaming. Abel called Ethel Wilcox from the hospital. Word hovered, hushed, over the telephone lines and in the post office and at café tables. Poor Gloria Denham . . . Ethel Wilcox found her practising in her music room. Gloria couldn't hear anything, except what she was playing, of course, and she didn't seem to understand what Ethel was saying, or so I heard. Really. Even once they got to the hospital, Gloria was still . . . Poor Gloria. Yes, they say the little girl died just as Ethel and Gloria got there. Terrible, of course. Of course the hospital wouldn't operate without permission. How could they? They had to wait, and she . . . Why didn't the other girl, Marcella, call Gloria? . . . Why didn't Marcella run to her grandmother? If she'd gone to Gloria first, maybe . . . She didn't, though, she ran out in the road. Abel Bowker stopped . . . No! Yes, he tore down the fence to get to the pool. Animals got in and drowned there. No! Really? . . . When Dorothea Jones came back, she found dead animals in the pool, raccoons and rabbits. Dorothea has put the house up for sale . . . She's going back to California . . . No wonder . . . She's tried to see the little girl, the other girl, Marcella. Dorothea

Jones has gone to the Denhams three times, but Gloria has forbidden anyone to let her in. Gloria won't even speak to her on the phone. Dorothea probably blames herself for leaving . . .

Gloria certainly blamed Dorothea. Gloria insisted Dorothea had turned Marcella against her, so much so that the child committed a colossal misjudgement that cost Rose-Renee her life. Gloria blamed Marcella for not coming to her first. *If only, if only, if only . . .* Mitch blamed Gloria for not looking after his little girl. Mitch's anguish was audible and visible to all. *How sharper than a serpent's tooth to have lost one's thankless child.* Valerie's grief was operatic. Her eyes red-rimmed with jet lag and sorrow, sleeplessness, her hair lank and unwashed, her face pale and ashen, Valerie wailed and wept. Valerie blamed Mitch for breaking up their marriage because, without the divorce, they would have been a happy little family, the four of them, Daddy, Mommy and two sweet little girls. Amid the bickering, Barry blamed Mitch for being an egocentric philanderer. Mitch's girl-friend Jackie blamed Valerie for running away, and not looking after her own kids. Marga and Sylvia didn't know who to blame, but they chirped and nattered with the rest of them. Sam and Elsie McNeill blamed Valerie for being exactly like her selfish mother, Gloria. Linda alone did not have the leisure to indulge in blame. Linda's grief was genuine, but buried, subsumed in the sheer weight of what she carried for others, a role she had never wanted, and she was astonished to discover she could

271

fulfil at all. She was strong, decisive, managerial, and when no one else would make all the sad arrangements, she made them. Soon it would all be over. The funeral. Tomorrow.

Linda found Marcella hiding in the garage, curled in the back seat of the Lincoln, wearing Rose-Renee's glasses and holding Cubbie and Barbie to her chest. Linda got in the back seat too, and rested her head against the seat. The car was airless and stuffy and hot with the windows rolled up. It was so quiet she thought she could hear the sweat prickling on her brow.

'Where's Dorothea?' Marcella asked at last.

'I don't know. I haven't seen her.'

'You mean she hasn't called or come for me? That's not true.'

'It's true that I have not seen her,' Linda said.

'Does she know?'

'She does. Ethel called her.'

'If she knows, then she'll be coming. She won't leave me here. She'll come and get me.'

'Get you? Like . . . take you away.'

'Yes. She won't leave me here.'

'She has her own boy to think about. She can't come running for you.'

'She won't leave me here.'

'She will, Marcella,' Linda said bluntly.

'She loves me.'

'She won't come after you.'

'I know. I don't deserve it. I don't deserve to be loved. I deserve to be punished for letting go of Putrid's hand.'

'That's not what I meant.' Linda sat up straight. 'What I meant is you have to be brave

272

now. This is a terrible thing and you shouldn't have to endure it, young as you are, but you must, honey. You have to be strong. Just like you were always strong for Rose-Renee. You always took care of her.'

'Not always. I broke my promise.'

'I've told you. No one blames you. It was . . . it was . . . no one could have prevented what happened.' Linda sighed. Just get through tonight and tomorrow, she told herself. 'Tomorrow is the funeral service. Ten o'clock. Mitch thinks you ought to go, and Valerie thinks you shouldn't. I've told them both, told them all, it's up to you. You're twelve years old and you can decide for yourself. After everything you've been through, you can decide this on your own.'

Marcella considered this. 'What'll happen to me if I don't?'

'Nothing. It's your decision.'

'Do I have to decide now?'

'No. Think on it.' Linda reached out and put her hand on Marcella's arm; she didn't flinch or draw away. A good sign, Linda thought. 'Here's what you do have to do now. You have to come in the house now and have a bath. You look terrible. You don't smell so good either.'

'To hell with you. I am Stinko. I am Putrid too.' Her dark eyes, magnified by Rose-Renee's glasses, were ringed with dusky circles and her lips were cracked and dry.

'Then you have to put on clean clothes and you have to have dinner with us tonight. It's time for you to rejoin the world even if you don't want to. This is what grown-up people have to do, and

I know you're not grown up, and it's not fair, but it's still what has to happen.'

'Why?'

'Because life goes on, sweets. Ask Tim.'

'How can I ask Tim? He sent us back our money, and we never heard another word from him.'

'How could he write back, Marcella? Just imagine what his life was like after his brother . . . You can't expect it. You shouldn't. Tim had to go back to Arkansas and be sad with his family, and help them. That's what you have to do.'

'I don't care. Not any more. I hate him too.'

'Tim didn't rage around like you're doing, did he? You saw what he did when his brother died. He didn't hide and hit and have tantrums and fight off everyone who wanted to help him. He did the right thing.'

'You were mad at him when he left. You hated him.'

'I never hated him, but I was angry. I'm sorry now for the things I said to him. I shouldn't have. I'm sorry that I didn't tell him goodbye at the train station. It's too late to change any of that, but I'm sorry just the same. When I look back at it, I admire him. Just like I admire you.'

'No one admires me. No one should. I am a stinking old frog, and I let go of her hand.'

'You are a remarkable girl, Marcella. Please don't say such cruel things.'

Marcella took the glasses off. 'How am I gonna live without Putrid, Linda? We were never apart. We could talk without talking. I was her eyes for a long time, and she was my . . . I don't know what. I don't have words.'

'I don't either, honey. I'm sorry. Come on, I got Twinkles for you. I ordered them specially. I remember how you liked them and Gloria wouldn't allow them.'

'You think I can be bought off with a Twinkie?'

'I'm not buying you off, Marcella. I just got through telling you that you are a grown-up girl now, and no one's buying you off. I want you to know I am thinking of you, that I want to be a help to you, to you more than anyone, really, though they've all had their paws on me, pulling me every which way. You have to take the bath whether you eat the Twinkie or not. You have to come down to dinner tonight.'

'I had my period,' Marcella said grimly.

'So, you see, you are growing up.'

'It wasn't any fun.'

'It never is. Come on, take my hand. You go in the bathroom and I'll bring you fresh clothes.'

'All right. I'll have a bath, but I won't like it.'

Marcella allowed herself to be coaxed from the car, from the garage, through the kitchen and deposited in the bathroom where she ran the hot water, threw her clothes on the floor by the wringer-washer, and got in the tub.

'I'll be back with your clothes,' said Linda.

On her way back into the kitchen, Linda was accosted by Grumpy Susan. 'It's that Mrs Jones, she's at the front door again,' Susan said in a low, irritated voice. 'She won't go away and she says she'll just stay there and knock till we let her in. Gloria, Mrs Denham, said she wasn't to

275

come in or talk to anyone, or see anyone. Mrs Denham will — '

'Just shut up, Susan. I'll take care of this.' Linda put the clothes in Susan's arms. 'Marcella's in the bathtub. You give her these clothes and tell her to finish and meet me in the sunroom. Tell her Dorothea is here.'

'It'll be on you, Linda.'

'Everything else is. Why not this?'

'If she finds out . . . '

'Are you going to run into the music room and tell Gloria? Are you? Upset her all over again, and get her in a state again? Are you going to barge in on Gloria? At last she's picked up the violin again. You want to change all that?'

Susan grumbled, took the clothes and went towards the bathroom.

Linda went into the grand foyer where the front door remained shut. She opened it to find Dorothea Jones there.

She wore a cool blue Oxford-cloth blouse, a cotton skirt, and sandals. Her sunglasses rested atop her head and when she saw Linda, her eyes lit with relief. 'I've called and called, for days, but people just hang up on me. I've come by three times before. No one would let me in. They slammed the door in my face,' she added, her voice catching in a sob.

'Follow me,' said Linda.

Marga passed through the foyer, pausing to look askance. Linda ignored her, took Dorothea's arm and led her to the sunroom, which was baking hot with the afternoon light streaming through the windows. 'Mother's left

276

orders you're not to be admitted. She blames you. Lots of people do.'

'Me?'

'It's not rational. I'm just telling you what's happening here.'

'It's just their grief talking. That's all. People are grieving.'

'There's certainly enough grief to go around,' Linda agreed. 'I'm just trying to keep a lid on everything here, to keep it all from careening out of control.'

'I'd like to help. I'll do anything you ask. Let me be of some assistance here.'

'I don't think that's possible.'

'Why not?'

'Didn't I just tell you? Are you deaf?'

'Why can't I talk to Gloria? Offer my condolences, to Valerie and Mitch too?'

'You just don't get it, do you? They all think you turned Marcella and Rose-Renee against them. They all think you interfered.'

'With what? What would Gloria have done with these children if I hadn't been here? What would have happened to them while she sawed away at that violin?'

'Look, Dorothea, you're preaching to the choir here, get it? I know what Mother's like. All I'm saying is, if you want to offer up your sympathy, send a card. It'll flip my mother out to see you, and Valerie is a mess too. Mitch, well, there's just too much anguish.'

'Anguish? Anguish from Gloria and Valerie and Mitch? Do you mean to tell me that they will really miss Rose-Renee, or care that's she's gone? They didn't care when she was here!'

'That's unkind.'

'Yes, but not undeserved.' Dorothea seemed to regret her tart observation, though she did not apologize. 'Please. At least let me see Marcella.'

Marcella, her hair still wet and uncombed, burst into the sunroom. 'Dorothea!' She ran headlong, flung herself against her, breathed in her banana suntan oil and the smell of her starched blouse. 'I knew you'd come! I knew you wouldn't forget me.'

'Forget you? How could I ever forget you or Rose-Renee?' Dorothea held her close, stroked her wet hair while Marcella wept, repeating that she knew Dorothea would come. Dorothea said yes, yes, she'd been trying for days, days and days. She put her hand beneath Marcella's chin and raised her face. 'Oh, you're wearing Rose-Renee's glasses. You mustn't.' She lifted the glasses from her face. 'You'll hurt your own vision if you wear her glasses.'

'I want to be blind like she was.'

'No, you don't. Oh, Marcella, Marcella,' and she hugged her, and whispered, 'Oh God, it must have been so terrible for you, so, so terrible, oh, my dear sweet girl. You are so brave, so very brave. Ethel told me everything you did, and I came as soon as I could, and I've tried to see you, Marcella, I've called, but no one would — '

'I knew you'd never leave me. I knew you'd come and take me with you.'

'Take you?'

Linda, who knew what was coming next, said

278

she would leave them alone. 'You'll be all right in here. Mother won't come in the sunroom.'

'I plan on coming to the funeral tomorrow,' said Dorothea firmly, still holding Marcella.

'Suit yourself. You'll get a cold reception. It's up to you. When you leave, you should go by that door.' Linda pointed to the French doors leading to the garden. 'I don't want my mother or anyone else to see you. Don't use the front.' She left them, closing the sunroom door behind her.

'It's my fault, Dorothea.' Marcella blurted out the truth, clinging to Dorothea, never wanting to part with her. 'My fault. I let go of her hand.'

'No. Never say that.'

'I broke my promise.'

'You never broke a promise to Rose-Renee. She was your little sister. You looked after her always.'

'I let go of her hand, Dorothea. I promised I wouldn't and I did.'

'You had to let go. God took her.'

'No, you don't understand, she said to me, promise you won't let go, and I promised and I let go.' She started to sob all over again.

Dorothea held her, kissed the top of her damp head. 'She loved you best of all. And you loved her. Your people let you down, but you never let Rose-Renee down, and you mustn't ever think you did. God took Rose-Renee because He loves her.'

'Please don't say that, Dorothea. I don't believe that. Neither do you.'

'I do. I do believe it. Rose-Renee is in Heaven. With Rodney's father, with Lee.'

'Did you believe it when he died?'

'Yes. They are in Heaven. God needs her.'

'I need Rose-Renee more than God needs her. More than God will ever need her. I will need her all my life and she won't be there.'

'God will be there.'

'I don't need God.' Marcella wiped her eyes roughly with the heel of her hand. She did not want to cry any more. She was sick of crying. 'Why isn't Rodney here? Where is he?'

'He's still in Claremont with my parents. He's too . . . it's too terrible, and he's too broken-hearted to come. Rodney is sick.'

'What do you mean, sick? He's never sick! You never say he's sick.'

'The news just left him devastated, Marcella. He's heartbroken. He just couldn't bear it, it's like when his father died. It would break your heart to see him suffering.'

'My heart? It would break my heart?'

'It breaks mine, Marcella. I can't tell you how it breaks mine.'

Marcella, suddenly, cruelly intent on wreaking more pain, lashed out, 'I always thought Rot would die! We were all waiting for him to die, and then he didn't, and it was Putrid who died! It wasn't supposed to be her! It was supposed to be him!'

Dorothea's blue eyes shone with tears and alarm. 'No one expected this terrible thing, Marcella. How could we? She was just a little girl.'

'But what about Rot? Will he live to grow up? Will he die?'

She did not answer for a bit, and then she said, 'I can't answer that. What I can answer for is the way he will live. I intend for him to be happy.'

'You're the kind of person who insists on being happy, aren't you? And you're going to take everyone with you. The streetcar named Dorothea. That's what we were there for, wasn't it?' She spoke slowly, horrified and mystified, and clairvoyant in the same moment. 'To make sure Rot ate like the Pig Sisters, and had friends to play with and go to school with, and even to fight with, to be sure he had friends at all. He didn't have anyone but you. That's why you wanted us. The only reason!' Marcella whirled out of her embrace, but Dorothea caught her hand, and held her shoulders. 'Just so you and Rot could make each other happy!'

'You're angry, Marcella, of course you're angry, and you don't understand this terrible thing that's happened. No one does. But you know I wanted you all three to be friends, and you are.'

'Not any more. There is no Putrid and Stinko and Rot. There's just me and Rot now, and . . . there's not even that.' Marcella quit thrashing. 'You didn't come back for me, did you? You didn't come back to take me with you.'

'I can't do that, Marcella. You're not my daughter. You're their daughter. I couldn't take you with me even if I wanted to.'

'But you don't want to.'

'You don't understand.'

'I do.' Marcella's eyes narrowed. 'As long as

we made Rodney happy, we were fine, weren't we, weren't we? And now we can't do that, and we aren't anything. We aren't even we. You can't be just one Pig Sister.'

Dorothea led her back to the loveseat, and sat down. She held Marcella's hands in hers. 'Listen to me. There are important things you have to understand. Rodney and I are not coming back here, Marcella. I'm selling the house. I put it on the market yesterday. We're staying in California. Rodney needs an operation. I have tried to avoid this operation, but they tell me if he doesn't have it . . . well, this is a last chance to save his life. He weighs ninety pounds. He can't eat. If he doesn't have this ileostomy, he'll die. This terrible Crohn's disease will kill him.' Her voice caught in her throat and she stifled a sob.

'Have a what?'

'It's an operation where they . . . ' Dorothea bit her lip and straightened her spine, an athlete's carriage. 'He'll have it at UCLA Medical Center, and I thought, why should I bring him back here? I never liked it. I only lived here because of Lee. I never even liked that house or Chadds Ford or the whole east coast. I don't know why I stayed after Lee died, but then, when we met you and Rose-Renee, suddenly everything was fine. And we had Flag School, but now . . . '

'Now everything is terrible.'

'Yes. Everything is terrible without you and Rose-Renee — '

'I'm not gone, Dorothea!' Marcella cried, frenzied. 'I'm here!'

'I'm selling the house. I'm going back to

282

Claremont, and we're going to live there.'

'Take me with you! Please, Dorothea, don't leave me here all alone.'

'You're not all alone. You have your mother now. Your father too. You have your own parents now.'

'Valerie? Ha! Mitch? *Mitch?* You think I want them? I don't want them and they don't want me!'

'She's your mother. Of course she wants you. She loves you.'

'But you don't? You don't love me. You never loved me.'

'I love you, Marcella. I love you both.'

'You loved Rot and you never loved us.'

'Listen to me, Marcella. Sometimes we have to learn to live with what God gives us, even if it seems unfair.'

'God hasn't given me nothing! God's taken away!'

'When God took my husband, my heart was broken, but I had Rodney and I would live for him. And then, God gave me the two of you. You were a gift to me! To us!'

'Why do you keep talking about God? I don't want to hear about God. I don't care about God. I never did. We only learned those stupid prayers for you. Oh, Dorothea, please, I'll say your stupid prayers every day, just take me with you. Please, please, please don't leave me here.'

Dorothea brushed Marcella's damp hair back from her forehead. 'One day you will be a lovely young woman. And we will see you again. I know we will. When Rodney is better, and has the strength, I know he will write to you. You can write to him. I'm proud of you. I will always be proud of you, and so will Rodney. He will never forget you and Rose-Renee. Never. And you will never forget him, us, but our lives are changing. We did not ask for this change, for this separation, but we must accept it. God's will.'

'Please don't! I hate God! I hate hearing about Him.'

But Dorothea went on, regardless. 'Perhaps I won't go to the funeral. Perhaps it would only upset Gloria and Valerie to see me. That would be unkind.'

'Who cares about Gloria? Who cares about Valerie?' Marcella was shouting, shrieking. '*What about me? Me!*'

'Perhaps it's best if you and I take this moment to say our farewells, but we will not say goodbye, Marcella.'

'Don't go, Dorothea. Don't leave me.'

'When I was in the Olympics, I learned a lovely phrase from the French. They say *au revoir*, till we meet again. So that's what I'll say. *Au revoir*, dear, sweet Marcella. Till we meet again. You say it too. *Au revoir*.'

Marcella slumped, silent.

'Please, Marcella.'

'Orvwa.' She released Dorothea's hands. Dorothea kissed her forehead.

Marcella watched as Dorothea left the room, left the house, not sneaking out through the sunroom door as requested, but through the foyer, and out of the front door like the champion she was.

Andantino

The eager-to-please Marcella vanished with Rose-Renee's death, and she took on her little sister's surly mantle. She was wary, self-absorbed, remaining resolutely an outsider at the various schools she attended, a stand-off socially, a stand-out academically. In high school she was a competitive solitary swimmer, competing only in solo events. She excelled at the piano, not genius, perhaps, but talent, and a vast capacity for practice — not rehearsal, she knew the difference. In keeping the solemn vow she and Rose-Renee had sworn not to be like Valerie, Linda, or Gloria, Marcella groomed herself to be like Dorothea, the champion: she set her sights on attending Scripps College for Women. Valerie, who knew nothing of Dorothea's connection with Scripps, laughed and teased Marcella. Really? Scripps College for Women? Was Marcella a dyke, or just a snob?

The autumn following Rose-Renee's death Marcella moved with Valerie to Vermont where Valerie got a teaching credential, and had affairs. After a couple of years Valerie fell in love again, this time with a man who was moving to take a job in Reno. Valerie and Marcella went with him, living with him till that broke up. Valerie became an emotional train-wreck: noisy, needy, indulging in alternating bouts of tears, drama, and drinking, until the next manlit her romantic fires.

Eventually — and to some extent, on the strength of the name — she had kept Denham

— she got a job as vocal studies instructor at a lacklustre community college in central California, a vast suburban sprawl of pastel stucco, strip malls, and smoggy palms. In a community theatre production of Guys and Dolls Valerie met her second husband, Gary, a Lockheed engineer, generally inoffensive, but odious to Marcella. As a sneering teen, Marcella had cruel words for her mother, for Gary, for the community college Valerie wanted her to attend after high school.

To attend Scripps, a private college, Marcella would need more than good grades: she needed scholarships. She used the writing skills she'd once lavished writing novels about pirates to write essays, florid, evocative pieces, variations on the Heidiesque tale in which the narrator went to live with her late lamented grandmother, how they had changed one another's lives, the narrator bringing joy to the shut-in grandmother, the grandmother inspiring the girl to achievement, especially in music. In the scholarship interviews Marcella took a page from Mitch, and all but looked heavenward when she spoke of her sweet grandmother, the famous violinist who had . . . Not a dry eye in the house. Augmenting her scholarship with loans and a summer job in the Tanglewood ticket office (thanks to nepotism and Linda, who had by now married her boyfriend, Mike), Marcella McNeill put greater San Jose behind her for ever, and in the fall of 1976, she enrolled at Scripps.

Like a wagon train encircled by hostile Indians, Scripps, a women's college, was surrounded by men's colleges. Men everywhere. Marcella tried out a number of these men, and while the boodling was fun, she didn't fall in love, and she had lost the instinct of tarting up her words and actions to please others. Too, at a women's college, there was an aspect of boodling that made it seem just one more competitive sport — among the women who competed for men.

Her real reason for going to Scripps was a house on 6th Street. She had not forgotten the address. She walked there more than once, but it took her a month to collect the courage to knock on the door.

The Lassiters remembered her name, of course! They were delighted she was at Scripps! They invited her in, gave her tea out by the pool. Everything looked much as she had imagined it. Professor Lassiter was the image of his daughter; Mrs Lassiter was pink and plump and jovial. They said Dorothea and Rodney had moved to Palo Alto where she was a swim coach at a private school, and he was a student at Stanford in physics.

'So,' Marcella said, sipping her Earl Grey, 'he didn't die after all.'

The Lassiters looked aghast. His health was good, they assured her. He was not sick. Dorothea had clearly taught them their lines.

Thanksgiving, 1976, Marcella joined the Lassiters and Dorothea and Rodney for the holiday. Rodney was a thin, hawk-nosed young man, stooped, scholarly, shy, prematurely middle-aged, his skin and hair the same dull

287

colour, his eyes hooded behind glasses. He still measured out his energies in teaspoons, like sugar into a cup. No one spoke of Crohn's disease. Nor his operation. If he had even had one. He and Marcella played chess. He was quiet, still deep, a thinker, but theoretical physics were not thoughts Marcella could share. He spoke of accelerating particles that Marcella could somehow see darting all about the room. He had not made an origami in years. Years. Rodney's sole remark testifying to his old dry wit or affection was that he could see she wouldn't be needing him to marry her, that she had grown up to be very pretty, even beautiful.

Dorothea's light-brown hair had faded, perhaps due to chlorine, and it had grown out. She wore it in a ponytail that bounced with her athletic walk, but her voice was shrill, as if she were calling continually out across a crowded pool, and had forgotten how to modulate. She seemed more exuberant than ever, but as her energies had no fixed purpose or goal — baking pies with her mother did not qualify — she seemed scattered, even flighty. Her insistent high spirits made everyone around her, her son, her mother, her father, seem tired and spent. Only Marcella could match her energy. Dorothea was delighted to learn that Marcella was a competitive swimmer, even if she had no Olympic ambitions. Their talk of swimming and competitions and great swimmers made Marcella happy. Dorothea was also delighted to know that Marcella had continued on in music, still playing the piano! She was delighted Marcella had a double major, psychology and music! Marcella felt herself standing on the Winner's Box. At Thanksgiving dinner, she could even still recite Dorothea's prayer; Dorothea gave her a radiant smile, the equivalent of a handful of M&Ms.

But the extravagant hopes Marcella had pinned on this weekend had little to do with the present. She wanted nothing less than that this reunion should recover the past they had shared. She wanted nothing less than that they should share and recreate their old alliances, bring back to life Rose-Renee's funny smile, her odd mannerisms, even her little brimstoney tantrums that now seemed so dear. But Dorothea would not recognize loss, and Rodney took his cue from her. They would not be drawn back into the past Marcella cherished, and desperately wanted to revisit. At any mention of Rose-Renee, the Pig Sisters, Putrid and Stinko or Gingerbread Girls or Flag School, of origami animals and model airplanes, of any of the myriad things that had once — just a few years before — united them, Dorothea and Rodney recoiled, rebelled. Mentally and socially they went elsewhere. They would not reciprocate. They remained resolutely tethered to the present, and the future, spoke at length about Scripps, spoke of Rodney's work in particle physics at Stanford, of the recent '76 Olympics. They, in effect, boxed up the past they had all once shared, gift-wrapped it, and gave it back to Marcella, be-ribboned, perhaps, but not to be opened in their presence.

True love may exist, but pure love is a poetic

fiction. Marcella finally understood, for good, for ever, that Dorothea's absolute, unswerving loyalty was to her son, his health, well-being and happiness. As long as the Pig Sisters were good for Rodney, Dorothea embraced them. Dorothea's love for Marcella and Rose-Renee was muddled with need, expedience, opportunism. But isn't love always a muddy swamp, a cloudy broth of needs, emotions, and hungers? Marcella had an unhappy glimmer that that was true.

After Thanksgiving Marcella and Dorothea and Rodney all parted with hugs and happy promises to write and have further reunions. Marcella never saw them again. The following year she left the cloistered confines of Scripps, and transferred to the urban sprawl of UCLA.

Marcella burned with shame at her childish love for Dorothea, her hunger for her approval, with or without M&Ms. She cringed to think of her quest to fashion herself in the image of someone who had finally and fundamentally betrayed her. Not until she married Tim Farleigh and became a mother to a boy and a girl, did she forgive her youthful self, did she take off the festering burden of pain that had overshadowed her youth and childhood. Ironically, as an adult, she became something of a streetcar named Marcella, and she regarded happiness as a performance art that required constant rehearsal.

13

Great Performances

After Dorothea left her alone in the sunroom, Marcella knew that Linda was the only possible ally she had in all the world. An imperfect, self-centered ally, true, but she needed Linda. As promised, she dressed, combed her hair, went down the back stairs and entered the kitchen before dinner. Linda and Elsie and Marga were bringing casseroles out of the oven, and plates of fried chicken, gifts brought by people who had not been to Gloria's house in more than a decade. Marcella's paternal grandmother, Elsie, embraced her in a great wave of Emeraude against pillowy breasts. Marcella squirmed, broke free, but she did not run away.

'Thank you for not wearing Rose-Renee's glasses, for seeing things clearly,' said Linda, putting a pitcher of iced tea in her hands. 'Take this into the dining room, will you?' She waited for an answer.

'Sure. But I'll wait for you. I'm not going in there without you.'

She followed Linda into the dining room where the windows were open, but the breeze was sluggish and fretful like the company. However, everyone said how happy they were to see Marcella again, and looking so clean and pretty. Marga and Elsie brought in the rest of the meal and sat down,

291

Elsie by her husband Sam, Marga by her married daughter Sylvia. Marcella took her place beside Linda. Barry was at one end of the table, Gloria at the other, as if between the two of them, the whole family was intact, and not as if they had been ironically drawn together because they were irrevocably shattered.

Linda passed the salad to Valerie on her left. 'This is the last time we're all going to be together for a very long time. We need to talk about Marcella. We need to think about Marcella and what's best for her. It's time,' she said firmly.

'Really, Linda,' said Barry, 'do you think we should have this conversation in front of her?'

'Why not? It's her life we're talking about. She can have a say in it.'

'She's a child.'

'She's twelve and she needs to be part of this.'

'Do we really need to discuss this now?'

'Yes. We can't put it off. It's important.' Under the table Linda patted Marcella's knee.

'So, Mitch, Valerie. What do you think?'

Mitch put on his Hamlet face, an expression at once knowing and quizzical. 'About . . . ?'

'Your daughter.' Linda restrained herself from adding, you asshole. 'We need to decide where Marcella will live, and who with.'

Mitch looked over at Valerie, who returned his glance and bit her lip. Otherwise silence reigned. Marga, Sylvia and the elder McNeills just passed the dishes among themselves, their eyes downcast amid a general shuffling of chairs and clinking of forks on plates, audible discomfort and evasion.

'Mitch and I have to catch a flight tomorrow,' Jackie began tentatively. 'Right after the . . . We're missing rehearsals, and the play opens soon, and they'll drop us if we're not rehearsed.'

'What's the play?' asked Marga, hoping for some less fraught topic of conversation.

'*Our Town*,' said Mitch. 'Part of the Ann Arbor Summer Arts Festival.'

'Oh God, *Our Town*!' Valerie laughed, a bitter, braying laugh. 'Are you really reduced to that old warhorse?'

'It's a classic,' he replied.

'Oh, you are desperate!'

'I am the narrator,' he said regally.

'No, you're pathetic!' cried Valerie.

'Listen,' said Linda sharply. 'What about Marcella?'

Marcella shoved macaroni and cheese into her mouth, gulping, surprised to find she was famished.

'You are not alone, Marcella,' said Barry, in his soothing way. 'We are your family.'

Marcella rolled her eyes, and swilled some iced tea.

Mitch cleared his throat. 'I'm not prepared — '

'Prepared?' said Valerie. 'What does that mean? Do you have to rehearse to be a father?'

Linda spoke very clearly, as if addressing unruly children. 'What needs to be discussed is what will happen to Marcella. Who will she live with? She needs someone to care for her.'

'I hate all of you,' said Marcella off-handedly and without passion, 'and I don't need any care from any of you. Ever.'

'She doesn't mean that,' said Linda.

'I do,' she replied with her mouth full. 'I hate all of you.'

'Tomorrow we will go our separate ways,' said Linda. 'I don't want to leave the table with this unsettled. What about Marcella?' Linda glanced at Valerie, who glanced away.

'I'm not staying here,' said Marcella, 'I promise you that.' She stuffed her mouth with more macaroni, and eyed them all as if daring them to chide her for bad manners. 'I'll run down to the road and throw myself in front of a car and kill myself. I'll get eaten up by the dogs like the Gingerbread Girl. I druther die like Rose-Renee than stay here with Gloria. I wish I was dead too. I wish Gloria was dead and Rose-Renee was alive.'

'How can you say these wicked things?' said Gloria.

'Now, Gloria,' said Barry. 'She didn't mean that.'

'Quit telling me what I think! Just because I'm a kid doesn't give you guys the right to shut me up. I hate Gloria. I do wish she was dead! I druther go to the orphanage than live with her. I druther go to California with Dorothea, but I can't. It doesn't mean I wouldn't. I druther live with Dorothea and Rot than any of you! Any day. Ever.'

'You see!' Gloria implored the whole table, crying out, 'Dorothea turned them against me! Dorothea made them hate me. I looked after you, Marcella! Both of you! You are a thankless little brat.'

'Gloria,' Barry remonstrated, 'you don't mean that. She didn't mean it, Marcella.'

'I am a brat,' she retorted, 'but Gloria is a bitch. I hate her music room, and I hate her music, and her violin, and I wish it would break in a thousand pieces. I hate this house. I hate all of you and everything else too. I will never stay here with Gloria, and you can't make me.'

'We've all just been through an ordeal,' said Marga gently. 'We have an ordeal tomorrow. We must be kind to one another.'

'We must,' said her wan daughter, Sylvia.

'You're being melodramatic, Marcella,' said Mitch.

'What's that mean?'

'You're overdoing it. Making things worse than they are.'

'Don't you guys get it? Things can't be any worse! Ever! I just want to know which one of you bastards is going to take me out of this damned house!'

'You ingrate!' Gloria drew herself up, her narrow shoulders quaking. She turned to the rest of them. 'Look at everything I gave up to take these children in when no one wanted them. I didn't want them, but I did my duty. Where was Valerie? Where was Mitch? You left me with nothing, no money, and two disrespectful brats. Where were you when I tried to put these girls in a regular school instead of that farce that Dorothea Jones ran? You could have found their papers, and put them in a proper school. Where were you when I tried to discipline them, or teach them, or see that they took baths or washed their clothes? Which they didn't. I can tell you that! They ran off to Dorothea's. I could not stop them. She turned them against me, filled their minds with poison against me. They ignored my every rule, wish, my every scruple, everything I told them, they disobeyed me. They were wilful and rebellious, and retarded! And where were their parents? Off studying opera! Off — '

'Following your example, Mother,' said Valerie, her eyes dry, her voice even.

'Don't do this, Valerie,' warned Linda.

'I was rehearsing,' Valerie went on, 'and Mitch was rehearsing, and we were all rehearsing for the wonderful performances, Mother, rehearsing, practising to achieve a standard of perfection you would never, never recognize. All through college, all those nasty, unheated rehearsal rooms, my throat swathed against the cold, singing, singing, singing for perfection! For performance!' Valerie ran up and down a few scales, and a well-known bit from *La Traviata*. 'And Mitch was repeating and reciting so he could perfect his role. Alas, poor fucking Yorick! I knew him well.' She turned to Mitch, her eyes blazing. 'How many years did I spend watching you rehearse and repeat and recite, and feeding you your god-damned lines so you could collect all the applause!'

'Mitch is a great actor,' said Jackie.

'Shut the hell up,' snapped Valerie. 'This doesn't concern you.'

Gloria scoffed. 'If you hadn't abandoned your own children, both of you, you could have signed the forms in the hospital. I even had to sign the death certificate. I took care of your children when you traipsed off.'

'Of course you took wonderful care of them, Gloria.' Mitch gave her his Richard III evil grin. 'Valerie knew what kind of care they'd get when she dropped them off here.' Then he turned his rich, theatrical villain's voice to Valerie. 'Being raised in this house was like living in a concert hall, that's what you told me. A big, cold, empty concert hall. But love? Care? Affection?' He looked up and down the table like Love, Care and Affection were proper names, guests, sitting there with forks in hand. 'This house was a whited sepulchre, a tomb, a mausoleum. You told me how you hated it, and yet you'd leave your own children, abandon them to a selfish bitch and a rotten mother who raised a daughter who is a selfish bitch and a rotten mother!'

'You heartless bastard! I am not a rotten mother!'

'But you'll cop to a selfish bitch?' he quipped. 'Sweden, Valerie? You'd dump your daughters with Gloria to go to Sweden, the home of opera?'

'Mitch,' said Linda, 'Valerie, please, not here, don't — '

Valerie ignored her. 'Where were you, Mr I'm-Such-An-Important-Actor that I'm screwing the costume girl on her ironing board?'

'Cherie?' Marcella said, surprised.

'Who?' said Jackie.

'Shut up!' snarled Mitch.

'Where were you, Mr Mitch Marlon Brando, when I was home with the kids, stuck with two

297

squalling brats in one-bedroom apartments while you walked the boards and screwed the costume girl? What makes my art less important than yours? All those years I gave up my art, Mitch, following you around from play to play, from city to city. You said you wanted us to be together and I stayed with you, and I lost years, Mitch, years!'

'You never lifted a hand to help us get by.'

'My hand? It wasn't my hand I wanted to lift, it was my voice!'

'So go stand in Gloria's goddamned music room and scream your goddamned guts out, Valerie. It's its own padded cell for the whole loony tribe of you.'

'Mitch,' said Barry. 'I resent that.'

'So fucking what, Barry? As soon as I took Valerie off your hands, you ran off with another woman.'

'Took me off their hands?' Valerie was hyperventilating. 'My parents supported us from the day we got married. What did your goddamned family do?' Valerie shot Sam and Elsie a vile look.

'I did not run off,' said Barry.

'Daddy, you're the only sane one in the bunch,' offered Linda blithely. 'Maybe Marcella should go live with you and Jean.'

Barry paled behind his napkin.

'Oh, yes, Barry and Jean.' Gloria cawed; whatever rattled out of her throat was so raw and unpractised, it could not have been laughter. 'Jean is a geriatric debutante, a talentless hack.'

Barry bristled. 'Jean is everything I want in a wife.'

'A slut who thought nothing of stealing another woman's husband. I watched her with you, I watched the two of you all those years we went to Palm Beach. The two of you sniffing one another out, just like dogs. Like dogs in heat. Old dogs. Disgusting old dogs.'

And so the squall turned to storm, and the great steamships all collided, no lifeboats in sight as their hulls cracked open, and emptied out steamer trunks filled with thirty years of betrayal, spilled after four days' worth of enforced intimacy. Brassy Jackie, timid Marga, stunned Sylvia, the rudderless and astonished Sam and Elsie McNeill, leapt protectively into the fray occasionally, only to find themselves wrecked, and drowning. Marcella, without a word, slid from her chair, under the table, and crawled among their feet to the beacon offered by the distant door.

★　★　★

Before ten the next morning, Marcella arrived with her McNeill grandparents at the funeral chapel, a neo-colonial brick building with a white porch held up by hollow columns. She wore the Wanamaker dress and patent-leather shoes she had worn to the recital; she carried Barbie and Cubbie. The day was intolerably muggy and humid; high, forbidding clouds gathered overhead, the hot breeze agitating the cigarette smoke of men clustered outside. Marcella did not know any of them. A sombre-looking man opened the door for them,

299

and gave her McNeill grandparents each a cream-coloured piece of paper. They entered the stale, air-conditioned chapel with its white walls and thick plush carpets absorbing dust and sweat and sorrows. The air was heavy, damp and floral; the light was soft, diffuse and dim. Two sets of pale-wood pews flanked a central aisle. The air-conditioning kicked in and went off in gusts. From unseen speakers in the ceiling tinny renditions of well-known hymns played, or if not exactly hymns, collections of conventional chord progressions calculated to cauterize emotion. At the front of the aisle there was a dais, a small stage with an electric organ to one side, a podium, bedecked with white flowers, daisies with yellow hearts, roses and sprays of filmy, small white flowers. Before the podium a white box with a bouquet of yellow daisies sat on a velvet-draped stand.

'Is that Rose-Renee?' Marcella asked her grandfather McNeill.

'Not Rose-Renee, only her body. Her spirit is in Heaven with the angels. With God.'

'I'm tired of God.' She walked to the front. She sat Barbie on top of the flowers, her legs splayed, her arms outstretched, her turquoise ball gown tattered and stained and her hair a mess. Beside Barbie she put Cubbie. He fell over. She sat down in the front pew beside her grandfather McNeill. 'She will need Barbie and Cubbie when she gets to Heaven,' she told him. 'She'll need the ammo.'

'Ammo?' he asked, his dry brow crinkling.

'For Doll Wars.'

'What's that?'

'Our game.'

'She's with the angels in Heaven. There won't be doll wars in Heaven, Marcella.'

'There will be when I get there.'

She turned and scanned the chapel, looking for Dorothea, but the faces she saw were not known to her save for Mrs Campbell, who came down the aisle clutching a sheaf of music. She put the music on the organ and sought out Marcella, giving her an intense hug of condolence and Tabu. She handed Marcella one of the cream-coloured programmes. On the front it said:

Rose-Renee McNeill
1960–1970

Marcella crumpled the programme in a damp fist.

The family arrived in groups, Linda bringing Valerie and Gloria. Seeing them at the end of the aisle, Mrs Campbell left the organ, and put her fleshy arms around Gloria, clinging to Gloria's thin frame with tender expressions of sympathy. Supporting Gloria, Mrs Campbell followed Linda to the front pew where she placed Gloria between her daughters. Barry, Marga and Sylvia were already seated. Barry reached for Valerie's hand.

Mitch and Jackie arrived, and Sam McNeill moved so Mitch could sit beside his daughter, but Marcella was having none of it. She got up and stalked across the aisle. Valerie held out her arms, but Marcella walked away from her too. Linda gestured for a place beside her and Gloria, but that was never going to happen. Marcella went to the furthest, unpopulated end of the pew, crossed her arms over her chest, stuck her hands in her armpits, and slumped. She kept her eyes on the floor so she wouldn't have to see the small white box up front, Barbie in her battered turquoise dress contrasting with the white flowers. She listened to the low hum of voices, to the air-conditioning gusting on and off, and the tinny, tuneless hymns.

Then the canned music stopped. A man in a black suit came to the front and welcomed all on behalf of the family of Rose-Renee McNeill. He was flushed and perspiring and a few strands of grey hair stretched across his gleaming pate. He wore a bow tie. He said they would all sing 'Amazing Grace', and that they would find the words in the Remembrance Book on the bench. He cued Mrs Campbell, who began on the organ and there was a shuffle of Remembrance Book pages. Marcella stayed put. She didn't want to remember. She wanted to forget that she had let go of Rose-Renee's hand.

They sang and sat down. Valerie came to the front. She composed herself with a deep breath, lifted her chin and her voice, and sang out, a cappella, 'Morning Has Broken', her clear, rich mezzo-soprano filling the room. When she finished, she turned and placed her hand on the white box. Then she sat down amid snuffles and nose-blowing and the snap of purses and the flutter of hankies.

The muggy weather broke and rain pelted the windows while Mitch was offering up the eulogy. Against his rich, rolling, sonorous farewell, they could hear the downpour outside. He offered a eulogy that trembled on soliloquy. He spoke of his youngest daughter, little Rose-Renee, of her happy personality, her lively sense of fun and her sweetly stubborn ways. Marcella wondered who he was talking about. She tried to peer over to Linda. Linda would know better. But Linda's lips were pressed together, her face washed clean of any emotion. Marcella wished that Rot were here; he would know the girl that Mitch described wasn't anyone they knew. Just some girl Mitch made up, like you would make up a girl in a play, like Stella or Blanche. Marcella couldn't bear to listen. She murmured under her breath, *Putrid Putrid Putrid* . . . creating a hum in her ears. *Putrid Putrid Putrid* . . .

Mitch said his last farewells, his voice catching in his throat, Jackie weeping loudly into her handkerchief, Valerie sobbing beside Linda. Not another sound in the house till he sat down, his hands placed on his knees, his gaze straightforwardly looking into the sad future. People surreptiously wiped their eyes and noses.

Gloria rose. She wore the black dress she'd worn to the recital, though without the pearls or piano scarf or gloves. Mrs Campbell took from the top of the organ the violin case, and gave it to her. Gloria opened it, removed the instrument and the bow. She stepped to the front, just to the side of the white box. She waited for low voices and snuffling to cease and for the paper programmes to quit rustling, and for a general expectant hush to fall upon those assembled. Then she raised her chin, tucked the violin in its accustomed spot and drew the bow across the strings.

The programme in Marcella's sweaty hand said *Pavanne For A Dead Princess*. She recognized it as one that Gloria continually rehearsed, but this was not rehearsal. Resonating from within the 1727 Stradivarius, the music measured, melodic and indelibly sad, there rose up from those 250 years of hope and pain, of loss and grandeur, the music of farewell and oblivion as you might watch the spiral of a leaf falling from a tree, or icicle melting, or the death of a firefly, something fleeting, unknowable and unformed, someone like Rose-Renee McNeill who, an unformed child, now unknowable, had left them. The cool lament tugged at Marcella's memory, the day that Tim left, the heartbroken busker, the lonely violinist without his lady: he had played *Pavanne For A Dead Princess*. It seemed to Marcella then, seemed now, the saddest song ever written. When Gloria finished there was a hushed, expectant quality in the room, and though no further piece was indicated on the sheet of paper, Gloria began again. Gloria's playing offered no cosy comfort to those present, but impressed instead the majesty of mortality: anyone born to live will surely die. She played for a very long time, how many pieces it was impossible to know, to differentiate amid the sorrow and the grandeur as they flowed from one piece to another, through time and the heavy-laden air. When at last she finished, or seemed to finish, Gloria stood unmoving, bow at her side, her head down. No one stirred at first, as though they had to wait to be released. And then everyone released their breath and their lifelong sorrows in one communal expiration; people turned to one another, and unleashed sobs they had suppressed for years, freed untainted emotion they had submerged for decades, pure love or pure pity, or pure passion. Their tears seemed to come in a swelling tide that engulfed the whole chapel, even perhaps the small white unmoving coffin at the front, all awash in human frailty, poor finite creatures joined here momentarily, helpless before infinite death.

★   ★   ★

Marcella did not accompany them to the cemetery to lay Rose-Renee to rest with the Denhams. She rode home with Grumpy Susan, who looked not at all like herself in her black moiré dress and a veiled, head-clutching hat from the Fifties. She wore black gloves instead of rubber gloves and she drove uncertainly, her tail-finned '59 Plymouth swerving over the narrow roads.

'It was the best send-off your little sister coulda hoped for. Oh, say what you will about Gloria Denham, ain't no one can play like that. I'll 'member that all my life, Marcella. I will.'

'Great.'

'And your daddy's speech. Oh, he did right by your little sister. He did. He said them words about her that was just, just golden.'

'It was from The Merchant of Venice.'

Marcella didn't know what it was from, save that it was not from the heart. 'I hated it.'

'You need to be nicer, Marcella. Think of your poor little sister, and be nicer.'

'She wasn't nice. She was putrid.'

Susan lit up a cigarette. Marcella rolled her window and let the rain-freshened wind blow in.

'Close that.'

'If you can smoke, I can have the wind. Blow, wind!'

'Close that window.'

'If I close it, I'll barf. Right here in your car. I hate your stupid old cigarettes.'

Susan grumbled all the way home till she pulled round to the kitchen entrance. Without a word to Marcella, Susan unlocked the door to the mudroom, plopped in a chair, took off her hat and kicked off her shoes. Marcella followed suit, kicking off her patent-leather shoes, then kicking them aside.

Susan slid into her workaday slippers. 'Well, now, we got all these people coming back to the house. I need your help out there serving. You wanna help?'

'I don't want to help you. I don't want to help anybody.'

'Listen, Marcella, everyone's been good to you this past week, all your tantrums, and saying how you hate everyone, and how you won't be nice — '

'And I won't.'

'Everyone's been good to you, but you can't go on like this. You're sad, we're all sad, but I been doing and going and fetching and cooking

306

for all these people, all your family for days, and I'm an old woman and I'm tired, my pet.'

'I'm not your pet.'

'You girls lived like little savages, and — '

'We're not girls! Don't you get it? We're not girls. There's only me!'

Marcella left her there, ran up the back stairs to the second floor, and wandered down the hall towards her room. Along the way, she opened all the bedroom doors; clouds of low-hanging cigarette smoke still hung in the air with the odour of cologne and mothballs. The beds remained unmade, but the rooms testified less to their recent occupants, and more to the distant past, the Wanamaker girl, Miss Manetti, Signor Massimo, the entourages of famous musicians, their wives and mistresses. Marcella heard her sister's voice, her laugh, her funny little snort. Marcella clump-clump-clumped down the hall, calling out, 'Where are my clothes? Where is my skin? Where are my eyes?' to frighten Rose-Renee, who was gone, and could never be frightened again.

Marcella ran downstairs to the music room, opened the St Cecilia doors and closed them behind her. She stood there in absolute darkness. No windows. No lights. No sounds save for her own breathing. The music room harboured no ghosts. This room was rarified and lacked all humanity. Gloria didn't count. Then she fumbled along the wall and found the light switch and the place illuminated. Even with light, the music room was its own enclosure that neither reflected the outside world, nor absorbed it, insulated from both the past and the future. Nothing echoed. Nothing endured. The piano was open. Marcella sat down and played Monsieur Armand's *Waltz*, beat it out viciously. Did performance require an audience? Rehearsing assumes performance. Practice does not. Performance is finite. You do it. It's over. But rehearsal is infinite. Endlessly, ceaselessly, you could rehearse for ever, infinite pains taken towards finite performance and applause that would die away just like Monsieur Armand's *Waltz*.

She wandered to one of the wing chairs, curled up in its embrace, and pressed her face into the smooth upholstery as if it were a shoulder, and as if the wings on the chair would enfold her. She wept quietly, and even that took on the quality of music, not lovely or formal, or well ordered, but simple, a repetition that assumed rhythmic measures. She cried herself to sleep.

Startled into wakefulness by a short scream, she was disoriented to see Gloria before her. 'Marcella! My God! What are you doing here? You frightened me.'

'Thinking.' She rubbed her eyes and wiped her hands on her dress.

Gloria's heels snapped on the teak floor as she walked to the table. She put her violin case down. 'You should join the others. They're here. Your mother is looking for you.'

'Fat lot I care.'

'Mitch and Jackie are leaving for the airport soon. You should go say goodbye to your father.'

'What for?'

'He is your father.'

Marcella stood and ambled towards the piano where she played a random trill. 'Should I tell him what a great performance he put on?'

'If you like.'

'Like your great performance. Did you have a wonderful time, Gloria? You got to play at last! Yay! Finally, someone heard you. You performed. Yay!' Marcella bowed deeply to a phantom audience 'Thank you, everyone. Thank you! Yes, Gloria, you've been rehearsing all these years, just waiting for Rose-Renee to die so you could play and people would love you.'

'How can you be so cruel?'

'You could finally be the great artist you think you are. You did it, Gloria, you were wonderful and no one could jump up and applaud, but everyone knew it. I knew it better than anyone. I've been listening to you rehearse for a year! Over and over and over! I hate your music, Gloria. I hate what you can do to people with that music! I hate that my sister had to die so you could have an audience and finally do something useful.'

'That's a very thankless thing to say. After everything I've done for you.'

'You never done anything for anyone in all your life.'

'Listen to you. Even your grammar has suffered at that school. If you could call it that.'

'Don't you go blaming Dorothea for what you did. You killed Rose-Renee.'

'You are a child, Marcella. You don't know what you're saying.'

'Oh yes, I do. I'm a woman now.'

'That's ridiculous.'

'I've had my period.'

'Hardly an achievement.'

'I'm grown up, and I know what I'm saying and what I feel, and I'm telling the truth. You killed her, and I killed her, and together we killed her.'

'Nonsense. I forgive you because you're grieving.'

'I don't forgive you, Gloria. I never will.' Marcella went up to her, close enough that her breath could puff almost visibly into Gloria's face. 'No one could find you. No one could reach you. They wouldn't do any operation and save her till you got there and you didn't get there till she died.'

'I came as quickly as I could. You ran into the road instead of coming back here. You got in a truck with a septic tank cleaner. If you had come here, I would have taken her to the hospital. I would have been there to sign the forms. It's your fault that I couldn't sign the forms.'

'I didn't know they'd need you to sign stuff! I didn't know!' Marcella swallowed the stones that collected in her throat, liquid tears turned to rock. 'But if I had kept hold of her hand, she would be here. She'd still be alive.'

'You've had a trying time. You ought to be thinking about how you can help your family, not make things worse than they already are.'

'How can they be any worse, Gloria?'

'Your mother is looking for you, Leave me alone.'

Marcella went to the St. Cecilia doors, and flung them both open. She turned back to her grandmother, and declared, 'No one has to leave you alone, Gloria. You are the alonest person in the world. And you always will be.'

Gloria did not reply, though she looked as though she had something to say. That's when Marcella knew — a stab of understanding as certain as if her own appendix had burst and flooded her life with toxins — that the other alonest person in the world was herself. Leaving the doors ajar, she ran away, down the hall, as fast and as far as she could, running away from the sure and certain knowledge that Marcella without Rose-Renee was destined to be solo for ever and ever, the broken off half of a once sustaining duet.

14

The Gingerbread Girl

She escaped the house, by using the back stairs, pausing where they opened into the kitchen. She peered round the corner, and luck was on her side. No Grumpy Susan. A good beginning. She dashed round the back of the garage, potting shed and other unused outbuildings, and down through the boxwood maze, staying clear of the long, paved drive up to the house. She could hear cars pulling up to the house and others leaving. She carried the small battered suitcase with which she had first come to Gloria's the year before. Into the suitcase she had swept all the origami animals from the top of the dresser, all the Polaroids and Instamatic snapshots of herself and Rose-Renee: Halloween, Christmas, standing on the Winner's Box, the lot of them. She took the silver bracelets Dorothea had given them for Christmas and the golden locket with an M that had been her birthday present. She wrapped Rose-Renee's glasses carefully in a T-shirt, along with some other clothes, useful clothes like the ones she was wearing, no frilly dresses. In the suitcase she also had a sock that held the twenty dollars Tim had repaid, her own and Rose-Renee's, forty total, the five-dollar bills they'd got from Mitch, as well as the spare change she had culled from the dressers of

Valerie's bedroom and Barry's and Linda's, and the room Mitch shared with Jackie, even Marga's and her McNeill grandparents'. Was that stealing? Yes. Well, what of it? She was through being good. She would be really bad. A true thief. The sock made a happy jingling noise she could hear as she ran downhill and towards the road. Once she came to the flowering cherry trees and the stone markers on either side of the drive, she plunged ahead, into the road, in the opposite direction from Dorothea's. *Run run, fast as you will, you can't catch me, I'm the Gingerbread Girl.* Moisture rose up off the fields and heat radiated in waves from the asphalt, shining prismatically in the oil slicks. When dogs raced down to the fences along the road, she hurried by, careful not to look at them. No one, not even a dog, should know she was afraid. Nor that she was hot and thirsty and hungry. She hadn't planned that far ahead.

How far had she walked before a car slowed and pulled up alongside her? Marcella had no idea, no concept of distance; she had stayed resolutely to the side of the road. No one had seemed the least bit interested in a girl walking beside the road, but this car, a station wagon full of noisy kids, with a big plastic cooler strapped to the top, stopped just up ahead. The driver was a young man with long hair in a ponytail. He rolled down the window and he called out to her. 'Hey, you! What're you doing all alone on the road?'

'My grandmother's dying in Wilmington and I have to get to see her.' She had rehearsed these

313

lines as she walked and now she delivered them well. They seemed to Marcella quite the joke on Gloria, and she felt a certain measure of justified glee simply to say that Gloria way dying. She had been thinking too of lovely elaborations to add to the story of Gloria's near-death.

'Well, we can take you part of the way. Hop in.'

He was a youth-group counsellor, and they were all going to a church picnic. His name was Jerry and she said hers was Shirley. They asked if she was saved, and having no idea what this meant, she said, sure. This pleased Jerry. He and the five or six kids broke into 'What A Friend We Have In Jesus', and 'His Eyes Is On The Sparrow' with the same enthusiasm that Valerie sang 'Oklahoma!' Marcella didn't know the tunes, but they were easy and soon she was singing along too. Jerry wanted her to come to their church picnic, but she told them again her grandmother was dying in Wilmington and she had to get there to say goodbye. Jerry pulled the station wagon to the side of the road to let her out, but first he insisted on a prayer. Marcella bowed her head.

'Oh Lord,' said Jerry, 'bless this child Shirley and bless her dying grandmother that she may be gathered up to glory and that Shirley will be safe under Your benevolent protection. Amen.'

'Amen.'

She waved goodbye to them, and walked for a while more, coming to a fork in the road. She realized she didn't know which way it was to the Wilmington train station. That's where she was bound. Once she got to the train station, she'd decide which train to take. She had money for the ticket. She was a true Gingerbread Girl, and they would never catch her. But how to get there? She had only been there twice, once when they first arrived, and once to take Tim. She thought about Tim, wondered what he was doing. He had lost his brother. He would know what she was feeling. But right now she was feeling lost. The low, rolling countryside didn't allow for vistas and there were no road signs. She licked her finger, and held it up to see which way the wind was blowing. Silly. The kind of thing Rose-Renee would have done, but better than nothing. The afternoon sun was hot overhead, and the woods and fields that bordered the roads seemed to hum, though maybe that was just the wires overhead. She wished she'd thought to bring some water. What's the worst that can happen, she thought. She put her thumb out.

A tiny convertible sports car pulled up beside her, a flashy green MGA. The driver wore a motoring cap, driving gloves, dark glasses, and a pressed shirt with a stiff collar. He had sideburns and a moustache and yellow teeth when he smiled. 'Where are you going, little girl?'

'I need to get to Wilmington to see my grandmother before she dies.'

'Well, you're walking in the wrong direction. But I'll take you a-ways and put you on the right path. Hop in. What's your name?'

'Heidi. What's yours.'

'Gordon.'

Marcella didn't especially like Gordon's looks,

but since the car had no roof, she figured she could always jump out if she needed to. She put her suitcase beneath her feet, got in the low seat, and pulled the door shut with a plastic cord.

'I never take the expressways if I can help it,' said Gordon, getting back on the road. 'The pleasures of a sports car are lost on a road like that. You need to feel, the car and the road, to be united, if you know what I mean.' And at that he leaned into a curve. He turned on the radio, and played with the dial while he drove. Marcella wished he would pay attention to the curves and the yellow line, but at last he found something he liked, and put both his gloved hands back on the wooden steering wheel. 'It's a '59 MGA,' he said. 'They don't make them any more. Classic.'

'What's that?' asked Marcella, pointing to the dashboard.

'The radio.'

'No, what's coming out of it?'

'Dave Brubeck. He's the best. You got to groove with him, though. 'Blue Rondo à La Turk.''

'Kind of makes you feel funny. Like . . . I don't know. Funny. I never heard anything like it.'

'Don't you know jazz?'

'We're a classical family,' she said with some pride. 'Opera. Violin. All the greats. In my family they're always rehearsing, rehearsing, rehearsing. They hardly ever perform, except . . . ' She let it go at that.

'Well, you're missing out, little lady. Jazz is the only real American music. Jazz is cool. Jazz will take you places that classical just leaves you at the station.'

316

Marcella smiled. She liked the image. She liked the music too. 'I've never ridden in a car so low to the ground. It's nothing like the Lincoln.'

Gordon laughed. 'You gotta be half dead to drive a Lincoln. It's nothing but a hearse. You wanna live, you drive a car like this, a '59 MGA. Of course, they're temperamental and expensive. But they're worth it.'

'They're noisy,' said Marcella.

'Hold on to the windshield and stand up,' said Gordon. 'Go on, you won't believe it.'

Marcella rose, and the wind whipped over and around her; she felt as though the wind blew her free of all sadness and the hair right off her head. For a single moment she let go of the windshield and held her arms aloft. Then she sat back down, smoothing her hair. 'Thanks, Gordon. I liked that. You got anything to drink?'

'Beer?'

'Coke?'

'I only have beer.' He reached in the small space behind the seat, and got out a can of Rolling Rock, which he popped. 'We'll share it.' He handed her the can. 'How can your family just let you hitch-hike down to Wilmington? Don't they know a little girl shouldn't be doing that?'

'I'm not a little girl. I can take care of myself.' She took a swig. Ugh. But at least it was wet. She gave it back to him.

'You want to watch out . . . what did you say your name was?'

'Heidi.'

'Heidi.' He took a big swill. 'You wanna watch

317

out. There are a lot of Big Bad Wolves out there who will pick you up just to take advantage of you.'

'Like what?'

He passed her the beer. 'Like . . . advantage. A girl on her own ought to be careful.' Gordon drove, picking up even more speed around the curves, chatting all the while about sports cars and rallies and how she would want to come with him to the sports-car rally he was going to. The car responded to every curve and pothole, and bouncing over one, the beer slopped out of the can and onto her T-shirt. She took another swill.

These were back roads, not heavily travelled, thick with woods and summer encroaching on either side. The beer dulled some of her senses and sharpened others. Marcella had a vision of the Gingerbread Girl eaten by the fox.

'Here's all right, Gordon,' she said, mustering some authority. 'I'll get out here,' she said when they came to a sign for a junction leading to Wilmington. 'This'll do fine,' she said, tensing when he did not immediately slow or pull to the side. 'Thanks for the ride,' she added, handing him the empty beer can. With the car still moving she put one hand on the plastic cord to open the door, the other on her suitcase in case she needed to make a Gingerbread Girl run for it. He down-shifted and in a great spray of dust and gravel pulled over. Marcella hopped out and he tooted his horn as he peeled away in a cloud of exhaust.

'Anyway,' she said as though Rose-Renee were present, 'we won't drink beer again. I druther smoke pot any day.' In the silence she could all but hear Rose-Renee's automatic echo: *Any day*.

Once she came to the junction, Marcella found a busier road, still two-lane but with more traffic. Cars passed, some honking, most just buzzing by. The dust had caked her hair and throat and the afternoon sun beat down on her head; thick humidity pressed around her and her feet were hot inside her sneakers and they were starting to pinch. She put out her thumb.

A Chevy with Delaware plates pulled over. This driver was a heavy-armed matron in a nurse's uniform with a name tag, Bess. She was on her way home from her shift. 'What hospital is your grandmother in?' Bess asked after hearing Marcella's sad circumstance.

'She's dying at home. It's what she wanted.'

'And why are you hitch-hiking?'

'The rest of them are all there with her. They didn't expect her to get so sick so fast. They didn't want me to come. They said I was too young. They tried to leave me with a neighbour, but she's my grandmother, you know? I love her.' Marcella felt the thrill of lying outright, the pleasure an actor must feel in the well-delivered line. Gratifying. She went on with the story, embellishing and adding to it, enjoying the sound of her own voice, complete with catch in her throat, thinking to herself Mitch could do it no better, careening along with her tale of woe until she looked over at the nurse. Bess's brows had creased into a deep frown, and her double chin pressed against her uniform. Marcella had said too much.

The nurse gave an almost inaudible grunt of disapproval. 'Seems like I'm catching a little whiff of beer, Anne. Have you been drinking? At your age.'

Marcella saw a 7-Eleven up ahead and asked to be let off, saying she needed to pee (true) and she wanted to call home (false).

'You had better do just that, Anne,' advised the nurse grimly. 'You had better get on home right this minute, you bad girl.'

Marcella said 'Yes, ma'am', delighted to have been identified as a bad girl.

At the 7-Eleven she went around to the side of the building, opened her suitcase and took a fiver out of the sock and shoved it in her pocket. She went in the store, found the bathroom, and after she peed, she loaded up on Twinkies, Fritos and Nesbit sodas, shoving the change in her pocket. No one paid her any mind. She sat outside on the kerb, the heated asphalt baking her bottom, and scarfed them all down. A black woman in a Ford Falcon parked in front of the 7-Eleven, went in and when she came out, Marcella asked the way to Wilmington.

'Well, Wilmington's a pretty big place. Where're you going?'

'Oh, downtown.'

'Downtown? Why would a child like you be going downtown?'

'Well, my grandmother lives there. You know, round there. Close enough to hear the trains, and I got to get to her house. She's dying, you see.' Marcella gave her the grandmother story, being careful not to add too much, and looking sad, even a little frightened, which wasn't how she felt at all. She felt strong and invincible.

'Get in, I can take you a-ways. Better me than some. I'm going to work. What's your name?'

'Shirley Anne. What's yours?'

'Tilda Washington.'

All the Falcon's windows were rolled down and the smell of its exhaust blew back in from the engine. The radio was on loud, and Marcella said that music made her just feel so good! 'Like you can't sit still.'

'It's the Temptations,' Tilda said, turning it up even louder. 'They make everyone feel good. Oh, listen to this one. Marvin.'

'Marvin?'

'Marvin Gaye. 'I Heard It Through The Grapevine.''

Marcella smiled, enjoying the wind blowing through the car and Temptations and Marvin Gaye on the radio, the songs all making her feet want to thump, while she enjoyed the sticky residue of orange soda on her lips, the beer and Twinkies in her tummy, and a happy conviction she was certain she shared with Rose-Renee. *Oh, Rose-Renee! We should have done this long ago, just like you said, run away and find the circus!*

'So, you all alone on the road, Shirley Anne?'

'Huh?'

'You all alone on the road?'

'My grandma's dying.'

'Yeah. That's what you said. Your mama know where you are?'

'Oh yes. She's with my grandma.'

'The dying one or the other one?'

'The dying one.'

'How come she leave you to hitch-hike?'

'Oh, she didn't, Tilda. They didn't know she was dying. They thought she was just sick. She been sick a lot before, so they left me with the neighbours, but then they called and said she was dying!' Marcella decided to shut up. Right there. To effect a little sniffle.

Tilda Washington said nothing. Just let the radio play for a bit. Aretha Franklin. The Four Tops. Then she said. 'I can't believe your mama would want you out here on the road.'

'I do this all the time.'

'All the time? You are one lying little girl. I gotta girl 'bout your age, and I can't imagine letting her wander all over the countryside with a suitcase. I'll bet your mama don't have any idea a'tall that you're out hitch-hiking. I'll bet you're running away, aren't you?'

'Oh no, ma'am. Not me.'

'I gotta daughter, and I can tell you this, Shirley Anne, you are breaking your mama's heart at this very minute. She is crying her eyes out, wishing you was home, and she is mad with worry for you.'

Marcella bristled at the memory of Valerie's hot, damp hugs, her grasping hands, her teary face begging for solace.

'Is that any way to treat your own mother?' Tilda demanded.

'I'm not running away. My grandmother's dying.'

'So you said. I turn here, Shirley Anne. You wanna get to the train station . . . well, follow the signs to downtown.'

Marcella scrambled out of the Ford Falcon as quickly as she could, and started walking. Her Temptations-Marvin-Gaye-Four-Tops-induced euphoria dried up and left her glum. Pretty soon she put her thumb out. Everyone passed her as though she were invisible. She fervently hoped Mrs Campbell wouldn't be driving back from the funeral, and see her, but then she remembered that was hours and hours ago. Days, it almost seemed like. The afternoon sun was sinking, though the heat had not let up. She wished she'd asked Tilda the time. Only why would it matter? It wouldn't. She didn't care about the time. She was repeatedly passed by big cars, propelling ahead, assured of their own important destinations: Cadillacs, Mercedes, Lincolns. None stopped, and she wondered if she could get to the train station before dark by walking. She hadn't much thought about dark. She had expected to be on the train by dark. To be on the train going to . . .

A '62 Plymouth Valiant, plastered with stickers like *Have a Nice Night* and peace symbols, passed and pulled to the side. The Valiant was full of hippies with long hair and beads and weird clothes like Tim and Linda wore, four of them, three girls and a boy. They stopped for Marcella without even asking where she was going, and she crammed in the back, suitcase on her lap, between the girls. They drove slowly, well under the speed limit, and the driver, a girl named Kathy with long, straight hair, hoop earrings and a serape, said they preferred the back roads because there weren't so many state police. The students were happy, chatty. They were on their way back to the

323

University of Delaware. They'd been to see Jefferson Airplane in a Philadelphia club last night. Really! Could you *believe* their luck? A band like that playing in a *club*?

Marcella recognized the beneficent effects of weed. 'I smoked a lot of pot with my big brother, Tim. He's an engineering student at Massachusetts Institute, and he brings the grass home with him, and we go outside and smoke, and our parents don't know the difference. Of course, they're drunk all the time, so how could they?'

'Alcohol's a vice, but pot is a social contract,' said the boy, Larry. He had bushy sideburns and a huge moustache. 'When you smoke with someone, you're making the implicit assumption of trust, that they're not a narc.'

'I hate narcs,' said Marcella.

'Sharing a joint means you're doing something intimate, important with one another.'

'Really important,' said one of the girls, breaking out a pre-rolled joint, lighting it and passing it around. They were careful to keep it beneath the window level when they weren't smoking. After Kathy had a few tokes, the Valiant slowed to twenty miles an hour.

Marcella (now calling herself Eva) told her dying grandmother story, told it well, having now rehearsed it several times, told just enough to make it poignant and to make her quest somehow noble. She knew enough now not to trip on the details. Her fellow passengers cared nothing for the details. They all said how sad it was to die. How sad it would be to grow old. How sad to be denied the rich, bright joys all

324

around them. How lovely to be alive. To be young and alive. They played a game with poems about being alive. They each had to make up a poem about being alive, only leaving off the last word, and the next person had to supply that as the first word in their poem. The poems didn't have to rhyme, but they did have to sound like poems. The rules were simple at first, but got complicated, and the game seemed to go on for a long time before everyone forgot what the rules were at all. Marcella told the story of how she defied all her family to find her way to her grandmother's bedside.

'You're a real rebel, Eva,' said Larry.

'We'll take you there, Eva,' declared Kathy. 'Yes, we will. Right to your grandmother's front door.' They would do it, they agreed, even though going through Wilmington proper was out of their way. They were going further south to Newark. They pronounced it New-ark. They were University of Delaware students, they said again, and they'd been to see Jefferson Airplane in Philly. In a club. Imagine a group like that playing in a club. Everyone felt good. Kathy had a tape deck under the driver's seat and she popped in an eight track, and they all had a fine time singing 'The Ballad of John And Yoko', which made Marcella really happy because she knew all the words.

★   ★   ★

By the time Marcella was being questioned by Bess, the heavy-set nurse, Mitch and Barry had gone to the Chadds Ford police, who took down the information the distraught men offered, but said they couldn't spare the manpower to investigate roadside ditches all over the greater Brandywine Valley. Besides, the cops advised the girl's father and grandfather, really she hadn't been gone that long. She'd come home when she got hungry. Mitch explained the situation, the death of her little sister, how upset she was, how they had already looked everywhere for her.

Not finding Marcella anywhere in the house, the family had got into cars and combed the area. Linda walked the path between the Denham place and Dorothea's, calling Marcella's name; she found Dorothea's house closed and locked and silent, the pool empty, a For Sale sign on the fence by the road. Valerie made phone calls to people like the Bowkers and Ethel and Susan. Barry and Mitch and Marga, Jackie, and the elder McNeills in separate cars drove every which way, up and down the country roads, looking in the woods and ditches, calling out her name. Gloria sat in the breakfast room with a cigarette, mute and alone.

The Chadds Ford police suggested that Barry and Mitch contact the television stations to get community support for the search. This proved to be a good idea. TV crews, Philadelphia affiliates of all three networks, came out to Gloria's and filmed Valerie and Mitch, standing side by side, holding hands, begging anyone who had word, news of Marcella to contact the police or the newspapers or television stations. They feared for the missing child's safety and for her state of mind. A picture of Marcella, aged nine, beaconed out across the greater tri-state area. The picture was at least three years old, one Valerie had carried in her wallet when she lived in Sweden. It was the only picture anyone had.

★　★　★

'Please be on the lookout for Marcella McNeill, of Chadds Ford, twelve years old. Brown curly hair. Brown eyes. Marcella is the granddaughter of Barry and Gloria Denham, a well-known Brandywine family, and the daughter of actor Mitch McNeill, and the singer Valerie Denham. Marcella is distraught over the recent death of her little sister. She disappeared after the funeral.'

The hawk-faced CBS commentator completed his coverage with the dire question: 'Do you know where your children are? Do you know where this child is?'

★　★　★

A local missing child was so much more immediate and dramatic than global travail. The appeal was irresistible. The calls came in. Some people, easily roused to the scent of a TV camera and a microphone, had nothing to offer, but finally, sifting through the true and the false, there emerged a picture of a hitch-hiking child. Though the child's name was different, four people all told the same story: she said her grandmother was dying and she had to get to

327

Wilmington. The nurse, Bess, berated the girl's parents because the child had smelled of beer. Jerry, the church youth director, wished he had pressed her on her feelings, certain that he could have assured her that her dead sister was in Heaven, and was shocked to learn that her grandmother was not dying at all. Gordon in the MGA said he would have contacted authorities about a girl hitch-hiking, but he was late to a sports-car rally; he feared a dark fate had found the girl. Tilda Washington phoned from her employer's house. She said the girl she had met did not seem to be upset or emotional at all; she was more, well, eager, even excited to be going to a dying grandmother's house in Wilmington somewhere. Maybe near downtown. The Wilmington police were alerted.

The stoned students in the Plymouth Valiant? They alone could have enlightened the police and the family as to Marcella's actual whereabouts, but they did not come forward. Perhaps they didn't watch the news. Perhaps they were paranoid, given the weed they smoked. Perhaps they were pissed off, and thought it served that brat right.

15

Destinations

The high was wearing off, and the students were cross. The Plymouth Valiant meandered towards downtown where they got lost and confused because Eva could not remember the street her goddamn grandmother lived on. They drove around neighbourhoods once grand but long since sunk into varying stages of decay, neighbourhoods that had been respectable, but had crumbled into slums. Pot made it hard to think, made it hard for Marcella to remember what she'd told them. Twilight had fallen, and the downtown streets they drove through were dreary, full of closed-up buildings, many with iron shutters, some boarded up, and men and women squatting in doorways smoking, barely visible in the dusk and shadows, some shuffling, lurching along the streets that were deserted of humanity, except for humanity like these sorry specimens. Marcella's courage faltered, but she had gone too far to turn back, and besides, what was there to return to?

'Second and French,' Marcella said at last, pulling from some deep recess of her mind a phrase that had a musical lilt to it.

'Isn't that like the train station?' one of the girls asked. 'Your grandmother lives at the goddamned train station?'

'Just leave me off at the train station. She lives right nearby and she'll come collect me.'

'How can she collect you, if she's dying?' asked Kathy.

'She is dying, but my aunt will come get me.'

'Why'd they let you hitch-hike all the way down here if they could just come and get you?'

'They would've taken me, but they didn't know she was going to die. Now they don't want to leave her bedside.'

'No one lets a kid hitch-hike,' said Larry. 'Besides, you got a suitcase, Eva.'

'You just never know how long it's going to take to die. Don't you have a grandmother?'

'Yeah, and at least I know where she fucking lives.'

'There! There!' Marcella shouted on seeing the train station with its iron posts and steep staircase and bilious green paint. 'Let me out here.'

'I don't think you know where the hell you are,' said Kathy.

'Or where the hell you're going,' added Larry.

'You are a lying little bitch, Eva.'

'Just let me out.'

'Don't fucking worry. Get out.'

If such a thing is possible, the Valiant pulled away in disgust.

Dusk had oozed into nightfall; the commuter rush was over. Marcella was disappointed to see that the corner where the violinist played was empty, and pigeons pecked the sidewalk unperturbed. She climbed the steep stairs and went right to the ladies' room which she very

330

much needed. She came out and checked the overhead departure-and-arrival board: nothing much leaving tonight, a local going back to Philadelphia. She wasn't going there for sure. She'd have to wait till morning to choose her destination.

At the station diner she took a place at the counter, ate a hot dog, and drank a Coke. The place was closing, and near empty, and she ate fast so as not to be in the way, and thus attract attention. She wandered into the waiting room, which was almost empty, a few lone travellers, and a middle-aged couple, everyone shuffling through newspapers, not talking. There was a young soldier too, in uniform, his legs set apart, his shaven head back, resting on the wall, his mouth open, snoring. Marcella remembered the soldier who had been nice to Valerie, now so long ago. A year ago. More. She saw a cop walk past the double doors. Then pass again. She had best leave. But where to go? On her way out, a homeless man came up to her, panhandling, his pale palm, his dirty hand held out. He asked for a cigarette and change.

'I'm twelve years old. Do I look like I'd be smoking?' She pushed past him with what she hoped was Olympic aplomb, but as she approached the closed-up newsstand, a perv stepped around the corner, stroking himself with unfeigned delight. He gave her an ecstatic smile, and moved towards her.

Marcella hotfooted towards the ladies' room. A heavily made-up woman was applying mascara in the mirror. Waves of perfume mixed with sweat wafted from her as Marcella walked past and into a stall. Marcella stayed in the stall till she heard her footsteps depart. Leaving her little suitcase atop the toilet tank, she moved to a bench, where she finished off the Fritos and Twinkies. She got a drink out of the faucet, and looked at herself in the grey mirror. 'Tomorrow,' she promised. 'Tomorrow we'll have lots of choices.' *Tomorrow*, she could all but hear Rose-Renee echo. *Tomorrow.*

Marcella heard the janitor's cart approaching, his radio on loud, his trash can clanging. She dashed into the stall. She locked the door and stood on the seat. Her heart began to thud as he pushed his cleaning trolley all around the bathroom, his transistor radio playing twangy guitars and a man's deep voice singing about being stuck in Folsom prison as the cart rattled among the cold metal stalls. When the song finished, a mellifluous male radio voice reminded listeners to be on the lookout for a missing girl, Marcella McNeill, age twelve, who had disappeared from her grandmother's house and who was thought to be in the Wilmington area.

The janitor flung open the door of every stall, sloshed the mop in the bucket, swabbed the floor and the toilet, flushed. The astringent smell of industrial cleaner snaked under the stalls and teased at Marcella's nose, daring her to sneeze. When he came to the door of her stall, locked, she quit breathing until he muttered, 'Goddamned kids,' and moved on. She breathed easier when at last she heard him slam the bathroom door, and turn an outside lock.

She semi-slept on the bench that night, waking often, alert to every sound. She dashed back into the stall and stood on the seat at dawn when a whistling security guard unlocked the door. Her heart pounded, but his whistle vanished as the door closed behind him.

A train station rouses early. The platforms were thronged with commuters as she stepped out of the ladies' room and into the bustle. Lots of weekday people with places to go collected and dispersed on the platforms. The very pigeons seemed to recognize the start of a new, important day, and fluttered noisily under the high, iron awnings, swooping down to peck at any bit of sugar fallen from a doughnut as commuters stood beside the tracks, ready to make their routine loops, their faces pale, their eyes inert with habit. I am not a commuter, Marcella thought with some pride. I am a real traveller going somewhere. But first the smell of frying bacon from the diner accosted her and her stomach rumbled.

At the station diner she ordered a huge breakfast and ate the whole thing. Just like one of the Pig Sisters. The waitress asked where she was bound, a little girl on her own, and Marcella again happily killed off Gloria. The food was wonderfully restorative and she anticipated the day ahead. Where would she go? She left a dime tip under her plate, and walked into the smoke, and summertime heat, the genial squalor of the station: the lights and noise of the overhead speakers, the heavy mechanical thrust of the locomotives, pulling in, panting hard for a while, as porters and passengers got on and off. *Five minutes! Five minutes!* blared out the overhead speakers, calling out the litany of landscape up and down the eastern seaboard: *Washington, Boston, Florida, New York,* further afield, names to crunch down on, *Chicago, Pittsburgh,* or roll over on your tongue, soft like a marshmallow, *Omaha.* Marcella stood looking up at the big board of Destinations. Where should she go? Where would the Gingerbread Girl go that no one would ever catch her? All these choices! She could almost hear Rose-Renee beside her voting for the circus, that they should tame lions and tell fortunes. She turned, expecting to see Rose-Renee squinting up at her, but strangers walked around her as though she were but a stone in midstream.

Then she heard the violinist tuning up; the sound caught her unaware, almost comforting, familiar. She clattered down the stairs to the street level where he stood, violin beneath his chin. He wore glasses, T-shirt and jeans and his long curly hair was pulled back in a rubber band. He was the same musician who had played when they'd first come here. The same one who played here when Tim left. She smiled to see a girl come stand beside him wearing a bright, full-length cotton dress splashed with many colours. The girl knelt and opened his velvet-lined violin case, and casually tossed two dollars in before she stood back up. She nodded to the violinist and they were about to launch into a song when Marcella went up to them.

''Member me?' Marcella said. 'I told you

she'd come back.' The violinist looked at her blankly. 'Member how I came here in March, and you were so sad and your music was so sad. I thought I'd never heard anyone play music that sad, and that includes Gloria. I mean, you wouldn't know who Gloria is, but believe me, she can break your heart into a hundred pieces with that thing.' Marcella pointed to the violin. She was about to say that Gloria had played the same piece at the funeral, but she could not bear to say the word funeral. 'You said your girl left you, and you would never be happy again, and I told you she'd come back, and look — ' Marcella grinned at the girl ' — she did.'

The girl regarded him quizzically. 'Who's this?'

'No one,' said the violinist. Then, to Marcella, 'I remember you. That was a long time ago. Months ago. I'm glad you liked my playing.'

'Are you happy now?'

'Yes. Thanks.'

'I'm glad she came back.'

'Yes.'

' 'Everybody's Talkin' At Me'?' asked the girl. 'Wanna start with that?'

'Sure.' He drew the bow up and across and began to play the lively pop song, perfect for the early-morning commuters to take with them through the long dark tunnels and industrial suburbs into the cities that would swallow them up.

As soon as the girl began to sing, Marcella realized her mistake. This was not the same girl. That girl sang opera. Sang like an angel. This

335

girl, Marcella watched her critically, substituted a lot of sass and shoulder movement, along with a tambourine, in place of a fine voice, or real feeling. Marcella watched the violinist, who played bright backup to the undemanding lyrics, and somehow she knew he was concealing his losses, his sadness, and he always would. Marcella dug into her pocket, and put a dollar bill in the velvet case. The violinist nodded. She went back upstairs.

While the buskers' light-hearted pop tunes floated up and around the platforms, Marcella paced and watched as the big board of Destinations changed, clacking every few minutes during the morning commuter crush. When that ended, more leisurely travellers took their places, parents with fussy children, students in congenial trios and quartets, the occasional granny furiously knitting while she sat in the waiting room. Marcella longed to ask them all: *Where are you going? Can I come with you?*

She sat on a bench and watched the names and destinations flicker across the arrivals-and-departure board and waft from the loudspeakers. She could sense Rose-Renee beside her speaking in their mute lingo; she could read Rose-Renee's sad face, her twitching expressions even without her glasses. Especially without her glasses. Claremont, she silently reminded Rose-Renee. 'Claremont, California. Sixth Street.' The words felt good on her tongue, but they dissolved there like ash in the hot wind that gusted in with each new arrival of a train, with the smoke that billowed out with each new departure. The

Destination board fluttered again and again, the letters making clattering sounds as they changed and new places showed up and new times and new opportunities. What was the point of going to Claremont? Dorothea did not love the Pig Sisters. She only loved that they had made Rodney happy. There were no more Pig Sisters. Rodney would never be happy. There was no streetcar named Dorothea. Not for Marcella McNeill. Her vibrant sense of possibility, freedom, withered, puckered, and she began to understand that a girl with all sorts of choices, with too many choices, in truth, had few. Maybe none. There was no place to go. No lighting out for the territory, like Huck. No raft. No river. No pirates. No mermaids or lost boys, all of which, she thought, slumping on a bench, were stories for boys. What were girls left with? Stories about making everything better for everyone else: white rolls for the dour grandfather, the orphan Anne of Green Gables lighting up the lives of two cranky old people, curly-headed Shirley Temple tap-dancing her way into the hearts of a lot of battle-hardened British soldiers, girls whose task — whose very reason and reward for living — was to make everyone else happy, happy, happy. Marcella hated happy. She kicked her suitcase and it fell over with a thud. She picked it up and walked up and down the platform.

There was no adventure in front of Marcella McNeill except growing up. No escaping, no matter how many lies she told. *Run run, fast as you will, you can't catch me, I'm a Gingerbread Girl* . . . . Wrong. All wrong. She would get

337

caught. She was no smarter than that stupid Gingerbread Boy who got gobbled up by the fox, pleased with himself till the end when his head got bit off. She bought some M&Ms at the newsstand and a newspaper and took it back in the waiting room and read all about herself. She read it again and again, anguished quotes from Mitch and Valerie, and Barry and Linda, the sad recent death of Rose-Renee McNeill, how frantic with worry the whole family was, how they begged that anyone with news of her would contact the police. Let them wait, she thought, let them look. I got nowhere to go, but at least I'm not in any kind of hurry. She knew that Rose-Renee agreed.

She went back out to the platform, and heard the trains roar in and out. Her back was to the waiting-room windows, her face was to the tracks. People surged all around her as the afternoon commute began. She watched the humid wind blow the cigarette butts and candy wrappers about, the detritus and debris shed by people with a thousand destinations and lives ahead. Marcella had no destination. And her life ahead? She thought to herself: this is your rehearsal, Marcella, for how alone you will be, how alone you will always be. You were a duet with Rose-Renee, a trio with Rot, a quartet with Dorothea. But from now on, and for a long time, you will be solo. Maybe for ever. The premonition chilled her.

A bag lady pawed through a nearby trash can, plucking at a half-eaten doughnut, and a cigarette butt. She had yellow fingernails and she was smacking her toothless gums, filthy and muttering to herself. Her hair was matted under a bandana and she wore layers of ill-fitting clothes, topped off with a greasy sweatshirt, even in the heat of a July afternoon. She turned and looked at Marcella. Blinked. Her rheumy eyes fastened on Marcella with recognition and malice.

Marcella glared back. After all, she'd bested the panhandler, and outrun the perv. She bent to pick up her suitcase, but just then the old woman galloped over to her, still clutching her bag. She used that bag like a weapon, whomping Marcella and pushing her, snatching, not at the suitcase but at the child, crying out, 'Mine! Mine!'

People nearby scrambled and shouted, and Marcella tried to run, but the old woman caught her shoulder. Marcella turned and swung her suitcase, hard, against the old woman's body, and she fell into a stinking heap and did not move. Marcella ran away.

A train steamed in, releasing its last long exhale of exhaust. The porter, stepping out near where the woman lay in a heap of rags on the platform, called 'Wilm-ing-ton, Dela-ware!' He blew a whistle and commuters got off the train. They stepped over the sprawling bag lady, and the porter tried to help her get up, but she would have none of it; she swore at him, a whole filthy litany. He blew his whistle twice and a cop came out of the diner. Marcella walked quickly to a line of payphones, went in and closed the door behind her. It squealed on its hinges. She put her

339

dime in and called her grandmother's house. But the dime came back. The call was long distance. She stood there trembling, wanting to put her arms around the phone and cry into its round dial face. She could hear from below the musicians lilting up wisps of 'The Ballad of John and Yoko'. Fingers shaking, she got the dime out of the cup and put it in again, dialled zero.

'Operator.'

'I need to call Chadds Ford. But I don't have any money.' This was not true. She had the whole sock full of money in her suitcase, but if she bent over to open it, she would fall over or pass out or throw up.

'You know you can reverse the charges,' said the operator, the tiniest inflection of kindness in her official voice. 'They can accept the call or not, but if they do, they'll pay for it. You don't have to. You can even make it person to person.'

'What's that mean?'

'That you'll only talk to that one person.'

'OK. I want to talk to Linda Denham.'

'What's your name?'

'Marcella McNeill.'

'What's the number?'

Marcella gave it to her, then listened when after two rings Valerie picked up and said, 'Yes! Yes?'

'Marcella McNeill calling person to person for Linda Denham,' said the operator.

Marcella could hear commotion, voices in the distance as Valerie gushed and wept and cried, surely there was a mistake, 'Marcella! Marcella, it's me!'

'I'm sorry, ma'am,' said the operator. 'I'll have to cut you off if you keep this up.'

'Marcella!'

'Ma'am. Please stop.'

Someone, Barry, took the phone from Valerie and the operator explained again the call was person to person for Linda Denham. Was Linda Denham there? The caller would only speak to Linda Denham.

At last, amid a background cacophony of tears and voices, Linda came to the phone. Linda was not crying. 'Yes, this is Linda Denham. Yes, I accept the charges. Marcella! Where are you?'

'Are they gone?'

'Who?'

'You know. Them.'

'Shit, no. Everyone's here worried sick about you. Now where the hell are you?'

'At the train station.'

'Are you all right?'

'I guess so. Listen, I meant it what I said about not going back to Gloria's. Not living there any more. I'd die there.' She swallowed a great lump in her throat. 'You tell Valerie.'

'Why didn't you tell her? Why didn't you talk to her?'

'Because she doesn't listen to me. No one does. They talk at me and no one hears a word I say. I might as well not exist at all. I might as well be dead like Rose-Renee.'

'Don't say that.'

'Tell them I mean it, Linda. I won't go back there.'

'It's OK. You and Valerie are coming with me,

at least for now. I wouldn't leave you here.'

'Are we going to the commune?'

'Tanglewood. Don't tell Mother, all right? I got a job at Tanglewood. I work in the ticket office for the music festival, but I don't want her to know.'

'You promise you'll take me with you?'

'I promise. You and Valerie are coming to Tanglewood to live with me, at least for the rest of the summer.'

'OK, then come get me. I'm at the train station. Where we left Tim off. Come alone. Don't bring anyone else when you come. I don't want to see any of them.'

'You should let me bring Valerie, Marcella. She's really broken up. She's already lost one daughter.'

'Fat lot she cared.'

'Look, you'll have your whole life to beat her up. Can't you just be nice to her now? She's a mess. She needs you.'

'Where was she when we needed her?' Marcella said, and then she remembered that they hadn't needed her. Not in the least. They hadn't wanted her. They hadn't even wanted her postcards. Grumpy Susan only wanted the stamps.

'If I bring Valerie with me, we can just keep going to Tanglewood,' said Linda. 'Otherwise, I'll have to come back here to get her.'

'All right. Bring Valerie if you want. No one else. I'll be waiting out front, and we're not going back to Gloria's. Promise?'

'Promise. We'll pick you up and keep going to Tanglewood.'

Marcella hung up and turned around, and there was the cop standing in front of the phone-booth door.

'Something tells me you're the girl whose picture's all over the paper. Marcella McNeill?'

'Yes. I just called my family. My mom is coming.'

'Has anyone hurt you, or bothered you, or . . .'

'That old hag nearly killed me.'

'She's harmless,' he said. 'Happens a lot. Always with a little girl. She sees a little girl and something just snaps in her brain.'

'Who did she think I was?'

He shrugged. 'Who knows?' He was perhaps forty, with pale blue eyes, his blond hair a stubbled crew cut, his clean-shaven jowls pink and pocked. 'I'm taking you to the station, Marcella.'

'No. Really. My mom and my aunt are coming from Chadds Ford. I'm supposed to wait downstairs for them.'

'All right. I'll go with you, but if they don't come, pretty soon, I'm taking you to the station.'

'Will I be in handcuffs?'

'I don't think so.' He lifted her suitcase.

Little more than a year after she first descended those stairs, Marcella McNeill once again walked down them with another man in uniform. She and Rose-Renee had played a game, swinging on the posts and splashing in the puddles. The violinist had played beautifully for a girl who sang Mozart and Puccini. Marcella stopped and stared at him and his new partner,

343

the girl with a brassy voice and more grit than feeling or technique, hips swinging as she belted out 'Cracklin' Rosie'. Marcella, unimpressed, returned her attention to the violinist. He played very well. But it was not the same. It would never be the same. Without losing a beat, he brought his gaze to Marcella, and nodded, and she silently acknowledged. She would never see the violinist again, but she would never forget him, and he would never forget her. She turned away and stood beside the cop, their backs to the musicians.

'Anyone can guess why you might have run away,' said the cop. 'We know you're heartbroken about your little sister, but you mustn't do this again. Your parents, well, think how heartbroken they are. They lost her. They don't want to lose you too.'

Marcella kept her gaze on the traffic at the intersection, on the litter in the street, on the drunks shuffling along the sidewalks so she wouldn't have to think about Mitch or Valerie. About losing Rose-Renee.

'I'm very sorry about your little sister, Rose.' He waited for her to speak. 'Very sorry.'

'Rose-Renee,' she said, gulping back a wad of tears that felt like a hairball, that finally erupted and spilled down her cheeks, though she did not move or turn to the cop or anyone else for comfort. She did not so much as wipe her eyes. The tears eased down her cheeks, and by the time Linda and Valerie arrived, the dirty wind had dried her face.

Standing there with that cop that July

afternoon, the humid, unforgiving heat wavering up off the pavement, and the noise and exhaust all around, the inane uptempo tunes playing behind her, Marcella could only guess at the years that lay ahead, knowing that she would grow up; everyone did, that is, everyone who didn't die. She remembered Rose-Renee taunting Rodney that they would grow up and he would die. But it was Rose-Renee who was gone, and Marcella was so tainted with this loss that, like a bit of grit lodged in an oyster, loss lodged itself in her heart and mind, and over all the years that followed, it irritated and vexed her, and she prodded and twisted and worked on it, and made of it a lonely pearl.

She framed the pictures that were in her suitcase on the day she ran away. She kept them by her bed for years. She would put them away when she slept with lovers so that she would not have to explain, to speak of Rose-Renee. She could not bear to speak of her. In the California home Marcella shared with her husband Tim, and their children, she kept the framed pictures of her sister along with the origami animals and the silver bracelets, and Rose-Renee's glasses, in a bureau drawer where she kept all precious things like her children's baby teeth in envelopes, their little notes on Mother's Day or Valentine's Day. When the Polaroids grew dim and the Instamatic photos waxed yellow, she had them copied and preserved. In these pictures, Rose-Renee, with her gap-toothed smile and her funny face, remained beached in childhood while Marcella sailed away on the inexorable tides of

345

adulthood — child to teen, to young woman, wife, mother, middle-aged matron, grandmother — while Rose-Renee remained stranded outside of time, caught for ever in a past where once these two were their own little country with their own customs, language and borders no one else could cross, though they had granted Rodney a temporary visa. Marcella McNeill was the last living native of that country.

Andantino

Marcella remained determined not to carry anything away from Gloria's house. Whatever might have been of value to her, she insisted to Linda, she had taken in 1970 when she ran away. She cared nothing for the rest of it. Personally, and though she did not say so, she feared carrying, unwillingly, even unknowingly, from the house the ineffable, the unseen, Gloria's spiritual effluvia. Nonetheless she finally capitulated to Linda's pressure, and accepted the silk-fringed ecru piano scarf. Folded, it fit in her backpack. She would leave as she had arrived, travelling lightly.

She came down the back stairs and put the backpack and her bag on the kitchen table. She was ready to go to the airport when Valerie and Linda returned from a late lunch. Marcella had resisted going with them. These three days — in a house they had all detested and were about to relinquish for ever — had eroded their affections, as though Gloria's last toxic gift to them would be the happiness they each felt in getting the hell away from one other.

Singly and together, they had made their way around Gloria's house amid a nameless army of contractors making notes for bids, men measuring, shouting, pacing, tapping, testing, prying, caring nothing for the ghosts they might disturb. Marcella was actually grateful for the presence of these strangers. When Valerie would weep and share her memories with the workmen, they listened, nodded, called her ma'am, and returned to their jobs. Valerie ricocheted between clinging to Marcella, and clinging to her cellphone, the lifeline to her new boyfriend, Robert or Roger or whatever his name was. Linda, brisk, cool and unerring, reminded Marcella uneasily of Gloria Denham herself. Between the two of them, Marcella was thrust back into the role of powerless child, torn between Valerie's pathos and Linda's crisp certainties. In this palace of remembered happiness, amid all this psychic uproar, flying dust, unearthed memory, upended artefacts, Marcella could not even speak of the hovering ghost of Rose-Renee, or the spectre of her own childhood. Valerie took everything personally, believing blame was being cast upon her, and this made her whimper. Linda did not believe in ghosts.

Marcella missed Tim's steadying presence, their wordless, reliable bond. But she also felt she could not speak of him, not even to mention his name. If she did, she was made to feel that she was flaunting her happy marriage in front of Valerie, whose four marriages and many relationships had all crumbled, and Linda whose husband of many years had left her for a woman half his age. Linda's impending divorce — or perhaps just being back in Gloria's house — unearthed Linda's long-dormant regret that, as she put it, she had let Tim Farleigh get away.

The night of their 1987 reunion at Tanglewood, the three had left the pizza parlour, and stood outside for their goodbyes. Tim said he was staying at a nearby B&B, that he had known it would be a late night, and he didn't want to start a long drive till the morning. He gave them each a quick fraternal kiss goodbye.

Driving home, Linda wondered aloud: Didn't Marcella think Tim was sort of extra-attentive to her, to Linda, that is, and maybe he wanted to have an affair? Marcella rolled her eyes and said only that attentive was his way. Linda went on that, of course, it was flattering, but what should she do? She'd been faithful to Mike. So far. She wouldn't give Mike up. She had a family and a place in the community. Of course she wouldn't! But didn't Marcella think Tim was still really attractive? Marcella agreed that he was. Still, Linda said pensively, he was always kind of slow, and he still is. Marcella said he was not slow, no more than Rose-Renee was retarded; he was laconic. That was just his style. Just like Linda's style was frenetic. Linda denied being frenetic and then worked herself into a froth, rattling on about what a fool she had been to give him up. Marcella finally had to remind her that she hadn't given him up; he had left her. His brother died, remember? Linda lapsed into a rueful funk. Besides, Marcella offered more gently, seventeen years is a long time, and maybe he's changed, maybe he's not like the old Tim we remember, maybe he's different.

But he wasn't different. He remained reliably Tim Farleigh, like an unswerving plumb line, used to measure the true and genuine, the things that don't change. Marcella felt her heart rise into her throat the next day when he showed up at the Tanglewood ticket booth and bought two tickets for that evening's concert. He asked if she would go with him. Marcella said she would be delighted. For the rest of that summer, the month of August, theirs was an unhurried pavanne of a courtship. Tim came up to Tanglewood every weekend, took her to concerts, went on walks and out to dinner. He even came to Linda's house for a barbecue, and met Mike and her sons. Linda drank too much that night, and went to bed early. Marcella and Tim did the dishes.

Marcella returned to California in September. Tim joined her in December, and they were quietly married in May. From their Napa Valley honeymoon, Marcella made the after-the-fact telephone calls. Mitch said something sonorous. Valerie wept. Linda let a short silence elapse, then laughed, a fine, good-natured laugh, and said she was happy to have Tim back in their lives. And ever after, she had been. Until now. Here. Gloria's house. Marcella hoped once this corrosive experience was behind them, she and Linda would return to their old mutual affection.

Standing at the kitchen window, waiting for the kettle to boil, Marcella moved aside the old dish-cloths on the string, all of them taut and dry and dirty as autumn leaves. The summer rainstorm

349

abated, leaving small pearly prisms gleaming on the windowpanes like the tears of saints or martyrs, gleaming on dark canvases. She was surprised to see a huge white Cadillac SUV splash through the puddles, and park at the back. A broad-bosomed woman got out and dashed, as best a stout woman could, to the back door. Mrs Campbell.

Mrs Campbell enfolded Marcella in a minty embrace, and many cries of how happy she was to see her again, at last! Her white hair was cut short; she had beautifully manicured hands, heavily ringed, and she wore a tailored suit in a washed-out mauve. She reminded Marcella of a great pale porpoise splashing about in a sea of sympathetic convention, which Marcella (taking the path of least resistance) reciprocated. The kettle whistled, and Mrs Campbell's face lit at the offer of a cup of tea.

Mrs Campbell sat herself down, her hands spread at the table as though it were a piano and she might any minute launch into playing scales. 'You must call me Eunice. We're all so close now. Practically family.'

'Are we?' asked Marcella, bringing the pot and the chipped cups to the table.

'I would have come to see you earlier, before this — I'm so glad I didn't miss you altogether, Marcella — but we've had back-to-back board meetings, and there is so much to get in order, and of course, I had to be there, and have all my notes. We have a major restoration plan in place, naturally, to do the place justice, but the particulars, well, who gets the contracts, that will be . . . well, there's just so much to be done. Contractors have till September fifteenth to get their bids in, and we'll take the fall to assess . . .' She babbled on at happy length about what Curtis Institute would do and make of the Gloria Denham Center for Performance.

Marcella sipped and nodded, made monosyllabic responses as though all of this was of any conceivable interest to her, which it emphatically was not. 'Ironic, I suppose,' she said when Mrs Campbell's litany dwindled to a close, 'that Gloria rehearsed here for, what, forty or fifty years, and never played, never performed.'

'Oh, but she did.'

'I do not count Rose-Renee's funeral.'

'Oh, I didn't mean that, Marcella. No. After Gloria bequeathed the house to us, that is, to Curtis — I am on the board now — they offered her a chair in the alumni orchestra, which she refused. By that time, of course, she was a soloist.'

'She was always a soloist, Mrs Campbell. I can't imagine Gloria acting in concert with anyone, ever.'

'Yes, well, we arranged an annual concert at Curtis for her.' Mrs Campbell beamed. 'She got lots of applause, encores, and really, given her age, it's astonishing how well she played almost to the end. I personally came out here to get her, to drive her into Philadelphia. They were wonderfully well-attended concerts. They were held in one of our more intimate performance spaces, naturally. They were gratifying experiences. For everyone.'

351

Marcella imagined the board of trustees and assorted hoary others hauled in, once a year, to listen to their benefactress, to applaud through many bows, and many encores, to stand at the end of the programme, to sate, annually, Gloria's terrible hungers. 'She would have thought it a fair trade, finally,' said Marcella, parching irony from her voice, 'the house for the opportunity to perform.'

'I wouldn't put it just like that.'

'No, I suppose not. Still, do you think it's worth it to give up everything that makes life messy and rich and memorable in the service of a Stradivarius and the conviction of your own genius?'

Mrs Campbell looked momentarily perplexed, then said she could not answer that question. She moved along briskly to a question that had not been asked. 'I must say, I brightened up her life these past thirty years, since 1970. I looked after her. I saw to things, to her care and such when her own family . . . well . . . '

'You'll get no mock repentance from me,' said Marcella with more asperity than she intended. 'She cared nothing for me and Rose-Renee. Why should we, why should I care anything for her?'

'I'm surprised at you, Marcella. One would think you would have some more compassion and understanding. I gave her your book, A Song for St Cecilia, and she was full of praise for it, well, for most of it. She had never thought of music as therapy. She said it was . . . ' Mrs Campbell sought the word. 'A unique insight, and how lucky you were to have found it.'

352

Marcella remembered passing out in the elevator. 'Was I?'

'You were rather hard on her in the book, you know. You didn't need to say . . . well, quite as much as you did. And honestly, to have heard Gloria play, day in, day out, listening to her music, well, that was a sort of gift, wasn't it? It was important to your life, your success.'

'Really? Like Mitch's soliloquies or Valerie's arias, or any of the arrogant people who cast me and my sister aside when we were inconvenient?'

'You don't think you learned anything from Gloria? I find that hard to believe.'

'I always pay the musicians, Mrs Campbell, no matter what they're playing, no matter where they're playing. I always put money in the hat. She taught me that.'

Mrs Campbell turned her board of trustees smile on Marcella. 'Whatever the source of your insight, your book has started all new sorts of dialogues! When it came out people at Curtis talked of nothing else.'

'The book doesn't pretend to be a scientific manual for music therapy. It's part memoir and part observations from my practice, anecdotes, not a string of successes.'

'Well, you perfectly captured the sense of that wonderful line, 'What passion cannot music raise or quell?'' declaimed Mrs Campbell, pleased with herself. 'Dryden's 'Song For St Cecilia's Day'', the epigraph from your book. And that's what you do, isn't it? Use music to rise or quell.'

'I suppose I do.'

'It's especially gratifying to me — in my small,

353

meagre way — since I gave you your start in music. And it's wonderful you dedicated it to your little sister. Poor little Rose-Renee, to be so young and go so swiftly. What a tragedy.'

'You have no idea,' said Marcella.

'She could be a stubborn little handful, and irritating, but she was lively, and impish, and dear in her way.'

'It's good of you to remember her.'

Mrs Campbell's plump, pink face brightened. 'Of course I remember her! I will always remember Rose-Renee. Who could forget her?'

Lots of people, Marcella wanted to say as she fought a rising lump in her throat, grateful that Rose-Renee lived on in the memory of someone other than herself and Tim. She paused, knowing if she lost this chance she would lose it for ever. 'Did she ever say she was sorry?'

'Sorry?'

'About Rose-Renee. Sorry that . . . Gloria, I mean, did she . . . ' The past, like a great, camphor-ridden lozenge, refused to melt on her tongue, to congeal into words that were and always would be unequal to their weight. 'Did Gloria ever say she was sorry that she didn't come earlier? To the hospital. That day. When Rose-Renee . . . '

'It wasn't Gloria's fault. It isn't as if . . . ' Mrs Campbell folded her glittering hands one over the other.

'Don't think I am pardoning myself, excusing myself. Don't you think I have asked myself, daily, for the past thirty years — what if? What if I hadn't run out to the road? What if I had run to Gloria's?' Marcella gulped down her pride.

354

'Look, you spent time with Gloria. I'd just like to know. Did she ever express regret?'

'She did not, I'm afraid. She never spoke of Rose-Renee. You, yes. Well, after you published your book. Not much before.'

Marcella nodded, relieved that at least she had been told the truth and not some bucket of bromides. Her old animosity against Mrs Campbell, which had hardened over years, crumbled. In securing the house for Curtis, Eunice Campbell had wheedled from Gloria Denham the only act of generosity she would ever make, and there was no contesting that the music room would serve a greater good than it ever had since the days of Igor and Andrés and Pablo and Darius.

Mrs Campbell took the paperback out of her purse along with a pen. 'Please write something nice.' She handed Marcella A Song for St Cecilia.

Marcella opened the flyleaf, and wrote: *To Eunice Campbell, my first and best teacher.* She gave it back.

'Do you mean that?'

'I do. Thank you. Thank you for coming by, and I wish you all the best with this performance centre.'

Marcella saw her to the mudroom door, and waved goodbye as Mrs Campbell's big engine started up and the Cadillac pulled away.

She walked down the long hall to the music room, cheered to think that the musty, unused smell everywhere, would soon change; contractors, carpenters, painters, plumbers, they would tear out the nasty carpets, and paint over the dirty walls, replumb and re-wire. The place would become new, refreshed, routing out the old phantoms. Music would come to life in this place, music and the people who made music and who loved it, and were willing to have their spirits raised or quelled.

She paused for the last time at the St Cecilia doors, her fingertips moving over the intricate carving, before she stepped in. She stood in the shard of light cast by the open door, and tensed, a woman in the lento of middle age gazing into a room where she had known the arpeggios of childhood. She strode to the centre, stood before the assembled metal folding chairs and imagined them filled, as though her own life, anyone's life, really, could be musically accounted for, starting out simply, the simplest of sounds, a triangle perhaps, small insignificant percussion pieces, little shakers to keep time over days and years as one by one various important players enter, parents, grandparents, peers, friends, lovers, adversaries, allies, the people who will contribute, for good or ill, the fleeting and the significant, the loving, the hateful, the lively and the doomed, people who will inspire, irritate, betray, amuse, enlighten, bring to tears and laughter. These people pick up instruments, tune up separately, take on the weight, polyphony, the melody, motifs and undercurrents of one's life in all its richness and rancour, its complex rhythms. It takes a long time to be able to listen, to understand the harmonies and dissonance, the counterpoint, the brassy cry, the reedy wail, the deep insistent rhythm, to fathom finally the shape and meaning of one's own life, to read the complete, the annotated score.

Acknowledgements

The author would like to thank Juliet Burton, and Pamela Malpas for their enthusiasm, dedication and wisdom. At Robert Hale Ltd and Buried River Press, I am grateful for Gill Jackson's lively support, and to Sarah Plows and Tom Lee with whom it has been a pleasure to work. Many thanks to the earliest reader for this novel, Alaine Borgias, for her insight. Ongoing affection and gratitude to my longtime east-coast friends, Judith Brown, Judy Hunt, Libby Nybakken and to Martha Oliver-Smith who offered inspiration. I am especially grateful to my sons, Bear and Brendan McCreary from whom I have learned so much about music.

We do hope that you have enjoyed reading this large print book.

Did you know that all of our titles are available for purchase?

We publish a wide range of high quality large print books including:
Romances, Mysteries, Classics
General Fiction
Non Fiction and Westerns

Special interest titles available in large print are:
The Little Oxford Dictionary
Music Book
Song Book
Hymn Book
Service Book

Also available from us courtesy of Oxford University Press:
Young Readers' Dictionary
(large print edition)
Young Readers' Thesaurus
(large print edition)

For further information or a free brochure, please contact us at:
Ulverscroft Large Print Books Ltd.,
The Green, Bradgate Road, Anstey,
Leicester, LE7 7FU, England.
Tel: (00 44) 0116 236 4325
Fax: (00 44) 0116 234 0205

Other titles published by Ulverscroft:

THE BONES OF YOU

Debbie Howells

When eighteen-year-old Rosie Anderson disappears, the idyllic village where she lived will never be the same again. Local gardener Kate had come to know Rosie well, and thought she understood her — perhaps even better than Rosie's own mother. Rosie was beautiful, kind and gentle. She came from a loving family, and she had her whole life ahead of her. Who could possibly want to harm her? And why? Kate is convinced the police are missing something, and that someone in the village knows more than they're letting on. As the investigation deepens, so does her obsession with solving the mystery of what happened to Rosie.

THE WORLD IS A WEDDING

Wendy Jones

It is 1925, and Wilfred Price, purveyor of superior funerals, is newly married to the beautiful Flora Myffanwy. His brief and painful marriage to Grace is in the past. He's busy with funerals — and preparing for fatherhood by reading a philosophy book and opening a paint and wallpaper business. As much as he loves Flora, he senses her distance from him — are marriage and fatherhood going to be very different from how Wilfred imagined? Meanwhile, Grace has fled from Narberth to London, where she is working as a chambermaid at the Ritz Hotel. But she has a secret — one that cannot be hidden forever, and which binds her to her old life in West Wales . . .

WEB OF DREAMS

Virginia Andrews

The novel that completes the Casteel-Tatterton saga. On her return to Farthinggale Manor, the luxury home of the Tatterton family, Annie discovers the diary of her grandmother, Leigh. Born into Boston's wealthy classes, Leigh hopes for a happy life, but her dreams are shattered when at the age of twelve, her parents divorce, and her mother marries Tony Tatterton. The shadow of the Tatterton family which is to envelop the next three generations is cast.

THE HOTEL ON MULBERRY BAY

Melissa Hill

Mulberry Hotel, perched on a clifftop above a sweeping bay, was once the heart and soul of pretty seaside town Mulberry Bay. Now it needs some love and attention, as do the Harte family who own it. As sisters Elle and Penny Harte reunite after years apart to face a crisis, they are unprepared for the reaction of their father, Ned. He steadfastly refuses to give up the family business, revealing that he's given up something equally precious once before. Startled by their father's revelation, and with the local community and hotel guests right behind them, the sisters realise they must do everything they can to save the hotel — and their family, too, in the process . . .